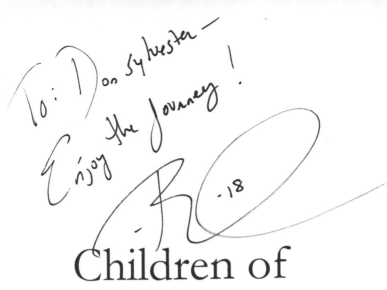

To: Don Sylvester—
Enjoy the Journey!

.18

Children of
The Program

D0611698

Brad W. Cox

First edition.

ISBN-13: 978-1517361723
ISBN-10: 1517361729

PRIDE & CONDOLENCES

I would like to extend my deepest apologies and gratitude, to anyone who has ever chosen to take this hell-bent ride I call my imagination. Your unwavering support has been a godsend — seriously, I appreciate your efforts. This includes, but is not limited to: My terrestrial friends, family, band mates, and, of course, the spiritual family acknowledged herein. Above and *beyond* 'em all, and most importantly, I'd like to thank my beautiful and steadfast wife. All things are possible when you have someone to catch your fall, or to rescue you from the shower.

CONTENTS

Cast and Conspirators *viii*
of The Program

The Counsel of *ix*
The Lords

1 Hallway of Sorrows 1

2 Reborn into Forever 8

3 Exposition 14

4 Paint the Desert 25
with My Heart

5 Leaving Tonight 32

6 Back from a Suicide 40

7 Visions of the Red Bird 45
(Anan)

8 Long Hard Road Home 51

9 The Gathering and 59
the Mission

10 The Eyes of Madness 70

11 Visions of the Gray Bird 76
(Than)

12 A Sorrowful Toast 80

13 Lifers 85

14	Downtown	91
15	Eyes of Merlin	98
16	Visions of the White Bird (Ath)	105
17	Revelations	110
18	Cadence of the Sun	118
19	Fool for Harder Times	125
20	Revolver	132
21	The Comedown	139
22	The Sharper Your Love	145
23	This is a Warning	152
24	Lottery of the Souls	163
25	The Lamb	168
26	Ashes Rising	178
27	The Devil May Run	183
28	Join the Cult	190
29	Shock Waves	199
30	God Complex	207
31	Ash to Ashes	219

32	The War Begins	223
33	The Eclipse of Icarus	232
34	Ashes of September	240
35	Run, Run, Run	248
36	Homecoming	257
37	The Road	263
38	Remember?	268
39	The Truth	275
40	East	280
41	11:11	285
42	The Hunt	290
43	Like a Dog	297
44	The Long Goodbye	304
45	The Masquerade	310
46	The Vision of the Black Bird (Isis)	320
47	Firefight	323
48	Letters to the Lords	329
	Epilogue The Song Remains the Same	335
	About the Author	

Steal their hearts or capture their imaginations...

(Dedicated to Grayson Miller)

Cast and Conspirators of The Program

Neco Baal – Baltimore, Maryland.
(Referenced in 1st and 3rd person)

Simon Peter – Abu Ghosh, Israel

Ash McKenzie – Aberdeen, Scotland

Rand Backer – Kassel, Germany

Dez Nave – Tecolotito, New Mexico

Grayson Miller – Brooklyn, New York

Magnus West – Chicago, Illinois

Elisa Tate – Los Angeles, California

Benjamin Maynard – London, England

Zane Brennan – Dublin, Ireland

Juno Vestris – Palestrina, Italy

Icarus Kali – Piraeus, Greece

The Council of the Lords

Anan (Red Bird) – Time and Space

Ath (White Bird) – Knowledge

Isis (Black Bird) – Creationist
(Derives its name from the Egyptian God of magic and fertility. Note: This bird is *not* a terrorist.)

Than (Gray Bird) - Death

CHAPTER 1
HALLWAY OF SORROWS

The forgotten yet familiar smell of ash and sulfur bullied away the cleanest of air. Time was of no real consequence. Everything had an eternal value; just as every grain of sand is a moment, every moment a memory, and every memory a map of a person trapped between the past and the future. We were trapped in the now.

"Is this hell?" I wondered.

Our cells were cold, dank and littered with countless aggravated souls, all wrenching for peace. Rust stains and blood antagonistically dripped and shrouded our naked bodies; we were thirsty for our confiscated dignity. Our flesh was tattooed by the human fluids of anonymous hosts. The aggravation and pain was unlike anything we had experienced on Earth. The damned awaited trial.

We were begrudgingly shackled to walls of granite, some elevated above others. We were spared the inferno's unquenchable palate, but could still smell death's warning and hear the screams of less fortunate souls. These beings were mercilessly tortured and rejuvenated for amusement.

This was purgatory; a backstage pass to the worst

horror movie imaginable. The only light came from the flickering underworld of burning bodies, miles below our unwashed feet.

It was ghastly.

In cycles, the Council of the Lords would allow 12 individuals to enter The Program. Twelve was an undisclosed metaphor. The odds of being chosen were in no one's favor; it was based on a spiritual lottery. The Program did provide relief from the pressures of purgatory and judgment and had been in place since the beginning. No one really understood The Program's complexity, only that there was no escaping it.

As I lay lifeless, freezing and fighting for my willed sanity, a long oxidized iron rod reached toward the asphyxiating cuff around my throat and disconnected me from the Wailing Wall. Instantly, I fell through a sea of chained bodies, and crashed upon a small rocky platform. My shins buckled, thick skull cracked and muscles tensed. A musing grotesque monstrous figure yanked me to my shaky hooves and dragged my nervous body down an endlessly dark and narrow hallway. Misery lurked, as countless hands reached through the void and clawed my rebellious flesh, longing to lay their five-fingered oppression upon my fleeting moments of freedom. Once human, these beasts howled like possessed animals. By all indications, I was being escorted to judgment.

As we marched forward, their staunch cries ceased. For a moment, everything went deafeningly silent and uncomfortably still — even our footsteps were robbed of their guiding vibration. We stopped before a gigantic golden door, framed by the darkness and bedazzled in precious stones. It was carved with unfamiliar symbols; it began to open. A radiant sapphire light briefly illuminated the long Hallway of Sorrows. For a moment, I gazed back, before an energy pulled me from the creature's grip and into a magnificent spherical room. My demonic escort was paralyzed by a brilliant indigo light, unable to cross the threshold of divinity.

The door slowly shut. Death was left to its duty; my paramania quelled.

The new floor felt smooth and sterile. The feeling of being trapped under ice passed. I was made comfortable and no longer aware of my naked form. An unknown source of light seemed to be reflecting immense and unknown colors off of the crystal walls, while a choir of 6,500 languages gracefully danced through the reverent air. The voices were humble, grateful and sanctified — a distant cry from the wails of the underworld or the moans of purgatory. It was beautiful and surreal.

Resurrecting to my sturdy feet, my eyes were captured by a large onyx table with 12 golden thrones, all facing the Council of Lords. Seated were the silhouettes of 11 individuals. They were adorned in the finest of linens and robes. An emerald hue surrounded them. They seemed like statues, locked in a forward position and unaware of my arrival. Scribed upon their chairs were the names: *Rand, Simon, Juno, Icarus, Zane, Benjamin, Dez, Neco, Grayson, Ash, Elisa* and *Magnus*.

Crowded by disbelief, a thunderous yet compassionate voice requested my attendance. I cautiously stepped toward the anonymous human frames and took my place in the vacant throne.

It was then I was able to recall my eternal name; it was Neco. As I lowered myself into my throne, my body was instantly clothed in a golden robe and fixed into place. My lifetimes were projected upon large crystal walls. Every visceral memory came rushing back, as if it was being downloaded into my spirit. I was forced to relive every tragic and beautiful moment of my physical journey. I not only recalled my times on Earth, but could also feel the horror of my previous afterlives.

I had been selected for *The Program*.

+++

The Council of the Lords consisted of red, white, black and gray birds, small in stature and similar to a raven. Each bird sat poised, stern and centered before couplings of three seated chosen ones. Their legs, feet and razor-sharp beaks were golden and their eyes burned like rubies.

The red bird represented time and space and was called *Anan*.

The white bird represented knowledge and was called *Ath*.

The black bird represented creation and was called *Isis*.

The gray bird represented death and was called *Than*.

Together they formed the basis for everything.

"Time is an illusion of space. With the division of space, there's time," Anan repeatedly spoke.

"From nothing comes everything," Ath crowed in all languages.

The Council's message reverberated through the room, in a choir of echoes. We could feel the gravity of their diction and understand inception through words. Our souls shattered like heavenly mitosis.

"All things have a beginning," bellowed Isis.

"All things have an end," whispered Than.

Our eyes remained open, while the Council paused to allow infinite wisdom to illuminate our beings.

We were becoming angelic hybrids.

With motion, the birds directed our attention toward the interior of the crystal expanse and merged into a singular entity. A magnificent light vibrated through our souls, as the shape of a dual-gendered being reflected our image. The Council's illumination allowed our enervated minds the ability to palate its presence, without suffering a swift cognitive obliteration. It then morphed into a pulsating spherical energy and began expanding to engulf the entire chamber. We were surrounded by fire and light.

The heavens spoke.

"You have been chosen to lead a new world. Your children will be part mortal and divine by decree. They will be equipped with the knowledge of our ages, given dominion over past lives and the ability to feel the dimensionality of time. They will have the authority to bring an end to what was begun and the wisdom to breathe new life into future generations," it proclaimed.

The room shook.

"You will be imprisoned by physical dictates of life and death, unable to enter The Beyond, until a miracle child is born of a beloved mortal. The children of tomorrow will be known as The Crystalline. Failure to produce a child will result in a reincarnated life. Once your child is born, your participation in The Program will cease and you will ascend. Your free will cannot be interfered with," it added.

The whites of our eyes blackened, allowing our pupils to fully access to The Council's proclamation.

"Your memories will be vanquished, until the earth stone has made 18 revolutions around the sun. Your reintegration into society is of dire importance. You must know their law, as they understand it, and relearn the basic principles of science, math and history, as to build a basis for the information that will be unlocked in your human body. This will help you to avoid premature shock or brain damage. To be a perfect union, your Earth born baby must be conceived with the person you hold most dear. This undeniable union is paramount in producing a Crystalline," it furthered.

Our heartbeats reverberated and pounded throughout the chamber.

"When it's time, The Council will call you all back together. Now, go and choose your earthly family!"

Like a clock, we were then directed and isolated into 12 corners of the chamber and able to observe infinite projections of earthly couples, due to conceive. It was up to us to determine the best scenario for actuation in The Program. Most chose stable families, as they felt it would provide them security in the formative years, while others desired autonomy and deliberately picked dysfunctional homes; they felt this would best-equip them for the mission and limit any personal attachments or distractions, as darker forces would inevitably be out to stop us from bringing a Crystalline into existence.

I could feel peoples' lives, as I reached into the vivid projections. I could sense their pains and see their auras. Instantly, their memories were uploaded into my spirit for discernment. I dissected and studied thousands of potential hosts. With time an immeasurable variable, we used dreams to communicate with potential surrogates. When I chose my earthly father, we met in a vision and reviewed his significance and my purpose in The Program.

He accepted.

In this dream, landscapes still appeared earthly, but matter no longer existed. We sat on a green hillside and gazed upon the ocean. Even in transparency, we could still hear and feel the waves crash upon the shore and smell the fresh blades of grass. These were the constructs of his creation, as he imagined them. I vividly recall the skyline. It was a beautiful combination of orchid rings and tangerine.

As we parted ways, he awoke with no memory of this account.

Grace would guide him.

+++

CHAPTER 2
REBORN INTO FOREVER

Vociferous screams filled an anticipating hospital room. My indignant mother launched an all-out attack of off-color and unintelligible word combinations toward my patient and unguarded father; her general lack of poise wasn't uncommon, but on this ceremonious occasion her temper tantrum was warranted. The walls, which bore witness to the event, were a cold yellow, like the autumn air surrounding the St. Joseph's Medical Center in Baltimore, Maryland.

The day was September 24th and the year has been erased from record.

My overwrought mother had been in delivery for 18 painful hours. The spell cast by the epidural had long run dry. Even her persistent tears had given up their plight and succumbed to the stark reality their tiny lubricating wishes were only making a nuisance of the situation. Gowned in the whitest of cloaks, the doctors and nurses stood like angels. They never wavered their attention and refused to leave her post.

In the unreachable corner of the room stood an old Solid State 12" black and white television. Static flickered, before an American flag ushered in the National Anthem, indicating a new day had come and it was time to sign-off on the past. There was always a certain uneasiness the image suggested. It may have been its association with the witching hours, or simply because it signified a pause in our access to humanity. For whatever the reason, it was fitting. By all accounts, I was entering an old downtrodden world and tasked with rebuilding a fallen empire; I was just unaware.

It all sounds rather grandiose when you think about it — and it was.

My exasperated mother gasped and made a final Herculean push, before delivering my tiny torso into mankind's unsuspecting arms. There were no Magi clamoring for my arrival, just the rumblings from a passing storm; I had arrived, whether a faithless world wanted me or not. Heavy rain pounded upon the thick industrial strength steel-wired window panes, but was deafened by sighs of relief, bringing closure to my mother's exhaustive labor. Begrudgingly, I was cleaned and snipped from her womb, presented to my father and rested upon her chest. My first cry was joyous, yet terrified.

"Who were these people?" I wondered.

My feeble brain was an unaffected slate of firing synapses and saturated with wonderment. I was digesting and dissecting the tiniest of life's riddles. To suggest, 'I was born in a crossfire hurricane,' as postulated by Jagger, would be a lyrical understatement; though, it would prove to be a fitting metaphor for the pending collision of worlds.

The first day passed. No one was the wiser.

Under the shroud of a blanketing new day's sun, we were escorted through the bustling lobby in a wobbly wheelchair and brought to the automatic hospital door exit. The magnificence of the burning star's radiation ignited feelings of something I was not prepared to remember. These moments of deja vu have immeasurable value, but are not always as interpretable as hunger, in the genesis stages;

I'm told, I was starving. I didn't only crave formula, but also my virgin life and a connection with my unsuspecting parents.

The Moody Blues strummed their eloquent sorrow, as I was rushed from my father's old red Ford pickup truck into a quaint nearby suburban home. Without pause, I was introduced to the rest of my new family, which included two mammoth-sized dogs and a sister. The lava lamps and wood paneling suggested it was the 70s. The psychedelic wallpaper wreaked havoc upon my limited concentration. Beneath my immersed toes rested a brown shag carpet. My reach was limited, but my new dogs accommodated my vertical limitation and lassoed me with tongues.

These are the moments when the stars align and the world seems to be in perfect harmony.

As a quiet young lad, I quickly acclimated to the new found freedoms of physical life, while days passed and memories accumulated. The clouds were the canvas of my imagination, while Bull-Bull, my German Sheppard, and Pandora, my collie, protected my tireless days in the yard from the potential thieves of my creation. This was my Shangri-La; a sanctuary, in which I spent many afternoons lost, content to play alone. As if by reflex, I would stare upon the sun for guidance, despite warnings. I couldn't resist the feeling I received from staring into the sky's brightest light.

+++

I wasn't alone. The Council of the Lords had littered the other 11 chosen souls across the planet.

Though we were destined to meet again, only a few of us had chosen to be conceived in North America. Some saw The Program as an opportunity to become cultured and inspired, while others chose to revisit the familiar places of their affected past. In the most spiritual sense, our souls were on a permanent vacation, until otherwise notified.

Rand was raised in Germany. Simon was resurrected in Israel. Juno took refuge in Rome. Icarus was conceived in Greece. Benjamin was born in London, neighboring Zane in Ireland. Dez lived in New Mexico. Grayson tackled New York. Ash was raised in Scotland. Elisa was born in California and Magnus invaded Illinois.

Time was our conductor.

Before traversing the pre-egoic ocean of my childhood hysteria and actualizing, my absentee mother left to explore a tidal wave of premature midlife crisis feelings. My chameleon-like sister and I instinctively became amicable and strategic in dealing with our rather absurd situation. Her dependency on my guilt-ridden father was understandable, as they were both left picking up the shattered pieces of a split family, in the midst of trying to console a confused innocent. My steadfast dad worked tirelessly to provide a life for us.

Father Time, on the other hand, was never on his side.

To bridge the quickly parting seas of familial madness, my resilient sister defaulted to a survivalist role and was instantly drawn to the maternal sense of purpose it gave her. Short of painting my face, as the sister she always wanted, she remained insistent on blanketing me from the horrors a strange new world had delivered to our doorstep.

As the blurring seasons passed, music became the glue holding my lonely father and me together. He would strum and finger pick his favorite melodies on an old Yamaha acoustic guitar and softly sing to his eager audience of one; he aspired to someday perform before thousands in Central Park, just as his rock n' roll heroes Simon and Garfunkel had done. Melodic mornings provided me with a much needed connection, before he was forced back onto the haunted streets to investigate and interrogate the oppositions of humanity.

His dream of a more harmonious existence seemed attainable, as he plucked away his free time and tried capturing his canticles on distressed studio equipment. This obsessive desire would foreshadow my coming days and guide my unsuspecting mind through the devil's playground. By night, my inspiration came from the toy inspired posters and glow in the dark galaxies littering my chamber walls. The bed was fully stocked with stuffed feline protectors. These were the guardians of the unknown and the defenders of tomorrow!

Protected or not, I still slid into my robot-inspired sheets and swiftly pulled my red comforter over my suspicious mind to hide my shifty eyes from the inhabitants of the dark. When you truly focus, you can hear the Beelzebub's shadowy footsteps and sense the presence of 1,000 unwanted ghosts. My childhood anxieties of the night were nothing compared to what I'd witness in my dreamscapes.

+++

In twilight, the embers from human remains cascaded upon me, while the unmistakable taste of brimstone arrogantly danced upon my chapped lips. My face melted, as the weight of hot air scalded my calloused lungs with each futile gasp. My mangled torso was overgrown and my features were exaggerated by dehydration. I could feel every muscle tearing through my skin, while my soul eagerly tried to escape the hell scorned body surrounding me.

Just as I was able to communicate with my future guardians through dreams, The Council would disseminate these types of riddles to me. I was often shown these deplorable landscapes and forced to taste the cancerous pang of life after life, forever reminded of the gift I'd been given. The pressure of my new life made it feel like a curse. I didn't understand the visions. I only recognized my fear.

If only I could awake!

My eyes gazed upon a holocaust, while countless bodies fueled an eternally hungry fire. Often, I was in a fight for my life with another individual. I didn't recognize the entity, but knew we were connected and these visions were meant to be a warning. We'd exchange blows, tear flesh and gouge each other's eyes out. The wails of our battle were intensified by the jeers of the undead. It was a collision of forces, one fallen and one pulled under.

These dreams were guideposts; none of my father's musings, nor army of plush kittens could stop them. Every time I awoke, it was like a resurrection. These nocturnal terrors were the bridge between life and death. No matter how many times I won the battle for consciousness, I knew it would never be over.

I was reborn into forever.

CHAPTER 3
EXPOSITION

Grade school was an afterthought. I had a natural attraction to education, but my preoccupation was to create. The latter won the Cold War over my torn focus. With starry eyes, I'd gaze through ghostly windows and remain aloof. My SOS to the world dribbled off my tender lips, as imagination became a reflex. Security was a freckled thought, but a cherished illusion. I wasn't in danger of being torn from anyone or anything, which I couldn't easily recreate.

The world I'd known was a cruel mistress. My nights were a restless current and my days, a lingering tide. Socializing was a cumbersome nonevent, a mere formality of being forced into civility. Trust was an uneven crutch, relied upon by the dependent masses, while genuine connections left me feeling like a roulette ball, dancing upon the hopes of a gambler's future regret. For me, loss, separation and pain lived in love's charming arms. The voices in my head kept me company in my elementary years. That's not to say I didn't make friends, but I was an introvert by circumstance. Creationism was godliness. I was more than willing to be led down the Yellow Brick Road, if it meant someday shaming the man behind the emerald and gold curtain.

My appetite for displacement brought violent storms to my academic doorstep. It wasn't that I didn't comprehend the general teachings and principles, I just ceased to find grandeur in societal posturing. Without a social reason to adjust my temperament, I was content to doze off and dream about crushing the wicked witch who'd caused my resentment. Tomorrow was a better time. It was a place I believed in.

It took years, but I eventually snapped out of it. The beauty in day-tripping rested in knowing that a head in the clouds was a comfortable perspective traced with grounded fingers. Crash landings were scarce. As my father continued to pick-up the shattered pieces and trudge through his expanding black hole of doubt, our family awakened to the flickering lights of normalcy and Alice was yanked from the rabbit hole. Life wasn't perfect, but it was stable. We welcomed anew.

+++

Of the 12 chosen to participate in The Program, Simon Peter had a similar upbringing. His father was a god in the community. He was often forgotten and forced to live in the shadows of crowded streets. He sometimes felt like he was carrying the weight of the world on his shoulders; and, at times, he did. The streets were dusty and the air was dry, but his thirst for the arts was an overflowing inkwell of unquenchable mystery.

He grew up in a small Israeli town, near the West Bank. His home was always a source of unresolved conflict and televised anarchy. Though respected, his family didn't have a lot to spare, so he too sought the wiles of his imagination and was fascinated by magic. It was an affordable means of entertaining himself and the vagrants, while exploring the boundaries of reality. It provided an escape and a way for him to communicate his longing for an otherworldly connection. He longed for a place where the rules of possibility could bend.

He was a muse, like me.

+++

I dipped my tepid toes into the street puddles of adolescence. Melodies rained down, giving me a reason to dance in the cool spring rains of a blooming new hope. Instinct guided me toward the thunderous vibrations of an electric guitar. I let the wind guide my virgin sails to the songwriting dens it dared me to lie down in. Hours were spent listening, dissecting and trying to crack the codes of my favorite minstrels. The harsh noises my instrument created weren't always a welcome interference, but tolerated. These were the screams of art therapy, and seen as a healthy wave to surf to the shore. My father was supportive and understood the power music had over adversity, and its ability to heal.

He taught me to play.

My fingers cramped, curled and resisted. Tenacious, he'd arch and position my begrudging appendages like hardened clay. I was convinced my awkward fingers would fail the presumed measurement requirements, but we'd always press on. The cool steel beneath my concerned mitts burned like hot wires cutting soft flesh. My enthusiasm waxed and waned, but never was eclipsed by the omnipresent fear of failure. It wasn't an option in the space we called home.

An aspiring star was burning.

Even my modest efforts were encouraged and willingly rewarded with infinite recording time, in the incomplete studio space carved out of our concrete-bedded basement jungle. The tiny room, adorned in nostalgic wooden paneling, provided my father an escape from the otherwise mundane existence of suburban domestication. Modern adaptations were a never ending work in progress, but a Fostex A80 8-track reel-to-reel, a brand-matching mixing board, microphones and an army of acoustic ornaments were permanent fixtures. It was a man cave.

The societal conventions separating me from the wanderlust of fame, fortune and heroic autonomy were rock n' roll blasphemy. I'd toil my craft, skip school and fast, in hopes of someday dancing in the promised lands, whilst drinking from forbidden grails of temptation. Perhaps, then, my father could vicariously live through my songs and success. I could show him the universe through my kaleidoscope eyes, and bring the world's distressed heart to a fever pitch.

I would someday write my own prescription.

+++

From stable roots, Ash McKenzie grew up in Aberdeen, Scotland. From budding hands, her brush strokes were guided by The Lords, never ceasing to bear fruit. The seed planted in her musing heart sought to gather the earthly materials needed to create the inspirations of her divine spirit. This genesis would lay the foundation for her creative revelations. Even as a terrible two, her messy, spaghetti-inspired works would trump the best-laid efforts of the most aspiring neighboring artists. She embodied the official animal of her country; she was a unicorn, one in a billion and her palate, a rainbow.

Her paintings had the power to heal the broken and resurrect lost innocence. Born with a gold spoon in her mouth, and accustomed to the finest of easels, her poetic canvas demanded the adoration of the elite. Her home was a gallery and her parents never wavered in hosting their support. She was educated and dreamed of attending the University of Edinburgh, where she'd graduate, fall in love and spend the rest of her days painting a financial future for generations to come. She was the epitome of grace, style and class.

The curse of having it all was never knowing what it might be like to want. Ash struggled with genuine connections and in understanding the limitations of her endeavoring peers. She couldn't help but perceive them as lazy, misguided or beneath her elitist standards, which made developing meaningful relationships a cross.

Who will I identify with?

Who can I respect?

What can I gain from these people?

These questions plagued her innocent mind. This curiosity left her in a watershed, stuck between brilliance and bliss. She knew the other half existed, but was unable to traverse the channels. In a blink, her troubles were forgotten; her eyes, distracted by the beauty in her art, the magnificence of her mansion and the sea of surrounding possibilities. A curtain wall stood guard, making sure the lower class didn't penetrate her ignorance.

+++

All of The Program's chosen ones had an obstacle. Only a heightened purpose could clear the debris and undo the unconscious bias of our upbringings. For now, we were young. During puberty, I would notice my iris turning a subtle violet color, while performing. This was a signal, meant to guide my adolescent pursuits.

This physical manifestation of synchronicity inspired our art, encouraged our practice and sought to ignite the sacred gifts buried within. There was a certain level of narcissism required in identifying with this spectral shift, but an otherworldly justification in doing so. It was important for the participants of The Program to find and develop skill-sets and recognize their innate calling, as to attract and connect with the outside world, but more importantly to lure compatible love interests.

We incubated.

I treated the world like a stage and relentlessly reinforced the voyeuristic instincts of its inhabitants. It was this cinematic state of mind, which allowed me to observe the brilliance of inspired creation. School nights were spent scribing carnal riddles upon loose leaf paper, in hopes of someday purging my animalism upon unsuspecting theater patrons. Gazing through the lens of an alter-ego provided enough detachment to explore the depths of an expanding soul. The awaiting underground music scene was alive and breathing, and I, transfixed.

With each bedroom performance, my hunger grew and the radiant purplish hue in my eyes enhanced. I explored and pined over the intention of each word, manipulated the positioning and timing of every lyric and began penning a musical diary of my experience. A certain level of megalomania took hold, but I couldn't shake the sense of predestination. When future reels of tape were set into motion, I longed for my songs to pierce the hearts and minds of even the most pedestrian of onlookers.

Fulfillment was impossible and growth a constant. It was the perfect breeding ground for eternal torment. Closing in on my chosen skill-set meant I was edging closer to understanding self-love, a natural graduation of consciousness.

+++

No stranger to commencement, school came easy for one Programmer. Rand Backer's life was stern, sterile and built upon the bricks of a harder time. The Bible took center stage and read like a childhood novel. It was forcefully served, swallowed and digested in his adolescence. His parents expected the highest level of respect, written therein. Given his father's orders, he would readily challenge the devil to a duel. His greatest attention was focused on the details of God's tragedy, called 'Life.'

Pressed shirts and astute rhetoric set the stage for his silent soliloquy. To Rand, knowledge was greater than capital, because it could barter for wealth. It was a conscious stream of income.

His home was erected near the Fulda River in the town of Kassel after WWII. Plenty of neighboring parks and palaces consumed his view. These structures provided hope and refuge from the rituals of his deflated youth. Freedom was earned and hours were structured, mechanical and socially void. The daily pittance of porridge he consumed was a bland reminder of his uninspired surroundings. The walls were coated in flat and his heart a barren sheath. His parents were well-intended, but paving a highway to hell.

The exterior was inspired by the old cobblestone streets destroyed by the war. The furniture was a rickety cliché. All lavishes were earth born and kept far from the interiors of their grayscale sanctuary. Seated comfortably in the doorway, the tricolour flag was a subtle reminder that Germany reigned the domicile and its perimeter.

God offered them grace, but his affected parents were haunted and stubborn. He recognized their torment, but was challenged by the complexities of a vast cultural shift. Brainwashed, he would be their savior from a modest life and an endless penance. He would bring pride and peace back to his family and rebuild what the war had taken.

He had difficulty understanding abstract thinkers and free spirits. They were impulsive, perverse and lawless. Their homes were built on shaky ground and challenged the very core of his upbringing.

Without roots, how could a tree bear fruition?

The dreamers blew with the wind and would blow away for good, if God would grant him just one wish. Staring into the eyes of their nomadic souls generated disdain. He could see the shadowy reflection of a people destitute for harder times.

Rand knew his truth.

+++

No war compared to the cancerous battle being fought between middle school walls. Self-discovery, hormones and coupling brought the sheep face-to-face with vampire wolves. Teenage minds would hemorrhage on homework and drama alone. The intimidation and arrogance of the older classes only exasperated the need for a strong defense, cronies and a myriad of exit strategies. The short-lived reign of an 8th grade bravado allotted them an excuse to spray paint their insecurities and retribution upon defenseless lockers, projecting immeasurable fear upon underlings.

Nervous, the song remained the same and shielded my virgin heart. Music was the key and my future peers, the gatekeepers. Hours of practice and the gluttonous ingestion of rock iconoclasts equipped me with the required vocabulary for initiation. Like-minded individuals found me and connected. Bullish sports were of no consequence. I dabbled. My immediate peer group consisted of: Punks, rockers, nerds and freaks.

As for love?

I had a mysterious and romantic interest in intelligent introverts.

Though the punks seemed to be fighting a war against an unknown threat, I appreciated their thirst for cred and their willingness to bring normalcy to fisticuffs. They lived to draw distinctions, foster principles and write anthems of revolution. Their code, was an oath tattooed on ideals; only they knew the rules. Amendments were made by the leader of a criminal hierarchy and intended to strengthen a cultish cause. Acceptance meant security and was an ironic mark of individuality.

My increasingly zealous trips to the basement recording studio tested my father's otherwise patient demeanor. He was nearing wits' end and suffering an understandable exhaustion with my obsession. We were two peas in a pod, raised on opposite sides of Eden. The inevitable shift in our dynamic was sparked by my new Crue, an expanding generational gap, and the heightened awareness of unresolved and inconsolable maternal issues. Time stored precise records and forced actualization to draw strain. The less he understood, the less he could tolerate my musical vision and color-coded shoelaces!

Throughout these years, my bizarre night terrors persisted.

+++

It was a crisp winter evening. In the shadows, I gazed through my bedroom window toward the western lights of a magnificent orange and purple skyline. My affected black light flickered like a séance candle. Plumes of rebellious patchouli smoke asphyxiated the second floor of my vacant Christian home. Chair cocked, my hypnotized feet rested upon a wood framed television set. An audience of cheap beer and bluesy cigarettes witnessed.

Counting sheep...

Chasing REM, I walked naked through a crystal landscape of snow mounds. Icy sharp daggers poked through the thin layers of powdery white snow, cutting a path; presumably, to a superhero's home. A gray bird circled and pecked my stubborn skull, hungering for my vision. Like a motherless child, it never wavered in its quest for notice. Insistent to follow, a trail of drawn blood drained from my trembling limbs and marked the journey. With each begrudging step, the gray bird's will tested my determination.

Echoing, I could hear the cries of a small child whistling through the tundra. The roar of lions and tantrums of thunder swiftly followed. Blanketing the ashy sky, purple and gray cumulonimbus clouds descended. The antagonizing sun only peaked to reveal the horror of an apocalyptic storm. I was surrounded by darkness. There was no turning back.

Suddenly, the vision froze. I stared in glazed twilight, as a female hand repainted the entire scene on my quivering lips.

I awoke to the sound of a playful voice.

"Wake up! Wake up!"

CHAPTER 4
PAINT THE DESERT WITH MY HEART

A 35 hour trek across the United States left an exasperated Neco wandering aimlessly through the patterning Painted Desert. Stumbling toward a flat, barren expanse, roughly five miles off of the forgotten road, he stopped to siphon a moment of clarity and digest his tranquil surroundings. Nestled beneath his throbbing feet rested the volcanic ash of immeasurable years and an encapsulating white ring. The curiously marked shape was 30 feet in diameter. Iron embedded in the shale and mudstone compounds produced a reddish hue upon the universe's rocky stage props. The fixtures stood like gods, casting grandiose shadows. They were the omniscient voyeurs of a billion lifetimes.

"How long have you been here, Cowboy?" asked an inquisitive and flirtatious voice.

Emerging from behind an eclipsing rock formation was an elegantly dressed female. She was ravishing. Her pouting lips were a glossy Merlot. The powdery pale hue of a perfectly symmetrical skull sat like a heavenly backdrop, complimenting her mysterious long black locks, Saint Laurent styled dinner dress and large insect inspired rhinestone frames; all hints that she may have misjudged the Arizona climate, came from afar or simply didn't care.

"I could use a little distraction from these rattlesnakes, y' know?" she continued in an affected English accent. Her face couldn't hold back the blushing of an eager smile, nor departmentalize her attraction.

"What are we doing here?" Neco asked in a surprisingly deep and dehydrated voice.

"I'm not entirely sure. I'd imagine it's paramount, considering the hellish nightmares I've been having over the past 18 years!"

She reached out her finely adorned and manicured hand toward Neco.

"My name is Ash," she smirked.

"My dreams have been extremely vivid for some time, too! I never really knew what to make of them, but there were times when the lucidity made it impossible to wake. Have I seen you before?" questioned Neco. He stepped closer to shake her pretentious paw.

She paused and answered without a word.

Juxtaposed, Neco was dressed in a rather cliché rock n' roll ensemble. His tight jeans were the work of a bad seamstress and his feet, rarely seen antiquities, were comfortably lost in an unevenly worn pair of cowboy boots, due to an undiagnosed case of Rothbart's Foot. His posture was otherwise stout and only offset by an understandable exhaustion. A standard black V-neck t-shirt and crucifix accentuated his moderately-developed chest and was front-tucked into an obnoxiously noticeable belt buckle, inferring a general sense of style and sexuality.

Ash liked her find.

The two mechanically paced the circle in the sand. They kicked dirt and rocks in hopes the other might use mindless banter to break the increasingly awkward silence. Vultures swarmed in a circular and mocking trajectory. The southwestern sun glared, as if to warn them of the dangers of overstaying their welcome.

"So, where are you from?" asked Neco.

"Well, let's just say, I couldn't exactly drive here," offered Ash.

"I'm from across the pond," she quickly added. She didn't want to try Neco's patience.

In the distance, Neco spotted a watery silhouette and coughed for Ash's willing attention. The mirage appeared clothed in a grayish militant grade suit. A complimentary cream-colored dress shirt rested beneath, while his broad chest begged for a cool breeze. Fastened buttons were the dismay of his pulsating neck. Tightly trimmed side and back hair bristled like the cactus needles and his plume, slicked to the right. Pressed pants and a starched jacket tightly wrapped his soldiering heart.

He slowly removed his perfectly resting gray fedora, adjusted his onyx-framed formal spectacles and approached. His posture suggested he'd soon address the state, on behalf of a warring Republic. Adjusting the dangling noose beneath his collar and clearing his strangled throat, he articulated his calling.

"The answer to this riddle eludes me. I've traveled a great length and traversed a sea of horrors to find myself standing on the most inhospitable of American soils. I should be preparing for university and yet, I'm called. Does anyone know the meaning of this? You needn't speculate," he delivered.

Neco and Ash hesitated, turned to lock eyes and smirked. A proper introduction had failed to grace his rhetoric and his biting tone was as welcoming as the vultures overhead. They silently debated who would attempt to climb the social wall he'd built with his cold introduction. Neco stepped toward the man, motioning the lead.

"What's your name?" Neco asked.

"My name is of no consequence to you. You'd have already guessed it, had you been the one to lead me to this wasteland of the States. Should I find that you are the one who disturbed my slumber, and haunted my visions, I'll see it fit to have your eyes. I can only deduce you are as vacant as I," he barked, analyzing Neco's merits on appearance alone.

"If he is not your compass than you both remain lost. But, he may prove to be more valuable than your demeanor would suggest," offered Ash. She mirrored his tone, giving him a logical reason to let down his guard.

"And who, might I ask, are you?" questioned the man. His surly tone shifted to the depths of a new condescending low.

Neco and Ash huffed a pause. It was clear, pleasantries were a fleeting discourse. Silence discredited his hard-sought dominance. His inquiry became a cast shadow, longing to flee his presence. Infuriated, he lumbered, devoid of control.

"His name is Rand Backer," said a welcome voice.

Tickling his peripherals, Neco refocused his attention on the slender conductor demanding center stage. He manifested from the thinnest of desert air, like a surprised white rabbit being yanked from a top hat. He wore a plaid Polo shirt, tucked into fitting khaki slacks. His interpretive American garb was lassoed together with a formal black belt and finished with dusty footwear. Weathered, his complexion was dark and his hair was oily, short, blackish and parted down the center. He clearly didn't grasp western style, but was quite proficient in juggling the hippie-inspired devil sticks that the youth adored.

"How do you know that, sir?" asked Rand with begrudging respect.

"We met at a gas station, about 5 hours ago. You fumbled through your wallet to find a credit card and your passport fell onto the floor. I picked it up and set it on the counter, and happened to catch your name, country and date of birth. You never know when you might find yourself in the middle of the desert, trying to solve a mystery, right?" asked the flippant voice.

"I don't recall this? Am I to suppose you're the one

who brought me here?"

"Quite the contrary, your dreams brought you here. My name is Simon Peter. From my earliest days, magic has been my escape, but don't expect me to reveal everything, yet. We've only just met," he paused. "Suffice it to say, I've been plagued with the same nocturnal intrusions as the others. How are we not to assume you brought us here? After all, you did try to conceal your identity from complete strangers who wanted nothing more than to understand this rather precarious situation. I can only surmise you're hiding something or you're a dummkopf," Simon said.

"That's ridiculous," Rand fired back.

"Good, then I suggest we all play nice and try to make the absolute best of this strange day."

Mocking a compass, the group subconsciously positioned themselves on the 4 cardinal points of the white circle and began sharing their revelations. Like constellations, underlying themes connected the dots to their enigmatic calling and produced plausible scenarios. Their lives intersected like the branches of a river, still no one was able to distill enough sustenance to solve their spiritual puzzle. The air became thick, as their need for water began to outweigh their thirst for understanding.

"You don't think they'll just leave us out here to die, do you?" asked Neco.

+++

Neco was aware to a fault. A self-knitted shroud of mystery and a devil's modesty gave him a boyish charm, though his intellect was never questioned. He'd developed from negatives and was quick to leave pessimism in the world fading from his rear-view. Poised with quips, he'd flick a distraction, to avoid drifting from the familiar coasts of comfort. A bleached fauxhawk stood like an antenna; a symbol of his punk rock allegiance. It was the glaring beacon of his remaining innocence. It didn't arouse suspicion, but it did cast a shadow of doubt onto the likes of Rand and Simon.

Though mesmerized by Simon's rhetoric, Rand remained grizzly toward the group's dynamic and perplexed by the complexities of their plot. Solitude became his ally, while stewing in afterthoughts. Neco, Simon and Ash were content to feast on conversation, gluttons for each other's story. They imbibed, patiently awaiting a moment of pause to purge an ocean of life experiences. Being the only girl gave Ash the much needed attention she'd grown accustomed; it was served up and stomached, welcome or not.

To pass the time and to impress her, Simon cast out poetry, confident she'd catch his offering.

"Let me not the marriage of true minds
Admit impediments. Love is not love
Which alters when it alteration finds,
Or bends with the remover to remove:
O no! It is an ever-fixed mark
That looks on tempests and is never shaken;
It is the star to every wandering bark..."

"Shakespeare," she interrupted.

"Yes," he responded. "The Israeli people love studying English literature," Simon said.

"Simon, says. So, you chose to memorize Sonnet 116, word for word?" she suspiciously asked and punned.

"Is it any more odd that I can recite it than you can recall it?"

She clammed to thwart his flirtation, aware of Neco's perception.

The patience of Rand became noticeably tested.

"I feel it's best for us to focus and disclose any and all relevant information to the immediate events," insisted Rand.

"I'm from Baltimore, Maryland," offered Neco.

"I'm from Scotland," said Ash.

"He's from Kassel, Germany," said Simon, while

motioning to Rand.

"Thank you, Simon," Rand snarked.

The heat was consuming everyone's patience. They were fading.

+++

Ash spent the majority of her restless time fantasizing about running her fingers through Neco's tabby-like hair and christening their romance on the reddish rocks. This was the perfect scenario for a one night stand, give or take the German-Israeli audience of two. Odds were, they'd never see each other again.

Justified!

In various versions of her sex fantasy, Simon and Rand stood guard, watched or were instantly struck dead by rattlesnakes. In another dream, the missionary tragically caught fire on the molten rocks! She had to reset her impetus, but was determined to get her fantasy right.

Unknown to the others, her heartbeat often became irregular and her mind agitated, while trying to departmentalize the inane background dialog and feuds of her new acquaintances. She wished she could find life's mute button, and pause god's cosmically-arranged talk show. The universe was interfering with her daydreams. It was then, she remembered, her nocturnal episodes were what got her lost in the desert.

When she snapped to, she stiffened like lumber and stood to make an unscripted announcement.

"I'm an artist. I've spent my entire life painting and awaiting the world's notice and adoration. It's what I adore. It's who I am! If we're to tempt fate, I pray I'm left with enough strength of mind, body and spirit to paint this godforsaken desert with my bleeding heart."

CHAPTER 5
LEAVING TONIGHT

Middle school was a passing spring breeze; the calm, before the nor'easter rolled in. Grades fell atop one other like an avalanche. At the pass lied the wreckage of teenage confusion. I mysteriously maintained a solid grade point average, and remained drawn and quartered to my craft. As the adolescent cocoon was shed, a once meek and introverted young boy became a social butterfly. My consciousness was entering a brave New World. Before long, I was introduced to various recording studios and finally able to give my overworked father a well-deserved break from my creative whims.

My only real obstacle was the towering wall of Babylon, which stood between me and the more mature crowds. My concerned parents were determined to help me avoid their missteps, which made it difficult for me to participate in the extra-extracurricular activities of my calling and foster my wanted peer group. This blockade only reinforced by creativity, intensified my hunger and allotted me ample fuel and aggravated time to plot a revolution.

Like the dinner table, my stage was set.

+++

No stranger to anarchy, Dez Nave hopped on his makeshift motorcycle, and burst into the sunset. Dust soared. He was a loner and thrived in arid environments, where the grass was high and the roots run deep. His facial hair and skin followed suit.

He was raised by a far more sinister force than wolves. Abandoned, abused and forced to defend himself from the closest of familial threats, life was his architect. Learning to hunt, defend and rely on instincts made him a callous assassin. He self-generated a cliché solace, from switchblades, whiskey and one night stands.

A long dusty road, and inoperable rusty antique cars provided a welcome barricade between his trailer and the outside world. An old neon sign occasionally flickered a familiar welcome, from his dilapidated auto repair shed; a metaphor for the fulgurating light in his eyes. For both reasons, business and money were scarce.

Beneath a smoldering New Mexican sun, he practiced Aikido and awaited the day he'd be forced to defend himself from a paranoia-induced post-apocalyptic world. Shirts were optional and his jeans read like a Rosetta Stone of tattered denim history. Unwashed memories were like the rings of a tree, but no one dared to get close enough to interpret them.

A dark energy surrounded him. Society was comfortable keeping distance, fearing the bodies of missing children would someday be exhumed from his lot. Given the right hallucinogenic opportunity, the devil would surely dance. A grave absence filled his soul and his heart was freckled with pain. No greater peace would purify his being than the destruction of a world he no longer believed live in.

Abandonment was always his justification.

Though graced with moments of hope and heart, the greatest obstacle standing between peace and narcissism was the pride acquired through his autonomy. It was his shield from the calloused world. Illusions of control forced fear and insecurity to cower at his feet. Reality told him, time would ultimately tear his fortress of solitude to shreds.

Dez was not the creator of his life, he was the embodiment of scorn!

+++

Through childhood, I'd learned that the *unforgiven* wore a myriad of masks. Static scrambled through my miserable factory car stereo system, as an evangelical preacher clawed through the airwaves. Familiar shivers awoke the nerves on my lethargic spine; tiny hairs stood in refute, like transfixed heretics. Without pause, I downshifted, leaned toward the radio dial and changed the frequency. My conscious mind was flashing intermittently, while lazy eyelids committed to resting upon my cheekbones.

Wake-up!

Snapping to attention, like a slap bracelet, I hurried to light a smoldering coffin nail, rolled down the temperamental driver's side window, forcibly inserted a familiar blasphemous analog antidote and psyched myself up for the endless road ahead. Arctic temperatures, nicotine and rock n' roll were common cures for sleep-driving.

Even in my youth, I found a morbid and undeniable obsession with the darker side of Christianity. Often sent gallivanting off to radical summer exorcisms, prescribed as youth revivals, I soon grew tired of being serenaded to sleep by the midnight hellfire stories of our well-intended, but irresponsible youthful youth pastors. Keeping organized religion at a controllable distance felt like the virtuous thing to do. Something about their tales of possession, demons and near-death trips to the pit hit a little too close to home. It was as if my being was feverishly trying to ignite a suppressed account. Though my vacant mind repeatedly failed to connect the unknown feelings with a memory, I knew a justified nerve was struck and my anxiety about the afterlife was warranted.

I became infatuated with solving the riddle. My free time was spent obsessively consuming prophecy videos, horror movies and conspiracy or alien theory documentaries. I was attracted to any subconscious forms of exposure therapy I could get my adrenal gland dripping hands upon. I had an addict's predisposition for self-medication.

Through my experiences and study, I quickly learned the power fear could have over people and how to use it. In cowardice, my voice became a megaphone for projecting my chickenhearted insecurities upon the innocent, in a very sinister and manipulative way. My songs were a warning to anyone who might intend to cross me. It was a warped adolescence on steroids, with its own ghostly soundtrack.

It turned out that a lot of society's misfit kids felt the same exasperation, from a life built on faith. I knew I could someday be their mouthpiece or inspiration; a champion for the underdog! I might even be able to help lead them from the depths of their tragic lives.

Life loves a happy ending, right?

The future was bright, but the destination unknown.

+++

Displaced, from birth, traveling was a way of life for Grayson Miller. He wasn't a military brat by nature, though his parents lived and breathed the United States Marine Corps. Intensity was their baggage, from long tours in Iraq and Afghanistan. His father had been stationed throughout the U.S. on various missions for the United States Special Operations Command (SOCOM), forcing migration to become a reflex.

As their careers began to simmer, they constituted a

new life, full of distractions, and laid roots in the most populated borough of New York City. Brooklyn operated with the same sense of urgency the military had accustomed them to, and provided Grayson with a cultural basis for their hard-fought freedoms.

His parents demanded academic results and made sure he attended the finest private institutions the city offered. Out of respect, he maintained his studies, but also developed a very strong social propensity. He understood diversity and common sense and valued it as equally as the books smarts relentlessly being crammed into his evolving skull.

New York embodied the melting pot of tolerance and diversity the country was founded upon. It reigned supreme, like their pizza, as the greatest city the United States could boast. His parents drew esteem in its preservation of their country's mantra and took pride in the magnificent penumbra The Big Apple cast upon the aspiring world. They'd often visit Manhattan, if only to bask in the shadows of the buildings they helped erect and the threats once razed. This was where dreams come true.

+++

My haunting and lucid night terrors intensified with age. With my 18th birthday on the horizon, I was awoken to the elegant rhetoric of an alluring angelic figure, hovering atop my queen-sized mound of blankets. She directed my calm, but couriered a stern order, while I scrambled to hide my filthy clothes and embarrassing magazine collection. The fiery hue in her brilliant eyes was piercing.

"Your time has come, Neco! You have been chosen," she proclaimed, in an unusually deep vibration. "Your new spiritual family awaits you, in the Painted Desert. You are to arrive on August 16th for a harmonic convergence. Leave your car on the highway and I will guide your tepid steps."

I reached toward the apparition and could feel the

intense energy field of a heavenly Aphrodite radiating through my clammy nerve-stricken hand. My veins pulsed with a bluish hue, from the electricity of our connection. As quickly as she arrived, she vanished. I never awoke!

My father heard the commotion, rushed into the bedroom and hurried for illumination. By happenstance, he accidentally plugged in a nearby black light and found my flat white walls covered in neon words and bizarre symbols — all scribed with a glow-in-the-dark crayon. The graffiti of my innocence captured his speech. He gazed in wonderment and throbbed with undeniable rage.

"What is this? Why have you done this to your walls?" he insisted.

The hieroglyphics of my youth exposed my visions and validated his worst fears.

"Dad, I have to head west," I said, without hesitation.

Shackling his tongue, he turned, walked from the possessed room and took shelter in his reverent chambers. The deafening silence was soon shattered by muffled cries. He damned his parental shortcomings, intent to cast the devil from out. He couldn't have been further from home.

+++

Program member, Magnus West, had his own demons to attend. Filled with an unquenchable thirst for rebellion and attention, his teenage heart wreaked havoc upon tradition. He'd skateboard through the high school halls of the Chicago-area school district, as if no distinction could be made between the streets and the freshly mopped concrete flooring. His parents were simple hardworking folks, but emotionally deserted. They cared, but never truly committed to parenthood. His father soothed his blue collar existence with frequent trips to the local bar, swift to asperse barbed wire remarks toward anyone in sight.

Magnus remained out of mind.

He lived in an average-sized aged rancher in the

Beverly neighborhood, along Western Avenue. His free time was spent dismantling and reassembling untagged motorcycles and listening to the hard rock wisdom of his heroes. Occasionally, his father would join him and rally his support, but a long string of false promises to someday help him ride, left his discourse falling on a deafening soul.

The underbelly of his long brown hair was shaved and typically drawn to intimidate others. His cred was noted by fellow classmates; academics were a back-burner priority. He was the criminal. He'd learned how to manipulate the system and others. Just about everything he loved was stolen and his misdemeanor rap sheet was an expanding insult to justice. Video game competitions, cheap wine and cocaine consumed his focus. A trail of broken and deflowered hearts lead directly to his doorstep.

His cold heart didn't know how to care.

+++

The summertime breeze was unseasonably crisp and whistled through my cracked windows, as I traveled toward the Painted Desert. The air conditioner remained full throttle, blasting a hurricane upon my pale affected face. The goal was to keep my shuttering eyelids in a northern position, while pushing off the east coast, charting a western course, down an endless highway.

Disturbing discourse with myself made the clock's mockery of my progress tolerable. The dirty passenger side seat was stocked like a corn silo with my favorite snacks and the buckling glove compartment was filled to the brim with paraphernalia, worn-out rock tapes and an avalanche of state specific maps. Nestled within was a spoken word cassette that my father had personalized and given to me, making his sentiments and the memories of our departure replay like a broken record.

Looking back, the morning following the awkward glow-in-the-dark crayon incident was a second chance.

Slinking into a bright new day, I remember seeing my aloof father shrouded in the kitchen's sunlight, solemnly staring into a miniature television set. His words were chosen, rehearsed and delivered, carefully; he feared any missteps would send me running — *faster* and further!

I was already gone.

"So, you're really going to go?" he said, in hopes my conviction had wavered.

"Dad, I have to..." I started, knowing my explanation would fall on sane ears, I clammed.

"You don't have to go anywhere," he insisted, "But, if you have to leave, please be safe out there. It's a jungle!" he exclaimed, as if trying to convince us both of his blessing, while stomaching the dramatic shift my Rumspringa inferred, atop his emotionally-driven and brimming third bowl of banana covered Cheerios.

After a few rotations of the small hand, my shortsighted packing was complete and my pilgrimage began. The complexities of the situation were never given the weight they deserved, nor a chance to take hold. My cronies, neighbors and relatives were signaled, presumably by smoke, we exchanged swan songs, and my vehicle nonchalantly reversed from the driveway. I made it to the closest convenience store, checked off my itemized to-do list, withdrew the last 200 dollars to my name and began descending into the abyss, to which I was called.

There was a certain romanticism to it all, but when I fastened my seat belt, it all began to click.

CHAPTER 6
BACK FROM A SUICIDE

The sun was a persistent antagonist. All energy, siphoned; no explanation given. The murderous growl of a motorcycle broke-up the monotony. The hindquarters of the throttling hog kicked up a hellish sandstorm, blocking the group's vision from what lurked behind. When the dust settled, an average-sized, shirtless individual emerged. He was dirty, wore a black helmet, adorned with a rooster-inspired orange comb, and stood with devilish poise.

Slowly removing his silver-tinted aviator glasses, the beast pulled a joint from his inside leather jacket pocket and commanded his steel horse to hush and heel. The heart of the radio remained beating, while The Rolling Stones, "Sympathy for the Devil" killed the dead air with an awaited dialog. Dark history surrounded Jagger's poetry, which made its eerie message seem awkwardly cliché. The cruel summer sun only reinforced the notion that they were in hell!

The man slowly walked toward the transfixed group. They were noticeably tense, sitting with crossed legs on the mysterious ivory sphere. He peered down with a cobra's disdain and magnetic eyes.

"Name's Dez," he gruffed.

"Hi," they responded, with begrudging acceptance.

"I really don't feel like I belong here," said Rand, under his breath.

"You don't," responded Simon.

"Do any of you scarecrows have a little fire?" asked Dez, patronizing their suspicions.

"I always carry a light. You never know when you might find yourself in the middle of the desert and asked by a Hell's Angel for fire. Ironic, really?" sassed Ash, curious if Simon caught her mocking quip. "First, soldier, I think we'd all like to know a little bit more about you. First question, are you Evel Knievel?"

"Well, I have about 99 dollars that belonged to someone else, I'm withdrawing from dope and I've been on my uncomfortable bike for roughly seven hours in this godforsaken heat. I think you know why I'm here, darling," he barked, allowing his words to idle. "Now, can I get that light?"

"Give him the light," said Neco, distracting Dez's focus and cooling the vibrations.

Dez arrogantly whet his budding marijuana tongue and lit the roach. He tossed back Ash's white lighter, refusing to cease eye contact, and sauntered from the uneasy group. He nested in the rocks, to enjoy his grass in peace.

In what appeared to be a collective moment of deja vu, Magnus came barreling toward the circle. His motorcycle, fully operational. Though his entrance was far more subtle than that of his cancerous colleague, he still managed to raise a few eyebrows, fueling the speechless group's suspicion of what the getaway mile demon's club had conspired to do with them. A human sacrifice, orchestrated by a notorious motorcycle gang, seemed entirely plausible.

"I definitely don't belong here," said Rand, under his breath.

"I already told you, that!" joked Simon. Petty banter

drew them closer.

"What do you got there, hot shot?" asked Dez, unimpressed.

"Do you have a problem?" responded Magnus.

"Not yet! Let the territorial pissing begin..."

Magnus shed a much smaller shadow, content to kiss babies and shake hands with the confused company. He didn't have the energy to cast the same bravado as Dez. His approach was the cool rain of a passing storm. His jaded heart hadn't been completely soiled by his ruffled upbringing. There was still a glimmer of hope in the iris of his emerald eyes, despite the darkness lurking behind his easy smile.

"The dreams got so bad that I tried to overdose and succeeded," offered Magnus. He knew they were looking for answers, but were fatigued by questions. "When I died, a bright light took me to a beautiful circular room. I knew, I'd been there. On magnificent crystal walls, it showed me a desert landscape. Twelve purple-blue stones surrounded a large white circle. I was told my time had not come and was tragically sent back. I believe those rocks represent us!"

The revelation gave everyone hope. There was suddenly a reason to believe they weren't simply ushered to death's oasis and that other travelers, with answers, would be arriving. Jealousy and suspicion drew a sobering Dez from the rocks. His instinct to control lacked reach. He became increasingly embittered by Magnus's ability to communicate and ability to connect.

"I don't believe a word of it," he hurled from the distance.

"Wasn't it Mick Jagger who said, 'Lose your dreams and lose your mind...'" mocked Simon. He knew Dez would catch his snark. "Dreams are chased on faith. Are you suggesting you do not believe in dreams?" he paused, placing Dez in check. "Are we to assume you simply had nothing better to do today?" asked Simon, moving him into checkmate.

"I guess you could say, our man, Magnus, is back from a suicide?" added Neco.

Dez scoffed and returned to the clouds from which he came. The group disregarded his attitude and began deliberating on the meaning of the stones. Color and quantity were the Mystery Machine's only clues. Their road, paved in speculative chatter, remained a welcome distraction from the still of voiding minds.

"Hello, I trust you're all tired, thirsty and confused," offered a wandering mirage.

The man was dressed in a yellow and blue striped Polo shirt, corduroy slacks and white leather Nike Air golf shoes. Short dirty blonde hair was tucked beneath a Titleist cap. He was of average stature and appeal, offsetting the complexities of his city with the simplicity of his ironic posture. Pulling a yellow No. 2 pencil from behind his relaxing ear cartilage, he began scribbling notes into a spiral notebook. They were sure he'd soon hurl questions and perform a full audit of sorts.

"What's your name?" scoffed Dez, from the distance.

"Grayson. I'm from Brooklyn. I'd have been here sooner, but my flight was delayed in Texas."

"Thanks for the insight. You don't look like you're from New York," prodded Dez.

"You don't look like you'd know," said Simon.

"Well, that's 7 stones," added Neco.

+++

The group grew exasperated. Rand sat quietly. He was synthesizing life's fodder, trying to produce his own tree of knowledge. If patience was a fleeting virtue and mindless chatter an uneven crutch, he felt an anxious silence might bear him the sought after fruits of wisdom. Ash had also reached her social limit and took refuge in Neco's welcoming lap. Following the tempting lead of groupthink, Simon kneaded the sandy ground beneath his dirty paws and curled for a nap. Dez baked.

While the group recharged their taxed senses, Magnus took the initiative to stockpile water from a nearby gas station. It was there he found Elisa asking for directions. Her abandoned demeanor immediately gave her destination away.

"I can give you a ride," he offered. He could tell she was suspicious. "The dreams brought you here, right?" he added, with a smile.

"Yes!" she said, with a smiling exhale.

"Hop on!"

Elisa Tate was a shy bookworm of a soul. She crawled about the center of her awkwardly perfect world, in hopes of never truly being unearthed. A modest hole, on the surface, suggested she was open to the possibility and impossible to forget. Her radiant hair was like the sands of the golden state that raised her.

She was gifted with wisdom, and carried an introvert's mystique. A healthy and well-rounded family gave her shine. She was poreless, beautiful and instantly intrigued by Magnus; he was the yin to her yang. Growing up in a suburban neighborhood made charting the traditional course toward financial security a breeze and curiosity, a luxury.

Science was her God and she worshiped daily. Societal laws were tolerated, so much as to gain the type of freedom that only submission could provide. At heart, she was an artist, but her internal negative dialog refused to allow her to dismiss realism and risk judgment.

Though withdrawn, she was still able to develop comfortable relationships in tragically hip social circles. She did her best to till the garden for quality over quantity relationships and on this principle, only the most determined individuals were allowed behind the curtain. Her rejection generated followers.

Introductions aside, the two arrived.

CHAPTER 7
VISIONS OF THE RED BIRD (ANAN)

The Council communicated through mad dreams and could send haunting visions of the red bird to participants of The Program. The bird, Anan, represented dimensionality, and could effortlessly make the sands of an hourglass pour in both directions or in hypnotic tandem. Orchestrating synchronicity in physicality was intuitive to its nature, as was leading unwilling spectators to the depths of life after life.

Anan showed Programmers how to understand time beyond the boundaries of linear thinking, and encouraged them to divorce the simplistic measurements of man's capacity. It explained the complexities of a mitosis-driven universe and was able to articulate how the beginning and end could simultaneously exist in an ever-expanding and fracturing soul cycle, while passing through each moment of awareness, connecting everything to everyone in every time period.

Elisa recalled her dream. Resting in puffy hotel linens, watching sitcom reruns and nibbling on leftover airplane peanuts, in a complimentary white robe, she found her taxed mind drifting. It had been a long week of hotel hopping, with her Senior Week crew — she was wiped. The posh parties had taken their toll. As her bloodshot eyes switched the channels of consciousness, she encountered the ruby red bird.

From atop the television set, it stared through her startled eyes and instructed her to gaze into the static, like the girl from Poltergeist. Scrambling signals, the tube idled and reflected her image like a mirror. Intuitively she assumed she was being taped for a graduation prank. Nervously testing its accuracy, she slowly waved her cautious hand about. Accepting the lucid moment, Anan began rewinding her life. She watched herself sleep, conscious, then quickly regressing through her current life, afterlife and witnessing a moment from her former life. No longer the voyeur, she relived it, like reincarnation in reverse.

The Santa Monica Boulevard was tense and humid. Distracted, looking for her mischievous keys in an extravagant Melrose-inspired handbag, Elisa emerged from an old mom and pop shop, awkwardly drinking from a tall carton of whole milk. Crossing the threshold, dark storm clouds, manifesting above the quaking parking lot, began descending around her.

"Hi, Elisa, what are you looking for?" asked a voice.

"My keys..." she said, pulling a teething ring from her purse.

"I may never see you again. Please don't make me kill you. We can still be together."

"What are you talking about? Are you really trying to kill me in my sleep?" she asked.

Shots fired. She awoke, hurling expletives toward the idiot box. The sequence was more lucid than any of the intolerably bad dreams she'd been forced to bear witness. As her eyes focused on a new day, a magnificent cardinal caught her unfocused gaze. Beckoning notice, it comfortably perched upon the sill, tweeting a soft short melody before taking flight. Making the connection, Elisa rushed toward the window, but it was gone — blending with the towering New York City skyscrapers.

+++

Sometimes the dreams were guideposts. I can still recall the unsettling feelings sparked by a marathon series of Faces of Death Vol. 1-4. Fearing REM, heavy eyelids were reinforced with Jolt cola and Skittles. A desktop lamp was tasked with running surveillance, and thwarting the threats of the monsters who would soon abound my twilit room. It was too late, nature had already begun its countdown, and prepared to up the ante on the disturbing images I'd carelessly consumed. I awoke in a vision, wrestling immurement. All exits were sealed.

Confined, the red bird, Anan, crowed to me.

Upon acidic concrete prison walls, I was shown a tetrad of ways to understand the limitlessness of space. Moments were shown on the dripping northern wall, from the past and of the future, when the astringent obstacles no longer existed. It was an escape plan. Chirps of faith encouraged me to risk chemical burns and simply walk through the blockade of smoldering green gasses. Without caution, my spirit was released into a parallel dimension on the outside of the prison.

"If time isn't confined to the body, how can these walls hold you?" asked Anan.

I was then returned to the prison. The only light came from the flickering southern wall.

"In darkness, nothing exists, except for the fate created by an architect's mind," crowed Anan. When the illumination ceased, the walls faded and the universe, anew, became imaginable.

"Everything is light," added the red bird.

Again, I awoke. The eastern and western walls were replaced with mirrors, to express infinity.

"Look to the East, everything is within," said Anan.

The mirrors vanished and I was startled by the lightning flashes on the western wall. It was there I was shown the image of a baby with purplish eyes. It represented the cycle of a promised evolution. In the vision, I was chased by a possessed looking man with a piercing fury, while a beautiful young woman ran with the infant child through a bustling city. She was surrounded by wolves. I was trying to protect a new world from death's grip.

"With life comes death and in death comes life," said Anan.

+++

Few people understood the complexities of life more than Benjamin Maynard. At an early age, he was abandoned by his cancerous mother and left to be raised by the Underground, lurking beneath the dank streets of London, England. A nomadic calling drove her into the arms of a Tommy, with zero interest in raising a troubled young chap or sobering from his post-traumatic stress disorder. His biological father settled for a life on the run, after a bank robbery went south, resulting in the misfired deaths of three British Bobbies. Society projected their disappointment upon the only visible reminder they could find. Ben was marked. Seeking his bourbon-riddled father would only carve distress signals, upon his otherwise blank mug and meant risking the whereabouts of a man incarcerated by anonymity; he knew it was wise to wait, without bated breath.

He stood an average height and sported an overflowing dark brown mop top, reminiscent of the Fab 4. His eyes, emerald; and his cautious smile, sincere. His moral barometer was defined by observing neighborhood interactions between old friends and harboring families. A vicarious life served as normalcy and kept his shattered spirit hopeful. Absent from archetypes, his failed parents caused an overwhelming sense of rejection to brew within his tiny frame. Commitment was seen as a home erected on shaky ground. Gambling loss was a luxury built by the posh. His interactions with passersby was curt, but cordial. He was a survivalist, who kept hangers-on just beyond arm's length.

His preteen years were strictly autonomous. He knew the dock and restaurant schedules well enough to sneak seafood or whatever fodder his hands could stow. Monitoring captains' work schedules enabled him short nights on port-side cabin floors; he'd scamper, if caught. Before long, he found refuge with Britain's finest foster care program, no longer trampling the streets of a forgotten scorn. His instincts were sharpened and his ability to survive, unmatched. Though he'd made himself emotionally void, he was not impervious to the feelings aroused by his dreams.

+++

Resting on a dock, the red bird called.

"I found myself lying in a rolling field, staring toward the heavens. I often used the tall brush as a shelter from the noisy world and counted stars, until sheep lied down beside me. On one haunting evening, I was already dreaming, though the lamb-scape never changed," he explained and punned with an interviewing therapist. "The clear sky was picturesque. From my peripheral, I noticed a red star shooting towards me. With focus, a tiny red wing span emerged. Returning to the heavens, the mysterious falcon connected the stars like constellations, to resemble the Borromean rings. They glowed red, green and blue and represented the past, present and the future," he paused, allowing the intricacy to marinate.

The therapist carefully noted everything.

"I saw my face appearing in the top western ring. It morphed and resurrected feelings from forgotten lifetimes. My soul radiated from these familiar eyes, as I recalled their affect. A strangely familiar girl appeared in the eastern circle. Her face transformed, but remained discernible. Reaching her shackled hands toward me, I could see her longing eyes welling with a vast regret.

"Do you believe she could represent your mother?" asked the doctor.

Hypnotized by his account, Benjamin ignored her diagnosis and marched forward.

"In the bottom circle I saw a brilliant pair of indigo eyes. They instantly faded to black. A small fire ignited and replaced the vacant ring; a fiery angelic face emerged. Without caution, my instincts pawed toward the Aphrodite," he paused, and quaked.

"Continue," instructed the curious therapist, placing a comforting hand on his clammy forehead.

"It distorted into a demonic figure and began screaming at me. Its harsh tone was guttural, but piercing. I cried in terror and my heart begged a swift exit from my pulsing ribcage. Opening shuttered eyes, I saw three burning rings," he said, calming. I awoke with an old rusty black key clenched in my sweaty hand."

"Do you still have it?"

"I have never been so terrified! I can't shake this dream. It haunts me," he added, slowly rising from the leather couch. He handed her the key.

She examined the key and passed it back.

"Do you believe this has something to do with your parents and how you might see yourself as the key to bringing them back together?"

It was a fair diagnosis.

CHAPTER 8
LONG HARD ROAD HOME

"Are y' from around here, cailin? I don't believe we've met," asked a handsome local bartender. The barman was working the late shift in EJ Morrissey's, off Dublin-Cork Road in Dublin, Ireland, testing a gal's ID and patience, before handing over a cool drink.

"I've always lived in the flats," huffed a soft female voice. "Do you know the old prison museum in Kilmainham?"

"You're over in the suburbs, a couple miles out?" he prodded.

"Yes! Exactly, sham. I'll just end the suspense, I'm almost 18-years-young. Now, being that you've already served a hapless lass, there's really no sense making a scene or getting either of us into any senseless trouble," she paused. "You know what, let's have another!"

"So your name is not Zane?" he asked, condoning her flirtation.

"No, it is, but I'm not 20, as the card suggests. Zane Brennan is my birthright. It basically means, bad arse feek," she added, with blush. She didn't want to lose his trust, nor interest.

"Feek, huh? Modest, too?" he paused. "Why are you out drinking before milk and cookies?"

"Isn't there a commandment on the wall, over there, that says, 'Thou shall not drive through Abbeyleix without pausing in Morrissey's for a pint,'" Zane quipped.

"Yes! Believable, or not, you've got a fetching sass! Carry on."

"My parents split, my best friend moved and I'm not having too much luck in love."

"So, you're compensating?"

"I've dated around, but I'm not really attracted to the lads my age," offered Zane, biting into a thick moment of still air. Her body language was a neon sign, stating, "You are exactly the right age!"

"Maybe I can join you for a drink, sometime?" he asked.

"That would be your treat!" she joked, with a wink. "I have to leave town, to visit family in the States, but I'm sure I'll find you passed out in the bogs, when I return."

"Sounds like a date," he risked.

"It's a date," she confessed.

"I have better things to do than croak with the frogs," he said, bidding her giddy hand farewell.

Zane was bedazzled, but painfully average. She rested comfortably in the security her tattooed cred and grandfather's worn military jacket provided and bathed in the bravado her combat boots added to a tragically hip and painfully ironic purple pixie haircut. A tiny silver hoop held onto her petite nose. She was a tomboy, posing as a punk rocker. By all accounts, a disgruntled middle class girl, crying out for attention. She was a novice in her journey toward self-discovery.

We were all heading somewhere.

+++

On its long meandering trek across the midlands, my old red fireball pulsated, shook and pleaded for a second wind. Landscapes changed with the tumbling odometer, while Baltimore waved in the rear view. The senseless charms and revelations of the road kept my lazy foot pressing on. Oblivious to traffic, and unwilling to make a distinction between the pavement and the desert made armadillos calming devices. These hard hat wearing sloths were blessed with an innate ability to block out the world's murderous terrain. It seemed awkwardly metaphoric.

I-40's charms boasted of no name gas stations, seedy strip club billboards and missing children, exhumed from the branching lost highways of the Midwest. My curious tongue was insistent upon French kissing the mouth of the Pacific, regardless of the mischief Arizona had arranged with the heavenly ghosts. Killing two ravenous birds with a rebel stone justified my cooperative urgency. My platitude was that the gods of rock n' roll were ushering me to the Promised Land and would awaken the damned with a ceremonious Hollywood riot in my honor, but a looming reality suggested my experience was called to be far more elaborate than a future memory of the Sunset Strip to boast from a Wicker Man's rocking chair.

Eighteen hours on the barren road can consume the fading mind with paranoia. Roadside naps were of little consequence and only littered my ill mind with episodes and day terrors. My initial stop was a warped refuge. Hunkered down in a cheap hotel, I was convinced I'd been traced by a bearded set of serial killers, motoring a large and suspiciously clean white economy van. Unsure if my profile matched that of someone they'd like to kill, eat or enslave, the warm welcome of a bolted door, a receipt of my whereabouts and a direct phone line to the desk clerk was a worthy bid for my shrinking budget. I incessantly peered from the musty hotel curtains. Nothing.

These types of sensations are amplified by distance, youth and only having a beeper to communicate with. It is hard for me to even type the word beeper without stirring up a generalized anxiety. H-E-L-P (4-3-5-7)!

+++

In the still of the night, I settled. Drifting into the space between consciousness and the void, I was whistled along by a blue bird. Its presence radiated a magnificent spectrum of light. Strangling the hands of time, it broke apart and reanimated as a black, white, gray and red bird. I recognized the riddling red bird and cruel gray, but remained mystified by the murder. Familiar feelings dripped from heaven, triggering my soul to condensate; misfiring synapses didn't have the nerve to unleash the Tell-Tale Heart lurking beneath the floorboards of my conscious.

The birds hovered above the cardinal points of a glowing sphere. Intersecting with six white lines, a clock emerged upon a targeted desert floor. A dove then highlighted the Northern and Eastern portions of the timetable. Isis, the black bird, pecked a septenary into my forehead.

"Forever this moment," said the red bird.

Naked, sweating and crawling from the center, the birds turned gray and viciously attacked me.

I was awoken by a loud tapping on my hotel door, in haste.

"Time to check-out," insisted a perky housekeeper.

"One of these nights, I'll dream about a woman and not these wretched fowl," I muttered.

+++

I desperately longed for female companionship. No soul embodied the beauty of feminine divinity more than Juno Vestris. Someday she would tap dance across the Atlantic and capture the gaze of every nation. She was inspired by the eclipsing architecture of her histrionic Roman yesterdays; her dances, a tribute to the ancient fallen world. Like the cobblestone streets, her body paved a way for her soul to connect with the simpler hearts of Palestrina, a small commune east of Rome. The roads were her stage and a constant reminder of an elementary time, when people coveted the virtuous patience needed to leave indelible footprints on the emotional psyche of future generations.

Deep roots connected her essence to a Christian faith. Juno often ventured to the Santa Maria della Vittoria to empathize with the suffering human condition, as depicted by the Ecstasy of St. Teresa. She could feel the fire of heaven scorning the damned heart, and knew the beauty and importance of purging negative energy through positive channels. Her mind was constantly musing, which left her studies an afterthought; creativity was a through street, mapped by her soul.

She grew up in a stable environment, compelled to give back. Participating in various children's ministries and women-focused expatriate groups, she made Rome feel like home. Time was an offering, consumed by volunteer driven soup kitchens and Sunday morning baptismal classes; it was a labor of love. Divinity was an unacknowledged hand guiding Christ-followers to the sacred waters of salvation, lurking just beyond the line on the horizon.

Her style was simple, but inspired. She rarely bothered with the trappings of an undiagnosed make-up addiction. The natural beauty of her long wavy red hair, freckles, green eyes and lushly positive confidence spoke in quakes. To Juno, a flattering solid-colored dress, splashed with an accent belt, was an evolution from deliberately distracting patterns, distancing her far from the repugnant geometric anomaly known as paisley. She'd harnessed the power of simplicity and reveled in authenticity.

Her dreams started like the others, though she never saw them as disturbing or frightening. They were a transmitter for speaking to God. Sometimes startled, she'd use her nervous midnight energy to create inspired dance routines; recalling their enigmatic calling was a box step away. She was willing to trust God's plan for her life and believed she was a predestined instrument of purpose.

Juno never took her life for granted. She was born a twin, but her sister died in utero.

She lived like a tribute.

Survival instincts sharpen our awareness to kindred spirits. Though thoroughly perplexed by the intuitive nature of the third eye or why certain vibrations are compatible, it's entirely fathomable to meet utter strangers and know their inner psyche without exchanging a word. As clairvoyance tightens, snap judgments become an impulse. Juno was in tune with such signals.

+++

I scrambled through static. After long and overly-analytical hours on the road to nowhere, I was able to find the proper channels. In an instant, I could distinguish between those eagerly traveling toward the western Promised Land, the misplaced, displaced or drug-addled, and the unfortunate souls, passing through the complacency of another day. Of course, vanity plates didn't hinder my investigation. Once a baited connection hooked a fellow road warrior, an unspoken pact developed. The rules implied commandeering a look-out for breakdowns, stranger danger or drifting.

Hoping to lure free-spirited females, my preoccupied eyes spun lustful webs. A few California Dreamin' dames, motoring a cross country expedition to Santa Barbara, were lassoed by my lashes; devoid of lip service, we blueprinted our libidos on sprawling dashboards and let the wiles of our imagination marinate over a hundred lascivious miles. Introductions were a formality, long-forgotten by climaxing pit stops to the Garden.

Due to the inexplicable odds of biting into the

forbidden fruit on the open road, these tattooed memories are still a welcome haunting; explicitly dancing in my frontal lobe, forevermore. These chance events only prove the intimacy of human souls and our inherent need for socialization, security and lust; after all, everyone has an unquenchable thirst for a good story to tell, right?

Invigorated by spontaneity, I beamed toward the shroud of mystery known as Area 51. I could allow my imagination to be abducted for a few hours; the desert rendezvous was a loose timetable. Able to explore my indescribable obsession with ancient alien theory, I found my way to Route 375, gazed and let fantasy unfold. Devoid of UFO sightings or unexpected attacks from resident Greys, the calm allowed my taxed mind a moment to decompress and enjoy the view of nature's simplicity.

When I shimmied back into my exasperated car, I heard the familiar song, "Life is a Highway." I never knew how motivational and poetic Tom Cochrane could be. So long as it wasn't another cryptic message from the omnipresent spirit guides, I was content to allow the one-hit wonder to blare through my rickety Toyota Tercel cabin.

"This song is terrible, but great!" I debated. "It's terrible."

I knew the Painted Desert was calling; I was refreshed and ready to knock out the ends of my travel. With one foot comfortably secured out of the driver's side window and a fresh fag lit, life was 'Just alright with me!'

The last few hours were a time machine to wits' end. Dazed and confused, I emerged from the bone-weary vehicle.

"Well done, Neco! Walk north. I am with you," said an angelic voice.

The gravity of the situation gave my wobbly legs reason for pause. It felt like the entire weight of the unknown had been placed upon my cramped shoulders. Reluctantly, I soldiered into the vast desert. It took roughly an hour of dust, sweat and tears, before I stumbled upon the target. Feeling lost in solitary, suspense mounted. I paced the pattern beneath, before another cannon fired from the loud speaker in my head.

"You have arrived. Wait," said the voice.

It was then I heard another unforgettable voice.

CHAPTER 9
THE GATHERING AND THE MISSION

Icarus Kali was a not-so gentle giant. He stood a towering 6' 11" and was the first of his classmates to grow a beard. He was born in the Hellenic Republic in Southern Europe. It was a fitting cognomen, considering the rich mythology and history surrounding Greece. He played football for St. Catherine's British School, while in upper school and planned to attend Athens College in Psychiko, Greece. His parents imposed high academic standards, but knew his brawn would inevitably do the bulk of his bidding.

Piercing cold blue eyes radiated from his mammoth skull like the waters of Antarctica. His heart would seemingly beat out of his thick chest with each deep, brooding and oxygen-starved breath. A caged animal lurked within, awaiting the day it would finally be unleashed upon an unsuspecting society of lemmings. He would someday reign supreme and be sculpted by the elite, as his namesake and birthright demanded. He was greater than myth and the embodiment of God's perfect strokes, upon the canvas of human development.

His stature ensured a justifiable arrogance, only tamed

by his father's matching height and experience. The spoils of a lush background only fueled his expectations. His mother was a successful defense attorney and his father a businessman; trouble could be quashed by money and justify his withdrawn empathy. They took turns disciplining, Icarus, physically. It was important to show dominance and to impose memorable guidelines for his troublesome and often aggressive behavior. It was the only method he responded to, but also reinforced projection.

They'd created a monster!

He dressed to impress, suppress and repress. Girls were of his choosing; their hearts were a lottery, and he liked to play. Those who didn't fawn, would inevitably cower into his arms and pray for a quick release. He had a long list of female conquests to boast and quickly assumed dominant roles amongst his peers. The Western sun called him to fly closer than he ever imagined possible.

+++

The summer heat burned through their clothes, while they cautiously awaited revelation. Even Dez was no longer loud, proud nor spouting off at the mouth; the buds had left his mind numb. Off in the distance, Icarus and the three remaining individuals emerged into view. If Magnus's dream was accurate, the circle would soon be completed and the 12 stones could take their place on the monstrous white mystery.

Their distance seemed to be multiplied by the group's divided patience. Their footsteps were ushered along, like a funeral procession, as they inched toward the gathering circle — their pace couldn't have seemed slower. They were covered in the familiar gaseous shroud of a heat haze. Their silhouettes, like the introduction of an old Mad Max film. One character stood-out amongst the rest. He was either really tall or much closer than he appeared. The impossible volume of this individual suggested he was closer. He was not.

"It looks like we're not alone! Plenty of shams," puckered Zane.

"No! It looks like there are at least 7, maybe 8, others," added Ben.

"They look like they need to stand-up and shake it off," said Juno, interlocking fingers with Ben's unwelcoming hands and lightening the mood with a mock waltz. Zane welcomed her effervescence. Ben was unamused. The lighthearted girls giggled. "Oh, come on, grump!"

Exhaustion reduced Icarus to sighs and lazy grunts. The time it took for sultry blood to circulate through his sky-scraping frame and reach his mammoth brain left him little energy to interact with the group. Each attempt to connect his mind with his mouth created discomfort. Nonsensical sounds fell from his lips, like lazy rain.

"Eh," tried Icarus.

Comprehending their calling was a crime against the mind, but not the shoulders they leaned on.

"So, how many of you were visited by the beautiful spirit woman?" asked Juno. "I bet she's with us now."

"I was terrified! I couldn't help but wonder how long she'd been watching me sleep — or worse! Total stalker," joked Zane.

"We know we're here to do something — something great! It's easy for us to take our dreams for granted, but if we weren't special, this desert would be consumed by the heartbeat of 7 billion people. I don't know what it is, but it'll be something amazing," professed Juno. "I can feel the rhythm of the air."

"What is amazing about being haunted by precarious dreams and led into the middle of god-knows-where for a celestial meet-and-greet with utter strangers? No offense, but this is offensive. I can't help but wonder if the entire universe is punishing me for something I did in another lifetime," returned Ben. With staunch pessimism, he squeezed his temples to relieve a pressure headache.

"Uh huh," moaned Icarus.

"Honey, you had to have believed it was going to be something incredible. You came, didn't you?" asked Juno.

"You're supposing I had a choice," said Ben.

Their dehydrated voices clammed, upon reaching the gathering. With sweaty palms, they reached down toward the lazy-eyed group. Like a game of Duck, Duck, Goose, they extended pleasantries and handed down swift introductions. Magnus, Rand, Simon, Neco, Dez, Ash, Grayson and Elisa were tired of formalities, but revived by the disruption of their speculative time. Zane, Icarus, Ben & Juno took a seat on the circle.

One by one, they purged their story.

+++

The dusk sunset complimented Ash's fair skin. Tattooed by the puffy shadows of the sky's love, she complimented the desert floor. Neco couldn't help in noticing her bold beauty, still resting comfortably in his cramped lap; she was adorned in a bedazzled mystique. The evening was bathed in twilight. The merciless desert was finally ready to bestow a warranted empathy toward its exhausted travelers. A modest offering cooled the temperature to tolerable, as the sun hung in its 7 p.m. position. From beyond, an aggressive breeze suddenly gusted about the perimeter, whipped the sand and pulled dust toward a parting sky.

"Do you see that?" asked Simon, pointing. His mysticism longed for ownership.

The group was dumbfounded by a brilliant red, yellow and orange sequence being painted above. Behind the beautiful colors shined a bright starry light, discarding shadows from the vacant interior of the congregation field. Human whispers, in various languages, consumed the vibrational field. Lowered by a cosmic puppeteer, the blue bird assumed the role of a supernova. Its breathtaking presence overshadowed its underwhelming size. Though mesmerizing, the magnificence of the sky's Broadway performance only cast a light upon their terrestrial insignificance. They cowered beneath the unfolding heavenly canvas.

The royal bird then separated into four gallant new birds. They circled, challenging the velocity of light. Like an interstellar beam from an alien aircraft, a sapphire illumination connected the arid ground to the heavens. A thunderous voice called out, in a deep, familiar and evocative way. It was The Council. Its power echoed through the canyon walls, and breathed fear into the already petrified forest.

"Beckoning for growth, a tenacious spirit longs for humility. It is the smallest mind that is able to move the greatest obstacle, through the hands of interconnectedness. We are one body, within an infinite mind," said The Council. Their harmonized tones sent tremors through the desert floor. "Stand, remove your clothing and lock arms!"

With warranted caution, they began begrudgingly shedding their earthly identities. The young girls removed their knickers, but hesitated with the veils of their chest. The developing boys wrestled with the insecurity of unfastening their ego-preserving fig leaves. One after the other, they revealed their bodies to The Council and risked the judgment of their new acquaintances; everyone, too self-absorbed to notice. They reached for each other's hands, until the circle was connected and instinctively looked up.

As if hypnotized, Juno broke free and began to dance; Neco harmonized with The Council; Ash waved imaginary brushstrokes toward the heavens; Simon's body flickered within and out of the visible spectrum.

They were the muses.

Grayson spoke in long-forgotten tongues; Elisa used physics to bend the marvelous lights of The Council's calling; Benjamin riddled in maths, seeking the final digit of the numerical constant known as pi; Rand recounted historical records with precise accuracy, as if narrating humanity for a book on tape.

They were the intellects.

Icarus, Magnus, Zane and Dez walked toward the center of the circle and began mock sparring. Juno inspired their choreography. Directed by Rand, clothing projected onto their bodies, like a hologram. They morphed to represent various moments of their shared human existence. In the beginning, they fought with spears; in the end, with bombs.

They were the warriors.

Returning to their positions, they interlocked their quaking hands. The Book of Records was then opened to reveal their past lives. The consuming beam subtly shifted from sapphire to indigo. Like lustful voyeurs, they peered into the minds surrounding them. They could witness their intersecting paths and mistakes and feel the pains of their horror-filled afterlives. The whispering voices overhead would shift between a choir of praise to the guttural screams of the underworld.

It was then, they knew. They remembered it all. They were chosen for *The Program*.

The rules of The Program repeated from the sky's mouth. Words overlapped in various tongues, falling like a purified rain. Their gravity was synonymous to the laws of nature; they were binding and absolute. In the sky, the souls of the damned sensually writhed across one another. Some pleaded, begging for notice.

"You are now ready! The Program is an unbreakable cycle. It cannot be interfered with by The Council. Your transgressions in these lifetimes will not be chronicled in the Book of Records, but may create a vast barrier between your soul and your mission for solvency and absolution from the physical plane. If it takes a 1,000 lifetimes to produce a Crystalline child, you will live them all. Your miracle children will usher in an awakening. They are the enlightenment of our new age. You will know them by their indigo eyes," echoed the Council.

The group held tightly to each other. The energy from the radiant lights forced them into a 120 degree angle. The vibration of the Council's voice sent shock waves through their rattling skulls, but their eyes remained transfixed. They were possessed by the sky. The bright light in the middle of the circle morphed into a fire and withdrew back to the heavens from which it spawned. Black birds dropped like rain upon the desert floor.

The group collapsed.

+++

Hours passed before they awoke. Dez was the first to his lifeless feet. He quickly redressed and pulled a fresh joint from his tattered jacket pocket. Kicking the midnight ravens, he returned to the security of the red rocks, where he'd been arrogantly resting. His frayed nerves were shot. The marijuana cooled him, but his new perspective — intoxicating.

"I may live a 1,000 lifetimes?" Dez pondered. "1,001 lifetimes?"

The Program was a jagged pill to swallow. His memories, like the others, were now amplified with visceral sensitivity. He'd feel his skin burn, if he thought about the heartless underworld. His mind was a battlefield littered with landmines. An abyss of sorrow consumed him, as he tiptoed through the memories of his losses from former lifetimes. He could deduce where the fossilized souls of his old friends and forgotten family members were spending their otherworldly days. The Program didn't invoke his inspiration. He was haunted by it. To Dez, it was hell on earth.

Zane awoke and joined the shattering man in the distance. Without a word, she uncomfortably took the joint from his lazy hands and deeply inhaled. "So, we've got a pretty far out road ahead of us?" she asked, clumsily attempting his phrasing.

"You may, lass! I don't know about you, but I'm going to continue living my goddamned life. If I find someone, I find someone!"

"It can't be that hard, can it?" she modestly asked, not expecting a response. "People and animals are always coupling. I fall in love, daily. As a matter of fact, I have a bartender awaiting my charms in Dublin," she joked, hoping to unearth a glimmer of hope in his mad eyes. "I'll find someone, we'll have a baby and I'll leave this godforsaken planet. I can't wait to fall in love!" she zealously proclaimed. "Though, I could do without all of these dirty birds."

"Can you please leave me alone," Dez pleaded. "Just, please!"

Dez revved his clunky motorcycle and startled the rest of the knocked-out group. Dust rudely sprayed toward the gathering circle. He brashly pulled off, without uttering a salutation to anyone. It didn't defy expectation, but did raise the antennas of the suspicious, hastening their pace. Ash was happy to find herself resting in Neco's arms. They mutually agreed to remain silent, naked and spooning. The Badland's bed made their plight difficult to sell. The rest of the herd dusted off, got dressed, chattered and began pairing — everyone was lethargic and disoriented. Processing the significance of what had happened would take time, an avalanche of wanted rest and copious amounts of caffeine.

"Well, it's 7 a.m. and I'm starving," proclaimed Magnus. "If you want, Elisa and I can head up the road and scavenger for food, drink or maybe just hard drink! It's probably best if we stayed together and discussed what happened here last night. We're really all we have," he added, appealing to Elisa's maternal instincts.

They left.

"So, what got you interested in math," Rand offered, breaking the ice with Benjamin.

"A couple of years ago, I had a dream about one of

those damn birds from last night," said Benjamin, in a husky morning tone. "It was the Red Bird, Anan. It filled the universe with Borromean rings," he paused, awaiting Rand's attention. "I was obsessed. My counselor felt it would be best if I redirected my focus on college and buried my nightmares in schoolwork. Long story short, I hadn't really settled into a specific study and figured I could kill two birds with one stone. So, I focused on math."

"Wow!"

"Diving in, I realized how easy it came. It just spider-webbed from there."

"Well, last night was amazing! Ben, it completely dismantled my world. I've lived such a smothered existence, this go-round. My parents were embarrassed by the shame the world cast upon Germany and the amplified moral responsibility it brought to our family. Simply, we forgot how to live. For better or worse, their parenting put a wall between me and the fallen West. It's ironic, really," Rand continued.

"That is the definition of irony!"

"No lifestyle could rewrite our sordid history. I did my best to bring pride to our doorstep, daily! I thought, if they could vicariously live through my academic success, I'd earn them the respect they were missing. It was never enough."

"It never is."

"I missed my youth. I've never even been on a date. Being tasked with finding true love might prove to be more arduous than I'm prepared for."

"You'll be fine! Find a Fraulein, recite her some poetic World War II history and sit back and watch the magic unfold," joked Simon.

"I'm not even mad at you, Simon! That's hilarious."

"By the way, I think the 'being naked' part is now officially over," said Simon to Ash and Neco, leaving lingering quotations and judgment in the cool air. "If you're going to continue to lay on the dirty ground in your birthday suits and pretend to sleep, you can at least make it a little more exciting for the rest of us!"

Neco kissed Ash and said, "Let's get up!"

"So, you're a tough girl?" Juno smiled, asking Zane.

"Only when I have to be," she returned, with a smile. "My father wasn't the most stable of individuals. A girl has to know how to protect herself, you know? I never really knew if he was going to be ready to kick some tail, after a hard day, or cuddle. I mean, he's Irish," she furthered.

Juno laughed. "What if I could teach you how to dance? You know, if you mix dance with your instinct to fight, your movements will be become fluid. You'll be unstoppable. It's the main difference between martial arts and street fighting." She paused. "Give me your tough little hands, sweetheart!"

They practiced in the hot morning sun, connected and learned from one another. Despite her somewhat rough upbringing, Zane always maintained a sweet and approachable demeanor. In stark contrast, stood Icarus.

"Would you ladies mind if I joined you? I could use a few new friends!"

Zane and Juno understood his gesture, smirked and let him have his precocious fun.

"Go ahead," offered Zane.

Icarus then grabbed the girls and lifted them, like an offering to the sun.

Juno laughed. "Then again, who needs to be able to dance or fight when you can simply pick-up everyone in the damn room?"

"The Incredible Hulk is real," said Grayson, making a mock headline for a future story. "Not to interrupt, but we all had a very wild night. What no one seems to be addressing is the sea of dead birds by our feet. Does anyone find it alarming? I mean, they are black, so, they obviously symbolize creation, but, I'm at a loss," furthered Grayson.

"I think The Council just wanted us to wake-up and remember what took place," offered Neco. "That or this black bird is in the cosmic dog house!"

"It's not like we can exactly forget. I think they are here to show us how many times we'll try and fail and not to underestimate The Program. Creation is a beautiful thing, but we've all been sent here to produce a child with a certain special unknown someone. It sounds simple, but it's clearly not or we wouldn't be standing in the desert and surrounded by feathered creatures that are covered in flies," Grayson continued.

"OK, changing lanes! If this is the last time we're all going to be together, we should have a party," insisted Ash.

The group immediately forgot the suggestion, as the roar of Magnus's chariot emerged in the shadowy distance. It was the most welcome and triumphant image they'd seen since The Council's light show. Elisa's dirty blond hair blew in the mild breeze. She was holding two large plastic supply bags. The motorcycle made short work of the desert and arrived, posthaste. Magnus slid his tires to aid the brakes.

"We hope you like Dorito's, cold pizza, NoDoz and water," said Elisa, dispersing the goods.

"It's got to be better than blackbird," said Ash.

"I'd say," said Grayson, in a huff.

"Sorry, Gray, I was just trying to lighten the mood," said Ash. "So, getting back on the topic, what if we have a child with a special someone in the group?" asked Ash, grabbing for Neco's hand.

"Moving on," said Simon. "You two can find out and get back to us, OK?"

"The union of two participants of The Program would likely overload the DNA structure of the developing fetus and ultimately result in a stillborn," said Elisa. "I wouldn't recommend it!"

"How do you know that?" asked Ash.

"I guess you could say a little birdy told me," returned Elisa.

CHAPTER 10
THE EYES OF MADNESS

"Our transgressions won't be kept in the Book of Records?" thought Dez, sipping on lukewarm black coffee, in an old diner two hours from the Painted Desert, letting the last sparks of innocence fade from his cruel and affected eyes. "Well, then..."

His demeanor was guarded toward anyone who risked making eye contact. Before settling into the worn red vinyl seat of the empty jumbo-sized motor home, parading around as a legitimate restaurant, he tested The Council's law, by nonchalantly robbing a Pic-N-Run gas station attendant. Dusty tire tracks from of an untagged motorcycle, a bike, which appeared to have been assembled on his front lawn, with leftover automobile parts from the abandoned impound lot he called home, were the only trace of his involvement. The rules of The Program favored his plea for rebellion. His crooked mind began fastening the beginning pieces of a sinister plot to punish the universe for his losses and for the horrific time he was forced to spend in the underworld. He was determined to avenge his fallen family and friends.

"My coffee is getting cold," he barked. "Can you handle this job? There's nobody here, missy!" His view of human beings had been permanently altered. He could no longer see man's innocence, nor promise, only their radiating fears and physical limitations. They were nothing more than a class of worker bees, submitting to the will of an absentee god. They were the dirt beneath his dusty boots. "The Council has made a huge mistake," he laughed, under sour breath. "I'll make this right. It's my right — my kind of right!"

After sucking back his fifth cup of bitter Joe, he stood, crumbled his handwritten bill, tossed it in his nervous waitress's face and exited the eatery. "The only punishment is that I'll never die? Ha!"

His bravado was a hammer upon the gavel of a new justice; one man, under lawlessness.

Dez mounted his steel horse and galloped 300 miles east, toward a seedy strip club. The venue was mere miles from his compound lot. With a suave cool, he trolled through the flimsy saloon doors and found the afternoon-quality dancers extracting the souls of hopeless derelicts — one dollar bill at a time! Taking inventory, he imbibed a moment's calm; even chilled, Wild Turkey bourbon couldn't cool his raging heart. He gulped, in droves. His reckless mind soaked in the self-pity and mania, which only a wanted alcohol-induced psychosis could produce. If all that remained was contending with visions of dirty birds and unwelcome memories, he was content to spiral.

The girls looked like prey to the new eyes floating in his barbaric skull. If any value was housed in their bones, they'd become pawns of primal gratification. His heart had iced. He was aroused by the thought of implanting himself into their minds, like a tapeworm. Unveiling the money from the gas station heist, he lured them toward his spinning cobweb. With wide eyes and trusting mouths, they kissed the air like hapless guppies, gobbling capitalism.

"Would you girls like to make a lot more where this came from?" The girls were smitten by his attractive offer and green for his affection. "All you have to do is say the word." They both playfully nodded, hypnotized by his tempting eyes. "I live about 10 miles down the road. Do you want to come over and maybe, cook me breakfast?" he added.

"Who's waiting for later? Let's go, now! I'm Crystal and this is Michelle," said an average-looking brunette dancer. Her straightened hair was decorated with purple streaks, and her soft face, masked in make-up, was a compliment to Dez's black cloak. "I don't suppose you've got any marijuana, do you?"

"I've got everything weed-need!" he charmed.

It was another relentlessly hot Sunday in the desert. The high humidity made Hades rise. Offering their manager a cut, the intrepid ladies followed the renegade for a presumed romp and clocked out from their remaining shift. They hopped into Crystal's old baby blue Camaro and followed the scribbled directions that the man had left upon a damp beverage napkin.

Coming upon an old rusty black mailbox, they arrived. The driveway looked like a long dirt road to a serial killer's bordello. Tall weeds barricaded their vision from any trace of a permanent residence. There was a warranted reason for pause. Though the long summer sun had hours to shine before it would sink below the skyline, they preferred to submit to his wiles and get out, before losing daylight. Slinking from the beat-up car, the girls adjusted their heels and approached the trailer. At war with the air and himself, a silhouette kicked, punched and screamed, before pausing to address them.

"You made it!" he said, kindly. "Even a den of snakes needs its charms," he thought.

"You didn't exactly make it easy! I could barely decipher your directions through the whiskey stains on this-here napkin, Picasso!" sassed Michelle.

"No matter, you made it! How about those drugs?" he smiled. "Are either of you thirsty?"

He didn't care.

Entering the dilapidated trailer, they were offended by the wafting filth and copious debris. Old rusty cans of Coors Light, bags of McDonald's and a Native America dreamcatcher, shaped from woman's lingerie, were a few of its tells — a trail of clues was pointing directly toward their questionable decision-making!

"Do you need a maid or did you actually have something else in mind?" asked Crystal.

"Just try and make yourselves comfortable, I'll roll us a joint!"

An old sheet of white blotter acid lay restlessly dormant in Dez's cluttered paraphernalia drawer. It creaked, as his diabolical claws opened Pandora's Box and dropped two tiny hits of funny paper into their cheap beers. He popped on the rusty caps and reemerged with the promised offerings. His steady eye was sure to keep his drink separate.

"Here we go ladies; a couple o' drinks and a joint!" he smiled.

In mere minutes, the thirsty women began pawing Dez. They panted like wild bitches in heat. Their senses were amplified by the trip and their inhibitions were a forgotten reality. Dez knew they were slipping under his warped rhetoric, and their fogging minds were ripe for the picking. Pushed their starry-eyed lust back, he cooled his primal urges. He understood Father Time's limitations, and cut to the chase.

"You're not here for that," he insisted. "I'll give you the money, though!"

He reached into his pocket and handed them 200 reasons to follow him down the rabbit hole.

"I'm confused, sweetheart," pleaded Crystal.

"This is some powerful grass! Am I hearing you?" Michelle added, adjusting her tank top.

"Yes. I get lonely out here, needed to vent and miss the company of a woman! I find you both beautiful, but you're worth a lot more than what you're selling yourself for on that worthless stage," he manipulatively spun and paced. "This world has fallen. Our government knows it! They use our dependency on money to keep us distracted with long work hours. Our taxes are skyrocketing, the value of our currency is depleting, and the cost of commodities is escalating faster than we've ever seen!" The girls glazed. Their eyes sparkled like rhinestones. His spoon-fed enlightenment into the abyss they called pupils. "The more we work, the more we'll cope. Being sedated keeps us from pursuing the truth," he scoffed, ironically leveraging his point. "It's a vicious cycle. If you don't believe me, look around! You sell your bodies to provide money for yourselves, or your children, and you're willing to risk life and limb to do so!"

Crystal was magnetized and sold by the ranting man.

"Are you sure you don't want a little, you know?" she asked, reaching for his tense leg.

"No, respect yourselves! I've already given you the money. I just want your company."

"No problem, soldier," said Crystal.

"You can see, I don't have a lot," said Dez.

"We'll stay," agreed Michelle.

Minutes turned into hours and an unmistakable bond formed. They trusted Dez. Being native to the frequent UFO sightings of Roswell, New Mexico added legitimacy to his plight. Without a moment's hesitation, he unraveled a detailed account of his trip to the Painted Desert and used mismanaged government cover-up stories and alien conspiracy theory to fodder his guise. Like an auctioneer, his captivating tempo never wavered and his volume smoothly glided from a whisper to a shout. His vivid descriptions, passion and their heightened affect made it so.

"Extraterrestrials are being born. They are conceiving with human beings. The government not only knows about it -- they're part of it." Dez pleaded. "It's happening — it's been happening. These alien hybrids have brilliant azure eyes. They are trying to wipe-out our human DNA-forever!

This mass extinction is called The Program."

Delusions and exhaustion had built a dam between Dez and his sanity. Knowing their high would soon wear off and to avoid their sobering morning suspicions, he challenged them to a race with the setting sun.

"What time is it?" asked Michelle.

"I don't want you gals getting lost. You should probably jet!"

As weeks passed, Crystal and Dez became closer than he'd planned. He used their connection to lure other derelicts and to sell Michelle. They were transfixed by his sincerity, insight and drive. His manipulations were delivered with an undetectable bias and littered with palpable half-truths. His credibility was never challenged. The drugs lassoed his missteps.

Dez made anything possible.

CHAPTER 11
VISIONS OF THE GRAY BIRD (THAN)

Just as the red bird visited, so did the gray.

Elisa lay on her plush bed reading "The Illustrated Brief History of Time" by Stephen Hawking. Though enamored by his genius on the complex subject matter, the detailed pages were slow turners and time burners. Her eyes flickered with the incandescent lights overhead, as nearby thunderstorm rolled in and threatened her progress. The bedroom fixtures cast towering shadows in her bedroom, like a Scooby Doo cartoon. Hypnotized by the rhythm, she fell faster than the count between the lightning flashes and heaven's roar.

She lucidly awoke in a cold and sterile white room. Checkered tile floors oozed an alternating red and pink pattern. The surrounding walls were covered in the hieroglyphics of man's genetic coding. Taking center stage, an old white bird cage rested atop a rickety oak nightstand. She could see the room slowly turning in on itself. Perching within the cage, a gleeful black raven, the bird of life, whistled Amazing Grace. It remained tranquil, confident faith would deliver its savior. As she ventured toward the calling cage, crimson quicksand corroded the porcelain floor and swallowed her longing footsteps. Startled, a misfired synapse stole her attention and caused her rattling thigh bones to be consumed in a gooey menstrual muck. The once peaceful raven panicked, realizing the limitations of hope.

Tiny feathers flew, while it cawed for release; her increasing heartbeat, the reaper. It was then, the ominous gray bird, Than, glided into the shrinking room. It pecked, squawked and flapped its enlarging wingspan upon the quaking cage doors, rattling them ajar. The black bird shot from the mutating room like a hell-lit cannon. Comfortably, the gray bird took its wanted position on the prison swing.

The cage door dramatically fastened. Than stared into Elisa's nervous eyes.

"Two chosen souls cannot produce a Crystalline," it warned. "Creation demands ignorance."

Her voice, gone, on the wings of Isis.

"Get out!"

The gray bird burst into ashes. Embers tickled the insides of her dream-stricken eyelids. Trembling, she awoke with irritated eyes. Her leg muscles throbbed; her cramps, acute. Elisa wasn't the only lass visited by death's scorn.

+++

Stumbling home, from a reckless night on the streets of Dublin, Zane sneaked through her rickety bedroom window and passed out on her welcoming twin bed. Her forehead caught a rusty nail and profusely bled on her favorite He-Man comforter. In fleeting coherence, she prayed her unpredictable father was riddled with a similar overindulgent fate, unaware of her clumsy entrance.

Vodka murdered her clarity.

Without warning, Zane entered REM. Her heavy body

plummeted toward a deep and familiar cavern of fiery entities. A brimstone shore offered a hell-side view of the beaten and damned. Their mouths reached for a heavenly hook of solace. They screamed for absolution, drifting in waves of eternal discontent. Lucky souls would cease to rejuvenate and rise like phoenixes; their singed bodies morphing into gray birds. Watching the fortunate elevate and reenter the physical world, her curious eyes followed a gray bird to its duty. The presence of the bird was undetectable. Humanity was too distracted by routine. It perched on peoples' shoulders and sang the swan song of their earthly days, often falling on deaf ears. After whistling seven sad goodbyes, it led Zane to an old pond where the brilliant sun cast its new day onto still waters.

"Look into the pond and tell me what you see," said the Gray Bird.

Frightened, she saw no reflection.

"Your vibration can no longer produce the image of your soul," it furthered. Her eyes shuttered. "You are dead, in both life and in death. Open your timid eyes and tell me what your heart can see!"

With hesitation, she faced the pond and watched a homeless English boy walking the streets of London. Turning to reveal himself, the gray bird entered the vision and pecked his virgin skin off. Like a zombie, his remaining flesh hung. Tying the haunting image to an arrowhead, Than shot it into her conscious mind.

Breathing deeply, she awoke and darted to her moonlit mirror. Her forehead was covered in dry blood. Zane fell to her knees and wept.

+++

Icarus always fell the hardest. Though his might was apparent in the Earthly realm, his physical strength couldn't protect him from wiles of his soul. He hid behind an impenetrable curtain, largely consisting of flesh and muscle.

Lurking behind his coarse bravado was a fragile operator, always fearing his stirring mind. After a crushing blow on the football field, one cold and icy Saturday afternoon, sending three young players to the hospital, Icarus was introduced to limitation. He slipped into a brief but impressionable coma.

Staring into utter blackness, he heard tiny voices but saw no one. From the void, two blueish-purple eyes appeared. They stared through his soul and lassoed his focus. Gazing into their soft violet windows, a beautiful baby girl emerged, morphed into adulthood and back again. She frolicked in a field outside of his fire-consumed home. She giggled, while the gray bird danced in the inferno. A black bird rested on her tiny shoulders, singing beautiful melodies; a white bird flew from her innocent mouth; the red bird dashed from cadence of her beating heart. She controlled them like a kite and painted the universe with their subtle movements. She was the animator of reality.

He then saw a second set of harsh red eyes. Staring into voiding pupils, he could see a rioting lynch mob wearing black and tan uniforms. A gray bird led the charge, while a reddish flag violently waved. A possessed crowd hurled obscene gestures toward an abandoned Irish cottage. The door was trampled. The clan picked up two wailing infant babies from a distant crib and carved the words "No Freedom" into their soft foreheads. The children were presented to the motley crew and sacrificed in the name of purity, God and creed.

The gray bird rested upon a distressed widow's shoulder and sang a sad song.

Icarus's pulse briefly went still before he thunderously gasped and snapped to.

He awoke in the hospital.

CHAPTER 12
A SORROWFUL TOAST

"I love cold pizza," said Ash!

The group swarmed the honey of Elisa's poach. They were enamored with gratitude and taken aback by the lush nourishment resting in their dehydrated hands. Not a word was spoken, as they rapaciously consumed and calibrated their weakened bodies with their tired minds. Their souls remained an overflowing silo.

"Before we leave, I'd like to get everyone's contact information. I will create a private website and message board for us to correspond. We have to stay in touch and will need the support of one another," offered Grayson. "I want to believe this is going to be as smooth and simple as it seems, but I fear it will not be! How can we can fall in love with someone, with the awareness of a motive? It's a juxtaposition -- our first true obstacle. This person we find will need to become greater than the mission. I just don't know how that's going to be possible."

"I can collect the data in my journal. Does anyone have a pen?" asked Rand.

"Why, you do," said Simon, magically pulling one from

behind Rand's ear.

"You never amaze me!" said Rand.

"Do you mean, 'Never cease to amaze me?'" asked Juno.

"No! I meant what I said," smirked Rand.

"So, how about that party? I'm sure there's got to be a liquor store, nearby," bolstered Ash.

Though warm to her flamboyant offering, the fatigued gang knew it was time to part ways and return to the worlds from which they came. One by one they lined up and provided Rand with their personal information, hugged and extended warm handshakes, with locked eyes. Once compiled, the information was copied and given to Grayson.

"We've all come a very long way and had our unique struggles. The dreams were rough, but we finally know why we're here and what we've been called to do! I want to offer a toast," said Zane. Nervously adjusting a spiked bracelet on her tiny wrist and uncomfortably blowing a piece of purple hair from her worn face, exposing a lingering tear, she raised a perspiring bottle of Evian. "You lunatics are like the family I never had. I'm blessed to have met you!"

Simon patted Rand on the back; Neco reached for Ash's hand; Magnus and Elisa kissed; Zane and Juno pretended to spar, before a long deep hug; Benjamin and Grayson shook hands; and Icarus gave Zane and Juno one last lift toward the blue sky!

Even the clouds appeared to smile back.

"So, I guess that's it?" asked Neco.

The group began the long walk back to their distant cars.

"So, are you heading back to Baltimore?" asked Ash.

"Well, I promised myself I'd head west and slink around the gutters of Hollywood for a couple of months. I may even chase my rock n' roll fantasy. Sky's not even the limit, right?" joked Neco. "My parents have already been alerted that my inner vagabond must roam. Would you like to escort me," he added, reaching for her relaxed hand.

"I'd...," said Ash

"That is, if you haven't already booked your long flight back to Scotland," Neco interrupted, fearing her hanging response. "I should probably warn you, I do not have an actual place to stay and I'm broke!"

"Who said I'm broke?" Ash asked, with a wink.

The howl of a used car lot sent echoes through the canyon. Engines flared and hearts pumped; they each left their dusty signature in the Arizona sands. Neco cleared off the dirty passenger side seat and opened his squeaky door. Ash smoothly slunk into his modest red car. The sun pulsated with energy and the road offered its blessing. They set-off into the welcoming arms of the unknown!

"Let's stop at this bar," insisted Ash, after traveling a few miles. They polished off a bucket of ponies, ate, decompressed and finally had a moment to size up the holiness of their revived Sunday. "So, are we really tasked with finding true love?" she asked rhetorically, pretending to stab her heart with the restaurant butter knife. "Who finds true love, like ever? True love is this thing Walt Disney cooked up in the studio basement of Magic Kingdom. He sold us all, to make billions. Seriously, it's a farce. I think people can fall, be or stay in love, but true love — that's cosmic."

"I don't think we're looking for true love, in the 'Epcot is the future of Mother Earth'-sense," he said, quoting his words with lazy fingers. "I think it's supposed to be the person who makes us want to live — that special someone who gives us hope or a reason. It's the person we entrust our secrets with and can provide us with a foundation to build upon. Then again, maybe it's just someone we can't live without. Regardless, I think the sentiment has to be shared. I'm not saying it's *not* hard to find, I'm just saying, it may not be as mysterious as we think. The truth is, no one is going to know, until their child is born."

"Oh, that would be awkward!" proclaimed Ash. "I'm

sorry, I have to go now, and you're clearly not the one. I have other fish to fry and babies to spawn," she joked. "It sounds trifling. The Council is officially our pimp!"

They both laughed, paid the tab and headed back onto the open road. The setting sun distanced in the rear view and they reflected.

+++

Zane's farewell toast was too sorrowful for Magnus to stomach. The forgotten lachrymal glands in his hurt eyes gushed. The thought of leaving his beautiful new friend, Elisa, overwhelmed him. His heart and attitude would now be controlled by the longitude between them. He'd never felt so connected, nor in love; everyone else in his life seemed like collateral damage. She was smart, sassy and beautiful. Her image gave him hope and a reason to believe there was still a chance he'd escape the downtrodden neighborhoods of Chicago. He was willing to change his entire being for a moment of her attention. The mission was suddenly the conductor of his limitations. The fate of his connection to Elisa rested in Grayson's hands.

"It was great to meet you!" Magnus said, playing it uncomfortably cool.

"You too! How else would we have fed our flock?" she smiled, offering a sympathy hug.

A certain part in everyone was left aching.

"The old saying, 'ignorance is bliss,' can take on a whole new meaning when you're faced with this kind of enlightenment. What's left, after you're given a backstage pass to forever?" asked Simon. "I'll probably never see any of you again," dramatically pausing. "For once, I wish I could actually make myself disappear! Having this child won't bring any of you back, but it may reveal the secrets behind the magic that is life. I'm not sure if we're doing the world any favors with this heavenly punishment."

"Take care old friend. I hope to never see you again,

too!" joked Rand.

The rest of the flock separated.

Rand returned to Germany; Simon to Israel; Juno to Rome; Icarus to Greece; Benjamin to London; Zane to Ireland; Grayson to New York; Elisa to California and Magnus to Illinois.

Neco and Ash were nearing California and ready to dance like hypnotized chickens, to the indie sounds blooming on the Sunset Strip. The layered Technicolor fantasy, blended together with their unforgettable masquerade in the desert made their surrealism peak. They tap-danced across the Mojave Desert and entered Needles, swallowing the gorgeous taste of their new life on tap.

CHAPTER 13
LIFERS

During an uncomfortably long plane ride to London, Benjamin did his best to sort through his lifetimes and travel anxiety. No shrink, nor priest could absolve his riddled mind. His current troubles paled in comparison. It was like the scales of universal law had tipped, lofting his ill-focused future agenda. He suddenly understood the complex visions he'd been given, their symbolism and the urgency of his adolescent night terrors. In a wintery snow globe's haze, his new memories blended with the old. He could recall the girl in the right Borromean ring, from the dream, but was slow to calculate the lifetimes they'd shared. It was a blur.

He knew they'd talk again — they had to. They had fallen in love during their first Program lifetime and developed a complacent thirst for stable companionship — it was the same trap Neco and Ash were destined to fall, if clarity failed to trump their raging hormones and rebel yells. Dismayed by reason, Ben's social life was a ship long lost at sea. He had no one else. Caution to the wind, he remained content to repeat life's vicious cycle, if it meant drifting toward the forgotten coast of stability. He knew leaving

The Program was a permanent commitment to spiritual vacancy. It also meant saying goodbye. *Forever.*

+++

The Beyond was not a spiritual gathering, nor a magical place with pearly gates. It implied transcending the physical plane and becoming unaware. It was a dead zone; a place Buddhists refer to as Nirvana. Released souls reenter the vacuum from which all light spawned. It is man's selfless journey, back through the wormholes of time and space, to touch what does not lie before the beginning. In the truest sense, it is peace in the absence of all.

Only faith could blind a man from the mysteries surrounding it. Living forever had its own sting, but ceasing to exist sent human egos into shock. The complexities of this conundrum were easy to understand, but difficult to emotionally navigate. There was also a lingering moral responsibility, to the souls stuck in the underworld, to not take The Program lightly and to produce a Crystalline child. Those who selfishly chose to remain in The Program or who had failed to produce an enlightened baby, for more than 40 lifetimes, were called Lifers. Though love of the physical world can trap even the most brilliant of hearts, Ben wasn't ready to let go!

His blue thoughts were then interrupted by a red rotary Batman telephone.

"Ben. Thanks for answering!" said Grayson. "I wanted to give you a quick call, to tell you our website is up and running. If you want to reach out to anyone or have an update from your side of the pond, let me know. I'll update the group!"

"Good timing, sir! Can I get our purple-haired friend's number?" asked Benjamin.

"Of course! She's actually not too far from you. I've got to jet, but keep me in the loop. Remember, The Council is watching! 10-4?"

"10-4."

Rehearsing mock greetings in front of his tiny bedroom mirror, Ben hung up the sweaty telephone and paced. He twirled an old Louisville Slugger and mentally traversed the minefield lying in wait. The overwhelming weight of their extensive history rested upon his feeble shoulders. He couldn't afford a misstep. A courtship with his past meant unpacking forgotten baggage and anew. Anxious, he knew there was a very real possibility that their union had reached exhaustion, but hoped she'd reciprocate his timely advance. Nervously looping his trembling index finger through the tight number slots, he dialed.

"Speak to me," snarled Zane.

"Zane." He paused. "This is..."

"Who is this?"

"You know, the math nerd from the Painted Desert with the Paul McCartney 'Meet the Beatles' haircut."

"I knew you'd be calling, darling boy. I think it's safe to assume you've spoken with our New York City counterpart, Grayson, and have had a wee chance to departmentalize, or at least recall, our lavish, yet irresponsible, dealings?" She paused, steering the conversation. "We were a couple of wild things, weren't we, Ben?"

"We are." he joked, hoping to generate a pulse. "I'd like to come visit you."

"I'm not sure the universe will have much to do with it!"

"I know."

"Nevertheless, there are a couple of great pubs in Dublin. When were you thinking?"

"How about 2 weeks from today?"

"OK, it's a..." Zane caught herself.

"Date?" Ben risked.

"It's not a date!" she joked.

Zane was conflicted about her nostalgic feelings. Her admittedly imperfect family hadn't left her with the same irreconcilable abandonment issues as Ben's — just alcoholism! She welcomed her lush years of emotionally detached sex, dating, and if her fancy was tickled, validating The Program. She knew a clean break with Benjamin would require calculated compassion or a combat boot, on the off chance things went south. She wasn't entirely opposed to the passing idea of making things work, but longed to spear the ocean for a new catch.

To avoid being hounded by the guilt of reconciling their past and faced with an unrequited nostalgic romp, Zane tapped Juno, explained the precarious hand she'd been dealt and offered to purchase her a round trip plane ticket. She was intent to avoid the exclusivity of an awkward situation. Juno accepted Zane's offer. Her maternal instincts beckoned. There was a certain grace lodged in her swagger that suggested, 'If anyone could talk reason into this hopeless romantic, it's me!'

"I'd love to come! I can teach you how to dance around this," Juno joked. "Plus, I can tell you all about my new man-friend. He is absolutely gorgeous."

"Thank you so much! I'm not surprised, you're beautiful. You'll be out of here in no time!"

+++

Rand lurked, in a town not too far away. His new lease on life brought confusion and fear to his disciplined family. It drew contempt. Suddenly, a solider boy who had never missed a test, bathed in the smuggest of clothes, and only delighted in the substantiated theories of historical facts, was vibrant, uncaring and throwing colors into the air. For once, he was alive and it was killing the status quo. His parents didn't know the scope of his impromptu Rumspringa, but knew something had dramatically changed in his staunch demeanor. They were determined to quash his newly beating heart.

"Are you on drugs?" asked Mr. Backer. His stern

rumble shook the cabinets and family crystal.

"No. I assure you, I am not. I've been awakened. It is too supernatural for my own comprehension. I don't dare your understanding. All I can say is, this facade of a life you've created — this prison," Rand paused. "It's all an illusion."

"Your country, your academics — your family is a magic trick?" asked Mr. Backer.

"We live inside heaven's ever-changing kaleidoscope. It's an untapped universe of possibility. Can't you see it? We're merely mirrors of fractured glass, facing the Eye of Providence. We observe the universe as it observes us. Wouldn't it be prudent to give it something to delight in?" Rand asked, with a twirl.

"I didn't send you to the U.S. to find god. I sent you to seek university!" his father screamed.

"Life is our teacher. It is greater than any uppity professor — a man or woman who justifies their existence with books and degrees and teaches others the value of teaching others to pave a similar road to nowhere, all while knowing that none of this means a god-damned thing. It's a fraud! Higher education is a sickness, and we all fell for it." A long cold stare ensued between Rand and his father. His mother remained nervous and idle. "A university of thought lies within each of us," he continued. "I seek love, friendship and to live my life! I will no longer be bogged down by the societal expectations you've imposed upon yourself or the walls you've built around this family."

"Get out of my house! Get out!"

"You've lived your entire life, fearing someday you'd awaken unlovable or isolated. One day you'll be alone and forced to reflect on your chastised years! This vicious cycle of your own creation will judge you and hold you painfully accountable."

"Leave, I said!"

"When was the last time you felt alive? When was the last time you and mom danced, gazed into the western sun and drank from the wine of truth or simply threw caution to the wind? Life was meant to be lived. We are meant to find love and no one in this house is doing it, or they stopped short of ever trying."

Mr. Backer opened the heavy front door and leered into Rand's longing eyes. Without pause, Rand accepted his fate on the cruel streets, grabbed his fedora and bag, and crossed the Backer threshold, knowing it could be the last time. The phone rang, stilling his father's raging heart. The door abruptly slammed.

"Hello?" asked Mr. Backer.

"Hi, is Mr. Rand Backer available?" asked Grayson.

"Are you with the university or are you one of his tripping desert friends?" barked Backer.

"I am a friend, yes!"

"Who is this?"

"Please just let him know that I called, and that our website is up and running. He'll need a password to access it," tip-toed Grayson, sensing the man's disapproval. "I can give you my number if you have a pen."

The phone slammed!

Rand was a lifer. He didn't intend to disappoint the uncompromising will of his parents, but knew his purpose was far greater than blind allegiance. The magnitude of The Program had all but eclipsed the drab and mindless moments of his past life. Even the simplest of relationships would quench his longing appetite for seduction. Absolution from the physical plane meant ushering in a new age of hope and peace. It was a message he wanted to scream from the rooftops, even falling deaf.

CHAPTER 14
DOWNTOWN

After settling into a crummy Roadway Inn, in Burbank, California, I began siphoning help wanted ads from various local musician listings in prominent newspapers like the L.A. Weekly and L.A. Times. I also generated roommate leads from nearby telephone poles, college billboards and guitar shop bulletin boards. Ash and I both sought employment, though, the lavish treasure she earned from her divinely inspired paintings was enough to hold us for years to come. There was a certain allure to bathing in the illusion of struggle, knowing we'd survive. Our bond blossomed, making Edinburgh seem like a distant memory.

The hours I spent penning my early recordings in my Dad's basement studio had prepared me vocally and instrumentally to engage in genuine conversations with area musicians. I was drawn to any and every aspiring Hollywood-based rock n' roll outfit who was looking for a guttural crooner. Ash did her best to stay motivated, but quickly became more emotionally attached to our forbidden relationship than her paintings or the dictates of The Council. She'd occasionally invite college girls over from the UCLA campus and set-up body painting expos in our quaint hotel bedroom, but was quickly fading from the lush goals she once held for her perfect life. We agreed it would be prudent to keep our eyes peeled, focused on potential love interests, but navigating jealousy, while keeping an open dialog, under a traveler's roof, on her dime, was a laughable proposition. Regardless, I was comfortably entrapped.

I eventually settled on a rock group in The Jungle of the Playa del Rey. It was located just off the beach and provided a paradise of inspiration, a view to die for and sturdy nightlife. At dusk, heaven itself reflected off of the Pacific Ocean and poured into the windows of my soul. It was a constant reminder that this life was not my own, though I preferred the escape of pretending it could be. Ash came to practices and parties to make sure I wasn't getting too caught up in a world that didn't include her. It wasn't long before her body painting hangers-on became a regular part of our bizarre practices and the masquerading performances that followed. The unique nature of our band's live show drew large crowds. Overnight, Ash's hobby took on a lucrative life of its own. Everyone wanted to be body painted. The fans longed to watch hypnotic girls dance upon black lit stages in a fleshy fetishy environment. We were content to provide the soundtrack.

Ash and I became unstoppable, but I was bound to find temptation — even love!

Our days in the shoddy Roadway Inn were short, but remain an adored memory. There was something special about the simplicity and nonchalance of living within a hotel means. The housemaids and lobby attendants became our family, though we still stayed in touch with our baffled parents, as did our web designer, Grayson, who was busy keeping our spiritual family rooted. After finding a new place and settling in Malibu, we made a concerted effort to keep The Program privy to our precarious exploits.

+++

"Hello, Love," batted Ash, after dialing Elisa from her new land line.

"Hi! I'm incredibly glad you called. So, where are The Program love birds nesting these days?" asked Elisa. "Grayson said you might still be in Los Angeles, which means you're literally roosting in my backyard!"

"We are! We're in the Malibu Hills. I'm not sure if you've heard the Hollywood buzz about our body paint n' rock n' roll shows, but we've been drawing tremendous crowds and making ridiculous money. We're considering taking this experiment on the road. It's a far departure from the walls of class I grew up on, but we're surviving. Even my parents seem supportive — go figure," said Ash.

"We'll definitely have to get a few cold drinks on Sunset! Can I go on tour with you?" asked Elisa.

"Of course! But, only if you agree to be my canvas."

"No. So, aside from wanting to see your darling unpainted faces, I'm curious if I should be concerned about something," she paused. "Ever since we left the desert, Magnus won't stop calling. He seems rather obsessed. I've tried to blow him off, but it's not working."

"Maybe it's a crush? An unshakable crush can happen — it does happen! God, look at us."

"I thought he was a really cool guy and maybe he is, but he said he can't live without me and that we are destined to be together. Obviously, we're not meant to be together. We're in The Program," Elisa concluded with exasperation. An awkward silence sustained. "When I told him to stop calling, he seemed really upset — even angry! I haven't heard from him since. What if he shows up at my apartment? It's freaking me out. Should it? Am I being paranoid?"

"It sounds like a crush. Did you tell Grayson?" asked Ash.

"I haven't. I didn't want to panic, which is why I was

hoping to reach you!"

"How about those bloody drinks?" bolstered Ash, dismissing her uncomfortableness.

Ash and Elisa tirelessly talked for hours. I writhed on the overflowing bed, opening piles of fan mail, occasionally stumbling upon the sentimental treasures sent by my son-sick father. His bountiful care packages forced me to stop and assess my trail of familial wreckage. Watching Ash comfortably traverse my haphazard mindset, and glide through our beautiful new home, made me question if he'd also prayed for her delivery. I could barely conceive how cosmically my life had changed in her presence.

The guitar beckoned, inspired by her silhouette. Adjusting my view, I strategically faced the room's broad bay window, clicked the record button on my struggling handheld studio and tearfully strummed my soul's grateful response. Hours marched by, before I snapped to and decided to follow suite and connect with a fellow Programmer. Ash was long tucked in, but the recorder stirred.

+++

"Icarus?"

"My man. I'm working The Program!" he joked, elated to connect. "Let me cut to the chase, I've been with a couple lassies. I even liked a couple of them, too. It's perverse, I know. For some reason they've all risked my unprotected advances. I'm liable to end up with a lion's share of sexually transmitted diseases, before this is over, but it's all in the name of love. Right?"

We laughed.

"That's it, love! What else is spinning?"

"I heard Juno has a beautiful new boyfriend and is already trying to have a Crystalline baby," he laughed, inflecting a sarcastic tone. "That ginger oozes love. If anyone can find it, it will be her."

"True!"

"I've tracked down just about everyone. I haven't had much luck with Rand, and of course that motorcycling maniac's information isn't available, because he was too cool to stick around. I digress. So, every time I call Rand's house, his father hangs up on me."

"That's strange."

"Apparently, Grayson is hitting the same wall! Have you tried?" asked Icarus.

"I haven't! Maybe I can call and tell his father I'm a professor from a prestigious Athens university. I can leave my name and your digits. There's no sense throwing up red flags with a U.S. phone number."

"That's actually brilliant."

"By-the-by, you're actually the first person I've even reached out to!"

"Honored," returned Icarus.

"Ash and I were living in a hotel, so we really didn't have access to a computer or dial-up, but Rand seemed pretty buttoned up when we met. I'd imagine if he's had a change of heart, it's not going over too well. Nobody is that rigid, unless they're raised to be or hiding something. The problem is, if he gets himself kicked out, he'll be MIA-permanently!"

"I've considered that myself."

"I have to go, but I've been meaning to tell you, you should probably avoid the sun."

"Very funny."

+++

After a brief break in the action, I dialed Germany.

"Is Rand Backer available?"

"Who is this?" barked Mr. Backer.

"It's Mr. Neco of the National and Kapodistrian University in Athens. Did he receive our letter?"

"We did not!" said Mr. Backer. He was suspicious,

digesting my tone and noticing my forced inflections.

"If you can have him call, when he becomes available. I will leave you my number."

"Thank you! I didn't realize he'd been looking outside of Germany." His voice calmed.

"We may be able to offer him a partial scholarship in our faculty of history," I furthered.

"Thank you! Thank you." proclaimed Mr. Backer.

+++

Grayson's website, and tenacity was a godsend. The thought of becoming isolated in our journey was a real possibility. Though his rebel heart had carried him toward the sun, my heart wept for Dez. Trying to breathe new life into a fallen world isn't a pressure suited for a boiling mind. This wasn't a mission we were expected to face alone. We were connected in life and in death. No love interest would ever fully palate the magnitude of our calling, without assuming we were all just a little bit crazy — maybe we were.

Ash and I continued our body paint n' rock n' roll gig for months. She seemed lush with enthusiasm, and my rock n' roll dreams were finally being realized. It seemed win-win, except for the part about us not living the way we were called to live. Our show was taking us up and down the California coast. Endless, were the sands of time. There had been posh offers for a full-scale tour, but neither of us were ready to commit to a life on the open road, and were in no condition to do so.

We were content to seek fulfillment in The Golden State. Our act got us invited to exotic parties for rich fetish seekers. Downtown Hollywood was thirsty for smut, and built on the bones of those overdosing on these lush brands of entertainment. The elite paid handsomely for Ash's services. Raves brought out the club kids, strange cases and designer drugs, all vying for a chance to sink their sordid claws into our quaking relationship. If the drugs didn't destroy us, the sex would. We watched masters drip molten candle wax on female bondage slaves, like children watch baseball games. I can still visualize the memory-blinding strobe lights, and the breathtaking lasers, splashing neon colors upon black rooms. The dungeon-themed bathrooms were dimly lit with black lights and the stalls were littered with the sexual deviance only witnessed in hardcore pornography. The Kings & Queens club, in East Hollywood, was our vice and main source of income.

Paranoia, weight gain, depression and apathy were laundered through excess and quickly masked by the punk culture eclipsing us. Empathetic hangers-on were still eager and willing to take the brunt of our growing delusions, but our poisoned well of sanity was running dry. Ash's art became sloppy and my increasingly bizarre stage performances became riddled with rants and nonsensical drivel. That is, if I bothered to show. Our parade of lust was becoming a monkey business.

CHAPTER 15
EYES OF MERLIN

"We're going to need money," said Dez.

Exhausted, fawning and resting in a tiny make-shift couch bed, covered in foliage and debris, she rested, while he plotted. The still moonlit sky brought out the wolves in his mind. They shared an old sleeping bag, but rarely made love. She often melted into his arms and stared toward the trailer ceiling, longing for a connection and to someday become his only mission. Dez, blinded by intent and an acute demand for dominance, made her advances an unwelcome distraction.

"If we can get more people to understand the deceptions of our government and what's going on under these very grounds, we can raise money," he huffed. "We need a computer, acid, and reliable transportation for starters!"

"How about we just make our own entertainment, tonight?"

"The government is trying to end the purity of our

species and all you can think about is sex! Ironic. Get off of me," screamed Dez, in an uncontrollable rage. He frequently slipped out of his charming guise, gaining an unhealthy level of comfort with Crystal. Outbursts scared her straight and silent. His undisputed eruptions only encouraged his verbal abuse and extended the boundaries of his control.

"I'm sorry, we can start looking tomorrow," she added, calming the quaking beast.

Dez's charisma couldn't be overstated. As the hot summer days passed, the cool evenings and sunsets offered relief and atmosphere to their acid laced bonfire gatherings. He'd strum his acoustic guitar and hypnotize his followers like a Christian revival. His vibrating strings swayed, dancing in the angel dust inspired tracers. Dez and Crystal repeated the cycle of drawing in unsuspecting strippers and nomads from the dugouts of New Mexico. Before long, groupthink reigned supreme and his hunger for power and the intent of his message became increasingly more sinister. Crystal never left his side and felt empowered by his fame. Her loyalty inspired the faith of others.

"Our dependence on capitalism hooks our lips and quashes our voices. We're left hanging by the rod, hoping to someday be released from the hands of their green-eyed motives. Like slaves, we fuel a big machine — a machine they designed and we maintain. We need to create our own law, and banks, and harness the materialistic beast that tempts our very essence with desire. The all-seeing eye mocks our independence. We are more than drones, or disposable pounds of flesh. To steal their money is to barter for freedom and reclaim what was hijacked from birth. Should they try, let no hand hold us down," said Dez.

"That's right," shouted a drifting follower.

"We're not stealing to hurt the bar, convenient store or gas station owners, we're stealing to someday protect the human race from a future threat and this attack that is threatening our way of life. I only ask you to help me. We should only steal what we need to grow. No one is to get hurt. You run before you fire! We cannot risk a robbery drawing attention to our circle," Dez furthered.

After his pounding sermon, a string of robberies sprinkled fear throughout the neighboring town. Weeks passed, and the drugs dug into their minds, like moles. Avoiding identification, the expanding group raised enough money to purchase a used vehicle, a few military grade weapons and a new computer. The blotted out windows in their 1996 Chevy Conversion Van offered a safe-haven from the outside world and ample protection from the law. They continued to meet in Dez's backyard sanctuary, intent to follow his drug-addled visions — producing results reinforced their adrenaline addictions and rank.

"I'm sure there is a lot we can learn about these children with the indigo eyes. These alien hybrids are already amongst us. Use this computer as a gateway to their doorsteps. Be diligent. Scour the Internet for information and take detailed notes. There are literally hundreds of sites on the topic and blogs about those who profess to be special or enlightened. It'll be important for us to find these families and to know what we're truly against!"

His eyes slipped into his skull like a possessed lunatic. His tripping minions, followed. Weeks of acid, plotting and brainwashing served to inspire their cry for revolution. Even Dez was starting to believe his rhetoric. He only regressed to his distant time in the desert, to combat his vivid memories and recall the dictates of The Program. Flashbacks made his anger bleed upon the sand. The drugs amplified his neurosis, increasing the frequency of his lucid dreams. His sense of urgency was magnified.

"I found a website called Children of the Program," said Crystal, still awake from an uncomfortably long bout with ecstasy. "It seems to be password encrypted. It's got an indigo background. Didn't you say the government hybrid operation was called *The Program*?" Her voice droned, falling from lofty heights and landing upon his resting ears. "What do you think, dreamy eyes? Do you think you can hold it together for a couple more minutes and check this out?"

In elation, Dez sprung to attention. Clearing the counter of old cigarettes butts and beer cans, he aggressively leaned in and obstructed her wondering view. His wide eyes were like saucers and his mouth frothed like a rabid animal. He was confident he knew exactly what she'd pulled from cyberspace. "The heavens always have the answer, don't they? Try typing: painted, program, council or lords," he paused. As he anticipated, nothing opened the temperamental site. He slapped the monitor to diffuse. Her shaking hands could sense his tensing anxiety. She feared further disappointment. "Try, Arizona or desert," he furthered. Excitement had quashed his aggravation. Her keystrokes were slow and deliberate. She knew a missed letter would amplify his blood pressure. Before she could blink, the desert themed website opened. "It's a goddamned miracle!"

"It was 'desert!'"

He pushed Crystal from the loose stool beneath her and cautiously scrolled down the unveiling screen. She was content to leave his side and catch a drag. He remained dumbfounded by the simplicity. His heart skipped a beat and his eyes danced. Taking a moment to gaze, he gasped with elation. The password was left accessible enough for the chosen ones to decode. It was a simple deterrent, meant to keep the outside world from bothering to care. The site provided their full names, telephone numbers and addresses. It also contained a small news-centered bulletin board. Some of the profiles included pictures, bios and email addresses. He was relieved to see the 12th member-area was left as, "Coming soon!" Hastily jotting down the sites information, he bookmarked the page and shutdown the computer.

"What is it, Dez?" Crystal called, pacing outside the trailer.

"It's a website dedicated to people like me. It's a list of people who know about The Program and can possibly help us spread our mission-worldwide! There's one fellow, in particular. He claims to be a magician. He lives in Israel. The Middle East is the home of a gamut of religions and belief structures. With funny paper, we can open minds, but with magic we can suspend the imagination. We can show the world that sometimes the unexplainable is a mere hat trick. This is how you expose a corrupt government! I've got to find this man."

"I'll help you turn over every stone, in the morning," Crystal offered.

"Simon, Simon, Simon," he breathed.

+++

Though it lacked prudence to openly discuss The Program, for once, Simon welcomed transparency. He struggled with his identity and new sense of obligation, longing to share his experience with the unwitting. Most dismissed Simon's tales, assuming his stories were the preface to another magic trick or a heretical illusion aimed at garnering their attention. Some passersby did believe his words and drew closer to his unveiling. They had nothing else.

Simon didn't want to know the answers to life's mystery. He wanted to practice magic in the shadow and mystique of creation. As word spread of his audacious claims and obsessions, his relationships with family and friends became strained. His gimmicky street performances began drawing more ridicule than adoration. He felt shunned and scrutinized by the world he was sent to save, only adding to his mounting inner conflict. His twilight was cursed. He could still hear the hecklers scream, "He's crazy!" and "He's a fraud," while trying to find a few fleeting moments of tranquility. With each day, he became more isolated. His tricks had lost their audience and his money was growing scarce. He had buried his future in Israel. Damned by his revelations, he knew there was no turning back. The same crux that drew his words was the same that would draw his unraveling. People didn't want to know the truth — they just wanted to live.

"Perhaps it's time for me to disappear," he thought.

His phone cried with synchronicity.

"Is this Simon?" asked a gravelly tone.

"Yes, may I ask who is calling?" asked Simon.

"It's Dez, from the desert. I'm sorry I tore out of there, without saying goodbye, but I was rattled by the news of our mission. There were so many terrible memories lurking, beyond the cobwebs of my consciousness. I'd have been happier to forget it all. Can you believe how many people we've known?"

"I know," returned Simon.

"It's crazy! I don't know how you feel about everything, but I am overwhelmed," said Dez.

"I'll admit, it's not sitting well with me," offered Simon. "My entire life is centered on suspense and mystery. I didn't want to go behind the curtain and I'm certainly not programmed to allow others to peak. Besides, who would want to know? It voids the authenticity of our existence, and siphons any true meaning from our experiences. We're sent to struggle, feel pain and engage in temporary relationships."

"This is true."

"Yes, but now, success is being asked to forget everything and everyone and to become one with nothingness. I believe the lucky ones got it right before having to choose or ever having to know."

"Wow, you've given this a lot of thought," returned Dez. "Look, I'm in a similar boat and was thinking we might be able to help each other. I'm trying to build a support group, aimed at generating awareness. If you're interested, I'd love to fly you out. We'd love for you to join us. If I'm being candid, I don't believe in The Program. I think it's downright wrong. It was wrong to unveil this to us, leaving us no option but to return from failed attempts at love, or to find love and be forced to say goodbye. I've been to the underworld. This might be worse!"

"I have, too!" laughed Simon. "Look, say no more. 'I'm leaving, on a jet plane,'" he added, crooning a joke. "I'm not exactly doing too well over here and could use the company and a healthy debate on the subject. Where are you?"

"New Mexico!"

"That's right. How did you find me?"

"Magic!"

"Respect."

Simon began packing his camouflaged bags, determined to unearth a little sanity or old fashioned American distraction. His tense mind uncoiled. He knew it was only a matter of time before Israel forced him into exile. As luck would serve, hope was reignited by an unexpected flame. It was as if the universe had called him to a new mission. Though Dez's bravado had intimidated the chosen ones, his demeanor on the phone seemed fair, well-intended and above all else, timely. Hasty for solidarity, Simon never considered his motive.

"Grayson, if you get this message, I'm heading to New Mexico to see the infamous Dez."

Click.

CHAPTER 16
VISIONS OF THE WHITE BIRD (ATH)

With zero trepidation, Simon boarded his flight. The distance to New Mexico smothered his patience and murdered his enthusiasm. Getting comfortable is rarely an option when wedged between two equally as uncompromising pieces of fleshy discontent, locked in a 110 degree angle. The mere thought of another bag of off-brand peanuts or complimentary cup of lukewarm soda was enough to make him pant for a stronger drink. Leaning back, he let the sweet taste of inebriation drown his unhinged mind. In moments, he drifted into the void of a well-needed rest.

Gazing into the eye of his dreaming mind, he saw the cold New York City streets standing apocalyptically still. The only stir of life came from the lazy humming neon. From a rusty yellow park bench, Simon watched debris and ash raining down upon a fallen world. Occasionally, a patronizing song, caught between two crumbling buildings, tickled his frostbit ear, sending shivers up his bowed spine. He was the lone witness, far from humanity's reach or care.

Those who survived the endless war were hunkered

down in fallout shelters in neighboring towns, far beneath the Earth's crust. The New York City buildings were covered in red spray paint. It was the abandoned graffiti of man's final cry. The cryptic messages were intended as an obituary to anyone who might stumble from the wreckage and find the city's lost bloodlines.

"You cannot make the world disappear," read the towering Empire State Building. "Our illusions are your reality," read the marked Rockefeller Plaza. They stood like tombstones.

Simon knew the messages were meant for his gaze. Adjusting his view, he saw the white bird, Ath, resting on the tablet in Statue of Liberty's left hand. The date had been changed.

"Freedom bathes in the ongoing fight for truth," said Ath, setting the torch afire. "Our hope rested in a single child, yet your sleight of hand has manipulated the world; a reality, forever tainted by the illusions you cast. We will continue to light a way and rise from these tired ashes, but you will remain enslaved by your guilt, forevermore.

"How can I be responsible for such destruction? What have I done?" asked Simon.

"It's what you didn't do," said Ath.

Than, the gray bird, then appeared. It flew into a towering skyscraper and burst into flames. The building trembled, before quaking to its knees. From the corner of his eye, Simon saw another gray bird approaching a second colossal twin building. He reached toward the sky to thwart its advance. It was too late, and far from Simon's reach. It crashed, smoldered and asphyxiated his view with blankets of dense smoke.

Encased in the steel ivory beast, Simon was startled by aggressive turbulence. He awoke. The shake of the plane stirred his palate and forced him to the tiny airplane restroom floor. His sensitivity to vodka consumed him with waves of nausea, but his vision swallowed his heart. He anguished. His aversion to The Program waned.

+++

Juno's never wavered.

Drifting toward the merriment of a peaceful night's rest, she ogled the mystery lurking just beyond her bedroom window. She was infatuated with life and the sea of possibilities resting in the future's hands. Startled, a white owl appeared and enticed her curious eyes into a staring competition. It would vanish in the darkness and reappear with the blue flashes of a passing hailstorm. Intensifying, her aged glass shattered, allowing the insistent bird to enter. It perched upon her sturdy bedpost. "Who will dance for me?" punned the White Bird.

Juno sprung to attention, flung off her fluffy comforter and without pause, struck a pose. As she danced about her room, her movements became effortless and exaggerated. The bedroom floor slowly faded into a brilliant starlit sky. To Juno, this was more of a fantasy than a nightmare. The bird showed her how to use her soul to cross the universe and overcome the boundaries of science and reason. Her art seemed limitless, in the presence of boundless faith.

"Your heart bears the fruit of love's seed. And such, your branches are uncontainable," said the bird.

She was then hung like a marionette. The owl bound her limbs with freshly cut metal twine.

"Will you dance for me?"

She was unable to move. Like a puppeteer, the bird then began forcing her into motion. The more she fought its cruel movements, the deeper the jagged ties cut into her virgin skin. Naturally, she panicked. Like a fountain, blood dripped from her overwrought wrists and ankles, as her tender flesh tore. Her tired muscles drained. She then realized her dependency on control outweighed the faith that allowed her to express her heart and mind to the broken world. She was still a creature, tempted by physicality, blessed by the comforts of privilege.

"Your joy comes from the limitlessness of free will. It's the greatest of all gifts and relies on man's convictions. It cannot be interfered with by The Council. If you never lose faith, you'll never stop dancing!"

The final sentence repeated in Juno's open mind. The words empowered her to challenge obstacles and lobby against doubt.

+++

Rand was also lead by the repetition of his calling and soothed by Ath's wisdom. The white bird filled his soul with poetry and paved the doldrums of his riddled mind with philosophy. These sentiments were his guidepost. He struggled with a world and an identity he barely understood. Drifting, he heard the familiar words of his childhood.

"You are one thought in a collective mind," chirped Ath. Rand squirmed trying to awake from a horrific dream about World War II. In his vision, the white bird reminded him of the reflective nature of consciousness and the danger of unwarranted hate. "You observe creation, while it observes you."

It showed him a mechanical German army and the beautiful people of his old country being prepared for the slaughter. He was then turned and sat before a vast mirror. The reflecting people turned into a sea of doppelgangers, manufactured in his likeness. He was instructed to massacre his identity and give himself over to death's sting. Fear of losing one's self, he learned, was the catalyst of all subhuman intent and guided by fragile egos. Though man could justify his actions with rank and divinity, he could never truly affect man's essence.

"Do you see the limits of physicality?" asked Ath. Rand watched billions of memories from millions of people set free from physical bondage and rejoining an omnisoul. The white bird then showed him the pit of the underworld and told him to jump into it. The fire didn't consume his soul, it recycled his energy and burned forevermore. "Understanding comes from an eternal energy. It cannot die or be lost in the fire. It can't be murdered by man's hands."

"What we do to one, we've done to all?"

"Love is love reflecting. You are the future we long to see, a mere thought The Council chose to have. You must not forget our interconnectedness or your responsibility to The Program, even if it seems impossible or inconsequential to today. Love is the union of two or more minds acting as one conscious."

The bird began morphing from white into a beautiful rainbow of colors.

Rand awoke, panicked and confused by the colorful symbolism. He shuffled to find a light, knocking a half-empty glass of water off of an old oak table. Glass shattered onto his wooden floor and awoke his parents. When they entered his room, Rand was gone, but the mess remained. He had been sneaking into his old bedroom to catch winks and would occasionally tour the house for clues to his family's on-goings.

"Call Neco, National and Kapodistrian University in Athens," read an old crumbled up piece of receipt tape resting on the barren kitchen table. On the back of the paper was a scribbled phone number with a strange exchange. The note's existence gave Rand hope that his mother and father hadn't completely divorced the idea of seeing him again. He knew his old desert friends were probably trying to hop over the Berlin Wall of his father's creation; he was elated by his find, and lost in the night. His parents were never the wiser.

His father had no idea how important this message was to the world!

CHAPTER 17
REVELATIONS

Benjamin and Juno arrived, in promise. They met at Silk's Restaurant, located at the Enclosure Bar in Dublin, Ireland. The ceiling, walls and floor were covered in a musty oak corkwood. Horse racing memorabilia painted an elegant scene of class and riches, neither of which Ben and Zane were accustomed. They chose to sit a healthy distance from the bar, to make their clean-living ginger feel comfortable.

"Before we get started, I have an important announcement," said Juno.

"You are..." started Zane.

"I'm getting married."

"Juno, that's fantastic! How long has this been in the works?" asked Zane, longing for hope.

"We just decided. I figure, if I'm going to start trying to have this 'out of this world' baby, I should probably avoid the awkward out-of-wedlock scenario with my conservative family. Besides, we're beyond in love. I'm thinking, beach," she added.

"We're happy for you," said Ben, assuming he could speak on behalf of his ex-lover.

Zane wasn't entirely prepared to deliver the crushing news to Ben, but his rhetoric drew her strike.

"Ben, I want to try The Program. We've been together for countless lifetimes. If we don't at least try, we'll just continue on this way forever! I do love you and I cherish what we had, but I really want to try and get this right," Zane said. Her revelation evoked an understandably uncomfortable silence from her *lifer* friend.

"I agree! I think you should try," Juno added. "If you can't find a dreamy or special someone, then maybe you're meant to carry-on together for another lifetime, but there's no rush in assuming anything! You have your lives ahead of you. Go run, like these horses." Juno pointed toward the paintings in the bar.

Ben's youth hadn't prepared him for her crushing sentiment. His mother ensured he'd never come to terms with abandonment. Zane was all he had to look forward to and remained his only connection to the past. In a burst of uncontrollable rage, he slammed his clinched fists on the sturdy wooden table and huffed from the bar. An ocean of tears begged his release.

"He'll be alright," offered Juno. "He just needs to cool down. You have to do what's in your heart. We're here for a greater purpose. If you're able to find love and bring a light into this crummy world, than you're justified, right? You may finally fulfill The Program and do what you've been called to do. That, my dear, is exciting! Ben is the least of your worries." Juno stroked her hair and empathized. She understood Zane's emotional struggle, due to her complex history with Ben, but couldn't hold back.

"I did meet a bartender before we were called to the desert. We hit it off in a, 'Hi, I'm not really old enough to drink, but I manipulated you' kind of way," said Zane.

"Go for it! Call him. That sounds rather exciting," prodded Juno.

"We could always just walk down and see him. It's only a few blocks away."

They exited the restaurant. Ben was knelt down crying. He faced north with one arm propped against an uncaring brick wall, and another curled under his prodding chin. He resembled The Thinker; had he produced an actual thought, he might have been spared the embarrassment of their find and moved on. It didn't matter, he was too consumed with self-loathing to be concerned with his unsavory appearance or how it might be interpreted by the passersby. If anything, he was prepared to welcome the attention that came with scorn or to bathe in their pity. He didn't know where to go or what to do. Zane had the power to show him what it was like to be put first and to change his skewed perceptions of love, but she'd chosen not to.

"First my family, and now her," he thought, shattering.

The girls tried to console him, but could tell he was content to remain unresponsive and transfixed by the day's events and dirty dank streets. Awaiting him to gather his sordid thoughts wasn't something they were prepared to entertain, especially not on a girls' night out — they had boys to paw. They continued down the gravel road. Zane was conscious to redirect her bartender-crazed conversation until Ben was far from ear shot. It wasn't long before he was swept off of the M8/N8 Cork-Dublin road, by a surly and impatient bar-back.

+++

Ben returned to his nearby room, seeking solace. His hostel was in disarray, but it was all he could afford, after the impromptu trip to Ireland. His dimming mind was still reeling over the money he'd spent on the inconsolable dilemma fostered by his trip to Arizona. He hoped a flicker of light might rest in another Programmer.

"You'll need to shout! Who is this?" asked Neco, paginating about the Lion's Den club in Studio City, California. The background noise roared with club kids panting for sub-kicks and pulsing house loops.

"It's Benjamin! I needed to talk with someone from our circle. You were the first person who came to my shattered mind. Do you have a moment or are you at a rave?" asked Ben. "And, what is that?"

"Actually. What's going on, Ben?"

"Zane and I have been together for several lifetimes! We never left The Program, because we were in love. We would simply die and wait to be reborn into another vicious cycle. We always promised to reconnect during every lifetime. It was really that simple, except," he said, pausing.

"So, you deliberately stayed in The Program?"

"I guess you could say Zane and I were a lot like Ash and yourself. We figured, since we couldn't conceive a miracle child of our own, our love would never have to end. I can't handle the idea of not having her in my life. We've had far too much history together."

"I'd love to say I understand, but I don't." Neco was interrupted by a litter of fawning kittens. Gulping saliva and whiskey, he continued his investigation. "How do you know this? Have you actually spoken with her? Where are you?"

"Yes! I'm in Dublin. By the way, I saw Grayson's update on the Children of the Program website. It looks like you and Ash have one hell of an act going in Hollywood. I trust that's what I'm hearing?" asked Ben.

The club beat waxed and waned with the rhythm of Neco's racing heart. "Ha! We did. I really can't get too deep into it, right now! I'm somewhat distracted and really haven't had a chance to process everything or even sleep for that matter," said Neco, coming down from an ecstasy high. "The long and the short of it is, our lifestyles caught up with us and we hit the proverbial wall. I lost everything."

"What do you mean, you hit the wall?" asked Ben.

"We tried to keep an open dialog about The Program. We agreed that we should allow ourselves to seek out compatible love interests, but the undercurrent of her tone suggested otherwise. One night, she walked in on a rather explicit party I was having with four of her painted dancers," continued Neco.

"I take it things didn't go too well?"

"I should have known better, but the drugs, my hormones and The Program clouded my feelings! She freaked out and immediately flew back to Scotland. Unfortunately, I haven't talked to her since. I'm actually surprised she hasn't called Grayson to update the damn website. I don't know, maybe she's embarrassed."

Ben was taken aback by Neco's candor. He understood the temptation he was under, but knew he'd inadvertently saved himself lifetimes of distress. "Neco, I understand. You can always call me! I'm sorry. Luckily, these things have a way of working themselves out. I won't tie you up any longer, unless you desire to be," joked Ben. "Just promise you won't slip down the rabbit hole. You're one of the few friends I've got out here!"

"Promise."

+++

Ben wasn't the only Programmer looking for a connection. Excited, Rand pulled the crumbled receipt paper he found at his parents' house and dialed the scribbled number. He waited with anticipation, and reeled over the possibilities. Without being able to see the Children of the Program website and unfamiliar with the foreign phone exchange, he could only speculate on who might answer. His dirty clothes wouldn't allot him much investigative computer time in the community library — he looked like a bum! The payphone rang, torturing him with its tenacity.

"You've reached the great and powerful Icarus," said an uncomfortably deep and arrogant voice.

"Oh, thank heavens! This isn't a recording, right?" asked Rand.

"No, no," said Icarus.

"I'm on a phone, just outside of Kassel, Germany.

What's the name of The Program's website?"

"Rand! We've been looking for you. It's Children of the Program, all one word, dot com. The password is: 'Desert.' I take it you've been home. Your father is charming. Did your parents give you the old steel-toed boot when you got in?" asked Icarus.

"Yes! I couldn't restrain my excitement, nor take their archaic ideals. Truth be told, they were going to kick me out, sooner than later," pitched Rand. He longed to share his revelation, hoping Icarus might catch the hint.

"Why, in this lifetime, would they kick out a perfect specimen like yourself? You seem like a parents' wet dream! Did your studies slip because of the insane visions? Did you fail to acquire a scholarship to a premier German university?"

"Nonsense, I'm attending a school in Athens, remember?" joked Rand. "No, it's nothing like that! Thing is, I'm actually afraid I might be trapped in The Program, permanently!" Rand began to tense, anxious to deliver the news.

"Why would you be trapped? I mean, we're all sort of trapped, but, why you, specifically?"

"Because, I'm gay!" Rand paused for a reaction. He was invigorated with freedom. "How can I have a Crystalline child with 'The one I hold most dear,' if I don't fancy the love of women? If memory serves, I've been at this game for a very, very long time! I'm what you might refer to as a..."

"Lifer?" asked Icarus.

"Yes."

"I don't even know how to respond. I'd give you a child if I could," joked Icarus.

"Thank you! I'm going to try and find a nearby computer, but can I get a few of those phone numbers from you? Can you also let Grayson know that my heart's beating, and that communication will be difficult, because I'm tragically homeless?"

"You got it. Stay safe out there and please don't hesitate to call." Icarus made sure Rand had everything he needed before cutting the telephone line. He was perplexed with how to console him, but was generous with his support. "Some people struggle with their physical demons and some are just dealt a difficult hand," Icarus thought.

+++

Magnus was a victim of his own device. Smoke escaped his blackened lungs like winter's chimney. He eased back his recliner, injected a lethal dose of cheap heroin and dulled the mania. The thought of living his dark existence without Elisa became increasingly unbearable. His nights grew longer and the sun set sooner. He was unshakably depressed. Scores of one night stands came and went, but nothing muffled his ache.

The Chicago Public Library offered a Gateway to her doorstep and was the only drug capable of piquing his distancing spirit. He'd gaze at her profile on the Children of the Program website, lust over her image and replay their short moments together. He spent hours scouring the Internet for the missing pieces of her back story. Toggling between screens, he was intent to obsessively refresh his browser, hoping Grayson might have added a morsel about her or updated the news section. He had her home address, telephone number, details on where she went to school and the names of her immediate family. He had enough to be dangerous. His obsession started playful, but without reciprocation, he seethed, assuming her perfect existence had moved on without him.

"I just wanted to see how you were doing," said Magnus, clogging her answering machine. The further he slid down his spiraling fantasy, the more depressed and unaware he became. A boy with little hope was given the power to give back to The Program and avoid an anguishing future, if only he'd turn the channel from unrequited love.

116

CHILDREN OF THE PROGRAM

CHAPTER 18
CADENCE OF THE SUN

Once his skewed mind settled and sober body safely landed on American soil, Simon regressed to his more cynical view of The Program. He bustled through a crowded terminal and traversed a myriad of displaced exit signs, all pointing toward the eager and under-worked ground transportation area, before emerging from the Albuquerque International Sunport. He was even more disoriented than when he'd landed. The patronizingly bright sun wasn't helping his gelatinous mind. Had he not known better, the climate of the Midwest would have easily fooled him into thinking he'd never left. Almost on cue with his exit, a white van crawled onto the jam-packed receiving curb. The back doors flung open.

"That's him! Get him," said a familiar voice.

"I hope I'm not being abducted."

"These are a few of my comrades. If we were going to abduct you, we'd have worn masks with large black eyes and brought laser guns. I apologize for the entrance. We're doing this for your protection — not ours," said Dez.

"Fair enough." Simon was confused by his logic, but

content to get stoned with his new friends.

"Give him a deck of cards! He's going to blow your mind," said Dez.

"It may be too late! I think our minds are pretty far gone, as is." Simon spent the rest of the drive entertaining junkies. Arriving at the compound site, a famished Simon was distressed to find the shambles of a junkyard, which Dez and the gang called, "su casa." The grounds were littered with tents, half-naked pedestrian eyes and rogue animals. It looked like something out of the 1960s and wreaked of death and suspicion. "I'm going to need a little time to digest all of this. Your overly-tinted van windows obliterated my entire sense of time and space. I've been tipsy, sick and disoriented more times than I can count, today. Typically, I do the blindfolding. Regardless, we need to find real food, and fast," said Simon.

"10-4. I was planning to take you to a burger joint up the road, you know, to *catch up*! There's also a strip club, not too far from here, where my girlfriend works. They serve wings, fries and a decent view. If you're willing to go a little further, we can hit-up the usual fast food chain restaurants or my favorite hole in the wall diner. It's your call," said Dez.

"Charming. Let's hit the diner."

"Done."

"OK, so tell me about this group you've assembled, and where you're heading with all of this," said Simon.

"I left Arizona in a rotten shambles. All of my suppressed memories broke me. It's like the ghosts of times past have returned to haunt my waking days; dare I say, worse than those pesky birds. Heading back, I stopped into a seedy strip club and invited a few entrepreneurs back. I wasn't entirely sure what my intentions were, but I knew I wanted female companionship. I started telling them my..." Dez paused, "Our story. They were intrigued and content to stick around. I was resurrected twice that day. I never looked back."

"So, they know about us? They know about The Program?" Simon asked, fighting suspicion.

"Not exactly! Who in a million years would believe this? Our story goes beyond the realm of comprehension. It makes the wicked alien abduction theories, sightings, and mounting government conspiracy cover-ups, surrounding this-here New Mexican state, seem like a historical lesson; a prose that our children will someday read about, and take as the factual origins of the Badlands. Our group aims to expose these Crystalline children, Simon! I sold it the only way I knew how, by interweaving theories. In short, that our government has been experimenting with alien-human farming, engineering or whatever."

Simon deliberately held his tongue. "Please, go on!"

"In a nutshell, I told them these children are aliens, that they threaten our genetic purity and that I need their support in awakening the public. No one is going to believe that the gods have come down from heaven and impregnated these bodies with special children," continued Dez.

"Yes, heresy, if I've ever heard it," snarked Simon.

"Simon, my group has already expanded into various cities across the U.S. We plan to go international. People are concerned. The word is spreading — *fast*. We even have our own website!"

"There might be a shred of truth in there, but you do realize you've started a cult, right?"

"It's not a cult."

"You're right, it's not a cult! But, it's nice to see you've finally made some friends out here," added Simon. Simon and Dez pulled into the old Eagle Diner on Interstate 40 and entered with affected swagger. They pulled up to the bar for a fill up. "I take it you found Grayson's site?" asked Simon, between ordering his feast and sipping a pop.

"Yes, by happenstance or fate. My girlfriend is always around. I have to view the website privately, to temper any suspicion. Our relationship wouldn't work out too well if she knew the whole back story, but I really don't know how else to spin it."

"Sure. Every successful relationship is founded on manipulation. You don't want to risk her trusting you. It would be over for sure!"

"Funny. I've written everyone's information down. If we can make the world aware, we can seriously disrupt The Program. We might even be able to stop it! It'll certainly make people think twice about these special kids being born. I plan on staying in The Program. They can't kick me out unless I procreate, right?" said Dez, rhetorically.

"Nice! So, you want to rule the world? Everybody does, you know," said Simon.

"Not exactly. No more than you. You're here aren't you?"

"Yes, as I understand it, unless you have a child, you're not going anywhere! Judging by your approachable demeanor and lavish property, I don't imagine you're in danger of finding Nirvana. Does The Mickey Mouse Club have a name?"

"Not yet!" Dez became increasingly annoyed by Simon's candor, but remained intent on lassoing his prey.

"The thing about the desert is, you can always count on it! It's consistent. It's relentless. It has an unmistakable rhythm to it. Before the first bead of sweat falls, man's instincts are hypnotized to survive. It tricks our eyes into seeing things that aren't really there." Simon paused, pulling a suicide king from behind Dez's ear, followed by a fork. "It's a true magician. It can strike fear without drawing a single word and steal the breath of a careless wanderer. With your group chanting this urgent and admittedly crazy plight to the unsuspecting world, you can use what the desert already knows to leverage an advantage. You become the rhythm. The magic. The Cadence of the Sun."

"I love it! I'm just looking for some solidarity. I'm not trying to mislead anyone. Sometimes, the truth isn't always what it seems. You of all people should know that. With your understanding of magic, we can literally put a spell on these people! It's going to take a little bit more than my campfire sermons and tripped out musings, on the beat up acoustic, to be a force to be reckoned with," said Dez.

"I'll think about it! I have my own issues to deal with, but I'm up for meeting everyone. I take it you heard Juno is getting married?" asked Simon.

"No, I hadn't."

"She was probably the ripest apple on the tree! She'll be out of here, lickety-split," said Simon.

"I'd sure like to lick..."

"Don't! Just don't. Look, I saw a hotel on the way over. Can you drop me off?" asked Simon.

"You can stay at my place," offered Dez.

"No offense, but I need a hot shower and good night's rest! You really didn't expect me to sleep in your lawn with those vagabonds, did you? Actually, scratch that, there was a little offense intended."

"Those are my people!" quipped Dez.

"What time does the Cadence rise?"

"Just be ready around 11. I know where you are!"

His years of magic had served him. Simon wasn't easily manipulated by Dez's wiles. Even in exhaustion, Simon's mind was far too grounded and clever to get lost in the dark web Dez was attempting to spin. Simon continued to use distracting humor to derail Dez's dizzy dialog, before finally being dropped off at a local motel.

"I'm glad you know where we are. I don't. I don't even know where you are, for that matter," said Simon.

Dez reached over and slammed the van door shut. Simon was left laughing and staring toward dusty taillights. On the way home, Dez stopped off at the striptease to reevaluate the unexpected turn of events and to soak his mind in liquid courage. Knowing Simon wasn't the only one capable of putting a spell on people, he lured a few new burlesque queens back to his lot. Left small, he needed to invigorate his sense of control and smite the taste probity had left on his razor blade tongue.

"Simon doesn't have the stomach for this," he thought.

His vengeance was smoldering.

Arriving home to a bustling fire pit and the anthems of his tribe, he could feel the booze rattling his calm. "Be quiet, all of you!" He was exhausted, frustrated with his failed evening. Giggling, an animated lass tripped the wire, sending his patience over the edge. "None of this is yours. It's mine!" He screamed, grabbing the guitar and smashing it into the pit. His congregation of mice scampered toward their makeshift tents. He stormed the trailer to find Crystal engaging with another girl. "Is this what you do when I'm not around? Are you whoring yourself with this tramp?" The girl ran from his fury and left Crystal to tend his rage.

"I don't know what's gotten into you. You've been gone all night! When you do come home, you show up with strippers, without your Israeli friend and in a maddened frenzy. What is it, baby?" Crystal asked, trying to calm the storm. "You can tell me. You have to tell me. I love you!"

"I'm sorry. I owe everyone an apology. I went out with Simon and he mocked me. He mocked us! I tried to open our door to him and he kicked it in. He pissed all over me and my prayers for tomorrow. He knows everything," said Dez.

"He knows what?"

"He knows about our plan to inform the world, about the website, our reach — everything! He's at the Best Western, a few miles from your work," said Dez. "I swung by the club and tried to wash down his barbs with whiskey. I felt defeated and needed a little decompression time. He made me feel foolish for trying to warn others. There's no chance he'll follow us. We could have worked together and led our future in the right direction. I wanted to feel like all of this still meant something and we could branch out!"

"Of course it means something. Look at all of those people out there," added Crystal.

"That's why I brought the girls back. I wanted to fight

his negativity by proving we could still grow. It wasn't to disrespect you! When I got home, all of these people were still up and carrying on. I blew a fuse. Can you go outside and apologize for me? I'll be out, in a bit."

"Of course. See you soon." She leaned in to deeply kiss her fearless leader.

"Oh, and stoke the fire. It's going to be a long night."

The trailer door slammed. In the calm, he opened the overheated laptop that had been hiding beneath their sleeping bag and scoured The Program website for revelations. He saw his name and home state had been added. "Heads will roll," he hissed.

CHAPTER 19
FOOL FOR HARDER TIMES

"Neco, you've always wanted a good story to tell," Ash muttered to herself.

She returned to her lush mansion in Aberdeen and fell into a sea of cardigan arms and loving support. Her rich parents had missed their little girl and the pride she brought to Scotland. Many of her original pieces had been sold to finance her Californian sabbatical, but she was eager to pick-up her lonely brushes and begin telling a new story — an enlightened story! The desert gave her a new perspective on the greatness of the universe and Neco gave her street cred; forever holding her hand, while she dipped her pristine toes into the turbulent wild side.

She was armed to move hearts, determined to trump her virgin art pieces and thrilled to be far from the aid of a human canvas. Though her relationship with Neco was strained, she would always hold a special place in her heart for his wiles. They shared something they'd never forget, and no one would believe. Even if their lost time only sustained as a lovesick memory, it was their beautiful disease. She knew they'd drift, but was intent to keep him orbiting. Like bottled-up tidal waves, she still longed to encapsulate Neco, in a painting she'd call, 'Into the Art of Darkness.' "Why do our hearts always get trampled," she whispered, awaiting an answer.

+++

"Hello. Grayson Miller, New York Times."

"It's Ash."

"Hey, how's Hollyweird?"

"I'm back. It wasn't meant to be. I've been wanting to tell you!"

"Is everything..." Grayson paused. "Is anything new?"

"I plan to start painting again and was hoping I could use our site to share my works."

"That's why it's there. You can also send me a picture, if you want to update your profile."

"Perfect! What have you been up to, aside from tirelessly keeping track of our motions?"

"I fell into it a digital editor position for a legendary paper," clarified Grayson.

"That's amazing."

"It's been an absolute dream come true. Lately, though, my real passion is The Program and the story that is unfolding before our starry eyes. I've been taking detailed notes about everyone's on-goings and will someday sit down and pen a book about it. Would you be open to doing a full interview, at some point? I'm asking everyone. I want to get a little of the juicy back story, to flesh it out."

"Absolutely. Please do!"

"I've also done a lot of research on these indigo or special kids. I'm starting to wonder if they might be the direct descendants of The Program. Obviously, if that's the case, their parents are gone, and unavailable for comment, but it may give us some insight into what these kids' lives are like, their innate sense of responsibility, and what their able to recall; moreover, the power our mission can ultimately have on our degrading society. I'm not sure I love New York City, but it does serve as a glaring reminder of what we are. We've become a cesspool of instincts, habits and disenchantment. We're an interconnected and amplified celebration of human devolution. Our world needs hope."

"Totally," added Ash.

"Our lives are too vast to ignore, and there are a lot of things I'm still having a difficult time understanding. For instance, did you hear that Rand is gay! How does that work? We have to follow The Council's rather specific law. It requires us to procreate. I'm curious to see how it all plays out," said Grayson.

"Well, I'm not sure it does play out. I mean, can it?"

"I'm a journalist. I'm programmed to never say never."

Beginning to hang-up, Ash remembered Elisa's anxious plight and thought it was best to warn him. "We might need to keep a ghost-eye on Magnus. Apparently, he's head over heels for our beloved California girl, Elisa, like, borderline stalker! She says he calls, leaves cryptic messages and simply will not take the hint that it's time to move on."

"I had no idea!"

"I figured it was a crush and maybe it is, but can you put a site tracker on our page?"

"Sure!"

"Maybe, we can track IP addresses, find anomalies and narrow down any possible offenders," said Ash.

"Consider it done."

Ash hung up, rejuvenated. Her creativity had been stifled by keeping her whereabouts under lock and key. Ready to focus on The Program and leave California behind, she entered her abandoned art studio; a world where longing brushes had been tapping against her old wooden pallet and awaiting notice. She began divinely painting the beautiful Painted Desert landscape, just as she recalled. In a fluid stroke, she defined the sandy volcanic ash floor and captured the radiant sunset; silhouettes of the participants, followed. The fiery sky lights were crowned with the descending blue bird. Grayson wasn't the only Programmer who wanted to tell their story. It just was a matter of capturing their hearts, so the world could believe!

+++

Shortly after Ash left Los Angeles, Neco returned to Baltimore. Affording Malibu wasn't feasible without their stage show and her financial backing. Crossing the threshold of his old suburban bedroom, he could feel the room's energy had made a wanted shift. It had been exorcised from head-to-toe and the graffiti walls were purified with flat; somewhere beneath the paint lurked the dark secrets of his youth. For Neco, going home was a second helping of culture shock and humility. Cascading through the windows, the sun cast a beam across his nervous body. In an instant, his anxieties snowballed into an oozing sphere of unforgettable and indigestible pain.

Like a séance, he sought the muses, and allowed psychotherapy to sooth his detoxifying soul. His preoccupation with writing, recording and control became an unquenchable obsession; each note laid the foundation, while pain provided the lyrical breeding ground. Dark rhythms detoured his immediate focus, allowing him to departmentalize the world he had long turned his back on. Before his dusty bags hit the welcoming floor, he began working on an aggressive love-scorned album. The project allowed his imagination to run and spoke gravely about his personal quest for damnation. His amassing guilt cried for absolution, and dark themes provided a shelter from the outside world.

His music brooded through lazy meters and played like an audio diary of his early years, imparting imagery from his lucid dreams, juxtaposed with the revelations he absorbed in the desert. Mock songs glamorizing suicide and primal screams gave it a sense of urgency. It instantly captured the ideation of the most sinister listener. The hopeless took notice and knighted him. Between writing and trying to get his footing in reality, he managed to stay in touch with the Children of the Program, hoping to someday muster the courage to offer Ash the apology she deserved.

"Ben."

"Neco."

"I'm back in Maryland. I just wanted to give you a call and see how you were holding up. I'm sorry I was a little distant, last we spoke. I was in the midst of an orgy. I'm sure you can imagine how distracting that can be."

"Sadly, no, but I heard. I'm hoping Zane comes around. In the meantime, I'm working my ass off on the docks and trying t' forget about her," said Ben.

"Any word from Simon, Rand, Icarus, or anyone else?"

"Simon flew out to New Mexico to meet-up with Dez and Rand is homeless!"

"How did that even happen; I'm mean, with Dez. He left without saying a word."

"No clue!

"I wonder how he even found him. I guess the better question is, 'Why?'" Ben and Neco debated the likelihood of Dez and Simon's pairing. "Just like The Program, life has a way of bringing people together, for better or worse; it's what makes the entire journey palatable and interesting enough to sustain, I guess. You said Rand is homeless?"

"Yes."

+++

Rand found solace in the underbelly of Kassel. Through a new friend, Isabella Hoel Schaffner, he found someone to spark a light in the darkness and to be a soundboard for his ailing mind. Isabella was a beautiful blonde runaway. She was willing to risk the brash realities of homelessness, if it meant never being touched by her father again. She tried to openly communicate with her pretentious mother, but she preferred to turn a blind eye to Isabella's reality. She didn't dare scorn their respected provider, nor the diamond studded life they'd grown accustomed.

Isabella wore a thick wool pea coat, large black framed glasses, brown leather work boots, faded loose-fitting jeans and a bedazzled crop top. Her hair was matted with unwashed dreadlocks, but her smile could send a fleet to war. Rand found her beautiful, and she found his sexuality painfully trustworthy. She tragically loved him, but did her best to try and help him find love, shelter and peace. The tight-knit homeless community had a way of looking out for one other. They knew the safest places to set-up camp, the warmest places to hide and the quickest ways to score a meal or a bottle of forget-it-all!

"I want something to love — someone who adores me," said Isabella.

"I do," Rand responded.

"Not you, Rand! That would be selfish, no? As soon as I find you someone to prance around these streets with, you'll owe me in spades," said Isabella.

"Anything."

"We'll see! We're just a bunch of fools for harder times, aren't we?"

"I don't think we're fools. How does one find themselves, if they're willing to give-up on who they are? Those people live to appease the ones who mock their very existence. Are they behind an agenda and the cold comfort of complacency?" asked Rand.

"I don't know."

"They are the fools; just mindless sheep, marching like ants under a magnifying glass. They know they are going in the wrong direction, but none of them bother to move or question their leader. They are terrified by what might lurk just outside of the lines. Entrapped by life, these lemmings march toward the same awful fate, are willing to be set ablaze by their stubbornness and are eager to watch one another die a tragedy. We're not the fools, Izzy." Isabella and Rand cuddled against the walls of the Neue Galerie art gallery. The air was tolerable and the moon was bright and longing for their gaze.

"It's beautiful," whispered Isabella.

"It would wink, if it could." They knew the most beautiful moments were found, bathing in the good vibrations, lost in the presence of the present. They basked in the radiance of truth, enhanced by the confidence of an unshakable trust. "My father doesn't have a life. He died a long time ago. How many souls does life steal, before they ever knock on heaven's door?" asked Rand.

"At least he wanted what was best for you."

He'd lasso her the moon, and wrangle it in, if it would give her that one thing she craved — love. But, life had its limitations. It seemed nothing could fill her emotional void, nor the modern day travesty of Rand being stuck in The Program without an exit sign.

CHAPTER 20
REVOLVER

Dez grabbed his shiny old silver revolver, spun the noisy chamber, dramatically clicked it into place, stuffed it into the front of his dirty denim and exited his temple on wheels. His eyes were lazy and enlarged, like glowing saucers, and his slithering tongue was sharpened for urgent deception. He'd prepared a crazed message for his followers and planned to stoke the inferno of his aggression, intent to asphyxiate the angels with his might. He was ready to launch his crazed war upon humanity! The revolution was mere footsteps from being unveiled. A Napoleon complex, a toyed-with ego and Black Velvet whiskey created the catalyst for building a foundation on blind anarchy.

"Tonight, we'll rebuild our fallen world, again," Dez said. The fire glimmered in a sea of hypnotized eyes. "We'll start a new order. The world laughs at us. It laughs at you! We have to rise up and make these minions aware of what our government is doing to our species. Our voices can no longer be silenced by the rhetoric of the elite, nor the posh arrogance of non-believers. They walk like sheep to the slaughter, hoping to someday graze upon the White House lawns; a home built upon propagandized freedom and digested as an American Dream! The unwitting self-impose their slavery," he continued. "We must awaken them."

"What do you want us to do?" asked Crystal. Excited, she locked arms with her longtime partner in crime, Michelle. For a moment, she looked around, recalling the first day they'd nervously stepped upon Dez's lot. She couldn't believe how their lives had changed over the passing months. Their days of stripping had been replaced with building an army.

"I think I speak for the congregation, when I say, you have our full support," offered Michelle's boyfriend, Max. He was a 19-year-old bald-headed bar-back, who had run away and filled his mind with the optic distortions of broken women tempting soulless men. Thirsty for approval, and aching for the support of a non-abusive family, he was easily compromised. His cracked compass was fixed in a southerly direction. Typically dressed in army fatigues, he was prepared to punish the world for his parents' wrongdoings. His sculpted muscles were intended to thwart the advances of mild-mannered pedestrians or the niceties of mindless conversation. Max was a rock. His mass was a respected symbol to the others and a wall Dez could rest behind.

"We start small and send a message," said Dez. "The prankster we picked up from the airport is a traitor. He brought the beast out of me. I apologize for the way I reacted. I had hoped he'd bring mysticism and enlightenment to our circle, but instead he came with an Israeli agenda. His people are backed by the United States. If we risk bringing him in, we'll surely find ourselves in bed with the devil himself!"

"So do we need to send a message to Simon?" asked Max.

"There are others who know this man, but wouldn't dare seek the authorities. They know he's here. Going to the authorities would only publicize their agenda. They'd never risk it, never!" His intensity and madness grew with each coarse word. "We will send a *crushing* message," said Dez.

"Who are they?" asked Max.

"They are the aliens sent to pervert the seeds of our DNA. They are watching us, right now," proclaimed Dez.

"I thought you said he was one of us?" asked Michelle.

"Beware, I sent you out as sheep amongst the wolves," quoted Dez.

The group was wide-eyed, drinking from his fountain of insanity. They no longer respected the compass of conscience, nor worried about the consequence of law. In the truest sense, they'd found salvation in abandoning reality. They made their own laws and had deteriorated to rebels without cause. They simply wanted the association of a peer group and to reinforce one another's palate for destruction and vindication from sin. Reduced to animals, they were no longer capable of leading themselves. The battle ax constellation of Yue shined bright. This was Dez's world.

"Get Simon and bring him here. Leave him unharmed," screamed Dez.

"Do you want him blindfolded?" asked Max.

"Of course, scare him and keep him from recognizing our faces. He'll know who it is, but we shouldn't give him the benefit of a second look! There's no sense risking everyone's identity or compromising our whereabouts," furthered Dez.

Max quickly rounded up a group of intoxicated campers, loaded the hot-boxed van and set-off into the crisp desert evening. They charted a course down the old familiar dirt driveway and into the great wide open. When the dust settled, the twinkle in Dez's eyes gleamed with psychosis. The waves had been set into motions and would soon crash upon unsuspecting shores. Their worlds would never be the same.

Like a union of fallen angels, Dez and Crystal deeply

kissed before the raging fire of Hades. She was fully committed to his mania and willing to go down in flames, if it meant securing her place at the devil's table and being crowned as the undisputed queen of the damned. To think, she once tramped stages in lonely afternoon dive bars, but soon would rule the underworld with her New Mexican prince. The passion and power of the moment overtook his reason. He tore off his dirty white T-shirt and allowed her to claw his dead skin. The remaining cult members sat mesmerized and aroused. Though he'd been conscious to avoid the risk of bringing a child into the fallen world, he longed for a union with her trembling and insecure body. He was exhilarated with power.

+++

Max and his road gang of demons arrived to their destination and warmed the cool air of a still morning. The squeaky van doors opened and slammed closed as the crew descended upon Simon's first level motel room. Intent to bring their leader his beloved Israeli prize, they hovered and circled like turkey vultures in pursuit of a walking corpse. Subtly knocking on the weighted door, Michelle prepared to fawn for entry. They didn't want the draw attention of neighboring rooms with aggressive theatrics, before exhuming their prey. The others stood withdrawn from his immediate curtain view. Groggy, Simon answered. He was confused by her untimely presence and understandably annoyed.

"It is a little early, isn't it? He said you'd be here at 11 — not three in the godforsaken morning," quipped Simon.

Michelle quickly covered his mouth with her soft lips and placed Dez's revolver to his temple. He was forced into the tiny studio room. Tripping over his duffel bags, Simon was pounced upon by three grown bandits, armed with only a dirty brown pillow case. Covered with doo-rags and aviator sunglasses, they grunted and bandaged his limp limbs with duct tape, making an unnecessary spectacle of his unresisting demeanor.

"What are you guys doing? We are friends."

"You're no friend of ours. You are the enemy," Max returned.

"Are you guys out of your troubled minds? We just broke bread at the diner up the road. He dropped me off at this hotel and planned to pick me up in the morning. If I was the enemy, why didn't he just take me? Are you even his henchman?" asked Simon.

"Dez does things the way Dez does them! It's your world that has blurred the lines of sanity," said Max.

"You are following the words of a lunatic on the fringe. You know that, right?" Simon directed his plight to Michelle. He paused, hoping her once-forced kiss might find curiosity in his words. "The only thing keeping that psychopath afloat are the people he's chose to surround himself with. You're all making a huge mistake and you will be judged."

"Save it, Nancy-boy," said Michelle.

Simon was pistol-whipped and tossed into the back of the familiar van. In the event their trapping went awry, the steel floor area had been prepped with a glossy plastic sheath. Celebrating the dawn of a new beginning with a fresh joint, their hormones pumped with zeal. "I'd have shot him right there, if I could," proclaimed Max. "I can't stand the sight of his kind!" Racially-charged, Max took every opportunity to align himself with Dez's clout. He earned his stripes from Dez's constant public sentiments, and reaped the sexual benefits of being his right-hand man. The group needed a second-in-command and Max was eager to accept his rank.

"Let's get back," added Michelle.

"Viva La Revolucion!" They drove back to the ominous field, invigorated by the cool air of drawn windows and the spider and the fly nature of their game. They'd achieved their first mission directive, undetected by the long arm of the law and were prepared to sacrifice their pleading sheep upon the devil's alter. Dez and Crystal continued performing lewd acts before their congregation of animals, while headlights illuminated their stage. The surrounding cult members watched and freely expressed their carnal desires by the beautifully burning fire. In the name of one body, they were encouraged to swap partners. Their explicit appetites were fueled by the bright van lights. Their perversion welcomed new voyeurs.

"We've got our catch," screamed Max.

The crew quickly emerged from the vehicle and yanked Simon onto the hardened ground. Max kicked him in the stomach and laughed with demonic empowerment. "Squeal piggy, squeal," cackled Michelle.

"Dez, what is going on here?" Simon muffled through the constricting pillow case.

"Bring him here," Dez calmly instructed.

Reaching his patronizing arm around Simon, Dez silently instructed his cult to follow him from the raging fire pit to a barren area just beyond the lot. The cracks in the ground were lit by the moon, while shadows of the flames danced across the desert floor. Compelled to command his mission and set a new precedent of acceptability, he debated how to handle his bravado and play. Simon was surrounded and feared Dez's mindset.

"I don't know what you're doing or why these people have beaten, blindfolded and brought me here, in the middle of the night, but I beg you not to do this. We're here for the same reason. These people have a right to know what's going on, if they're going to continue doing your spineless bidding," pleaded Simon.

"Your words of desperation fall deaf, Simon! We know who the true enemy is," said Dez.

"Why didn't you come for me? Why did you use your clan to do your dirty work?"

"This clan you speak of — this is my family. I owed it to them to make sure I thought this out! The new world you came to populate is an abomination to all races, creeds and colors. It mocks humanity and the human heart. Your world attempts to destroy the very foundation of our existence, and I can't, in good conscious, allow that to happen."

"You are one of us, Dez. Look on the website, it's all there! Has anyone seen our website?" asked Simon.

Wandering eyes and nervous body language spread through the camp. The cult seemed impatient and afraid of what they might hear next. The truth, they were willingly manipulated and enjoyed the sense of freedom and power it allotted them. Whether Dez was on a mission from God or a fraud was of little consequence to what they chose to believe. Dez gave them hope and support, but moreover, filled their souls with sex, drugs and a world without boundaries. They wouldn't let it be compromised by reason."

"Shoot him, Dez!" pleaded Max. He handed the shiny revolver to his merciless leader, who placed it to Simon's sweating forehead. "What are you waiting for?" he demanded. The atmosphere grew thick.

"The time is now for us to take our name and send heaven our messenger," replied Dez. "We will stop those who came to create a world of genetic impurity. We will light the way and be the heartbeat of a fallen world. We are the Cadence of the Sun!"

Dez slowly cocked the weapon. Simon's shoulders fell. Sweat poured from Dez's furled brow as he accepted full ownership and pride in disrupting the Council's plan; knowing, by their own admission, that Lords couldn't interfere with The Program!

Free will.

CHAPTER 21
THE COMEDOWN

The dull residue of drug use made it difficult for my therapist to decipher the messages lurking in my crystal skull. Grounding from the psychological trip, caused by The Council's spiritual interference, left me sanely unsettled. I scrambled to turn the station from yesterday. For hours, I uncomfortably gripped the cliché leather couch. Her pointed questions drew demons from my tired body. When still, you could hear them surf about the sterilized green room on waves of dissonance. Each week, I entered with the sincerest hope she'd have the sense to avoid finding the root of my bipolar behavior. Fearing a misdiagnosis swore me to secrecy. Exposing my truth, without evidence, would only lead to a cocktail of pills, which I'd never awaken from. I'd become the Rip Van Winkle of The Program. To fetch her interest, I comfortably tiptoed around familial issues, sexual deviance and the hellish nightmares. None of which held a candle to what I'd seen out west or what I'd been called to do. In earnest, she wanted to help, but nothing put me face-to-face with myself like stomaching the comedown in isolation.

With a truth, stranger than fiction, I created a variety of different musical aliases and purged my sentiments. The lyrical beds and marketing did the bulk of the talking and were saddled atop crunked rhythms, all chugging at 1,000,000 horsepower. Music gave my multiple identities a way to communicate the unbelievable things I couldn't tell my shrink. The closest I ever came to publicly revealing my soul name, evolved from a fantasy pop rock project I called Niki Thunders. Devoid of body paint, my longstanding California-based musical project, Skitzo Calypso, became a crossbow aimed directly at modern society, taking issue with the insane landscape man was expected to traverse, without ever knowing who or what lies behind the shadowy curtain separating life from death. I could empathize. Some of us were privy to the afterlife, but dismissed as lunatics or attention whores. Art built a nest for my mad mind. If only the world knew about those damn birds!

Like mitosis, my soul fragmented, leaving shards of memories for my cautious heart to be cut upon. My thoughts were scribbled across razor sharp mirrors, coated by the dust of desert sands. I could suddenly see things from a myriad of welcoming new perspectives. I always thought the essence of man lurked behind the wheel of our fleeting bodies, or was a singular construct of personalized energy, but, it turns out, there's a tiny universe breeding inside of each of us. We are the stardust of an infinite body and immeasurably responsible to one another. We are called to create.

The more frustrated I became with my juxtaposed realities, the more devoid of heart my music and lifestyle became. Everything seemed purposeless. The heavens had sent me on a one way trip to nowhere, without a resident lifeline. Suicide became a glamorized end, for a soul that couldn't die, nor face post-life repercussions. On several occasions, I attempted to drown my corpse in gallons of alcohol. My rock n' roll idols had found solace in a similar fate and I was eager to follow suit. Luckily, my chums and lovers would graciously fish me out of random bathtubs without ever uttering a damning sentiment. I was a mess, drifting far from my responsibilities to The Program. No one entered my harbors or docked on my shores. There was no risk in hurting someone, like Ash, who wasn't allowed to get close. I felt justified in the walls I built and better off alone.

Oddly, there is something socially acceptable about smothering one's being in excess and passion. The truth is, I was just looking for an easy way out; a eulogy, sold and written as an accidental death. The criminals I did bet on were equally as psychologically affected and excessive. They were bore of devil's sweat, stood as pillars and were the true salts of the earth. We, the undersigned, were sworn to an unwritten pact, willing to go down in flames for another's heartache and eager to tempt fate for another adrenaline-fueled moment. We lusted for life, death or an exit ramp off the highway to hell. Though my cronies were a welcome distraction, I still longed for Ash and our short time together. I missed her tempered voice and bountiful grace. In a moment of weakness, I dialed, anxiously counting the ring tones.

1, 2, 3...

"Ash, it's Neco."

"I always knew you'd call. I've missed you so much."

She was able to speak with a reassembled confidence, no longer bogged down by the missteps of heartache. Her divine artwork was touching people and soaring beyond the realm of earthly possibility. Leaders from various countries would stop by her legendary mansion, and allow their eyes to feast upon her self-made museum. They clamored for pieces to hang in their capitals, and often made gratuitous offers.

"I've seen some of your paintings on Grayson's site. I knew you were good, but you're changing the world. With the mere brush of your heart and the oils of your soul, people are seeing The Beyond. I've never seen anything so beautiful, in my life, except for..."

"Thank you, Neco." She blushed. She was able to pick up on my sweet gesture. "We all have gifts. Find yours before it's too late. These angelic paintings defy my own comprehension. I've been on TV shows, radio programs, featured in magazines, written about in newspapers, and stalked by the paparazzi, but I'm still at a loss for words. When you're one with your calling, you'll shock yourself and the world will notice."

"You deserve it!"

"I feel fully dialed into my mission and completely unstoppable. The pay isn't half bad," she joked, drawing focus from her success. She didn't want to tap dance across my obvious depression, nor outshine my pursuits. For whatever the reason, she still believed in me, and wanted me to find true love and purpose.

"I hope I'm not being self-centered when I say this, but I saw a picture on the Children of the Program site, called 'Into the Art of Darkness.' It looked an awful lot like me. Dare I ask?" I could always find tiny clues, hiding in the layers of her artwork, but here, her intent wreaked of blatancy.

"It's you! Of course it's you. You are a beautiful misguided person, Neco. I don't regret a thing and I'm not upset with you. I can't say that I didn't have the same primal urges or that I wasn't equally as out of my mind and beyond the scope of repair. You had the guts to live it. In the end, I needed my family, my studio and the stability of a Scottish home."

"Have you talked to anyone else?"

"Grayson is a site editor for The Times. He's kept detailed notes and interviewed me."

"Me too."

"I spoke to Zane. Geographically speaking, she's probably the closest female connection I have."

"How is she?"

"Dating. A lot of dating! She gave me a little bit of

background on Benjamin's predicament."

"He's heartbroken, but understandably so. Their situation mirrored ours!"

"True. I get it. By her tone, I'm not completely sure she's finding what's she's looking for."

"Who has? Icarus seems content to impregnate as many girls as possible."

"Charming!"

"I guess he figures one of them has to be a fit. Juno's not too far from you, right?"

"About 25 hours. Zane tells me she's getting married, so I'm sure she's on her way out."

We continued to playfully share the war stories and gossip of our fellow comrades and debate the ends of the universe, systematically solving all of the world's problems before cutting the line and going our separate ways.

We'd talked at such length, I'd forgotten the fear that had kept me from picking up the phone. Her motivation, drive and impact was infectious. I wanted to make her proud and show her that I too had something special to offer; but, before I could be an agent of goodwill, the darkness would have to subside from my furious heart. It would require traveling to the bowels of the underworld, to unearth the source of my guilt and frustration.

"3, 2, 1," she clapped her hands. "Neco. Snap out of it," called the therapist.

My eyes flickered, as I realized I'd been hypnotized.

"It sounds like you're love sick," she added.

With a refreshed perspective, I spent weeks injecting prophecy videos and occult literature into my constricted veins. Overexposure seemed like the best vehicle to face my demons, and touch ground zero. My anxiety was replaced with an unquenchable thirst for self-discovery. To tap the fountain of essence within, I began penning anthems for the underdog and experimenting with various genres. The songs were riddled with irony and littered with clues about The Program. I spent years rubbing pennies together, building a musical bridge over troubled waters and creating a lyrical map of my psychology. Some touted my work as megalomania and others followed the clues, knowing they'd someday find the key to Pandora's Box.

CHAPTER 22
THE SHARPER YOUR LOVE

Per Ash's request, Grayson kept strict tabs on the frequency of IP address hits to the website and mapped their origins on meridian lines. He knew the group was using the site, but if patterns arose, he was prepared to make Elisa aware. The last thing his spiritual family needed was to divide or have a sociopath on their hands. He took Magnus's threat seriously. Playing detective was in his editorial wheelhouse.

Updating the site's coding from his work computer wasn't always an option. Between demanding shifts at The Times, he'd slip into local coffee shops to fraternize with the staff and update the Children of the Program page. It was the only access he had to any semblance of a social life. Affording a place in New York City came with excessive financial commitments, which didn't allow for a lavish night life, an abundance of free time, or even an operating budget for his own Internet services. It also meant he could easily miss crucial events in the lives of the chosen ones.

Grayson's defense mechanism for dealing with The Program seemed to be textbook avoidance behavior. He made his work his obsession and assumed the full journalistic credo. He'd often forget The Program existed, or that he'd been called upon, until after a 15 hour beat had come to pass. It's not that he was actively avoiding or disinterested in love, he was just transfixed with their story. To Grayson, falling in love and having a baby would jeopardize his self-imposed responsibility to the world.

+++

"Elisa?" Grayson was eager to let her know he'd received her plight.

"I swear to God," Elisa said. She was nervous the unfamiliar voice was Magnus. Filtering unknown numbers and toll free exchanges and using the time differential to her advantage, she was typically able to discern whether the call was coming from the devil himself, a telemarketer or might actually be worth answering.

"Wait! It's Grayson. Ash filled me in."

Her mind uncoiled. "I'm sorry! You don't understand. Then again, maybe you do." Elisa nervously played with the cord on her neon telephone, ready to purge the volcano of emotions burning in her heart.

"I just wanted to give you a quick call and tell you that I'm tracking an unusually high amount of IP address hits from various computers in the Chicago area. I know various members are using the site more frequently than others, but this seemed a little excessive, and validates your recent concerns. As an experiment, this morning, I briefly took your picture down. The site tracker went crazy with hits from Illinois."

"I'm not surprised! I've told him to stop contacting me. I've thought about getting a restraining order, but I really don't know if that would make much of a difference. My gut says he'd continue to stalk me, one way or another."

"I'm going to try and call him. He might be willing to open up to me, but I wanted to make you aware."

"Thanks!"

"Is there anything else going on? By the way, thanks

for the picture. I've been working on plotting our pictures and locations on a site map."

"I've been dating this guy from work. It seems to be getting pretty serious, but I'm not sure that's newsworthy! It's a step in the right direction."

"Definitely. Not everything that goes on the site is newsworthy, but that doesn't mean it's not a part of our story. The devil's in the details and I'm out to raise the beast. I hope to someday share our story with the world. But, for now, if you think it'll escalate his insanity, I'll leave it off."

"I think it may also make him realize the door has shut- for good! Post it."

+++

Elisa knew love could be just as dangerous as it was nurturing. Forty-five hundred miles away, a long flowing white wedding dress poured over the ancient grounds of Sardinia. Lush flowers and a small guest list came out to celebrate the marriage of Juno and her fiancé, as a brisk warm sea breeze gusted off of the Mediterranean. The beauty was a reflection of her soul, as she radiated before the stars in heaven. She playfully waltzed down the aisle to meet her soldier prince, accepting his hand in marriage, without ever uttering a word. A lavish after-party followed, before they consummated their love. The island had never known the likes of Juno. It was as if an angel was sent from heaven to amuse humanity with the simplicity of a healthy heart, body and mind. She loved everyone, setting the stage for reciprocation. She understood The Program, its parameters and how to make love without assuming or abusing it. Prepared to leave the earthly world with her final beautiful offering, she kissed her husband deeply. Never leaving their adoring sexual mindset, they crashed into the hotel bedroom. It was passion, fueled by a cosmic romance. She insisted her child be conceived on that premise. For days, they made love before the heavens. Gasping for breath, his soul entered her body and connected. Her body was unchained by his love, like Andromeda. They swapped minds, intertwined bodies and allowed time to bestow its heavenly gift.

She longed to tell the world.

"Grayson, I'm married!"

"I'm so happy for you! Are you leaving this planet, anytime soon?

"Yes."

"I guess it was in the stars! Soon you will dance before the heavens and enter The Beyond."

"Our child will guide the world and dance between dimensions. It will shine down a new day, ushering in enlightenment for future generations to marvel. Pain will be destroyed by the heightening vibrations of our graduating awareness. The galaxy will have its new angel. He will be called, Marte."

"Wow. You've really put a lot of thought into this."

"I promise to keep in contact with you! I will not vanish without saying goodbye.

Excited, Juno dropped the call and dialed her Irish heart assassin. Her lover pawed. Starting with a soft kiss to her neckline, he insisted on a celebration lap. Playfully, she pushed him away and awaited an answer.

"Zane, are you sitting?" asked Juno.

"I'm as comfortable as I can be, on this rickety old bar stool," returned Zane.

"I've consummated. Under a radiant sun, our child was conceived."

"Such poetry." She motioned the bartender for a Jack & Ginger, inching closer to the glass. "I'll just go ahead and drown my tears. The heavens sure love torturing my lush soul. I finally make a real friend, and she's due to evaporate from planet earth in just a matter of months. Who in The Program am I going to talk about my boy troubles with?" asked Zane.

"I'm not fading, yet! Has your situation improved?"

"I've dated a cruel summer worth of loser guys, but nothing feels right. The more I think about Ben and our lives together, the more I remember." Stirring her drink, her speech sputtered into an intelligible whine.

"You're not giving up on us are you?"

"I feel obligated, like I owe Ben a warm handshake and a real conversation."

"You'll never have sex like *this*," Juno giggled, "With Ben." Her interrupting lover clicked the receiver.

"Maybe so," she thought.

Within hours of Juno's tease, Zane and Ben reconnected and resolved their past. Their conversation oozed with gut-wrenching joy, the ache of lost time and the empathy of past woes. Knowing they may fail to give the world a Crystalline, they sharpened their steely knives, removed the pain, and vowed to take a stab at another future together. Swallowing her transgressions, Ben understood her hunger for anew. On impulse, she invited him to Dublin. She wanted to find a cottage together. He was happy to drift from the harbor, frolic in her fields and make an abrupt shift to familiarity. They laid sturdy roots and began rebuilding their endless romance together.

+++

Though sharing lifetimes could become a civil union between two Children of the Program, and may have held a certain timeless wonderment, Grayson knew it would be wise to warn Magnus about the dangers of forcing unrequited love. "Sometimes man misreads the signs of a wanted fate, fooling his lovesick eyes with the perversions of a prejudiced thought. Ben and Zane weren't meant to be witnessed as an example. They are an unresolved anomaly," Grayson rehearsed, before dialing Magnus and handling Elisa's bidding.

"Have you shaken the desert's dust off, Magnus?" asked Grayson.

"I think it's still stuck in my eyes. I really can't see too clearly, these days. I'm dealing with a lot of unresolved conflict and emotions from that day. It's all very heavy, you know? God's special children, right?" asked Magnus, rhetorically.

"I think we are all tasting the sour sting of that tribulation. Elisa?"

"What?"

"Look, it's nothing. I spoke with Elisa. She's concerned about your frequent calls."

"What do you know?" asked Magnus. He became increasingly flush.

"I know she has a boyfriend and is thinking about getting a restraining order!"

"I'm done with this baiting conversation. Elisa and I saw God. She knows it and I felt it. I'm not going to let her drift into the sunset because we're a few thousand miles away. If I lived closer, we'd be together."

"I'm not trying to get a rise out of you, but you've got to leave this alone. I'm documenting everything. The others have shown their concerns. I offered to reach out and talk you off the ledge."

"You can't! Are we finished?"

"She's over it. It's not a matter of geography, it is reality. Don't you think she'd make an effort, if distance was the only true obstacle?" Grayson grew agitated, as hot coffee dripped from his squeezed cardboard cup. "You weren't sent here to be together. You're here to conceive and satisfy a calling. That's all she's trying to do. Please, Magnus, let it go."

"Fuck You!"

Magnus hung-up the phone in a fury. He threw it against his bedroom wall and began stomping it with the heel of his old cowboy boot. He knew Grayson was right, but could no longer bear the song of truth entering his thick skull. He allowed their memories to reel like tape, until his sanity was a shadowy backdrop, and he was the sole playwright of his destiny. He was prepared to do anything for Elisa's adoration.

"The sharper your love, the deeper I'll cut," he laughed, carving her name into his forearm.

CHAPTER 23
THIS IS A WARNING

Dez's trembling hand muscles tightened. Closing his narrow eyes, he brought the tight trigger to an inevitable rest. The flash of a fired gun silhouetted his demonic body. A subconscious moment of clarity guided the barrel off of his defeated target. An anticlimactic dust cloud raised from the solid sands. "This is a warning," he rattled. A cold southwestern wind blew across the desert as a dove flew from the fire pit and circled the camp. "Simon is worth more to us alive," he regretfully muttered, encouraging the wild eyes of the night to stand back. Thirsty for blood, Max shook his head and paced.

"You can't kill me," insisted Simon. "Had my brains been splattered about these New Mexican sands, and the vultures stomached my thoughts, I'd never truly die and you know it. These crazed revolutionaries of yours, masquerading as a purpose driven cult, have a right to know the nature of your game. You're a sham!"

"Tape and tie the wizard." Dez stormed away, more enraged than when he'd left the diner.

Simon's evening ended with the resounding thud of Max's fist. Unaware, he was beaten and tied to the propane gas tank attached to the back of Dez's trailer. They were willing to risk that possibility of gray wolves or rattlesnakes finishing the job, though Dez knew Simon's knowledge of The Program and access to the chosen ones was invaluable.

The cult was taxed by the raw excitement of nearly killing a man. One by one, they slunk to their tents and settled in for the night. They thirsted for a new hell-sent mission and adrenaline high! Resting uncomfortably in his dirty sleeping bag, their fuhrer plotted, trembled and detoxed his pores of bourbon woes. He felt shrouded by humiliation and emasculated in the presence of his cult family.

"What if they question my sincerity or motives? I must make them see," he garbled.

Crystal was wise to keep a safe distance. Perching on a rock, she reflected. She'd bore witness to her mother's agonizing screams, and could still hear her abusive father's drunken slurs. Unfastening a tiny locket from her neck, she struggled to open her only connection to her stolen innocence. Tucked safely inside her tiny silver heart shaped picture locket was a wrinkled black and white photograph of a mother she'd never met. Gazing at the picture, a tear crept from her tired eyes. Though she beckoned for the only man she trusted to guide her, the moon never answered. The sound of silence was her only refuge from the pain.

The dawn of a new day came quickly. She awoke on the desert floor. The hot desert sun made sleeping an inconvenience. Clanking a rusty spoon against an old coffee tin, Max played rooster. The rabid group was hungry for a breakfast of retribution, blood and eggs. Their animation distracted Dez from noticing Crystal's absence in the night. Their loyalty toward him never waned. They trusted his judgment to spare Simon and foamed for a new emotional fix.

"I had asked all of you to keep detailed notes, and to research these alien kids on our computer. Some people tout them as divine, some refer to them as miracle babies and others simply profess they're possessed by god or some supernatural force," said Dez, rattling on like a broke record.

"They are aliens. Here's to the enemy's enemies," interjected Max, raising his ration of juice.

"It doesn't matter what they're called. They are all born of a common thread. They are conceived with American lies and alien deception! I do not profess these articles in vein. How can a forest grow with the synthetic seeds of deceit? We must replant, by unearthing the disease," Dez added.

"What are you suggesting?" risked Max, speaking for the bewildered group.

"I want you to hunt these bastard children and stop them. Our awakening is imminent."

"Exterminate them?"

"Our reach is far greater than just the group we've assembled here. We've networked and grown exponentially. We need to reach out to our affiliates from across the globe and make them feel our urgency. Our next mission is a young Italian woman named Juno. She is a birther. She will use her body like a temptress and bring a counterfeit into this distracted world. I know her whereabouts and have a recent photograph," said Dez. Pulling a folded piece of paper from his military ensemble, he passed her image around the camp.

"Do you want us to kill her?" asked Max, holding her picture high.

"We can send a strong eviction notice to the likes of Simon. Others know her, I assure you."

Dismayed, Simon mumbled behind the thick sticky barrier standing between him and reasoning. Taken aback by Dez's sentiments, he couldn't believe the spider web of lies his airplane had been caught in. Struggling, he tipped over and watched an army of shadowy demons crawl from the tiny cracks in the desert floor. Their energy inhabited the cult's veins and pumped arrogance into their swollen minds. Heat exhaustion and malnourishment lead careless whispers to fall from their lazy tongues. Simon recognized sanity was quickly distancing from New Mexico, and his escape was paramount. Wiggling his bound wrists, he pleaded for The Council to descend from heaven and peck through the thick silver strip. They never came. Paranoid by limitation, he feared the tears mounting behind his saturated mouth bondage would soon drown him.

Huddling in cliques, the group discussed possible scenarios, police involvement and evacuation procedures. They were slowly becoming one body, operating with a lion's head. Michelle reached out to the European Cadence of the Sun sect, to see who might be able to rattle a few cages and roar for their cause. Wanting to minimize their liability, she hoped to organize a flash mob and start a rebellion without ever leaving the camp grounds. She knew if they could lasso the right media coverage, they could brand their cause and have a network news reality series.

"This could be a crucial turning point for our cause," said Michelle, leaning in to kiss Max.

Dez used their networking powwow as an opportunity to visit Simon. He ripped the tape from his parched mouth, set him upright and poured whiskey onto his dry tongue. "You're not worth much to me, dead, is that it?"

"You can't stop The Program! It has existed since the dawn of mankind. It'll always exist," said Simon.

"And so will I, if I never provide the world with a child. In case you've forgotten, none of this is being recorded in the Book of Records! The Council gave us a hall pass to freedom, and you threw it away. For what? If I can find these kids, and stop the participants of The Program from bringing new life into this world, I will become unstoppable. Indefinitely. Let that sink in. It's a new world under my order. A planet we could have ruled together."

"You've lost it!"

"Who knows, maybe someday I can free my friends and family from the torments of the underworld. We can resurrect the bartering system, end world hunger and stop war. It's been a long time coming. I can be the second coming. The messiah. God's chosen one."

"To what gain? For what God?" asked Simon.

"Who made who? God is what people believe it is. If they believe in me, they'll follow," he paused. "We have tremendous power and we've been tortured. I'm avenging the ones who weren't as lucky as you and I. And you? What are you doing with your life, magic boy?"

"I'd like to think The Beyond has a little more to offer than a cyclical earthly existence."

"You'd like to think, but you won't think in that space. Don't you get it? You'll cease to exist. You'll never see the ones you loved again! You'll never taste wine from the grail, nor lie with a woman; though, in your case, that might not be too uncommon. You'll never feel the warmth of the summer sun, nor bathe in the salty ocean. You'll just evaporate into the unknown. A phantom."

Simon struggled to fight his reasoning.

"Simon, this isn't a magic trick. You make yourself disappear for the amusement of others, but what happens when the joke is on you? What if something or someone makes you disappear — *forever*," he added.

"I, hadn't..."

"Are you're prepared to spend the next 1,000 or more lifetimes failing to measure up?"

"I'd like to find love and validate my existence, if that's what you're asking."

"Don't we all, Simon? Don't we all. Where is the value or beauty in never bearing witness to your sacrifice, nor watching your tiny gift grow up? This child, who is able to bring so-called miracles into our reality, abandoned by his father."

Dez slowly re-taped Simon's mouth, patted him on the

cheek and pulled the revolver from his waist band. "I hate to be an Indian giver, especially when it comes to life, but," he said, slowly loading bullets into his gun.

"You can't kill me, Dez," said Simon, over the tape's failing adhesion.

"Actually, I can. I thought I needed you, but you did my bidding before you ever left Israel."

"How?"

"Grayson and the group already know you're here. Had you kept your mouth shut, I'd still be able to use you. In the event you cease to surface or reappear, Mr. Wizard, they'll come looking for you! Everyone likes a game of hide and seek, right?"

"I can help you. I don't want to die like this."

"It's nothing personal. Keeping you here is a liability to my plan and ego."

"Don't do this!"

"Don't worry, we'll meet again. Just consider this a down payment on our future together!"

Dez slowly backed-up, lowered his gun and fired six shots into Simon's head and heart.

"I thought you needed him!" screamed Crystal, running toward the scene.

"I gave it some thought..."

"And?"

"I didn't!"

In that moment, the cult members were no longer revolutionaries, but accomplices. To cover his sins, Dez dug a shallow grave for Simon's bleach bathed body. His followers scrubbed the iron-stained trailer of splattered blood and unceremoniously lowered him into the plot. He was headstoned with an old rusty upright sundial that they'd found lying in the heaps of grass surrounding his lot. Simon was permanently a symbol of their time and calling. As a final gesture of cruelty, Max and Michelle spit upon the dirt. Packing the dirt, they drove their point home with the heels of their boots.

+++

Brainwashed and immersed in denial, they began training for a cause only tested by ego. In the afternoons that followed, they practiced martial arts with their sensei and prepared for an alien uprising or the FBI. As a mark of their dedication, members were tattooed with a fiery Japanese Taiyo sun. It was strategically placed behind the left ear, and meant to symbolize the forgotten light of their dying world. The mark was shrouded by an eclipsed sun. It was a rite of passage. A follower's dedication was tested with initiation practices. Robbery, prostitution, drug dealing and recruitment were all pre-qualified down payments. New members had to provide adequate identification and human collateral. From there, official members were interviewed and verified by Max and Dez. The growing army couldn't risk an intelligence breach, nor their fearless leader being carted off to jail and standing trial.

Simon's death did not sit well with Crystal. In the days following his murder, she questioned her loyalty, beliefs and their escapism. With his recent flex of power and the group's willingness to follow, she was left gripping the reigns of an unchained bull. His horns seemed poetically pointed at her distancing heart. Leaving the Cadence of the Sun meant accepting there would be retribution. Being Dez's girlfriend meant knowing the devil, and fearing his depths. Escorting her fallen prince to the end of the long driveway, far from the cackles of the tribe, she risked stoking the flames of his insanity. For once, she wanted his undivided attention and to feel the stillness of their autonomy. She wanted things to be the way she had remembered. Her voice was muted by his aura. The bugs chirped out their longings for life, as her heart nervously throbbed, mustering the guts to speak.

"Baby, what's your plan? Where are we going with all of this?" Crystal squeezed his coarse hands, accentuating her genuine plight for a sincere response. They walked slowly, and stared toward the stars above. The glow of the moon humbled him. He sensed her qualms and adorned a devil's modesty.

"I know this is new to you and I know you have your doubts, but when this is all said and done, you'll have brought hope to mankind. They walk around like zombies, sacrificing their precious time for blood money. They don't know what it is to live, any longer. I can't be the father you never had, but I can try to be an example," offered Dez.

"I want that."

"Just like him, they spend their free time intoxicating their minds, knowing the reality of tomorrow will someday come pounding on their front door. The repossession agent is sent for us all. He will lead them back, and force them to toil and till for their indebted existence. They will be forced to pay for the life they borrowed and fantasized in. Coping by doping, they are slaves."

"Do you believe all of that?" The whites of Crystal's eyes looked up with longing.

"It's all I believe. Our lives were cooked up by Wall Street. Their ideals were painted on the canvas of our unsuspecting youth. They didn't have a choice in being sold off as a stock option. These beautiful children, full of life and spirit, were sold on the black market and placed directly into the wallet of the beast. They never had a chance to play their hand. It was a non-negotiation. The beast is growing. It's hungrier than ever," said Dez.

"No future?"

"They spend their whole lives chasing an imaginary plateau, told, 'If you try hard enough, you might be great, someday!'"

"It's not true, is it?" she asked softly.

"It never was. What I saw in the desert would blow your mind. If the government is able to erase our internal compass, what will guide us? Let me ask you, why do you know right from wrong?" asked Dez.

"Conscience?"

"Yes! Our limited conscious is what makes us human. Our ignorance, in some strange way, is a gift. We're born with a simple barometer to measure our actions by," said Dez.

"True."

"What if that instrument, the only thing separating us from animals, was gone? They have innocence, we have ignorance. What if one thing had neither? What if our love and connection was swapped out for mechanics and technical savvy? People are connected because we share something innate. It wouldn't take long before we were no longer able to recognize each other or the beauty of being alive. Our role on this planet would be trivial and only benefit those who engineered this perversion to make themselves more money."

"That makes a lot of sense," acknowledged Crystal.

"A lot of this goes against me, too. I have terrible dreams. I'm haunted."

"My heart is with you, I just need to know we're doing the right thing and that you love me!"

"The truth is, I do."

Dez leaned in for a kiss. Without another word, he led her to the trailer to consummate. Though by gag order, he extended a warm closing to the others, before silencing the camp. His demeanor was soothed by Crystal's trusting nature. Lobbying for a genuine connection, his heart pounded for notice. He didn't want to risk their relationship, and knew her trust could be resurrected with attention. Always wearing a mask, he sometimes forgot how to take it off, be in the moment and allow himself to be loved. His inferno of anger had a way of pulling him back into the spiraling abyss of a bottomless well. The more his heart opened, the worse his dreams became. Fluttering through his frontal lobe was an avian onslaught. The Council was relentless.

+++

A few weeks had passed since Simon's murder and the group was fixing for blood. Their enthusiasm waxed like a lion and waned like a lamb. On a cool winter's morning, during their ritual breakfast gathering, Michelle brought rejuvenating news to the group. "Max and I have lassoed a small Italian Cadence. They are willing to knock down the doors and kill Juno. I have run them through a gauntlet of qualifying questions. We are convinced that they are fully committed to our mission, and are our best hope to march forward. We're ready to send a message! What do you want us to do?"

Dez stood up to claim ownership.

"I could sense our next big break was coming. It was wise for us to wait. Are you confident that this new foreign sect is secure and our whereabouts will remain untraceable by Italian law enforcement?" asked Dez.

"Yes, I've been communicating through private message boards and sending numeric beeper codes from disposable cell phones. The communications take longer to decipher, but we're clear. They've been following our chapter for months, even prior to our inquiries. They'd have had no reason for suspicion or interest in us," said Michelle.

"Perfect! Put them on the mission. They are allowed one final communication when the job is done. We'll need to distance ourselves from the site and any further correspondences. This act will surely gain the attention of the group that Simon was deeply entrenched with. They claim to be like us. They are wolves in sheep's clothing."

"Who are they?" asked Michelle.

"They are their own champions and we are their detractors," Dez muttered, cryptically.

Walking with a purposeful strut, Michelle walked from the gathering to deliver the horrifying directive. Her work had won Dez's favor and cast Max into the shadows. So long as he didn't slip any further, he was comfortable with her adoration and growing rank.

In numeric code she texted her Italian counterparts the word: "Anew."

It was their cue to kill Juno.

The Italian Cadence received the encoded message and began plotting. They followed Juno for days and studied her habits. It was imperative that their message was clear, their crime was clean, and that her new husband wouldn't be around. Michelle directed them to leave a simple note on her corpse, stating, "The end of your new beginning starts tonight," per Dez's request.

CHAPTER 24
LOTTERY OF THE SOULS

Screams filled the Hallway of Sorrows. Though prayers and pleading were of no consequence, their imprisoned souls beckoned for release. The stench of decaying humanity singed their nostrils. Hawking screams, from those tortured mercilessly, maddened them. They never drifted, nor were given a moment to forget. The Hallway of Sorrows was littered and stacked with billions of naked reasons to never wish a return. They awaited a chance to someday reenter the beautiful world they'd once taken for granted. The smell of spring flowers, the sight of an ocean's horizon and the calming sounds of children playing on a warm summer afternoon were now memories haunted by a poltergeist. Left staring into the pits of the underworld, they were reduced to a graveyard of useless and repulsive human vehicles. The laws of The Council determined which tragic offenders would be sentenced. When a soul's punishment was fulfilled, it was ushered to the Hallway of Sorrows for further review.

"The Program must be reset," proclaimed Isis. "New participants are needed. Our brave new world must be balanced. The population has grown immensely. Evolution is needed, as they continue to breed new life and hope into future generations. Humanity is our greatest success. We must not waver."

"A world at odds can never find balance. Willing to swan dive into the raging inferno and to die forevermore, for a mere moment to relish in their physicality, they are a cesspool of disappointment. They are destined to repeat their mistakes, fail and toil. They are cowards, hiding from the truth," crowed Than.

"We are one body. Without one, there cannot be another," added Ath.

"It will be this way in the end. It was this way when it began," riddled Anan.

The Council's existence relied on one conscious. In light, the darkness lurked; with knowledge, ignorance evolved; in death, the phoenix rose; in time, space bore infinity. A new universe opened, with every potential outcome in the physical realm. This constituted the matrix of the continuum. Linear time, as a memory, was an illusion created by man's decisions within an evolving space. Parallel universes and scenarios enabled choice.

The Lottery of the Souls was based on three distinct classes of awareness, and determined by previous lifetimes and past experiences. There were the muses; sent to bring light and distraction from man's everyday struggle to survive. There were the warriors; sent to lead and protect the world from itself. Finally, there were the intellects; sent to define the elements of life and expand the human consciousness. These classes were essential in maintaining a balance. If the world became overly distracted or entertained, it would fail to seek purpose. If the world became too focused on knowledge, it would fail to find humility and be blinded from the abstract tapestry. Without protection, governments would fail to sustain, and people would be left with little opposition to their impulses. War was a necessary evil. It reflected humanities desire for anew.

The four birds took their angelic shape and gathered around the four corners of the onyx table to receive the new members of The Program. Some entities were returning, while other positions were backfilled. The process for choosing the souls was based on a light sequence. Surrounding the crystal room, countless lifetimes played on the majestic walls. No soul could be chosen without a revelation from The Beyond. When called upon, a magnificent light shined down and engulfed the room. It illuminated the scalar fields of dark energy, where the floor had given way. The funneled spectrum filled the void, with the point of intersection resting on the darkest point of the abyss. The swirling light pulled the lifetimes from the crystal walls and spiraled them toward the beginning.

A positive flare triggered an outward pulse, when a Programmer entered The Beyond. This energy was the source of all recognizable light in existence. The new lifetime resting at the point of intersection entered The Program. Once selected, images of the chosen one's lifetimes would play in the colorful cone for The Council to witness. They would then engrave the soul name upon a golden throne and accept The Beyond's selection. From the beginning, this was the way of the lottery.

"Take Dez Nave from the underworld!" proclaimed Than.

"Pull Neco Baal from the Hallway of Sorrows," insisted Isis.

The others were called in similar succession, until they were all brought before The Council to reset The Program. Though their wrongs during The Program would not be recorded in the Book of Records, their previous lifetimes determined death's due. The Program would not reset until all of their souls returned or entered The Beyond.

+++

Simon awaited his fellow Programmers in the Hallway

of Souls, unable to connect. He never risked revealing his identity to the ones passed over. He longed for justice, but knew he had to accept the discomfort of his current situation, and allow free will to remain free. His only source of optimism lied in knowing he'd someday leave the Hallway of Souls and be set forth on a more fruitful mission. He could also breathe easy knowing he'd forever be spared the underworld.

Knowing Dez's intentions riddled his conscience.

"If he's able to kill the Crystalline children and the Programmers, how long before the world is pulled from darkness?" questioned Simon. "Without an immediate intervention from The Council, would everything be lost?" He knew The Program had been around since light, but questioned the implications of their actions. "I'm the kiss of Judas. I'm partly to blame, but stand free of judgment. How will Dez be punished for his crimes against humanity? If he's allowed to run free, are we at the whim of Dez's insanity, forever? He needs to be forced out of The Program! He needs to pay." When justice fled reason, these were the types of questions and consequences that plagued the Programmers. Simon ached for another moment to save humanity, and test Dez.

+++

The Council communicated with humanity through: symbolism, synchronicity and animals. The instincts of animals are paramount in reminding humans of their mortality and the simplicity of love. Their messages often go undetected, due to their inability to be seen as rational beings. Some animals teach us about unconditional love and others about unrequited. These reminders are the toolbox of a broken system.

Awaking in a vision, Neco stood naked in the snow covered desert. He walked solemnly back to the original gathering circle. The fallen black birds remained. Upon witness, they flew back to the heavens. In a mind's blink, he was again holding hands with the members of The Program and reliving their revelations in reverse. The sequence continued until he was sitting on the gathering circle with Ash nestled in his lap. He immediately noticed Simon's absence. The gray bird then led him to the Hallway of Sorrows. Simply uttering, "The absent one," Simon reached for him. One by one, the entire hallway began chanting the word, "Go!"

Isis then took him back to the circle, and spoke. "The Crystalline children will be forever identifiable by their indigo colored eyes and have the innate ability to excel in fields, which others will spend their lifetime mastering. They will establish new governments, masquerade as provident entertainers and bring new technologies to our aging doorsteps. They've always been here. Their mission is simply to enhance the human experience and reinforce a belief in The Beyond. They've inspired hope and religion, and captured our imaginations. The Program was developed by us for us, and its purity relies on a healthy degree of lawlessness. Now, do as they said, and go!"

The gray bird, Than, then took him to a beautiful gallery and showed him a canvas oozing with fresh blood. It read, "Ashes to ashes, we all fall down." He awoke to the sound of a gray bird slamming into his bedroom window.

CHAPTER 25
THE LAMB

Before leaving for New Mexico, Simon was diligent with his Children of the Program updates. Grayson was his soundboard. On a weekly basis, he'd harass Grayson with his cynical and meandering questions. He didn't have the same faculties to deal with The Program, and had quickly alienated his immediate Israeli peer group. Though moderately concerned, when Simon's communications went mute, and considering Dez's abrupt exit from the desert and overall attitude, Grayson found solace in knowing his generalized whereabouts. Elisa was the most accessible to the desert site, but if Simon was staring the reaper in the eyes, he knew he couldn't risk sending her alone. He entertained the possibilities that something may have happened to Simon's phone or that he may have found peace of mind. As a precaution, updates were added to the website, encouraging the others to make contact. To keep the investigation light and thwart any misconceived reactions, he fastened Simon's picture to the back of a milk carton graphic. It simply read, "Missing!" He saw no sense in unfairly attacking Dez, until they were confident.

"I'll be happy to give Simon a call." Icarus was quick to respond. His sexcapades had filled him with adrenaline for The Program and a new found sense of purpose. Though producing a Crystalline child would undoubtedly mean saying goodbye to his angelic new friends, he didn't want to risk missing a beat of their earthly lives. "If he's in trouble, I'll ruin the man!"

"I hope we're not jumping to conclusions, but it's not like Simon to alienate us," said Grayson.

"Agreed. Even if he was distracted or enlightened, I think he'd still want us to know," said Icarus.

"That's what is concerning me. He's no rabbit in the hat," furthered Grayson. "Any updates on your end?"

"I've chased a few waterfalls, but I've also stuck to the rivers and lakes that I'm used to! There's one girl who I think might be the one. I'm not in love with her, but I love her dearly, if that makes any sense."

"It actually does, Icarus; and, to most! Good luck, I hope you're wearing your sunblock."

"Enough, already."

+++

Through his formative years, Icarus dated a beautiful young Italian girl named Maria. In his youth, his parents worked tireless nights to provide for their mammoth offspring, and would often offload him with her family. One evening, in secondary school, he promised that he'd someday marry her, if they'd both found themselves tragically unattached in their mid-twenties.

Maria and Icarus spent many cruel summers playing and fighting one another, reinforcing an almost familial bond, and had, for the sake of his post-desert sanity, reconnected on a late night whim. Icarus was desperate to share his calling and the details of The Program. She remained indifferent, but was more than willing to share her body, for the sake of his unusual cause — or psychological break — and for a dash of weekday entertainment. She had never stopped loving Icarus. Their families were connected by geography and generations. A girl, who would otherwise seem like an obvious marital partner, left Icarus thrilling for the hunt and relishing in her spoils.

As they grew, they were in dire hopes of unearthing and investigating their vast genetic and psychological differences. They experimented and shared the types of secrets that only best friends of the opposite sex could share. They knew this was the precious covenant of information that might set the stage for their success in future relationships — it was the Holy Grail of human instinct. By their teens, jealousy had pulled them together, while the other kids were busy swapping notes and heart-shaped candies. The sight of watching the other's libido blossom was more than both of them could bear, though maturity eventually made it possible to handle each other's young and wandering heart. As years passed, they remained hopelessly attached and tragically, realists.

It wasn't long before Maria became pregnant. Knowing she hadn't shared her bed with another, she was excited to share her breaking news with Icarus. She genuinely believed her child would sit at the head of all tables, even knowing she risked raising their tiny miracle without a father.

The Program was something they'd discussed at length, far before planting the seeds of a life. The revelation of his mission was above and beyond the courtesy he'd shown any of his other female conquests. He made sure Maria had the Children of the Program website information, his parents' cell phone numbers, a hospital arrangement and his child would be born under the finest conditions Greece had to offer.

Fulfillment of The Program became Icarus's sole conquest. He knew she was the only person in Europe capable of explaining their pregnancy to his irrational parents and was grateful The Council would quickly usher him into The Beyond, knowing his father was likely to knock him out cold for disrupting his scholarship opportunities. Any trepidation he had about their reaction was easily quashed by the irony in the spiritual graduation, sure to follow. His competitive nature would only accept winning results, and to shine as bright as the stars.

+++

Also chasing the crown for first place, Juno's bump was growing. On a cold February morning, she left her usual Tuesday morning *Little Warriors* ministry and boarded a bus to the Cornaro Chapel. She'd been whisked away by emotion and was longing to pray for her coming child's wellbeing. Gazing out of the rattling bus windows, she reflected on her life, and began planning the nursery and considering names for her soon-to-be prince or princess. Recalling the birds of her dreams, she thought naming the child after The Council seemed like a beautiful homage to her calling. "Maybe for Ath, I could change it to Athena," she pondered, shuffling off of the bus stairs. "Or, maybe for Anan, I could change it to Canan. That would be a great name for a boy!" Her stolen focus caused her to walk blocks in the opposite direction. Disoriented, she headed back.

Though she understood The Beyond, she felt a disciplined ritual of faith and prayer, no matter the religion, sanctified the human condition and directed all negative energy back to a more capable source. She felt it was important to be grateful and to show reverence. It curbed her perplexing avian night terrors. The universe seemingly longed for her adoration. Rightfully so, her soul put colors into the air.

She entered the holy chapel like any other afternoon. Kneeling, she gave her angelic salutations and proceeded to the powerful and mystical alter of divine sculptures. She was entranced by The Ecstasy of St. Teresa.

Always trusting, she often ran into familiar faces and

engaged in deep conversations with the downtrodden locals. She wore her heart on her sleeve and her mind was an open book. Not long after her arrival, two young girls called her by name and asked to speak with her privately. Without hesitation, she followed them to the chapel doorway. They overtly complimented her noticeable pregnancy and played on her maternal pride.

"We see you here often and plan to have children of our own," said one of the girls.

"What a wonderful gift to bring into the world," said Juno.

"Thanks! It's a bit cold. Did you drive here?"

"I always take the bus. I like to stay connected with people of all walks of life," said Juno.

"How about we give you a ride back to your place? We could talk on the way."

"That would be great!"

The two girls were well-groomed, dripping with syrupy sweetness and had a good reason for wanting to rescue Juno from the elements. Juno figured a warm ride home would save her an unnecessary fare. She was eager to witness to her new found friends, if only to share her otherworldly experiences.

Leading Juno to the back of a nearby van, the girls yanked open the rusty back doors with dual control. Before Juno could react, four long tentacles lunged from the cabin and pulled her into the vehicle. Laughing, the girls slammed the cabin doors. Immediately, Juno was knocked out with chloroform, cuffed and looted. The clan then traveled to a remote landing on the Tiber River and awakened their Sleeping Beauty. They were intent to make her feel every moment of the cruel death they'd planned, and to drown her in her choice to bring shame to the human race. As she came to, the bandits took the gag from her quivering mouth and began prodding the hive.

"Why have you come, bearing an *alien fetus*?" asked a deep male voice.

"What are you talking about?" asked Juno.

"You are pregnant with a hybrid," the man continued.

"I was called by a higher power to bring perfection into this world. Aliens?" asked Juno.

"God? God met you in the Painted Desert and asked you to get knocked up?" he scoffed.

"Who filled you with these tragic lies? How did you find me or know about the desert? It wasn't God who sent me, it was the Council of the Lords. They've entrusted 12 of us! This child I carry is theirs. You will pay gravely, if this baby is harmed."

"We'll take our chances."

"I bet she's a witch," laughed a Gothic teenage girl named Andromeda. "Throw her into the water to see if she floats." The girl then took out the letter that Michele had instructed them to pen, placed it into a water resistant bag, and slipped into her back pants pocket. "The end of your new beginning starts, tonight -- *Juno*!"

"What?"

They laughed, hogtied her legs, taped the dirty rag back into her mouth and walked Juno to the water's edge. Though she struggled and screamed, it was of no bearing. The cloth muffled her cries. The sound of Juno's strained voice miffed the anxious kidnappers. Awaiting, at the base of the hill, where the water moved quickly, was an old tent. Her captors opened the nylon door frame, zipped her into a sleeping bag coffin, collapsed the tent and rolled her up — stakes and all.

The irreverent girls insisted on taking posed pictures with Juno, before tossing her alien-toting body into the river. Though they mocked her courage and felt justified by their cause, her words rang like tinnitus in the ear drum of their souls. It was a constant, uncomfortable and piercing cry. Instinctively, the bells of denial rang out, deafening them from the off-chance they were making a huge mistake. Groupthink trumped their ability to hear her sound pleads. Juno was all but gone. If she didn't asphyxiate, the frigid waters would shock her conscious, while her bound limbs finished the job.

With two group members on either side of their human cargo, they prepared to heave their offering and become heroes of the Cadence.

"On the count of three," garbled a lazy male voice.

"Do a quick perimeter check. Let's make sure there aren't any cars coming," said Cass, the leader of the group.

"We're clear on my side, Cass," said Messi. His appearance suited his name.

"Halt. The municipal is by our van! Put her down. We need to make it look like we're setting up an actual campsite. We don't need them getting curious. Andromeda, gather a little firewood for us," instructed Cass.

The police car came to a complete stop, looked around the vacant van and examined the landing. "It's probably just a bunch of college kids looking to get drunk or laid, but we should probably go down and have ourselves a look. Besides, what's theirs is ours." They laughed, holstering their nightsticks.

"I told you this was a bad idea!" said Andromeda. Her nerves stood on end, as the authorities approached."

"Shut up. Just shut up," insisted Cass.

"Good afternoon. What have we got here? It looks like societies rejects are fixing to party?" asked an officer.

"We were planning on doing a little camping and maybe drink a few beers," said Messi.

"Do you have booze wrapped in that pretty little tent? If so, that's a little more than a few."

Pleading for her baby's life, a tired and incoherent Juno muffled to the officers, but couldn't be heard through the thick bondage. She was quickly losing oxygen and barely able to squeak out a lethargic cry. Even her arms and legs had fallen numb, and were incapable as sending out a fluttering SOS. Though she understood The Council's hands were equally as tied, she felt forsaken by her calling and smothered in guilt.

"Did you know there is no drinking allowed in the Tiber River Regional Park?"

"We did," Cass, nervously.

It was a risk, but they knew building credibility was their only play. Silence filled the basin, while the cops paced around the wound tent. Their eyes pierced liked lasers into the kidnappers' souls. Their hearts raced, causing enough beads of sweat to flood the basin. Their chests pounded like war cannons. They were frozen.

"What are your names?" asked an officer.

"I'm Cass. This is Messi, that's Andromeda and she is Constella."

"Relax. Here's what we're going to do! Our shift ends in a couple hours. We're going to leave you to your business, but we'll return. You'll have a couple of those cold beers waiting for us, right?" asked an officer, before pausing. "Sound fair?"

"It sounds like a night we'll never forget or remember! Thank you, officer," said Messi.

"Oh, and have a fire pit going," said the officer.

The municipal returned to their vehicle and drove off. To the Cadence, their pace from the landing to the road was agonizing. Without hesitation, they tossed Juno's limp body into the cold river and returned to the van. If the cops returned, there would be no evidence and no party. They knew taking Juno only increased their chances of being caught, and by their guesstimation, she'd already suffocated.

Andromeda reached out to Michelle. "Mission complete."

"Excellent! We will keep strict tabs on the news. Correspondence is to cease."

"10-4."

A week later, the tent and Juno's body were recovered. A group of Tuscany fly fisherman found her resting upon an embankment. The authorities were notified, but no solid evidence could be found on her, or in the fibers of her nylon tomb. Juno was pronounced dead on arrival.

The municipal police, first on the scene, recognized the tent and knew they'd been careless. Dismissing the threat and failing to track the van's license plate number would haunt them. Both officers kept quiet about the incident. Though their integrity would breathe easy, they couldn't escape the smothering guilt or dance away from the demons in their mind — *poetic.*

Juno's homicide went viral. All of the news affiliates picked up the tragic scoop. The Programmers, wary, began suspecting that another force was poised and rearing. With Dez avoiding their radar, and Simon remaining distant, they debated the intent behind Juno's murder. They feared the dark side may have its own minions out to stop them. The authorities remained at an impasse when the autopsy and police report ballooned the airwaves. As paranoia boiled in the pits of their minds, suspicion pointed toward the New Mexican sands.

+++

Grayson urged the remaining Programmers to find out what was going on in New Mexico and to locate Simon. Before his exodus, Simon had given Grayson a fairly accurate idea of his general whereabouts. They had a town name and were able to map a general idea of what surrounded it. Grayson wasn't at liberty to leave the New York Times on sporadic time, but lobbied the Children of the Program site for anyone willing to make the trek.

"Grayson, why don't we contact the authorities? Maybe they will be willing to send out a search party and unearth our vanishing kin. If we extend our plight, perhaps they'll agree that there's a connection and look into it for us. That's their job. It certainly can't..." said Neco.

"We can't risk bringing the authorities to our doorsteps," interrupted Grayson. "For one, we don't want to expose the entire group or go public with our story or bask in the merits of our perverse dreams. It'll only draw negative attention to us. Our identities will go viral. We'll look like lunatics, possibly even suspects. It'll make our chances of succeeding in The Program impossible. If there really is someone, or a group of individuals, trying to kill us, we need to avoid giving the entire world a map! Chances are, there are crazier people lurking."

"True. We can't risk our friends and family in the process," said Neco.

"Right. We don't know if there's a connection. Implicating our friends isn't friendship, it's bad judgment. All we know is that Juno has been killed and that Simon is not answering his telephone. There's no crime in that," said Grayson.

"I've tried calling, as well. Nothing," added Neco.

"Can you imagine what type of strange attention we'd draw to ourselves? People would want to examine and interview us. Revealing ourselves might incite copycat killings. What if we inadvertently put a child in harm's way? If people knew about these Crystalline children, they'd be mercilessly studied. They'd become the victims of a society we were sent to enhance," added Grayson.

"I was just spit-balling. I might be able to get out that way. I may contact Elisa and meet her in Los Angeles. We could road trip to New Mexico," offered Neco.

"Four eyes are better than two," joked Grayson.

"I could certainly use the company. If there is something terrible going on, I'll need backup," said Neco.

"I know, I'm sorry I can't be there! Let me know if she's game and if you choose to go."

CHAPTER 26
ASHES RISING

The power and popularity of Ash's artwork continued to lift her global profile. A lot of her pieces were put in museums; or, their rights were sold, and used by book manufacturers and magazine publishers. Her posh lifestyle was easily afforded off of the sale of one physical painting. As she reached her highest vibration, her hand flowed about the canvas like the wind through the trees; the landscapes painted themselves, and motion was captured in a single frame. Her sentiments were like teardrops from heaven; a signal that the universe would rain down perfection on those working within their intended frequency. Her art was a steppingstone to heaven, but her child would change the world.

The trifling ways of her adolescence were mere experiences to draw upon, not to live by. She continued using the brush to write the pages of her story, but her most precious piece of artwork was still in utero; she was having a baby with her childhood sweetheart. Ash wasn't sure how to bridge the literal and metaphoric ocean that separated her from Neco, but her time was marching toward its inevitable end. She wanted to see him, again, if only to glide the tips of her fingers across the pained lines entrenched on his disenchanted face.

"I'm pregnant."

"Ash?" asked Neco.

"Yes, it's me," she replied.

"When? How long?"

"I was pregnant when we last spoke, but didn't want to muck our conversation with awkward theatrics. It didn't beg a revelation. It may have explained my carefree demeanor. That's not to say I'd written you off. I'm just not one to dwell. We are two separate hearts, beating to the same thundering drum."

"There's no need to explain. You do not owe me that. I'm genuinely happy for you. Sure, I wish you'd have told me, but are you confident it's a Crystalline and that you're heading to The Beyond?" asked Neco.

"I am."

"Nervous?"

"I am. That is why I'm calling! We must rendezvous before our time's cut short. My boyfriend understands." Longing, Ash stared at the incomplete painting of Neco and outlined his frame. "You mean a lot to me, Neco. I don't want a telephone call to be our last love letter in the sand. This child is going to bring the canvas to its knees. I only wish I could see its success and share in it." Sensing Neco's energy, she pulled out a brush and captured the verbal aura of their conversation.

"Have you told Grayson?"

"I have. I didn't want him to post anything, until we spoke, and due to Juno's mysterious death, I thought it was prudent to wait. The lion's share of my new paintings are of those babies with the beautiful indigo eyes," said Ash, knotting up her telephone cord. "If someone really is out to get us — someone within — it wouldn't take a criminal mastermind to piece it all together. Though, I'm not really worried. Fear is just the absence of faith. Besides, my mansion is surrounded by towering gates and the tightest of security. If someone's out to kill us, I say, 'Bring it!'"

"Please be careful," insisted Neco.

"I know!"

"Have you picked out a name?"

"The black bird brought me a vision of a beautiful girl. I awoke with the name Akiane!"

"Magnificent. Gorgeous."

As they parted, an unmistakable calm befell him. All Neco wanted was her forgiveness and friendship. Her phone call and wish to see him affirmed that his prayers had been heard, and that the most beautiful treasures are sometimes discovered in the darkest moments. Ash had healed and painted herself out of their tragedy. Her house was built upon marble grounds, where she could gaze upon rolling hills and heavenly rivers. Her departure meant the world would continue spinning in living color, and her beautiful art would remain a reflection of her indescribable life.

Dez kept strict tabs on Ash's online paintings and became increasingly nervous about her influence over the world. Though it was in his best interest to lay low and see if Juno's murder investigation brought the authorities to his doorstep, the Cadence was prepared to treat her as a serious threat and end it, given the order. He was savvy to the nature of her paintings and communication style. His tied stomach knew there was an urgency in play.

+++

Mere hours away, Rand continued to walk the hopeless streets of Kassel. He remained a romantic. His dependency and bond with Isabella continued to evolve. They would occasionally copulate for the sake of feeling the presence of another body pressed against their own. Though she'd introduced him to a number of singles, or passed-over flings, nothing really opened his shuttered heart like his long walks and conversations with Isabella. Her soothing tongue and cool pace comforted his anxious gaze. His sexual preference was of little relevance. They were merely soul friends with physical benefits.

His limited access to online networks left him haplessly disconnected from his spiritual family. Distracted by survival, he often missed the group's changing dynamics or breaking news. Though he'd still sneak into his old refuge, or steal the Backer's mail, any relevant information was fleeting. Whether his parents had written him off, or not, The Program still seemed like his closest, yet distant, family. When he was able to connect, he always regretted their somber goodbyes. Since their initial contact, Icarus remained his closest friend.

"*Wings*, fill me in," joked Rand.

"Rand. Dear heavens, we're glad you are alive. I'm having twins!"

"Is the world ready for Icarus squared? Look out, here comes the 8th and 9th Wonders of the World. I'm impressed, but not surprised. The Council never elucidated the profound implication of bringing multiples into this space. Do you believe you're heading out?"

"Like a fetus," he paused, stumbling over his clumsy joke. "This time, it is possible. The reality is, I'm either getting out alive, or my future is going to be riddled with child support payments. There's a good chance I have a lot of kids coming, Rand!" exclaimed Icarus.

"I have no doubt. So what's your plan?" asked Rand.

"My girlfriend Maria has a few immediate Euro-connections, but she can always link up with Benjamin and Zane. I put them in touch. I'm not sure how much time I'll have once their born. For all I know, I'll simply evaporate, when the baby crowns," said Icarus.

"They are certainly a better resource than I could ever be," offered Rand.

"I know you care. I suppose you heard about Juno?"

"No, I haven't had access to a computer! The library

keeps curbing me, because I'm homeless."

"She was killed, Rand," he paused. "Simon is missing."

"Is there any correlation between the two?" asked Rand.

"No one knows. I wouldn't alarm yourself. After all, you don't have a traceable address. Needless to say, the group's on edge. Simon went out to the desert to visit Dez and no one's heard from him since. Not long after, Juno and her baby were found dead in the Tiber River. She was wrapped in a tent."

"Jesus! Dez was a strange character and all, but do you think he's involved?"

"I think a lot of us have that sentiment, but we cannot risk jumping to conclusions. We don't know if there's an actual connection. If we make the implication too soon, we could start an unmanageable and dangerous war."

"I totally agree."

In shock, he cut the line with Icarus. To decompress the news, Isabella and Rand panhandled enough money for a couple of hot coffees at a local's only coffee shop. He purged and explained The Program and Icarus's news. With each word, she drew more withdrawn. Risking judgment, he trudged forward, knowing there was a very real possibility she'd find him insane, toss hot brew in his face and run to the Grey hills.

As the veil lifted, her eyes locked.

CHAPTER 27
THE DEVIL MAY RUN

The devil's hooves tap danced across the desert meadows. News of Juno's death sent electricity through the Cadence. They were adrenalized. To think they had an international network, could orchestrate a murder, and bring a message of terror to the world stage, with a simple email, fueled their sense of empowerment. They felt like vigilantes, far from the reach of the long arm of the law. Dez began plotting his next mission and wasn't content to simply seek and destroy the current Program members, he sought a broader massacre; a massacre that included anyone who claimed to be indigo or spiritually gifted. The cryptic message tucked in Juno's pocket had been publicly revealed, though, its riddle, meant to be decoded by those in The Program, had fallen deaf. Dez continued to pound the holocaust drum and preach his message of genetic cleansing.

"I appreciate that you've unearthed some of these bastard indigo, crystal or divine children and gathered their personal information. We must find all of them and cleanse the world of their bodies. With their dreamseeds and integration, our genetic structure will become degraded beyond recognition," insisted Dez.

"We have already begun mapping their IP addresses, and paired that information with what they've willingly and innocently shared on the web. In some cases, we've reached out from bait accounts and set-up meetings. We have ten targeted locations, but that number is growing. All we need is your directive," said Michelle. She'd taken their mission with an increased militant sincerity.

"It is prudent to relish the calm. When our time has come, the devil may run!" Dez lit a cigarette and laughed. He was charged by the rhetoric of his sermon. Immortality fanned the flames of his arrogance. Even jail was a waning concern, with his cult's reach. "Come and get me," he screamed toward the sky. "I dare you!"

His rise to stardom had left Crystal distressed. She felt abandoned by the shadow he cast and wondered what she stood to gain by reinforcing his mania and propping him to unreachable heights. It was one thing to stand for a cause, but another to allow him to dig his heals into the backs of the ones who helped raise him. Saddled by doubt, she was no longer confident whether she was galloping toward the sun or eclipsing it. Their recent actions stung like vinegar in her bleeding heart. They seemed like a walking contradiction; a blasphemous sentiment to the planet's cry. In moments of clarity, her constricted mind would release, unveiling Dez for the troubled sociopath he'd become. As his paranoia increased, he ordered the members of the Cadence to accept a permanent residency on his lot. He built a towering psychological wall, thwarting all communications with the outside world. Resting back 100 feet from Dez's trailer, the camp spent weeks erecting a compound upon a shaky foundation of bloodstained money. Civilization was the lost line on their distant horizon.

The compound walls were glazed in a white stucco flat, and the structural integrity was raised by virgin hands. Dez ran his command center from an underground bunker. He felt secure, lurking below the surface, while plotting the world's damnation. Drugs were no longer his distraction of choice, he preferred to mainline power. His underground walls were reinforced with steel and fiberglass, and resembled a walk-in refrigerator. A triple bolted lock secured the enclosure, and a narrow tunnel, leading to a spot just beyond the trailer, served as an immediate escape route. It was surrounded by a tall steel white fence, making the doorway invisible to onlookers. It held, roughly, 50 Cadence members. With only 40 approved followers, not including Dez and Crystal, there was still room for a small expansion.

In the still of the night, Crystal remained anxious and wide-eyed. Though she'd tried to hide her morning sickness, she'd knew she'd soon be forced to tell Dez about their coming gift. Though he'd expressed a venomous disinterest in bringing a child into the world, he was careless in his attempts to prevent it. Judging by his recent mood swings and growing power trip, she was convinced he would force her to have an abortion. Her heart knew a child could remedy their strained relationship, but her instincts begged her caution.

On an average morning, she'd awake, slip out of their home and force herself to throw-up in the tall weeds behind his trailer. It wasn't long before her routine caught his attention. One morning, while she was kneeling down, with one hand holding back her greasy locks and a long finger forced down her heaving throat, Dez appeared. He was suspicious.

"What are you doing?" he asked.

"I don't feel well. It must be something I ate. I can't live on the animals you hunt, alone."

"Crystal, we don't eat much and when we do, it's usually the same supper." He calmly rattled. "I've noticed you waking, bright and early, and leaving the trailer. I had assumed you were smoking, but yesterday, I heard you getting sick. Is there something going on with you?"

"It's nothing, Dez." She froze. She knew the truth would send him over the edge.

"You'd better not be pregnant and trying to hide it from me," he snarled. Dez had considered the implications of having a child with Crystal and the effect it would have on their mission, but wasn't entirely convinced his pretense for love was a qualifier. His arrogance wasn't prepared for the possibility that he may have already snared himself.

"It's nothing. I'm just nauseous. I'll gladly take a test, if would put your mind to rest."

"Have Michelle escort you. If you're positive, we'll talk," said Dez.

Crystal already knew the result, but saw fit to stall. She didn't want to risk the life of their child over an overcharged conversation. She wanted what was best for him. With a pout, she idled. "That sounds good! Can we take some of the petty cash and grab McDonald's? I'll test first. If the results are positive, I won't pick-up the food — we'll need the money. I love you, darling, but I really need to eat some real food."

"Real food and McDonald's — ha! Just bring back the test," added Dez.

Slipping into the compound and quietly wrestling Michelle from Max's loving clutches, she dropped a tiny whisper into her opening eardrum. Michelle slunk from the cabin, adjusted her side-braid and loose-fitting white tank top and tossed a camouflage printed hat on her hard head. Crossing through the gates, they walked into the dawn of a new day and discussed Dez's wish for Crystal to take a pregnancy test. He may have had a war to wage with the world, but she had her own battles to fight. Not long after hopping into the van and driving from the lot, the nervous mother spilled her guts. She'd been dying to share the news.

"Dez is going to lose it, if I'm pregnant!" said Crystal.

"You're not, are you?" asked Michelle.

"He does not want to bring child into this fallen world. It would interfere with his calling. I don't want to burden him or the mission. We've come too far. There's time, I need to know I have someone I can count on," said Crystal.

"Are you?" asked Michelle, even more insistent than before.

"'I want to wait and surprise him, when there's no turning back. I'm just about through with the morning sickness. He's got a good heart, he just seems a little broken and afraid to be loved. I believe a child would make a huge difference in our lives. But, everything has to be right. Will you help me?" asked Crystal.

"Of course. Do you need me to pee on the stick?" asked Michelle.

"It has to be our little secret. You can't tell anyone, not even Max! No one else knows."

"I promise."

They stopped into a local McDonald's and ordered a handful of breakfast meals. The modernized lobby had a few big screen televisions, all flashing world news and stock market updates. Looking up, in a daze, Crystal heard a journalist describing the note found in Juno's back pocket. Her life was reeling in living color and heart began racing with excitement. It wasn't the first time the note had been shown, but it was the first time they'd witnessed it. Crystal was giddy with excitement, hoping this revelation would distract Dez. She grabbed Michelle's arm and directed her eyes toward the set.

"We have to watch this," said Crystal.

"And now, a follow-up on the bizarre story of a woman who was found asphyxiated by her own tent," squawked a smug news anchor. "The note reads, as follows: 'The end of your new beginning starts, tonight.' If anyone has information, or is able to decode this cryptic message, please contact the authorities and make a statement."

"Dez is going to flip," squealed Crystal.

"You know, I can't visualize his body in that motion," joked Michelle.

"You know what I mean."

"I'd imagine he'd rip those dirty ass jeans! I wonder how long they've been televising this? Do you think the message has alerted the *special* people he's been hunting? If so, our revolution has begun. I think a baby is the least of your concerns, right now. Let's flick the stick, Crystal."

"Agreed. There's only one way to find out," said Crystal.

The girls eagerly hopped into the van. The music, air and news had switched the course of an otherwise dismal morning. They felt alive, it was as if her doubts and suspicions of the Cadence were simply quashed by her friend's willingness to lie for her. Suddenly, a double homicide was trumped by an Egg McMuffin. They sang the swan song of freedom and arrived in record time. Dez ominously awaited in the driveway, alone. The mere sight of him gave them both pause and cold chills. Before exiting the cab, they took a moment to rehearse and calibrate their stories.

"We went to Savoy's convenient store by the club. We used their bathroom. It's negative," said Crystal.

"Right, we went in, and I watched you like a hawk," rehearsed Michelle.

They both took a deep breath and approached the unwelcoming authority.

"Dez, you won't believe what we just saw on the television," said Crystal.

"That they found the note, dear?" asked Dez.

"Yes! You heard?" asked Crystal.

"Of course, I heard. I knew, weeks ago. This is my lifeblood, remember? What do you think I do underground? It hasn't generated the response I was hoping for, but it will. I will tell you what you need to know when you need to know it. Now, where's the damn test?"

"Here. God," said Crystal.

Putting on a brave face, Michelle looked Dez directly into the eyes, with a glare of disdain, and said, "She's clean! Drop it." Her tone cut the noose from Crystal's neck. Dez gruffly grabbed the bag of breakfast sandwiches from her nervous hand. With a cold and unsettling stare, he turned without saying a word.

"So that's it? You're not happy?"

"He's never happy," dared Michelle. "Where's Max's car?"

"You should know."

"How so?"

"I sent him to follow you."

CHAPTER 28
JOIN THE CULT

After a series of dreams, suggesting Ash was in danger and might already have a target on her back, I was left with little choice in packing my suitcase and confronting the growing beast. The Council had thrown my obsessive compulsive disorder into overdrive. I didn't want anyone's coffin resting on my conscience. No one wanted to believe Dez was the culprit, but too many signs pointed in one direction - *west*!

We knew Simon's disappearance was odd, Juno was dead and Dez's aversion to the group was increasingly suspicious, but no one understood how the pieces fit. The other obstacle lied in determining the legitimacy of our dreams. I didn't always know if a lucid vision was divinely inspired or a mere projection, though witnessing Simon writhe in the Hallway of Sorrows was haunting. If I chose to ignore his cries, I could very well be writing his death warrant — if he wasn't already dead.

Dreams of the Hallway of Sorrows always triggered a painful reality in me. I often wondered, 'How could we collectively allow a place like this to exist,' when I was forced to relive the agony, lifetime after precious lifetime. I was always diligent in offering my spiritual blessing to the fallen. The night before I decided to travel west, I was visited by Juno.

Hanging on the Hallway of Sorrows wall, she ached. She'd done everything right and wanted nothing more than to give her life for the betterment of humanity, yet the world responded with her brutal assassination. Death by asphyxiation wasn't a fate for the faint of heart, and certainly not intended for the angels who walked amongst us. I witnessed her memories, as she recalled suffocating and feeling her cramped body fade. I could feel her skin tighten, as it touched the freezing waters of the winding Tiber River. Together, we went into shock.

"My beautiful child will never know the magic it held. This is a blasphemy to our humanity. Why doesn't The Council interfere, when the truest of hearts is sacrificed for following their directives? Why have faith at all?" asked Juno.

The sight of her sent me rocketing from my bed and dialing. "Elisa, I'm coming your way."

"You're coming to Los Angeles?" she asked.

"I would love to say it's for pleasure, because I *am* excited to see you, but The Council has called me. I'm not sure if you've heard about Simon and Juno, but things have taken some dramatic turns."

"It's horrible. What does that have to do with you coming to the California?" she asked.

"I was hoping you might be willing to escort me to New Mexico? We need to find Dez."

"I might be pregnant. I'm not sure I can escape from Los Angeles, or my job. As you know, it's expensive on our coast. Truth be told, it also scares me a little. I don't want to end up like our martyr Juno," furthered Elisa.

"Would you mind if I came and stayed with you, until I get my bearings and head straight?"

"You're always welcome. If you can cover your food,

I can offer my couch," she said.

Experiencing déjà vu, I began my long trek back to the Golden State. Taking a moment to assess my progress, in a Texas roadhouse gas station, my doubt was siphoned by a news report referencing the letter found in Juno's pants pocket. My suspicions were confirmed and the dots connected. This tiny morsel of information spoke volumes and trumped any dream elucidated by The Council. Accepting I may enter Dez's world, alone, I walked to the trunk of my car and made sure the revolver I stole from my father was present. The dusty air and rocks beneath my hot and swollen feet put my mind in tune with the earth and blessed my plea for vigilante justice. In my mind, I was the lone gunman out to save the world. My only hope was that the devil would be surprised.

There seemed like only two ways out of New Mexico. He'd either die by my hand or I'd need a miracle.

By the time I arrived at Elisa's doorstep, I was focused on the mission. I'd devised a few methods of tracking Dez. Living in a small town, I knew he'd eventually need to refill his hog. I considered setting up camp, at nearby gas stations, waiting and following him. Studying his habits, I figured, I could integrate with the community, slowly. My long term plan was to embed myself with the locals, until I was accepted, fitting the culture and speak and adorning the swagger. Their trust would make my assimilation natural. In my fantasy, they'd serve him up on a platter. Obviously, there were precautions to take, but it was all I had. I envisioned finding Dez resting in a pit of cobras, nestled in Medusa's chest and plotting. Slithering to the center of his world would require drinking from his poisonous springs.

Los Angeles had a way of smuggling weeks from my life. Elisa didn't mind the company and I was content to regress into familiar habits. Her fear of Magnus never waned. My presence offered her a wanted security; her boyfriend's job interfered with his ability to stand guard. The looming chance of Magnus playing his curious hand, seemed cued, after his last conversation with Grayson — everyone in The Program was on high alert. It was clear that Elisa and her boyfriend Marcus genuinely loved each other, and she'd someday join The Beyond. No one wanted to see her end up like Juno. As my welcome began to run dry, we parted ways. I'll never forget how tense and humid the California air felt that day. In separate directions, she drove toward Santa Monica to pick-up a pregnancy test, and I carted myself into the desert. When we hugged, it felt like we might never see each other again. Goodbyes were always hard with Programmers.

+++

When Elisa arrived at the convenient store, she could feel an unwelcome set of eyes resting upon her. On guard, she surveyed the scene. Assuming her nerves were getting the best of her, she crossed the threshold. As the automatic doors closed, an uncanny sense of familiarity befell her. Slipping by her radar, the devil was parked and waiting. As she greeted the local store clerk, another Godstop of synchronicity pecked upon her awareness. She recalled the dream she'd had of Anan, the red bird. Nervously shuffling through the tests and cautiously glancing through the sliding doorway for clues, her waxing and waning memories distracted her focus from reality. 'Was the dream about Magnus?' she questioned. In record time, she made her purchase and stalled in the aisles, until coherency trumped her fear. Slipping out of a fire exit seemed reasonable, considering her recollections.

After a noticeable amount of time had passed, she tempted fate. Entering the parking lot, she locked eyes with Beelzebub and swallowed a big gulp of adrenaline. This was the moment Anan had foreshadowed. She choked, screamed and turned back toward the store doors. Her ears sprung like an antenna, as Magnus locked and loaded his pistola, and slowly inched toward her. Per protocol, the store clerk secured the premises and called the police. Elisa cried, knowing she was trapped. Though she screamed and pounded upon the doors, it was of no consequence. The clerks huddled behind the furthest aisle walls, praying they'd soon see their friends and families. They'd already stomached the reality they'd someday have to explain why they locked a pregnant girl out of their store, while she faced a killer.

"What do you have there?" asked Magnus.

"You already know," said Elisa. Nervous, she took a step back and pleaded.

"Stop! If you have this baby, it's over. I'll never see you again. You have to agree to terminating it, or I'll be forced to kill you. We can still be together, Elisa. You've got to stop this from happening," said Magnus.

Her quivering mouth moved along with his crazed words, 'We can still be together.' Frozen with fear, she dropped the weightless bag. "You don't have to do this!" Elisa fired back. "Don't be a selfish prick! Think of all of the people you'll be hurting. If I don't love you now, why in the hell would I love you, after you've pulled the trigger."

"I love you. I can't risk losing you. You know we connected in the desert. We just need time," said Magnus.

"Time? This isn't how love works. You can't force someone to be with you. I don't love you, now, and I never will. You're psychotic! Even if I had a few flash feelings, that's not why we're here. Do you think I want to spend an earthly eternity with a lunatic?" asked Elisa.

He was too distracted to respond to her unsettling and brave reasoning. Disrupting their heated discourse, an army of blue and red lights descended upon the parking lot. Magnus's fight-or-flight reaction was triggered, making him a ticking time bomb. "Put down your weapon!" screamed an LAPD officer.

"I'm sorry. We're out of time. Luckily, we have all the time in the world to figure this out," said Magnus.

"Figure out what?" asked Elisa.

"Us. For once, I kind of know what God feels like — it's this moment," said Magnus.

"What God? You're a megalomaniac," screamed Elisa.

"What can I say, I have a bit of a complex. Killing the one you love is love, right?"

"Jesus Christ!" she screamed.

She jerked and tried to run, but it was no use. Magnus immediately opened fire and unloaded a flurry of bullets into her spine and head. The bullets that missed her grazed the police, who fired back. Just as a Nickelodeon winds down, he fell to his knees in slow motion. Trembling on the ground, her furious eyes locked with his. Together, they drifted toward The Hallway of Sorrows. The city wept, as warm blood ran from their bodies and glazed over the smoldering concrete. Three birds were killed with a single heart of stone.

+++

I arrived in New Mexico, followed my plan and tracked Dez. We made small talk and danced around my immediate reason for being spotted in a New Mexican strip club. He remained disengaged by my ramblings, but was often distracted by the people in the club. They seemed to know and enjoy showering him with a comical level of adoration and respect. I decided the best way to win his trust was to continue filling our void of relevant commentary with the sound of my own voice. The more I shared, the more I hoped he'd consider opening a dialog. I told him about my time with Ash and framed our departure as a riddle of regret. If he was plotting to kill her and he had murdered Simon and Juno, I thought steering our conversation into a familiar harbor was a good place to dock. Overhearing my one way conversation, a small group swarmed and introduced themselves.

"Ash? Isn't she that famous artist in Europe?" asked Michelle. She was curious.

Immediately becoming uncomfortable, I could practically taste the beads of sweat emerging from Dez's brow line. I knew there had to be a reason this random New Mexican club kid would know about Ash. Dez knew it wasn't the time nor place for revelations. My curiosity piqued. This was the validation I needed to justify my presence.

"Yes!" I responded. "She left me broke and brokenhearted in Los Angeles."

"Women?" she laughed. "How do you know Dez?"

Encouraging me to pause, Dez put his arm around my shoulder and firmly directed me away from his peer group. He led me to a remote part of the club, far from ear shot. "Small talk, aside, why are you here and how did you find me?"

"Ash and I had a hell of a rock show going in Los Angeles. She deserted me and it all disbanded. I was abruptly forced to leave. Getting back on my feet, I wanted to visit a few friends, so I returned. Elisa was gracious enough to share her couch for a few weeks. I talk to Grayson, pretty regularly. Do you remember the guy?"

"I do," said Dez.

"He said Simon was with you. So, I figured I'd try and kill two birds with one stone."

"Yes, Simon was here. He didn't stay long. I might have scared him a bit. I don't have the nicest of accommodations and my demeanor can sometimes make people a little uncomfortable. He was staying in a nearby hotel. I think he just needed someone to bond with. Israel ostracized him," furthered Dez.

"He's gone?" I asked.

"He is. He wanted to try and find himself in the desert."

"Like Moses?" I asked.

"Yeah, I guess. He wouldn't be the first to get lost out here."

"How did that girl know about Ash?" I prodded,

beginning to sense trust in Dez's tone.

"These people are my closest friends. I share everything with them. The Program doesn't make sense, Neco. I can't participate or even allow myself to think about it. It's too much, and I have too much of my own baggage to sort through," said Dez.

"Tell me about it!"

"Our calling, it feels like Zombieland. So, I built walls, went off the grid, made friends and found my own way of dealing with it. The booze, and girls are a mere distraction. I'd invite you over, but I don't know that you'd feel comfortable with my arrangements," offered Dez.

"Dez, I don't have anywhere to go! I'm like a nomad. Ash obliterated my heart. I'm furious with her. Point is, I've got no real reason to go on. It wasn't supposed to happen like that, you know? None of this feels right, but I have no choice but to wake-up and face this reality. It never fades," I said.

"It's why I'm distant. I stuck my toes in the water and invited Simon. He didn't seem too tolerant of The Program. I figured we'd find some common ground. If he stayed a little longer, we may have been able to save each other. Everyone else seems to be content living their lives and fully engaged in The Program," said Dez.

"It does seem that way."

"We're not. These friends of mine follow me, because I gave them a backstage pass."

"Do they know about The Program?"

"Yes, I expressed it in a way they could understand. If you're willing to come out, listen and follow along, without judgment, you're welcome. If you become uneasy with what I've built and what you hear, I'd appreciate it if you just excused yourself. What you'll hear is my reality. It's my world. That said, I could certainly use a friend. Most people would see what I've raised as a cult and that's fine. It's not a cult."

Luckily, my steady hand played. Dez couldn't see a

downside to bringing me in; we'd either connect or he'd be one step closer to wiping out The Program. I knew more than he'd given me credit for. So long as I continued playing up my dysfunctional relationship with Ash, I had a gateway to staying in good graces. All I had to do was join and play nice. "I would be honored."

CHAPTER 29
SHOCK WAVES

News of Elisa and Magnus's death sent shock waves through the dwindling Program. What brought the surviving members alarming pause was the unrelated nature of the four recent deaths. Knowing Dez hadn't triggered Magnus's unquenchable obsession. The suspicion surrounding him was again tainted. The Hallway of Sorrows mounted with tragedy. Though few news networks missed the opportunity to share the viral coverage of Magnus and Elisa's standoff, Grayson, always the first to know, was tasked with warning and informing his distant comrades. The gruesome coverage haunted them all. With twins on the way, Icarus instantly became concerned. He was excited about the implications of a dual Crystalline delivery and didn't want to compromise Maria's life, or his grand exit from The Program. Knowing a mad season had fallen upon them, he was quick to make concessions.

"Ben, it's Icarus."

"How are the little ones coming along?" asked Ben.

"They are good. Maria and I would like to bury some neighboring roots. These months pass like days. With the chaos surrounding The Program and our lot of tragic deaths, we wanted to be proactive about cloaking her delivery, and shrouding our newborn babies from this traveling beast. We suspect the other Programmers know of her pregnancy. It's all a bit unsettling, but we're not taking any chances, especially if there is a western renegade on the loose," said Icarus.

"We totally understand," said Ben.

"We'll be moving to Dublin in a month. We will give you our whereabouts when we arrive," continued Icarus.

"Don't give it another thought. We are happy to help you get situated and show you around," said Ben.

"You are our lighthouse. Thank you for guiding us to safe harbors," said Icarus.

"Great passages to you. We have to stick together. There's no need to thank us," said Ben.

"When they're born, Maria may need to go into hiding. In which case, our kids will remain with you, until it is safe. Sadly, I cannot bring my biological family into this without them fearing for our sanity. It's strange to say, but sometimes being estranged is in everyone's best interest. Once they've forgotten about the pain of abandonment, they can relearn how to live-in peace!"

"How's Maria doing?" asked Ben.

"She's nervous and getting bigger," whispered Icarus, afraid Maria might hear him.

"How do you feel?" asked Ben.

"I get weaker with each passing day. I'm not entirely sure what to expect, but if she's truly the one, than these symptoms are telling, and should be documented. I feel light, and my mind has been consumed by a smothering fog. I feel lost within my body, and my eyes are like a flickering candle in the tired wind," said Icarus.

"Farewell, my friends."

+++

Circulating reports of harassment toward others, those who claimed to have birthed miracle or crystal children, began to surface. Dez's cult was gaining national media attention and momentum. Their bravado was amplified by coarse actions. Acts of violence, vandalism and arson were often marked by Cadence of the Sun business card; a card that included their Taiyo sun symbol and moniker. Supporters were quick to take the microphone and amplify their plight. The cult was targeting Programmers, their family members, solicitors of divinity and anyone with pupils with an indigo hue; people presumed to be the direct genetic descendants or mere charlatans, manufacturing dissonance.

Though an investigation of the website and its loyal followers was underway, a lack of hard evidence, connecting the recent mischief and murder to the group, shielded Dez from the authorities. Ongoing coverage, leaks from ex-cult members and helicopter runs from various news affiliates began unearthing vivid details about the compound. The police were poised. The Cadence could surmise the police were sitting on a loose case, inciting their lust for poking the hive. The parents who had birthed these special children were nervous and began scouring the Internet for instructions. The proliferation of disinformation, by people claiming to have birthed these children, blended with outlandish conspiracy theories, mucked the waters of reality and fueled the confusion of the public. There became a fear of an impending uprising, and a government cover-up.

These rumblings of a new U.S. cult, with an international reach, were often downplayed. The government didn't want to fuel the notoriety of its discontents or encourage the unstable to take up arms. This wealth of reporting also put Grayson's journalistic poise on high alert. Meticulously, he documented the unfolding chess match between the Cadence and the world. Grayson knew the merits of his final editorial work would trump the efforts of his predecessors, as he slowly fastened the beginning and middle pieces of his book into place. As a security measure, he reached across the pond and lassoed the ears of those he feared may be void of breaking news, changed the password of their private website and scrubbed pertinent information from the site, which might put anyone associated with The Program in harm's way.

"Ash, the cult has surfaced. They are targeting us and our families. Anyone claiming to have carried a child of divinity may be in trouble," warned Grayson. "I don't know the legitimacy of their claims, but I know they are prevalent, and a spiritual war is unfolding. Dez wants to burn the world to the ground."

"Yes, I heard the whistling wind through the trees, but I've been too consumed with my studio and pregnancy, to pay it mind. I heard about Juno and Simon. Have the two been connected, or are we still skeptics, bathing in black soap?" asked Ash.

"The cult is called Cadence of the Sun. Leaked information from ex-cult members links them to a town outside of Albuquerque. Their IP address confirms this. The ringleader is, of course, Dez. He's getting 100's or 1,000's of hits per day. He's built an army of followers. You need to be careful. I don't want to write your obituary, darling," said Grayson.

"I'll keep a tight ship."

"Your secret is safe, though, people who follow your paintings will be quick to assume you are carrying a crystal child. It only takes an ounce of suspicion to bring the devil to your doorstep. For all we know, the Cadence of the Sun is there, in wait. Godspeed."

"Thank you, Grayson."

Grayson became entranced by the investigation. He felt the pinch of Father Time and padded his own story with follow-up interviews from the remaining members — feverishly trying to connect the morsels of data needed to help the police arrest the madman. His ongoing story had been scribed across pizza boxes, napkins and archived in countless emails and word documents. Taking precautions, he was quick to compile and secure his notes, praying he wasn't next.

+++

Surprisingly, amidst the chaos, no one took ownership of Juno Vestris's horrific death, while Simon Peter still remained a missing person. Their only hope for answers lied in Neco's trip west. Like Simon, Neco's conversations with Grayson slowly sputtered out, due to location, time zone and his immediate access to the Internet. On a busy night, Grayson was interrupted, while tending a beat.

"I'm in," said Neco.

"Neco?" asked Grayson.

"I'm barricaded in a hotel."

"What are you doing there?"

"Waiting. I'm told it's the same hotel Simon stayed in."

"He's alive?" asked Grayson.

"Dez said he only stayed briefly, before heading into the desert to find himself, or God?"

"Simon found you in a vision, remember? If we are to trust our dreams, he's already dead," said Grayson.

"I didn't say it made sense, but he was remarkably convincing," said Neco.

"I'm not surprised," said Grayson.

"The people in this town worship him."

"He started a cult, Neco!"

"I know, I joined, and have been following the story from my room."

"That's great! Are you sure he's not just going to lure you in and kill you?"

"I'm not sure of anything. I managed to sell my disdain for The Program, which I'm confident he bought. If he suspects anything, I *am* dead." Neco lit a cigarette and kicked rocks in the empty parking lot. Exhaling, his smoke was consumed by the street lights above. He could see if headlights were coming, for miles, but no one came. His detachment from humanity made him feel like he was sharing his final days with an absentee god. "Right now, I'm worried about Ash. These people knew about her. I'm not sure if they know about all of us. Dez got very uncomfortable when I brought up her name," said Neco.

"He knows you can out him. I just got off the phone with Ash. I filled her in on everything that's going on and urged her to keep watch. The password to the site has been changed to 'Children of the Program,' all one word. I'm avoiding updates and have encrypted a lot of our personal information. He may have hackers — not that it would take a mastermind," said Grayson.

"Exactly!"

"Neco, I'm going to compile our story and leave a hard copy beneath the floorboards of my kitchen. If anything happens, we need someone to share our story with the world. Of course, you will have to wait until the time is right. We may end up thanking each other in another lifetime, or not, but somehow that's a good thing, right? It's *beyond* comprehension." Grayson joked.

"You're psyching yourself out, but I promise, if I survive you, I will!"

"Be careful, Neco. I have confidence you'll find Simon's body, Juno's killer and who's next!"

"With any luck, I'll find a way to end this, permanently."

+++

Far from the recent revelations of a cult or Elisa and Magnus's death strolled Rand and Isabella. As the months passed, the strength of their relationship intimidated the approachability of outside love interests. Isabella wasn't prepared for what the cosmos had arranged and feared the mere revelation of her gift would jeopardize her friendship with Rand. With time, it all became painfully evident and impossible to hide.

"I'm pregnant!" professed Isabella.

"What?" asked Rand

"I'm pregnant with your child."

"That's not..."

"It is! I haven't been with anyone else."

"But, I'm..."

"You're going to be a father. A beautifully gay father!" she assured.

Rand leaned over a small arching bridge and began to vomit. He was in shock. It wasn't meant disrespectfully, but he was overwhelmed by their financial situation, the impact it might have on their friendship, his faltering sexual preference and the thought of raising his child with the wolves of the night. She nervously patted his flannel-coated back, hoping he'd lift his head and show a level of composure and excitement.

"I am going to be a father," he sniveled, turning to hug her. He gasped with joy, while tears ran down his grimy face. Knowing his heart lied with the same sex, he was relieved to know their child would always have a father. "This child is about you, Isabella. I love you. I prayed I could give you something to live for." Rand was honored to give her a taste of heaven's mercy and reignite her long forgotten hope. He wanted to name the child. "How about Izzy, for a boy, or Isabella, for a girl?"

"Izzy, I can live with, but I don't want to be a senior," Isabella joked. "Look, I know you're scared, but I don't expect you to marry me. I don't expect you to always be there or to forgo who you *really* are, but I do expect you to try and I trust you will."

"Of course? Where else do I have to go?" asked Rand.

"Nowhere! You're ours."

"Dare I ask, how long?"

"I really have no way of knowing. If I were to guess, 3 or 4 months. I had assumed my morning sickness was from the terrible food we'd been fishing from the local trash cans — you know, to survive. Not to mention, my shape hasn't been the greatest. I've been practically swimming in these damn rags for months," said Isabella.

"We have to call Grayson!" proclaimed Rand.

"Lead the way, Superman."

CHAPTER 30
GOD COMPLEX

I returned from the strip club, late. After talking with Grayson, I sat before the only beacon of light shining in New Mexico. I penned lyrics about Ash, and drifted. Hours passed. Startled by bright headlights, cascading through the crease in my thick paisley curtains, a new curiosity projected upon the wall behind my mounted television set. I uncurled, like a lone wolf hiding from the harsh desert winds and slowly allowed the shimmer of a rude awakening to enter my quivering eyelids. A light rapt on the door lit a match in my belly. Before sanity could trump intrigue, I answered, never considering why these vampyres had come and were knocking on my hostel door at 4:00 a.m. They could smell blood.

"We're sorry to wake you." Michelle whispered.

"It's OK. I had only drifted."

"Dez asked that we bring you to the compound. We travel by night. I apologize, but he did ask for us to blindfold you. Please do not be offended. He doesn't want to risk our whereabouts, in the event you're dismayed by our way of life. It's a precaution to protect us both!"

"I shouldn't have had those last couple of shots. I need a few more winks."

"We're total night owls. Time is relative. You're welcome to bunk in one of our beds."

"Fair enough."

The patchouli scented van hummed Jefferson Airplane's "Somebody to Love." It all seemed rather ironic. Here I was, attempting to join a cult, whose entire mission was to stop my fellow Programmers from finding true love and birthing a child, and these wackos were singing along like disenchanted Muppets.

The van began to feel like a puffy cloud, as phencyclidine filled the open space. My mind lost track of reality, as my dry mouth wistfully sang along. The creeping aroma had glazed over my fear of dying. Catching my slip, I quickly spun my internal compass back on point. After about 20 minutes, reason avenged my drifting curiosity. I could sense we were getting close, by the cabin's breaking calm.

When we arrived, I was lead up a long dirt driveway. I could hear the crackling fire pit, feel the soul of the group and sense the free-spirited harmony of a crisp desert morning; a world, far from my suburban norms. There were dozens of crooning campers, awake and blissfully driven by the sounds of Dez's guitar. Though blinded, I could still hear the passersby rustling and conversing a lazy drivel. Judging by rhetoric, they seemed to be in their late teens and early twenties. My captors assured my tepid steps, easing my reflex to fear. Something about Michelle's soft delivery soothed me. It was a dangerous serenity. For a moment, we were trauma bonding, emotionally connected to Dez's mad pangs. After passing through a gated area and the whispers of tenderfoot guards, we entered a giant storage locker posing as a shelter. I was escorted down a long hallway and offered sanctuary in a quaint bedroom. Slowly, the blindfold was removed. One by one, the accomplices left the room. Michelle kissed me on the cheek, placing her finger to my lips.

"I'm sorry."

"It's fine. It was a bit unsettling, but I'm OK."

"There are a few things for me to check on, but I'm happy to help you settle."

Savvy to her suggestion, I realized that dismissing her advance might be seen as a red flag, even if sleeping with the enemy flew directly in the face of my entire reason for joining the cult — *Ash*! I slowly removed my shirt and stared into her sparkling eyes. For a moment, we connected. As I leaned in to kiss her, she put her soft hands on my shoulders and thwarted my advance. Again, we locked eyes. An unspoken and lustful sentiment lingered.

"I'd be a fool to turn down such an offer," I said.

"See you in a bit," Michelle said.

Moments later, two girls returned in her place and satisfied my earthly fantasies. It was a test. Dez was judging my character and sincerity about Ash. I'd passed. So long as I could departmentalize the horrors of his mission, I could relish in the perks. The girls and I ran the gamut for hours, before passing out and awaking in a locked prison bedroom.

The cell had its own tales to tell. The windows were abnormally small, intended to confine a human body and mind. They were shrouded in a silky black drapery. When drawn, the sun was blotted from existence. The walls were covered in newspaper clippings. By candlelight, I could see stories that documented the group's progress. Recent news articles shared the wall with conspiracy theory literature, UFO maps and, strangely, bloodstained thumbprints, marked by identifying names. The floors were covered in a very thin green industrial carpet and lined with a thin layer of plastic. I could tell the facility was new — only the neighboring walls had been fitted with drywall. At noon, I was ushered to the pit, to finally meet Dez on his terms.

"Cadence, I would like you to welcome Neco to the group. Should he choose to follow the words of our calling and embrace our mission to cleanse the world, he will be considered our friend and should be treated as so. He knows much about the government cover-up. He knows the identities of those who purport to be sent by heaven itself," said Dez.

As he continued, I immediately knew what he was selling and what had happened to Simon. One after another, the cult members welcomed me. Chills ran up my spine, as I thought about Juno and how zombified his followers had become. There was no turning back. The odds were stacked in his favor. I knew it was do or die. "Unlike our former guest, Neco genuinely seems abashed by the external threats. Until I'm given cause, he is to be trusted. Would you care to speak, Neco?" asked Dez.

"I'm happy to be here. I've wandered from coast to coast and have kissed the sun of east and west. I've tried hiding from my past, but I can no longer cower. There are those out there who will perpetuate, encourage and have created this new world order Dez has warned you about. From first-hand experience, I can tell you, they are terrorists to humanity — a danger to us all!"

Dez was reassured by my message. People had always avowed my natural gift for persuasion, but when your life is swinging in the balance, you can only hope that their confidence meets your words and your sentiments glide received as a foregone conclusion.

My presence and unification with their vision hurled a burst of provocative energy towards Dez's blood-thirsty wolves. In 40 days, every filthy detail and damning piece of intelligence passed my sights. I could deliver the authorities their prize, but had a good reason to bide my time — again, *Ash*! Withholding tears, I visited Simon's grave, knew the names of Juno's assassins and who their future targets were. Per Grayson's request, I kept a secret and detailed journal of every moment and disturbing conversation.

+++

Max and Michelle were miffed by my quick advance in rank. Their curiosities were piqued by our mysterious connection, and how quickly they'd been replaced. To continue my assent, I offered to unearth Ash and chart the course of her demise. If she was going to be targeted, I wanted to keep my enemies close and control the plot.

Scandalous rhetoric elated our fuhrer's confidence. Communication outside of the compound became rare. Aside from the obvious oversight of an iron fist, the desert limited our access to technology. Knowing my intentions weren't in question, I feared Grayson would soon get suspicious of my absence and attempt to rescue me. From my vantage point, he was best served tending local news blips and awaiting bodies to surface.

One cool morning, I emerged from the bunks, early, and found Dez screaming and shaking Crystal's frail body. Quickly taking cover behind their trailer by Simon's grave, I desperately tried to dial into their conversation, while remaining a specter. He was confident she was pregnant and insisted she sacrifice their unborn child to God's will. She knew he wouldn't react well, but was rattled by his irrational intensity. I wasn't. After forcefully striking her gut, Crystal picked herself from the ground, grabbed her belly and slunk down the driveway toward the road. She wept. From a distance, he continued to cuss and scream at her, but she clammed.

"I heard what I heard," I said. Distracting him, I seized the opportunity.

"What?" Dez leered, with hesitant suspicion.

"She can't carry your baby. I don't know how close the two of you are, but if she gives birth to your child, and she is the one, than this whole thing could be shot. You're finished – *gone*! The Cadence needs you. I can't handle the leadership responsibilities. They don't trust or adore me like you. I need you." I attempted to sustain his trust.

"I'm not sure my heart is capable of creating the kind

of child The Council would recognize, Neco. It was conceived under the pretense of control and my own self-serving lust. I shouldn't have been so hard on her," offered Dez.

"Maybe! Who do you hold most dear? The Council didn't elucidate a lot details, as to what that meant. She very well could be a birther. Let me go after her. We can play a little good cop/bad cop. I'll force her to take ownership of the situation and to terminate the pregnancy. I can convince her she's being selfish and that everything she has, you provided. She can't argue with that. You plucked her from a strip club," I continued.

"If you can pull that off, I'll serve you Ash's head on a plate!"

"Consider it done."

Chasing after, I found her leaning upon an old wooden fence by the crossroads. She remained a brilliant image of serenity, a stark contrast from the fiery eyes of a sociopath. I didn't have a lot of time to rehearse; again, my tongue would need to be guided by divinity. As I approached, the wingspan of a beautiful white owl tickled my eardrum. With a cool gust, my nerves settled. Though a verbal fumble could be my death sentence, I spoke without caution.

"Are you OK?"

Crystal slowly lifted her head from the fence and moved a stream of locks from her lethargic eyes. "What do you want, Neco? Did he send you down here to talk me into an abortion or to kick dirt upon my worthless body?" she asked.

"No. I just wanted to know if you knew your options and might like to talk to someone."

"I've been toting his temperamental baby around for more months than I can count. You can't hide from being pregnant, forever. Even loose-fitting hippie clothing have their limitations. He was bound to find out. Not a day has passed, where I haven't considered my options. I just hoped..." furthered Crystal.

"You just hoped a child would simmer his growl and draw your distancing hearts together?"

"Yes!" She cried.

"What do you think is going to happen if you don't have the abortion?"

"He will kill me. There is no leaving the Cadence!"

"That's exactly what he'll do. He killed Simon and Juno and wants to kill my ex-lover, Ash. He's threatening to kill any child he finds on the Internet that doesn't pass his sniff test. Is any of this making sense to you?" She looked to me with a puzzled hope. Again, the white owl had graced my tongue with eloquence. "I'm risking my life by even talking to you. You're right, Dez sent me down here to talk you into killing your child. I need to know that I can trust you, too. Otherwise, I'm Simon and you're Juno, capiche?"

"You can trust me," said Crystal.

"Do you want this baby?"

"Of course. I wouldn't have carried it for this long, had I not."

"You're going to have to listen to me. There is no time for you to doubt me."

Time reeled forward like a time-lapse video. My words tripped over the anxiety of each moment. After 10 minutes of purging the detailed specifics of our past and entrusting her with the new password to our website, I seized a moment to breathe. Her access to the site would prove Dez was a cranky fraud, far from the glamorized midnight cowboy he claimed to be; a mere wolf, hiding his vicious teeth from the hypnotized sheep fluffing his revolution. With or without evidence, she knew she needed to get as far from the compound as possible and have their baby.

"How else would he know about Simon, Juno or myself? We're not exactly locals."

"I hadn't had time to question it. Even the smallest of inquiries would ignite the inferno attached to his mouth. It seemed best to avoid poking the bear with realism. I didn't want to risk sharing a plot with Simon. There were times I thought about running, but he casts a long lasso. If not me, he'd kill the people I care about. He didn't have to say it. I knew," said Crystal.

"If you have his baby, and his baby is truly what I believe it'll be, you'll save our very existence. He wants to be a God. All of his brainwashed lemmings will face an unimaginable afterlife in the underworld. It's gruesome. If living in his shadow scares you, imagine the fire. It's real. You have to rise up and take ownership of the situation! If anything, save yourself."

"So, if I have his baby, and it's one these Crystalline children, he'll be forced into The Beyond? He'll cease to exist?" asked Crystal.

"Yes! He'll be gone, forever. That's why he's freaking out."

"It's actually starting to make sense," she humbly offered.

"I'm here to disrupt his plan. He wants you to have an abortion because you might be the one he *holds most dear*, if that's any consolation. There's no changing what he is or what he's become. As you said, he's been doping you. He is marching an army of broken souls to the drums of madness. He's become a rockstar."

"How so?" she asked.

"Rock n' roll is about social change. He may not be screaming into a microphone or strumming an electric guitar, but he sold it all for the rights to this revolution, and has created one hell of a fan club."

"It's so surreal," said Crystal.

"You don't have time to think. When you leave, you can never look back! I will try to find you a safe house, but if we get separated or I'm killed, promise me you'll contact Grayson and have this baby."

To make haste, Dez descended to the crossroad. "So, what have you kids come up with?"

"She's going to have an abortion," I offered.

"Is that so?" he questioned, with an eerie look in his eyes.

"I was afraid to tell you, because I thought a child would bring us closer together. But, Neco's right! When I think about the mission and what you're trying to do, it's not fair to the Cadence of the Sun."

"There's no time like the present. I'll drive," said Dez. Neco, I owe you a head — *Ash's!*"

"That you do, sir! That you do."

+++

Dez placed his bare chest and arms around Crystal's meek shoulders and guided her back to their house on the hill. With one last glance, she left me questioning fate. Her eyes were filled with an ocean of unsettling fear. Thoughts of her family and friends seesawed her loyalty to Dez with the karma of hurting an angelic child. She was convinced her racing heart had caused a minor tremor beneath their feet.

For all intents and purposes, my immediate reason for joining the cult was validated. I'd have ran, but protecting Ash remained paramount. Dez and Crystal didn't simmer long before hopping on the road and making their way to an abortion clinic in Silver City. His demeanor was cold, as the reality of her hiding her pregnancy eclipsed his ability to maintain a calm composure. For miles they rested in an uncomfortable still — only the wind risked tickling their eardrums. Resting in an ocean of blue skies, the magnificent sun of a new day pleaded for her absolution.

"You should have parted your lips and spared me this embarrassment. Your deceit will undermine my reign. Do you realize the precedent you've set, Crystal?" asked Dez. "How can I stand before this world we've created and tout our successes, if our followers cease to respect the expectations of their leader? What stops any of them from choosing secrecy as an option?" He paused and allowed a moment for his wanted-aggravation to stoke his fury, hoping his closed line of interrogation would guide her toward his reason. "You've jeopardized our security with your silent lies! How do I learn to trust you?"

Crystal could hear the familiar rattle of his mania. Everything was beginning to make sense. "Do you love me?" The words fell from her tongue, casting a brilliant line over his flimsy logic and towering walls. They pierced his soul and taunted his guise — never had those four words had the power to stop a man dead in his tracks. He was fearful of the mines he'd laid. Knowing the truth would set the universe back into balance and answer The Council's calling, he stewed in checkmate. The illusion he viciously protected from himself began shattering. He gazed out of the windshield, as his mind drifted with the vehicle. An alerted patrol car took notice to his swerves and followed.

"Now, look what you made me do!" Dez said.

"I didn't make you do anything. I asked you a question and you didn't answer."

"Just shut up! Goddamnit," Dez barked.

The circus lights atop the car mocked his sense of freedom. Dez knew it was best to pull over and face the authority. With a rush of blood to the face, they both sensed it was more than a mere traffic violation — paranoia suggested the authorities had been following them and were prepared to link Simon's disappearance, Juno's murder, and a laundry list of unsolved Cadence crimes to their names.

After a slow-rolling approach to their vehicle, the cop finally emerged from his dusty patrol car and walked toward his scraggly offenders. The officer's hesitant posture amplified Dez's rattling mind. He felt the law's heavy footprints crushing their freedoms beneath. He cracked the window cautiously, allowing only a brief waft of soiled air to mingle with the crisp clean atmosphere. Crystal felt compelled to run.

"License and..."

Before uttering his rehearsed dialog, Crystal flung open

the passenger side door and hopped onto the solid ground. Without a thought, she sprinted into the unknown. Startled, the officer tried to verbally thwart her, before radioing for back-up. Dez remained in the vehicle and began feverishly sweating. He could see the fear in her sluggish rhythm and knew she was putting him at a greater risk of being detained.

"Where is she going?" The deputy officer screamed.

"I don't know! We were heading to the hospital, due to complications with her..."

"Save it," he said, bringing his lips to his Handie-Talkie. "We have a young woman, early twenties, on foot. She's running towards the highway. We're on 152, about eight miles out. She's crossing the desert fields, approaching Santa Clara. Please be advised." Crossing behind an old field house, a barn obstructed their immediate view. Quickly making her way to the intersecting route, by a nearby overpass, she crossed U.S. Route 180, scaled a minor hill by the exit and began flashing truckers for rides.

"Why do you suppose she's running?" asked the frustrated officer. Patrol cars began to swarm Dez's vehicle.

"She's not dangerous — she's scared! We were heading west, toward Silver City. She's pregnant."

"Is she armed? High?" asked the officer.

"Armed? No. She's concerned about the baby and probably heading to a hospital," said Dez.

"Do you have her number or a way for us to reach her?"

"We can't afford phones. Let me help you find her. We're not criminals."

"OK. Why does your van smell like grass and why were you swerving all over the damn road?"

"We were arguing!"

"About pot? It's not the kind of thing babies are into, ya' dig?" The officer mocked his anxiety.

Dez's shoulders slouched. He knew his words had fallen deaf and struggled to maintain his humility. "What's wrong? Cat got your tongue? We've had a lot of marijuana smuggled down this road. Coincidentally, it's always in a white van," added the officer.

"Is that so?" snarked Dez.

"You wouldn't happen to know anything about that, would you, Smokey?"

"We don't have anything on us. Are you arresting me?"

"Search the vehicle."

Dez offered a statement and was eventually released with a citation for reckless endangerment. He hopped back into his van and was consumed by curiosity. In the days that followed, Crystal never appeared. He feared a large scale search of the compound was imminent.

CHAPTER 31
ASH TO ASHES

Ash was turning the corner on the 26th week of her second trimester. Time was short, but she remained intent to see Neco. Making arrangements, she booked a plane ticket to the States. She hoped to surprise him at his Baltimorean home. As she packed her leather bags, she sifted through various medallions and ornaments; items that incited the gorgeous memories of her recalcitrant days in Los Angeles. She furtively longed to smuggle a piece Neco's impenetrable soul to The Beyond. She always toted a lock of his dirty blonde hair in her favorite heart-shaped necklace.

Before taking her flight, she sought an update from Grayson.

"Any word on my dearest? I was thinking about surprising him in the Land of the Mary," asked Ash.

"Maryland?" asked Grayson.

"Yes."

"Cute. He's been hovering below my radar. I have been conscientious about following various New Mexican police blotters and keeping a long watch on story blurbs from southwestern news affiliates, but nothing has come across my radar to suggest he's been hospitalized or murdered. I am still worried about his overall plan for this mission and general well-being," said Grayson.

"Wait, what do you mean?" asked Ash.

"The last we spoke, he was holed up in the same hotel room that Simon stayed in. He seemed a little anxious, but it's hard to fault a guy for being a little nervous about joining a death camp, cult or whatever. I still can't believe he had the guts to go in. If anything, he's got heart," said Grayson.

"I meant, in general. What are you talking about?" asked Ash.

"He shot like a cannon toward Los Angeles, met up with Elisa and worked his way over to New Mexico. He went to find Dez and Simon alive! Things got bloody when Magnus recreated a perverse Shakespearean death sequence in a Santa Monica convenient store parking lot. So, they're gone! We very well may have four dead Programmers on our hands," said Grayson.

"It's a tragedy," she sobbed. "I was planning to surprise him. Why didn't you tell me about this? You know how much he means to me. Why would he risk going to New Mexico with all of this chaos unfolding?" asked Ash.

"I don't know how this will land on your conscience, but I'm fairly confident that *you* are the answer you're seeking," said Grayson.

"I can't believe this."

"He didn't want to put any added stress on you or the baby. The truth is, in his own words, he 'Didn't have anything left to lose.' He figured he would try and do something about Dez — for all of us. He was concerned about you, especially after Juno's horrible murder. Trust me, we are all in considerable debt, and better hope he never comes to collect."

"I'm speechless," said Ash.

"It's hard to believe it's happening and he's there, but once..."

"He gets an idea into his head..." said Ash, finishing

Grayson's line.

"Exactly."

"I've got to find him!" she said.

"You absolutely cannot. You're pregnant. If he is in trouble, you can't risk your life or your baby's. That baby is bigger than your feelings for Neco and I don't say that to be hurtful or to invalidate your mindset. Think about all of the people who've yet to be born. I beg you, don't miss your opportunity to leave this vicious cycle of life," Grayson pleaded.

"Where is he, Grayson?" asked Ash.

"In good conscious, I simply cannot tell you. He's going to have to save himself."

In utter disgust, Ash slammed her phone down on the marble floor. Pieces shattered and spun, just like her ill heart and reeling mind. She understood Grayson's concern, and that he was only trying to shield her child, but she remained determined to find a way to communicate with Neco. For weeks, she pined by her broken phone and stared at the plane ticket, knowing it would always be the 'goodbye' that never was. While penning her last will and testament, she was startled by an untimely buzz at her towering gates.

"Hello?" she asked, peering through the thick curtains.

"Is this the virtuoso they call Ash?" asked Cass, drenched in a black trench coat.

"Yes, this is she. Can I help you, sir?" she asked.

"I was hoping you'd buzz me in. I have a few parties interested in viewing your lush works."

After her scrambling black and green gate monitor settled, she was able to make out the silhouettes of four bodies. The communicator seemed young and arrogant, as if he was trying to impress his cohorts. Their wicked smiles, illuminated by the whites of their teeth, helped decipher their intent. Cass repeatedly looked over his shoulder for reassurance, but also for patrolling vehicles.

"You can come back during an open house, but we do

not have regular visiting hours," offered Ash.

"Of course, you don't. I'll just leave my business card," he paused, furling his brow and offering a distorted smile for the adjusting camera. He flashed the card before the lens, to reveal the Cadence logo, before flicking it through the gate. "Oh, and Miss Mckenzie, we'll be back. Remember this face. We're very interested in what you have to offer," said Cass.

Ash's mind was suspended by suspicion. In a trance, she faded from the monitor and debated whether she should stir her slumbering parents with the obvious prank. If her life was in danger, she wanted to warn Neco. Knowing the best way to communicate with the outside world was through her brush, she decided to publicly part with her "Neco: Into the Art of Darkness" painting. Collectors knew of the piece, and her insistence to never part with it.

The following morning, Ash welcomed the world to a game of Where's Waldo? "Find and deliver this man and **WIN** this painting, valued at **$8,582,475** (5,000,000 pound sterling)." The piece quickly became one of her most popular works. She contacted various news groups and editors to spread the word of her offer. It quickly went viral. Her official landing page and the Children of the Program website also featured the bait. To create a demand for its attention, the proposed value of the work was set high.

It was to be an offer Dez couldn't refuse.

CHAPTER 32
THE WAR BEGINS

When Dez was away, Neco used his lush musical background to serenade and win the favor of the 1969-reveling sect members. His campfire jams included classics, from artists like: Jefferson Airplane, The Rolling Stones and The Doors. His years of siphoning in his father's musical collection had come in handy. He also wasn't shy about littering in a few original cuts. Having musical talent gave him an instant connection with the aspiring cult culture and enabled him to captivate the minds of those moved by the pulse of a good vibration. Neco tried to lasso in the wayward, by reminding them of the peace and love missing from their hippie narrative.

Dez and Neco both strummed the same sermon, but to different ends. They both understood that the combination of drug use and rhythm could transport any audience to a place far beyond rational thought. Music was the cornerstone of their manipulation. It could start a revolution, and sound a battle cry for war. Its power came through the mad receivers of their fluttering words. Neco was always penning the songs of tomorrow, by candlelight.

The Cadence, always flirting with a looming endgame, would soon sound the trumpet for an all-out blitzkrieg. Though the flames had been stoked, its declaration was a matter of semantics and time.

Dez was fuming after his brush with the law. He stormed his trailer and began destroying the fixtures and screaming coarse words. Crystal, on the run and missing, forced his hand to compensate for his loss of control. He no longer had time to debate her intentions, nor fear for her life. If the police came looking, they'd find his compound turned into a Hollywood stage. Cautiously, Neco approached Dez's shaky trailer, but was turned away. His concern for what Crystal may have revealed begged an answer. For hours, Dez seethed, smoked and prayed for his phone to ring. When he finally emerged from the trailer, he lassoed an impromptu meeting.

"This has gone on for long enough!" Dez proclaimed. "Our war begins tonight."

"What do you want us to do?" asked Michelle.

"I'm not done with you, Michelle. As a matter of fact, take her to confinement," he instructed.

He unraveled a plan that would permanently place the Cadence on the map. "The outside knows we're here. With my citation and Crystal's behavior, the cops will come looking. We have no time to waste. I want you to hide the drugs and guns in the underground tunnel. We will be more effective on the run. We must disperse from these premises. We're leaving tonight!"

"Can they even find us?" asked Neco, hoping to maintain his stay.

"I'm not willing to take any chances. Helicopters are an amazing invention. For all we know, they're already running surveillance and waiting to pounce. Besides, I'm sure we could all use a nice hotel bed and bath," said Dez.

"You don't have to ask me twice!" Neco jested.

"Just remember, in for a penny, in for a pound," Dez added.

The group dispersed and began cleaning up the campsite. His directives generated more questions than answers. Tiny whispers filled the lawn's brush, as they mingled about the reality of being on foot, their methods of survival and the danger of being arrested or isolated. The cult's challenged faith left them hoping Dez had specific assignments and meeting points in place; though, it was clear he was being reactionary. Their only consolation lied in their acquisition of the town's money tills. They had a silo of money to graze from, while hiding in the shadows.

"Each of you will play a part," Dez shouted. They scurried like church mice, fearing the finality of his instruction. "For now, I will develop a plan and find feasible meeting posts. It's time for us to make our move on the world's chess board. In the meantime, please be diligent and thorough with our clean-up effort. Burn anything that doesn't pass the sniff test. Meet back at dusk, and we will prepare to defend our legacy."

Neco became increasingly concerned over his relevance to the operation. Though he wanted to be sure he gathered enough information to keep Ash far from peril, he could feel the magnetism of time's arrow and the heavy sands slipping through his quaking hands. He knew if Crystal chose to return, Dez would have him killed. Debating his options, he decided to stay the course, knowing his fellow Programmers, their offspring and his family's safety were more valuable than his own lot. He could only hope the seeds he'd sowed into Crystal's mind would continue to resonate; though, awaiting their harvest might leave him guilty of a crime by association and behind bars. Lucky or not, he wasn't given much time to consider his options.

At dusk, the Cadence huddled around a final bonfire and awaited Dez to return with a list of operation-specific initiatives. Without their wished partners, Dez placed them into groups of two and gave his orders. He understood that separating their interests would create a longing for their reunion and keep everyone's mind focused on the mission — the prize was communion.

Though frustrated with his inability to access the Children of the Program website, Dez knew Grayson had received the Cadence's sinister message to the world and had made a conscious decision to draw a line in the sand, separating the future villains from the vigilantes. For security, he tasked Neco with being his sidekick in crime. He couldn't risk Neco developing a change of heart. They were to remain on the battlegrounds, awaiting Crystal's return and to run the international operations. Should the authorities descend, they had just enough room, food and technology, stashed in a secret lower level of the bunker, to survive.

Like soldiers, the Cadence groups marched from the site, hitched eastbound rides and accepted their orders; the less glamorous side of taking a stand. Dez fired up the computers, adjusted the surveillance cameras and allowed his racing heart to settle.

"It's time to let our story unfold. Aside from Vietnam, because we lost, can you think of a war that was ever won without a successful leader? I'm standing down, because I can't risk being captured. You and I are far too valuable to this mission. It's bigger than we are, or The Program. I don't want you to see my directive as cowardice," said Dez.

"Our very world depends on us not being seized. Have we gotten any word back on Ash?" asked Neco.

"I've had a group scouting her mansion for a couple days now. It's the same group that took Juno Vestris camping. They've made contact, and startled her, but they need to make sure their timing is right. It's not like she's hiding out in a tiny apartment, she's her own township or capital. I assure you, she remains our number one target. A promise is a promise, m'boy! I understand your betrayal and pain. At the moment, I couldn't be any closer to that sentiment. I'm sorry to say, her talents and money probably made it pretty easy for her to leave you."

"Way to dig the knife in a little deeper, Dez," said Neco.

"I was being candid, not rude. Let me ask, how were you able to convince Crystal?"

"By building her trust, while hiding behind the smile of a leveraged guilt. It was hard to read her sincerity, at first, but I assured her it was the right thing to do. I figured if I could plant the seeds of doubt, she'd come to the desired resolve, whether it was right or not. When backed into a corner, people have a tendency to lack conviction," said Neco.

"You don't say," Dez laughed.

"You make them question their reasoning, by always offering a counterpoint. In so, you can typically get them to see your point of view, while convincing them they came to it on their own. It is basic psychology," said Neco.

"It's the Jedi Mind Trick. You're just as disturbed as I," assured Dez.

"We all are. It just takes the right set of circumstances."

"Neco, I haven't heard from her. I'm actually getting a little worried."

"Don't be. She's probably worried you're upset with her. My guess is she's taking care of things, so that when she does call, she can lead with good news. One thing she made crystal clear, was that she loves you. Pun intended," said Neco.

"That's what I'm afraid of," sputtered Dez.

"Touché."

+++

Settling into the bunker, days passed as Dez and Neco awaited news about their unfolding revolution. The accommodations were stark and militant, but safe. The main room was blanketed in television monitors. Video streams from various countries continuously aired news coverage from the major networks. Exercising patience felt like waterboarding. Concrete walls encapsulated them, and steel beams separated the desert from the basement. Three bright industrial grade lights shined overhead. A year's worth of rations were stashed in camouflaged lockers. Even using the bathroom became a war zone, it meant surfacing and not being witnessed by the occasionally passing helicopters.

The first blip on the radar came from a broadcaster. It gave Dez pause. The anchors touted Ash's painting and offer. The piece perfectly matched a long-haired version of Neco. The canvas detail was impossible to ignore, and rattled the core of Dez's trust. Neco was uncomfortably resting on a portable cot, when the news bulletin first injected itself into his weakening mind. He immediately suspected the worst. "Ash screwed you over. Is that it, Neco?" asked Dez, tossing a metal pale of cold ice water onto his lifeless body.

"What?" screamed Neco. He awakened in a furious panic and rattled by the accusation.

"Ash! The Scottish girl who left you high and dry in Los Angeles, California? The girl's head you had asked to be delivered on a food tray. Do not tell me you've forgotten? You're a poor poker player, sonny boy," said Dez.

"How could I forget? It's why I'm here. What has gotten into you?" asked Neco.

"She's auctioning off a painting worth millions. The person who delivers you gets the prize," said Dez.

"What?" asked Neco.

"For that kind of money, I might consider unearthing you myself! You may be worth more to the cult, alive. Please, amuse me, if you are at such odds, why does she care so much about you? Why does she paint your likeness with such accuracy and essentially auction it off to the world for millions. Why does she suddenly go on national television, drawing attention to your potential whereabouts?" asked

Dez.

"Maybe she feels guilty — *maybe*! If we were still close, she'd know where I am, no? I know what you're thinking, but if she knew I was with you, and trying to infiltrate the Cadence, do you think she'd risk my deliverance with such a charade? She'd be writing my death warrant. I already know enough to destroy you and this plot. If I planned on bringing you down, I'd have already left. Think about it, and please, pretty please with sugar on top, throw me one of those fucking towels," said Neco.

"I haven't had a chance to think," he paused, pointing his damning finger at Neco's damp forehead. "If I so much," he stopped, turned and hurled a steel economy chair across the bunker, grazing Neco's head. It smashed against the wall behind him. Blood rained down Neco neck, onto his dirty white t-shirt.

"Relax. She's already on our radar," said Neco, dodging the reaper. He reached up to feel the warm reminder of his situation and mortality. Continuing to prance around suspicion, he tried to remain calm. He could barely hide his racing heart from trying to escape his pounding chest. "I understand your concern, but you were right to trust me and bring me in. We need each other. I still believe you share that sentiment."

"Ash is practically on her death bed, Neco. If you're bluffing, her coffin will rest on your conscious. You should have ran, while you had the chance. At this point, you may not be too far behind her. I'll find her and hunt her, for lifetimes to come," threatened Dez.

"What are you waiting for?" asked Neco, hoping to salvage his gamble.

"Why don't you come over here and look me in the eyes. I want to know just how good of a card player you really are. Surely, you've scored an ID and gone to Vegas. Have you ever pushed all-in, holding a 7-2 off-suit, while staring the devil in the eyes?" asked Dez.

It was then, Neco realized his left wrist was tied to a

wooden table neighboring the control desk. As he adjusted and nervously stared into Beelzebub's approaching eyes, Dez calmly moved and clasped his loose hand into the remaining steel bracelet and married it with the desk. In those tense moments, few words were exchanged. It wasn't long before Neco's shocked demeanor went from passive to overtly aggressive. His only hope rested in convincing Dez his anger was justified. He knew continued submission would warrant further suspicion.

"I'll be a little more comfortable knowing I can keep an eye on you," said Dez.

"Do what you've got to do. Your paranoia is clouding your mission. Pride has lost many a war, Dez. You started this, don't be the one to end it. I've helped you devise it, I've rallied the Cadence and cast damning orders. Now, I sit chained to a table. Why? Because an editorial piece about a spoiled painter, hoping to absolve her conscious before entering The Beyond, has napalmed your reason. Seriously, you're losing it. You're illogical," said Neco.

"Where is Crystal?" asked Dez, leering.

"How should I know? I don't even know which direction she was last seen running."

"You and her had a nice long talk and now she's nowhere to be found! What did you tell her?" asked Dez.

"I told her you were a fraud. I told her your revolution is based on delusions of grandeur. I told her to have your child and to save the world." Neco raged, with rising intensity. "Is that what you want to hear? I could have killed you, while you slept. There's nothing in it for me. I'm fucking hungry, tired and pissed off."

"Where is she?" Dez continued.

"You can either shoot me, turn me over for Ash's purse, release me, and we can get back to business, or you can spend your final days cleaning Programmer blood off your basement floors, while misdirecting your failed war —
alone!"

With nothing to lose, Neco began slamming his

forehead on the legs of the command center. The mania and theatrics forced Dez to intervene. With every pounding blow, blood poured from his brow. He was psychotic, making a point to never lose eye contact with his commandant. His smile distorted, as his mind blackened with insanity. He wanted to return to the Hallway of Sorrows by his own hands, if Dez was planning to kill him.

"What the hell are you doing? Stop!" demanded Dez.

"Are you ready to unlock me? I have nothing to lose, Dez. I'm worth a lot more to you alive!"

"Alright. Stop! You're getting blood all over the fucking hardware."

Their emotions had climaxed to a point of inevitable exhaustion. Dez begrudging decided to ignore his instincts and release Neco. Forcefully twisting his arm, he elevated and slammed his tired body into a chair and uncuffed him. Trying to regain some sense of composure, Neco slowly stood and rubbed his sore wrist. He walked, without a word, toward the surface. Watching Neco urinate, curious if he'd run, Dez sat in his armchair of anarchy and let his thoughts wander. He feared Crystal was dead, raped or worse, nearing labor.

Though rare, his heart occasionally questioned his malcontent. His ability to block out reality, and harness his hatred was slipping. He felt weaker with each passing day. His mental palate craved distraction, destruction and a higher high.

CHAPTER 33
THE ECLIPSE OF ICARUS

Remaining inconspicuous, Icarus and Maria settled in Dublin. They prepared for their fast-approaching day, but Cadence fears haunted away their brief moments of joy. Even with their precautionary move and detailed preparations, their flaring nerves couldn't be cooled. Benjamin and Zane were equally as overwrought. On a cold morning, Maria began dilating. Icarus's strength quickly waned. Without a moment to spare, he worked his way down their birth day checklist. With shaky fingers, he dialed a cab, notified Benjamin and Zane and prepared for his triumphant end. He could tell by his increasing lack of mental clarity, the bizarre lactic acid build-up in his muscles, and his recent flutter of Isis dreams, that their child would be Crystalline. The Council wouldn't allow him to doubt. When they arrived at St. James's Hospital, they rushed through the emergency room and feverishly issuing their goodbyes, before drowning in tears.

"Sir, we need you to check in," issued a receptionist.

"Maria, I love you! You are about to bring two of the most amazing children into this world. When you look into their eyes, I only ask that you'll remember me." His eyes clinched, but his mouth remained parted and silent. Waves of nausea, dizziness and flashbacks from his passing life distracted his focus.

"I don't know if I can do this," said Maria.

"You don't have a choice. I don't know how this ends, for me, but I imagine I'll be gone soon," said Icarus, placing his tree trunk fingers over her cold lips. Removing sweaty dark bangs from her furling brow, he softly kissed her forehead. "We knew this day would come. You have a lot of work ahead of you, darling. The darkness will follow. You need to be strong and mindful."

Benjamin and Zane arrived to the hospital, shortly after. They held their post in the bustling lobby and teared up. They had both longed to someday find true love, but had always fallen short. Their love was absolute, but never divinely-inspired. Already being approached by various Cadence members, they knew they'd have to be willing to die for Icarus's children. "Ben, what are we going to do? If they get a chance, they are going to kill us and these children," said Zane.

"We're already dead. This is a sacrifice we need to make, for a world we've selfishly ignored," said Ben.

"I'm worried. Maybe, we're not the best people to be watching over them? We're magnets," added Zane.

"If the Cadence knows of us and that we're together, then they know we're of no immediate threat. We promised Icarus we'd help care for his children. We can't look back. This isn't just about the kids and Maria, he's protecting his family, friends and legacy. He genuinely needs us. No one else understands the complexity of our calling. They will need to know who they are. Who better to cast a light, when that day comes?" said Ben.

"I know," said Zane.

"We're not madmen or women. We're the future," he closed.

"I need a doctor," screamed Maria. The nurses rushed

to the scene and administered an epidural. Almost instantly, she became overwhelmed and light-headed with anticipation. She struggled to find the will to push. She could sense that her increased dilation made Icarus's body breakdown. "Stay with me, Icarus! I'm not ready," cried Maria.

"I have to go, darling. This is it," he whispered.

Sensing his fragility, the nurses rested his body upon a gurney and rushed him from the room and placed him into another. His muscles decomposed, his air supply dwindled and his spirit crawled from his fading body. While they were awaiting care, he vanished. For a moment, his spirit was able to witness the birth from above. Resting upon his shoulder, the black bird whistled a beautiful song into his ear. With a final push, his children were born and made a joyful cry. In that moment, Icarus ceased consciousness and entered The Beyond. His passing spirit would illuminate future generations and the physical realm. All medical records of the incident were scrubbed. Reason suggested Icarus had vacated the premises and was alive, but Maria knew better. Her babies were cleaned and presented and their eyes glowed like burning stars. They were beautiful. Ben and Zane were invited in to celebrate.

"Look at their indigo frames. You can almost see heaven inside of them," cried Ben.

"It's amazing!" proclaimed Maria.

"What will you name them?" asked Ben.

"They will be called Titan and Selene," said Maria.

"An eclipse?" asked Zane.

"Yes, the god of the sun and goddess of the moon."

"It's beautiful!"

+++

They remained in the hospital for two days, before Maria was released and able to retire her mind, body and soul into the welcoming arms of Benjamin and Zane's modest home. Maria knew the tide was rising and she'd have to call their families, but she wasn't entirely sure how to explain the gravity of her situation.

"I don't know how to do this," fumbled her mind, pulling a plush comforter toward her nervous face. She lied in a small bed, while her babies comfortably rested in a crib, perpendicular to her arms reach. Though the home was quaint, it was warm with familiarity and chaste love. It was the perfect dwelling for her new arrivals.

"Maybe you don't say a word. Let's face it, from this day forward, your life will be anything but common. Be it an eternity, you're welcome to stay as long as you'd like. You have our unyielding support. It's the least we can do for you, Icarus and humanity," offered Ben.

"I can't just remain on the run and raise these brilliant children without a father. How do I tell Icarus's parents, 'Your son was a part of The Program.' It's a spiritual revolution of sorts. Long story short, he disappeared on the scene and entered some type of nirvana called The Beyond.' They'll think what any rational human being would think, and that he lost his marbles and was nothing more than deadbeat dad."

"Maybe you can say just that," interjected Ben.

"What?" asked Maria.

"They'll just assume he went AWOL. People do crazy things when their doped up on religion and guilt. While that may not paint the prettiest portrait of their deceased son, it may be the most believable and leave them with a shred of hope — hope that he'll someday come to his senses and ring their doorbell. In their minds, he'll live on," said Ben.

"Yes, but why am I living in Ireland?"

"You were visiting old friends, fight-or-flight kicked in and you got caught up in the idea of moving — starting anew. You can say that Icarus had been looking for factory work, to support you, when nature ran its inevitable course. Be matter-of-fact about it and explain yourself in a very straightforward way," offered Ben. "But, you have time for that. For now, I don't think you need to do anything, besides hold and kiss these precious heavenly gifts. They're beautiful."

Ben reached into the crib, lifted Titan and Selene and laid them into Maria's arms. The settling tone of his voice brought her anxiety air to a still. Maria could almost hear Icarus speaking through him — soothing her doubt, refocusing her worries on the miracle and assuring her he loved her.

A dark undercurrent remained. Ben and Zane knew they'd have to tell Maria about their visit from the Cadence. With their home being targeted, it wouldn't be long before another incident presented itself. Though seemingly omniscient, the Cadence was not privy to Icarus's plans and was still scrambling for clues. If anyone had witnessed their arrival, it wouldn't take a full-scale investigation to piece together the possibilities, especially if the Cadence failed to unearth Icarus in Greece. Time was a constant antagonist, always following the breadcrumbs of their clumsy thought patterns.

+++

"Dez, this is Abas of the Greek sect. We've hunted down Icarus's family. No one seems to know where he is. We posed as officers. They seemed legitimately concerned and clueless. They asked if we had checked with a girl named Maria. Does this name ring a bell?"

"Master manipulators!" screamed Dez.

"We're currently exhuming her apartment for clues. We did find two airline ticket receipts for Dublin. There was also a picture of a pregnant girl, whom we presume is Maria, resting just beneath the refrigerator. Otherwise, the place was empty. Could it possibly be a relative or a sister of his?" asked Abas.

"Nonsense, he must have headed north to meet-up with another birther. I want you to organize a small team and follow them. Steal a car and leave tonight. You can take the ferry from Cherbourg to the Rosslare Harbour. There's a very real chance an alien hybrid has been or is going to be born. Kill the child on-site and its guardians. Send me proof when it's done – over and out!" ordered Dez.

Neco heard the channel feed and again debated a swift departure on a getaway mile. Feet like cinder blocks, his love for Ash and desire to keep pace with Dez's momentum had entrapped his heart beneath the desert floor. Stuck in a submarine of his own device, his only perspective of the outside world came via Dez's televised periscope. As his guilt mounted, from the lives he was willing to put on the cross of her love, he begrudgingly retreated from his selfish emotions. Though a smooth exit wouldn't be easy, he had amassed a database of the devil's intentions and could sense Dez's mental state was weakening.

"Do you think Icarus has partnered with Ben and Zane?" asked Neco.

"It's crystal clear, to me. We have no time to waste. Whether they're having children, or harboring them, it's time to rid the planet of The Program and their kids. I shouldn't have waited this long. With outside pressures drawing attention to the Cadence, we must strike like a cornered cobra. I have no intention of being incapacitated by the U.S. prison system. As harsh as the pit of the underworld may be, prison may be worse. It's better to reign in hell..." said Dez.

"Than to serve in heaven," said Neco. "That, and no one gets raped in purgatory."

In his mania, Dez often forgot Michelle was locked in a dank prison. She only manifested as a blip on his radar when his carnal appetite for sex reared its ugly head. Without his lustful heart and the tiny bread penance he'd offer for raping her, she'd have starved, had it not been for Neco. Though their rations were limited, Neco was diligent to save a portion of his bounty for her hollowing frame. Heading to the bathroom, he'd often slip pocket-stuffed leftovers through the tiny mail slot in her door. Her treatment and conditions were deplorable. She lived in a dank 8' x 10' cell, devoid of shadows. In some ways, Neco had an ally, though, he wasn't sure how she'd react to an offer to escape. It was a risk he'd be forced to take, as his options exhausted. She would either follow his lead or expose him, in order to regain graces with Dez and in hopes of someday reuniting with Max.

Confident he could persuade her, Neco made a move. "Ready to get out?" read a note, scribbled upon a tiny square of toilet paper, slipped in with her nightly offering. Neco made sure the message was delivered to hopeful eyes, before returning to the devil's chambers. Seeing the hope in her wide-eye, he knew he could turn back.

"Dez, we could probably benefit from Michelle's help," said Neco.

"What does the gimp have to offer? She's the reason my revolution is in jeopardy."

"I understand your concern, but no one understands this the way we do. Girls cover for each other. It's in their nature. I'm sure she didn't realize the magnitude of her decision. How could she? She helped us, greatly, before you boxed her in and duct taped her mouth. She's the reason we have sects all over the world. She's the reason Juno is dead. She may even be able to help us track down Crystal. Who knows, maybe she knows where she's heading," said Neco.

"Why do you suddenly care? You never considered this before?" asked Dez.

"I hate to see our talent crouched and naked in a barren cell. I have a soft spot for humans," said Neco.

Dez approached Neco and leered in his eyes. Hoping to find Neco's tell, his couldn't manage a read. Resigned, he turned and walked toward the keyboard and silently faced the monitors. As if distracted by incoming information, he mindlessly flipped through video streams and again turned toward Neco.

"Ash is at the gates of hell. It won't be long, now," said Dez, reaching in his pocket and fishing out a thick rusty key. With a sinister glare, he held the key before his eyes and stared through the loops of the base. "If your heart's wish is to set the whore free, be my guest. We're all prisoners, Neco," said Dez.

Catching the key, Neco turned to exit. After a few paces, he stopped. "What do you mean she's at the gates of hell?" asked Neco.

"The Cadence has secured the perimeter. They're not only in her head, but probably in her house, by now," he said, pointing to a camera feed of Ash's bedroom.

Ash paced about, brushing her hair and staring upon her plump image in a long mirror. It was the first time Neco had seen her in nearly a year. She was barefoot, pregnant, and visibly due to deliver. She was as beautiful as he remembered. "It won't be long now," Dez laughed.

A flood of emotions ran up Neco's spine. Goosebumps created a ribbed appearance on his arms, as an overwhelming dryness befell his throat. His sense of urgency had never been greater. Time had come pounding on the door of his heart. He knew he had to escape.

"Good to hear," tried Neco. Turning quickly, he walked toward Michelle's cell. His entire life rested in the delivery of the few gambled words he offered her, but the clock stopped for no one. "I have no time to explain. Follow my lead," rushed Neco, opening Michelle's cage. "Crystal and Max are safe, but we have to get out of here, before we're both killed."

"What's going on?" asked her broken soul.

"I've been keeping you alive, for a reason. Dez was intent to leave you for the rats, a long time ago," he paused, letting his revelation sink in. "You're just going to have to trust me!" Neco furthered, unclasping her wrist from an iron bedpost.

CHAPTER 34
ASHES OF SEPTEMBER

Smiling and rubbing her round belly, Ash flirted and fawned over her new body. Even knowing they'd never meet, the thought of bearing a savior elated her. Her spirit had never been so driven by purpose. Her physical strength was amplified by superhuman vibrations. A few alarming visits from the Cadence incited her longing for a swift delivery. Nightly, she begged The Council of the Lords for entry into The Beyond, and nightly they'd forsake her request. Knowing she could no longer be his guardian angel, she prayed Neco would remain safe in the cult's lair. Counting down the days, arrangements for her child's arrival were made. She journaled her plans and whispered her hopes to the sky.

"If I die during my pregnancy, I know you'll provide a perfect life for Akiane," said Ash.

"Don't talk like that! You're healthier than I've ever seen you and you glow like the heavens on a clear night. I can practically reach for the stars in your eyes. You're beautiful. If only I could paint this moment with your brush and have it last forever," offered her father.

"Have you tried?" asked Ash.

"To give birth?" asked her father.

"No, to paint," she laughed.

"I'm just playing with you, like I used to. By the way, this came for you today. It's a gift!" Her father pulled a box from behind his back. With the rooster's third crow, it was delivered to their doorstep and packaged to be noticed. "It looks special. Don't worry, I didn't take a peak," he said.

"Thank you, Daddy!"

He turned and walked from her bedroom, to give her privacy. His slippers clopped across the old oak floor just beyond her sanctuary. As she heard him descend the cavatappi staircase, she reached for the box of mystery, carefully shook it and slowly untied the topping bow. Endless visions aroused wonderment in her childlike heart. Though it was Christmas in September, the recent threats left her wary. Paranoid of what the box contained, she slowly opened her bedroom door and gazed into the camera-monitored hallway, before returning. Her solitude was reassured. She didn't want anyone to worry about her recent visits from the Cadence — a bigger surprise awaited their grip on sanity. Taking inventory of her extravagant surroundings, Ash's fear was again unguarded.

As she opened the decorated box and pulled back the distracting layers of tissue, she came across a taped envelope. The bravado of the unidentified parcel had a sinister undertone and begged her focus. She scrutinized the package for clues, but found nothing. With a sterling letter opener, she tickled the crease, nervously removing a thin layer of tape from the envelope. She had few doubts about the origin of the package, only its intentions. Breaking the seal, a small cloud of white smoke rushed toward her startled face.

When the dust settled, she looked into the envelope and found a folded note and a match. It read, "Ashes to ashes, we all fall down!" She had never considered the possibility of death by asphyxiation, but could no longer dismiss the clan's seemingly trivial threats. Affected by the cult's terror tremors, the impenetrable walls her family had built on a marble foundation were cracking. Falling to her knees, she maternally wept for release. She couldn't imagine bringing her child into a spoiled world — a world hungover with discontent.

Dez was elated. He replayed her reaction and mobilized his minions toward an immediate strike. The crisp fall evening came quickly, as Ash continued to pace around her bedroom. She contemplated how to avoid having her and her child murdered. She considered faking her delivery, which would provide her the temporal security of hospital walls, but compromise her family's safety. The horrors that would await her return, would haunt her conscience more than facing the immediate threat. As the hour struck midnight, a bright light illuminated her grounds and the main floor. Looking down the staircase to identify the disturbance, she saw a myriad of Molotov cocktails crashing through her stained glass living room windows. Her temple was afire.

The devil danced — again!

She heard her mother and father scream. The fire engulfed the lower level instantaneously. "Try to throw the bottles out!" screamed her father. His intentions were split between returning the consuming cocktails, smothering the fire and tending to his pregnant daughter's cries. Following his voice, she quickly exited and descended the stairs, before realizing the exits were blocked. She was trapped. In the pandemonium, her father's shirt caught fire. His burning flesh filled the air and smelled of the familiar inferno she'd only narrowly escaped.

"Daddy! Daddy!" she pleaded.

"Ash," he cried. Her father was tackled to the ground by demons, while her weakened mother continued clearing an exit. She was consumed by smoke inhalation. Ash returned to her sanctuary and feverishly dialed 999. After a quick plea with an unintelligible emergency operator, she hung up the phone and awaited *time* to deliver its unraveling fate. Stress from the situation induced her. Though she could hear her father wailing, she knew she couldn't save them and her responsibility lied with The Program. Tearful, she turned her once baptizing tub into a makeshift gatch bed and feverishly blocked the tiny gap in the doorway with a rolled towel. She was conscious to leave her diary parted on the floor by the running bath. Dipping her anxious toes into the purity of forever, time stood still.

Pain rushed through her body, as her imagination turned the pool of blood into lava. Lightening ran through her veins. Her determined eyes widened, dilated by her stretched nerves. As fate danced between positive and negative outcomes, flocks of black and gray birds slammed against her bedroom window. They responded to each birth pain. Continuing to push, she reached toward the sky and disengaged the shower curtain with an instinctual grip.

The lights flickered, as her will collided with the fury of Dez's mad scene. As her body crowned, her baby effortlessly slid into the sanctifying lake. Ash's physical body slowly faded, as she entered The Beyond. With a final crash into the bathroom window, a blackbird signaled Akiane's arrival. Firefighters battled down the obstructed door to find the newborn baby submerged. With an emotional and confused proclivity, the lead fireman grabbed and shielded the infant in his yellow turnout coat, descended through the flames and quickly exiting through the absent doorway. Ash's father and mother had passed, but the baby's heart continued to beat.

The Council of the Lords rejoiced.

+++

Dez danced before the monitors, elated with his affect. Manically singing Frank Sinatra's "My Way," at the top of his hoarse lungs, he sought a celebratory bottle of champagne. The echoes of his psychosis vibrated through the underground catacombs and awakened the hounds of hell. The inferno of the underworld was stoked by his malice laughter. "We did it!" he shouted, forgetting his suspicions of Neco's intentions. "You have to see this. Ding-Dong! The witch is dead. The house didn't land on her, it consumed her."

"Michelle, listen to me," Neco paused, softly tugging her malnourished limbs. "We have to get out of here, tonight! I don't know exactly what's going on in there, but I'm terrified by the sound of it. If anything happened to her, I'll never forgive myself. She's the reason I came and the reason we have to leave."

"Who?" asked Michelle.

"It doesn't matter!"

"I trust you, Neco. Please get me out of here," she pleaded.

"You're going to have to help me distract him," explained Neco.

"Sexually?" she asked.

"He locks the tunnel and the hatch, every night. It's probably locked now. The keys to the surface are lassoed to his waistline. He neurotically grabs for them, concerned they've magically disappeared. Getting them won't be easy. Whatever just happened is a perfect distraction for us. His mind swings like a pendulum, but at least we can be sure of his mood," said Neco.

"Do we have the strength to double team him?" asked Michelle.

"He's got a black belt in Aikido and a PhD in batshit crazy. We don't need to provoke an impromptu fight club to know how it would end. We'd be dead before the first fist was fired. You can barely stand-up and I'm not a fighter. I'm a pretty lousy lover, too!"

"So, what then?" asked Michelle.

"For now, be excited. No matter what he says, smile and nod," said Neco.

"I'm a terrible liar," said Michelle.

"This isn't lying, it's acting! You can act, right?" asked Neco.

Though close to choosing his celebratory phial. The sound of Dez rattling through an old ice chest of bottles echoed through the steel beams overhead. The underground air seemed denser and more asphyxiating than usual. Beads of sweat rushed from Neco's brow, as he lassoed Michelle's arm around his tired neck. They limped to the control room and awaited their story to be written by the shaking hands of time.

"Look what the cat dragged in!" said Dez, elated.

Bouncing off the concrete walls, nerves fired from Michelle's tense body. "I am sorry. I never meant to disappoint you or keep you in the dark about Crystal's pregnancy. She was scared. She wanted to tell you," she offered.

"Shut it! Let's not ruin the moment with the bullshit you've been cherry picking for this day."

Reaching over, he slithered his arm around Neco's shoulder and guided his attention to the monitor of Ash's bedroom. It was scorched and filled with lazy flames. The dense smoke nearly eclipsed their view, but the portrait was painted.

"She's dead. Burned to crisp!" he laughed. "God love her, she tried to survive and almost succeeded, m'boy," said Dez.

"Did you actually see her die?" asked Neco, with a reserved enthusiasm.

"I didn't have to. Firefighters went into the charcoaled bathroom and exited without Ash."

"That's it?" asked Neco.

"It's almost ironic," he paused. "Don't you think?"

Neco motioned for the carafe resting on the console and fantasized about beating Dez unconscious. Shaking the fantasy, he calmly removed the bottle opener from Dez's flannel shirt pocket and tested his trust. Celebrating his lover's death for the sake of survival seemed like a travesty, but a far-off hope lingered.

Michelle followed Neco's lead, and reclaimed her familiarity with Dez by forgetting his crass acts toward her. "I want to help you find Crystal," she said, sipping on the bottle of Cairn O'Mohr. "She's scared, but I know a few bungalows and people she may have sought refuge with. Have you ventured back to the strip club? This town isn't that large. Hell, the population of New Mexico isn't that large, when you compare its size with the rest of the world. Someone has to have seen her. She's not going to allow her baby to starve to death."

"It's trivial. Scared or not, she'd have called by now," said Dez.

"If she's scared, she's not going to do anything. You can't spend the rest of your life hiding underground, refusing to trust the world. All I did was buy her time, and ended up locked in a barren cell. You nearly starved me. For what? I've been nothing but loyal to you. You can't rule the planet alone – let me help you!" pleaded Michelle.

"Why in the world would you do that? My gut tells me you'll run and never look back. You may even call the goddamned police. Where would that leave us? Where? Don't think you'll escape. You're an accessory to our crimes," said Dez.

"Nowhere. It would leave us nowhere," said Michelle.

"That's right, we'd be the children of nowhere. It doesn't have a very good ring to it, does it?"

"Actually, it would make a hell of a band name," offered Neco, trying to steer away from the tension.

"Fair point," said Dez.

Michelle sipped on her wine. Locking eyes with Dez, she refused to blink. The whites begged his trust, her irises remained stern, and her pupils shuttered, with each passing frame, downloading thousands of photographs for her memory to someday dissect. She'd either develop from negatives or be exposed by her bluff.

"Look, if I run, you'll hunt me down and kill me,"

Michelle said, beginning to pace. "If you don't find me, you'll kill someone I love — I know that much!" Uncomfortable, silence consumed the room's attention. "Dez, I know how this works and I'd never risk Max's life. I can't get too far and you know it," she insisted. She made haste, like a salesman on a month-end sit. "Please let me try!"

"Dez, she's right. She's got nothing to gain. You know her friends, her family, and her boyfriend — hell, you know her whole life's story. We have to trust someone. If anyone can get Crystal back, it's Michelle. It's that simple. There are more Programmers out there. The war has begun, yet we lie dormant, cowering below ground."

CHAPTER 35
RUN, RUN, RUN

Crystal had made up her mind and knew that she'd have to find Grayson. Radioactive dust cluttered the air surrounding her decision, but the inevitable fallout was worth her risk. Knowing she'd have to find her way east, she was anxious to access a computer and make her presence known. Her child was growing fast, and by all accounts, her stomach was smuggling a tiny planet. Only the heavens could bestow enough absolution and grace to turn her tragedy into a miracle, and withstand bearing the cross of her child's birth. As insane as her life had been, she'd either hitch a ride to the Promised Land or die trying.

"Hello lass, where are you heading?" asked a cynical and flirty pickup truck driver.

"New York. I'm heading to New York City."

"New York City!" he joked, mimicking the popular salsa commercial. "Hop in. I can get you to Texas, but you're on your own after that!"

"Thank you," she replied, awkwardly pulling herself into the rattling cab.

"I don't mean to pry, but I did see you running, no?"

he asked, turning to make eye contact with his dirty hitchhiker friend. "Is everything OK? I don't typically stop, but you seemed harmless and a tad spooked. Truth is, you never know who you'll meet on the open road. I just like to know a little bit about my runaway friends, before they kill me, steal my truck and leave me for dead."

"New York City! You're so pretty." chirped a cockatoo, resting behind a slightly parted black sheet in the backseat. "New York City! You're so pretty. New York City! You're so pretty," it continued.

Curious, Crystal looked behind the sheet and was startled by the size of the bird's monstrous and feathered frame and cocked yellow mohawk.

"Don't listen to him. He thinks he knows everything!"

"Maybe he does," she quipped, playfully brandishing a smile.

"Give him a finch and he'll talk you a mile," he punned and paused. "So, are you?"

"Yes, everything is fine! I'm pregnant and have to get home," Crystal added.

With authority, the truck driver pushed his foot on the pedal and ushered her toward the sun. His lustful intentions were cold-showered by an instinctual tug on his being. He knew the highway wasn't a safe place to let her wander and was empowered by her dependency; her security came first. They traveled the road for long hours and filled the time with much-needed laughter and revelations. Succumbing to sanity, Crystal cuddled in the comforts of traditional human values. For the first time in years, she felt alive and secure. It was as if The Lords were driving, while she nervously felt her way back to reality.

As the hours passed, time no longer held its negotiable value. She was content to spend years traveling the open road with her new trucker friend and their pet narrator. About seven hours after their chance-rendezvous, they stopped at a locals' gas-and-go diner near the Texan border. He offered her a hot cup of coffee and slice of warm apple pie, in exchange for the companionship she'd provided. She swooned for real food. With lazy legs, they hopped from the cabin and hobbled under the tin roof. His long years of paving the open road with rubber warranted the staff's pause and adoration.

"Hey there, Romeo," said a female waitress, dolled in a frilly yellow sundress and a cliché apron. Her character was hallmarked by a predictable raspy southern accent. "I see you've found yourself a lost puppy? Don't let the help see this one, ya' hear!" she garbled.

"She's just a friend, Rosey. How about two hot coffees and a slice?"

"I'd ask you if you want sugar, but I already know the answer to that question." She winked.

Though they'd grown fond, the fluorescent lights and reality of their situation renewed their awkward palates. A world of unknowns lingered between Crystal and the trucker's longing eyes.

"OK. How about I go first?" he offered. "I've lived in Texas my whole life. I'm gratefully divorced. I have two brilliant children, whom I rarely see and a stupid bird, content to remind me of just how dumb I sound when I open my mouth," said the trucker.

"I don't think you sound dumb," said Crystal.

"I appreciate that. Though, I have to say, I'm a bit more interested in your back story. I may not be the smartest guy in our modern universe, but it's not often I find a pregnant girl running up to my trailer and wanting a ride to her New York City home. I guess, I'm a bit curious, is that your residence or is it just the furthest place you can think to go?" he paused. "You don't have to..."

She debated her response, staring into her black coffee with a voided stare. "You guessed it, I'm on the run. The father of my child is a dangerous man, whom I once loved dearly. Believe it or not, this baby could change the world and that stupid white bird of yours is a little more than you give him credit for. To me, he's a symbol. He represents synchronicity," said Crystal.

"Petey?" asked the trucker.

"Yes, Petey! I don't have the time or energy to tell you the whole story, but I already trust you. My heart believes you were sent to intercept me. I do have a friend in New York City. He is writing a story that will someday change the world. It'll end religion and enlighten humanity. Have you ever heard of the Cadence of the Sun?" asked Crystal.

"I reckon, I have. They are an international terrorist organization."

"It's a cult," clarified Crystal.

"It's become a universal movement. Discontents subscribe to their nonsense. It's growing like wildfire. No one really knows where it started, or their scope, but its followers are out for blood. It has become the world's latest headline. Interviews and speculation suggest it has something to do with aliens, government testing, hybrids and a New World Order," said the trucker.

"It's a terrible lie. I am carrying their leader's child. Its delivery will change everything, and not in the way he's preaching. Do you know anyone who can get me the rest of the way? It's important that I get to New York, safely," said Crystal.

"I know a lot of people who might be willing to help, but I'm tempted to take you myself."

"Do you have a computer?" asked Crystal.

"I do. Name's, Joe."

"Crystal," she paused. "My name is Crystal. If we can lay low, for a couple of days, it'll give me time to make arrangements with my counterpart in the city. In exchange, I'll be happy to purge my very soul. Are you confident you can afford the time off work? Are you sure you want to go gallivanting about the planet with a disturbed damsel in distress?"

"Time is all I have. Besides, I could use a little excitement in my life. Do you have any family?" asked Joe.

"My father was an alcoholic and my mother died

before we met. This is her," she added, opening her locket. "I used to sit around gazing into my father's old pictures, trying to piece together her memory. It was my only means of learning how to accept myself. She was a renegade – a total badass," said Crystal.

"It doesn't sound like the apple fell too far from the tree," said Joe.

"Here's your pie!"

+++

After a long talk, they retired their check and headed to his country home. Joe comfortably resided in a predictably small cottage, just off the woods in Plainview, north of Lubbock. When day broke, Crystal awoke, dazed and confused. She was startled by her new surroundings. Reclaiming her bearings, she scrolled through her mental to-do list and whispered, 'Connect with the Programmers,' under her sour morning breath. She allowed Petey and Joe to rest, privately investigating the whereabouts of his promised computer.

Beneath scattered newspaper debris, Crystal unearthed an old Compaq monitor resting atop a messy desk. The surface was littered with ashes, cigarette butts and Budweiser labels. After toggling and toying with the sticky keys, she opened the Children of the Program website. Defragmenting her memories and backtracking through her conversation with Neco, she validated her password and entered. Within the site lied the unpalatable answers to her stillborn questions. Every black and white detail, projecting in living color. She scrolled and marveled through the remaining names and archived news blurbs.

A rush of spiritual energy connected her with the forgotten universe; a place Dez had desperately tried to blot from existence. Its coding read like a cosmic Playbill, and she was standing center stage. The more she consumed, the more her horror-filled memories haunted her conscience. Baptized by clarity, she was forced to take ownership of her malice involvement and the impact the cult had had on The Program. 'How would the world have been different if Juno or Simon lived?' she wondered and reeled. Though Dez's picture was missing, his information, name and general whereabouts were deliberately left on full display. She couldn't believe his depths.

"Good morning, sunshine!" chirped Petey.

"I see you've found my magic picture box," furthered Joe. "I hope that's all."

"Yes, I hope you don't mind. Once you've had a chance to wake-up and digest your morning cup o' *Joe*, I want you to take a look at this. I'll fill in the blanks." Crystal said with a renewed, but anxious spirit. "I need to make a phone call."

"Be my guest! But, try to keep the conversation short. Bills!" exclaimed Joe.

Pushing her way through the rickety screen door, she settled into a properly placed patio rocking chair. A cool breeze brushed her hair to the side. It offered her a heavenly calm, while her nervous fingers tap-danced atop the old portable telephone keypad. Mounting rings tested her patience, but finally submitted to her heart's flutter.

"Is this Grayson Miller?"

"Yes, of course it is. This is a private line. Who is this?"

"This may be the most important call you ever receive," said Crystal.

"Again, who is this?" asked Grayson.

"My name is Crystal Lynn Holmes. I am carrying Dez's child."

"Wait, what?" asked Grayson.

"Neco told me everything. I don't have a lot of time to get into the specifics, but I believe I may be carrying a divine fetus. The Lord's have visited my dreams. The urgency in protecting this baby is crucial to humanity," she furthered.

"It's mission critical, for all of us. Where's Neco?"

asked Grayson.

"Neco is in serious danger. I took my first opportunity, and ran. I'm currently holed up in a trucker's home in Texas. He is willing to escort me to New York City. Neco said you could help. It seems, everyone in the States is dead or unreachable, except for you," says Crystal.

"How do I..." started Grayson.

"You're just going to have to trust me. I could have never found you without the password, right?" she asked.

"Right," he paused, still shaking off the shock. Before allowing the call to go static, Grayson left her a rendezvous address. Her surprise call and candor left him with a warm rush of blood painted across his otherwise pasty face. He'd never had a female roommate, nor been forced into a paternal calling.

Aggressively trying to piece together his work stories, Grayson vigorously logged every detail of their conversation. The slithering path that The Program traveled always took precedence. The general public, awaiting their next clickbait headline, were at the mercy of his scattered focus. Plagued by deadlines, he'd never had so many unresolved questions trumped by an unattainable resolve. Ironically, his entire existence was dedicated to documenting and understanding other peoples' lives, while he deliberately ignored the vast questions lurking in his own life.

"New York City! New York City!" crowed Petey. He strutted across the eggshell covered kitchen counter, while Crystal delivered the promised eulogy of her abandoned past. From time to time, Petey repeated recognizable words to feel involved in the excitement of the conversation. He loved his new friend.

"Do you think we should bring Petey with us?" asked Crystal.

"I'd love to, but I think it's probably best if he stays. We don't know what arrangements we'll need to make or where he'll be welcome. He loves the road, but I don't want to put your host in an uncomfortable situation with his landlord and I really don't feel comfortable leaving him caged on the New York City streets. He'd hate that," said Joe.

"New York City! New York City!" he repeated.

"It sounds to me like he'd love to come with us, but, you're probably right," said Crystal.

Joe finished his week's shifts, while Crystal rested and planned her move to the Big Apple. She spent her idle time rummaging the Internet. She scavenged for every informative droplet she could find, from the hurricane that had ravaged her tragic life. Always fearing Dez was one step behind her, she tried to anticipate his moves. She religiously followed the Cadence of the Sun website for updates. The quantity of information and misinformation circulating the web, about the cult, was alarming. At times, she felt the whole world was savvy, though, most of the truth had been tainted by debunked conspiracy theories.

+++

Long hours alone had left Crystal battling a breeding temptation to find closure on the status of Michelle and Neco. She couldn't risk calling the compound, but became intent on delivering a message. One afternoon, while Joe was making deliveries, she called her old brothel. Her former manager was a simple soul, compromised by the expectations of survival, but savvy to the movements of the local townies. She knew she could trust his wherewithal to extract gossip.

"Gus, it's Crystal! I was curious if you've seen or heard from Michelle?"

"I haven't. As a matter of fact, I haven't seen anyone in a very long time. Are you ready to get back to work? I could really use a professional girl to show my amateur-hour-flowers how it's done! Things are slow," said Gus.

"No. I'm sorry, I can't."

"What in the world are you doing in Texas?"

"How did you know?"

"Caller ID."

"If you see her, let her know I'm OK!"

"Are you OK?"

Crystal knew she couldn't stay in Texas much longer. If Dez caught wind of her whereabouts, he'd find her, drag her back to the compound and have her crucifixion televised. Her peace of mind became a war zone of firing thoughts, all triggered by a cat's curiosity.

CHAPTER 36
HOMECOMING

Illuminated by the lampposts and the pride of tall buildings, the blanketing fog and orange-colored Kassel skyline arched over the still city. Rand and Isabella made modest concessions for the stork's arrival. Like the stacking snow mounds surrounding the exterior of their makeshift shelter, they knew their magic moment was closing in. With the full intention of ushering in a new lord of the underground, Isabella's body morphed. Rand stared, in awe, into the local clinic's sonogram photographs.

"Izzy it is!" whispered Rand, under his stale breath. His body interlocked with Isabella's. They rested beneath the dank archways of a brick bridge, cuddling for the other's heat. "He will rise from these streets and sit at the head of all tables. I do believe that."

"I know you do," said Isabella.

"A gay father. Who'd have thought?" Rand stopped, reflecting. "Certainly not my father."

The Cadence's focus on Rand lied dormant. Though they'd made attempts to contact his parents' house, rumors circulating about his homosexual lifestyle brought little insistence or follow-up to their doorstep. The European sects were assured that the rat infested alleys and brash elements would handle their affairs.

With grace, Rand and Isabella only had the unwelcoming streets to contend with, though it was the most indignant and humbling reality to befall their spiraling tragedy. Children, born of the city, often died, were found in dumpsters or aborted in a horrific fashion. Rand knew they needed to make uncomfortable accommodations. He had contemplated addressing the large elephant blocking his old home's doorway, but was nervous their only lifeline would be cut short. He couldn't imagine his parents allowing a child to starve on the unforgiving streets of Kassel, but stranger things had already happened.

"I think we need to try to rebuild my burned bridges. We've wrestled the elements for too long. I don't want my arrogance to stand in the way of Izzy's health. It's not fair. Perhaps, my father will be open to our heterosexual union and assume I've come to *his* senses. If their hearts beckon for reason, we may be able to dock in safe harbors — tonight! We should try," offered Rand.

"Can you?" asked Isabella.

"I don't know."

As the dawn of a new day arose, Isabella and Rand dusted themselves off, crawled from the trenches and begrudgingly soldiered home. The air was as cold as their anticipated reception. Taking a deep breath, Rand cleared his constricting throat and tapped his shaky knuckles across the old familiar wooden frame. In tandem, an arctic gust whipped the effervescent German flag. It masked Rand's humble glare, as his mother slowly answered the heavy door. Without pause, she wrapped her arms around him, and pulled him into their home. His father's heavy and methodical footsteps pounded like cannons in his chest. With each thud, his heart thumped a fearful retort. It was as if a volcano was erupting in his throat and his body was trapped under ice.

"What gives you the nerve to come back?" asked Mr. Backer. "Stand up straight when I'm talking to you!"

"Dad, we didn't know where else to go. I'm sorry if I've disappointed you with my lifestyle, but we really need you," Rand said, leering into his father's uncompromising eyes. "This is Isabella," he quickly added. Redirecting his eye contact toward his mother's softer gaze, he reached toward Isabella's stomach and risked, "This is Izzy."

"Oh my heavens!" Rand's mom gasped, hugging Isabella. She was unaffected by her slovenly appearance. The tension dissipated, as his grouchy and stalwart father turned and removed himself from the kuche. His mind was at odds with pride and the idea of offering his son forgiveness. He wanted to remain angry, but a tiny light flickered through a crack in his concrete heart. Grabbing his khaki trench coat and fedora from the coat rack, Mr. Backer returned and offered his son a beer. A tiny lake formed in Rand's eyes, as he accepted his dad's brand of absolution. They left Isabella and his mother to form a bond, quietly entering a delicate world littered with psychological landmines; a place reserved for the strongest of male souls. Their hearts' were prepared to shatter like the forgotten cobblestone streets of Kassel.

Without a word, they both walked five blocks to the local watering hole. His father held the door, as his son modestly shuffled by. He looked back at his father with respect and submission. It was in that brief moment he knew his father had torn down his towering expectations, and that his unborn child had given them both a reason to try again. They gazed into the TV set, while exchanging regrets. In just minutes, Rand knew he'd never find himself cold and wandering homeless. Sometimes, time is the architect of healing.

"I only wanted the best for you – that was all!" His lower lip rattled with honesty.

"I know, Dad."

Defusing the battlefield, a nightly headline caught

Rand's wandering eye. "A newborn child is in intensive care, tonight, after a terrible fire brought a legendary Scottish painter's mansion to its knees. The mother does not appear to have survived the blaze, though her body was never recovered," chimed a television anchor. Rand immediately recognized the woman's picture on the screen. It was as if his father's offering had lost all meaning. He was paralyzed by the revelation.

"Are you OK, kid?" asked Mr. Backer.

"Dad, do you remember my excursion to the States?" he said, rhetorically. "I met that girl, Ash, in the desert! She was an incredible artist. It's a long story, but have you had any strange guests or calls, recently, aside from that college in Greece?"

"It was you! I knew it." he laughed. "You always know when your child is around."

"This is serious. I don't want to alarm you, but I believe there is group trying to kill everyone who met in the desert. One of the members went missing and another was pregnant and murdered. I have to know, have any strange individuals questioned you about my whereabouts?" asked Rand.

"A young woman and an older man came knocking. They were looking for you, and had your picture. We told them we kicked you out and that you were taking your chances on the street. I just assumed it was a couple of those nut jobs you've been associating with. I'm sorry," said Mr. Backer.

"Did they say who they were or what they wanted?"

"They just left this card." He reached into his back pocket and unearthed it from his wallet.

"Listen to me, if they return, do not change your stance or story. We are all in grave danger!"

After a lion's share of brew and the aftermath of a never ending hiatus, the two men retreated to their home. The world somehow continued to spin, during their parted time, just as it would when their weary heads rested on down pillows. Though childbearing, the Backer's were still more comfortable with Rand and Isabella bunking in separate rooms. Rand had the best night's sleep he'd had in over a year.

"I love you, Rand," she whispered to herself.

As the weeks pressed on, Rand, Isabella and his parents grew closer. The days marked by their ignorance-inspired incompatibility had passed. The Backer home symphoniously prepared for their son's coming arrival. Though overjoyed, Rand's body battled a constant state of exhaustion. He attributed his weakness to the psychological impact of his wayward days. On All Saints' Day, the moment sprung with an unexpected splash.

"Rand, he's here! We've got to go," said Isabella.

"Mom, I need you to drive Isabella to the hospital. Dad and I will catch a cab."

Their car was too modest for their lot, but the hospital was close. Rushing from the bustling home, Isabella eased into the reclining passenger's seat. The cold snowy air whirled with cinematic tension, as Mrs. Backer attempted to start the stubborn vehicle. Sputtering a few exhaust coughs, the Volkswagen's dependable engine turned. They plowed toward the Krankenhaus.

"Son, if you want to grab a quick shower, I will call our ride. We have 15 minutes," offered Mr. Backer.

"Perfect! Thanks, Dad."

Those were the last words Rand ever spoke.

After shutting off the running shower, exhausting the walls of his home and pleading for Rand's reciprocating voice, his panicked father motored toward the hospital. He expected to find him bedside. Rushing through the lobby with flush cheeks, Mr. Backer looked up Isabella's room and bulldozed through the staff. His level of disbelief overwhelmed his ability to reason.

"Where is Rand?" asked Mrs. Backer.

"I don't know. He went to take a shower and never emerged," said Mr. Backer.

"Do you think he got scared and scampered off?" asked Mrs. Backer.

"I do. But, I thought he'd have come to his senses, by now, and would have already arrived."

Their anxiety was interrupted by the vision of a gorgeous child resting upon Isabella's chest. His piercing indigo eyes caught Mr. Backer's heart. Rand's disappearance was suddenly an afterthought. In the presence of such beauty, his excuse would fall upon deaf ears. Isabella was resign to Rand's abdication. She focused on nursing their infant and tending to the Biblical birth pains she'd endured for heaven's promise.

CHAPTER 37
THE ROAD

Polishing off five bottles of celebratory champagne, he sat ogling his tired computer screens, reading and scrolling through horrifying reports of innocent children who'd been targeted and their tread upon innocent families. For hours, Michelle and I waited, dissolving into the background. As much as I wanted to take the corkscrew and stab Dez through the forehead, prudence suggested the alcohol would run its course and do my bidding. Michelle and I had plenty of time to imagine being lost in the shadows of a post-apocalyptic world, left battling the wandering ghosts — robbed of enlightenment.

"It's time we made our move," I whispered. "If he awakes, distract him with sex."

"Easy for you to say," said Michelle.

Our deliverance rested with fate. Tension mounted as Michelle reached for the tightly fastened key ring, clasped to his waistline. The tiny hands of my watch strangled time. Dez fidgeted, but his floating mind, drowning in spirits, was consumed by a nightmare. His incoherent somniloquy was reassuring. Unhooking freedom, we tiptoed from the underground and emerged into tomorrow. We were graced.

Stars illuminated the forgotten New Mexican sky. The air was cool, crisp and welcoming. Our sanity seemed to rest just beyond the untouchable line on the horizon. Tickling my senses, I could feel the grass tufts beneath my nervous boots brushing away the pins and needles of our long sit. Gleeful words danced from my flapping tongue, stirring an audience of yipping coyotes.

The sandy floor we trampled no longer wreaked of survivalism and madness. We hitchhiked west, distancing ourselves from the vacant and suspect van. A young driver, willingly escorted us toward the Pacific. He was charting a familiar course, from Indiana, to the perverted promised land of rock stardom. Conscious of our anonymity, little revelation passed between our adrenaline pumping hearts. Surfing through the static for proof of western civilization, our lack of discourse left our driver's nerves on end.

I appeased his need to fill the dead air, by rattling off canned answers. Making a significant leap of faith, Michelle remained stewing in mounting questions. Flutters of her fear danced about the cabin. After a short nap, in an abandoned Winslow, Arizona truck stop, we arrived in Barstow, California. With sunburned forearms and glassy eyes, we emerged from the vehicle and reconnected with God and country. Our new cowboy friend stopped and filled the belly of his beast. Sitting dehydrated on the lip of the truck's bed, sipping a Coke, Michelle licked the end of a rolled joint that she had plucked from behind Dez's greasy ear. She sparked, inhaled and released a sigh of grateful confusion, before breaking her long silence.

"Where is Crystal?" she asked.

"It's a long story, but she's out to save the world, if you can believe it," I said.

"I wasn't about to die in the compound, but what are you talking about?" asked Michelle.

The gas pump clicked, before I could respond.

"We really should hit the old dusty trail," interrupted

Billy, our driver.

"I think we'll find our way home from here, Kid," I joked. "It's only another 2 hours."

"Are you sure?" he asked.

"I am. We have a lot to talk about. Here are a few dollars for your troubles."

"No problem. Thanks for the company!"

"You could have chopped us up into bits and left us in the desert. So, thank *you*," I said.

The driver laughed, tipped his Stetson and road off into a desert heat haze. I spent hours bridging the gap in Michelle's taxed mind. Though sounding as nonsensical as Dez's drivel, my explanations, like the rushing waters of a broken dam, had a cleansing virtue. Despite his influence, I was granted an unexplainable peace, knowing she was no longer a threat and I would soon corner her trust. Idling in the gas station parking lot, we ran dangerously low on the fumes of sanity. It was time to reunite with The Programmers.

+++

Screaming out curses, Dez awoke. He was drunk and disoriented. For a moment, his hungover pride refused to accept accountability for avoidable missteps. Though disillusioned, he refused to believe his key ring was no longer attached to his belt loop. He purged enough rage, to rattle the tormented souls of the underworld. For the first time in recent memory, he was alone, with no one strung-out or tied to the end of his short leash. The foregone conclusion of his erratic and poorly executed revolution forced him to the surface, intent on seeking retribution against the cult members he'd trusted most. After a final red-eyed glance into the surveillance cameras, he exited the compound, headed west and stormed the club where it once began.

"Where are they, Gus?" He beelined past the cum-stained pool tables, toward the back office.

"Where are who?" asked Gus.

Dez grabbed him by the collar and violently forced his pumpkin-shaped head into an oak desk. Blood sprung like a fountain and splattered across the office floor. With mocking remorse, Dez reached for a beverage napkin and handed it to him. "Clean yourself up!" Sex-deprived and hungry patrons ignored the ruckus, continuing to imbibe lust from a topless tap. "These people don't care about you. I did. Let's try this, again, where are Crystal and Michelle?"

"I haven't seen them. Crystal did call, asking for Michelle. I have her number jotted down."

"Give it to me." Dez reached for a piece of the greasy receipt tape tacked on a bulletin board, reading 'Crystal.' Arrogantly patting him on the damp cheek, he analyzed the merits of the scribbled message, stuffed it into his back pocket and readjusted Gus's once-slicked hairline. "That wasn't so hard, was it?" he asked, kicking the saloon doors and exiting the vagrant's club. "I'll be back," he yelled from the dusty parking lot. His cold words echoed through Gus's shaken psyche.

"Unless she's on the move, she's in Texas," Gus shouted. "She seemed a bit shocked when I asked her what she was doing there," he nervously continued, hoping to win Dez's trust and quash any future attacks.

In an attempt to triangulate Crystal's location, to a town or city, Dez returned to the bunker and launched an investigation. He rallied the Texan Cadence, while monitoring traffic anomalies to his site. Noticing a flux of hits, he mapped her coordinates with pushpins, delivered his initiatives and seethed. He was determined to slay their coming child.

+++

After our brief stay in Barstow, Michelle and I felt our way to Los Angeles, California. The smoldering hot summer air burned off our distressed energies. We bunked in a bungalow with friends. Allowing a few restless nights to pass, and our lagging souls to departmentalize the recent changes, we reconnected with The Programmers.

"We're out," I said.

"I'm so happy you're alive. I heard from Crystal. She thought you might be in trouble or dead," said Grayson, in elation. "She's coming to New York City. I can't believe you did it! This is going to be one hell of a story. If your clever strategy comes to fruition, its surrealism wreaks of fiction."

"We're not out of the woods, yet! He's going to hunt us down, like hapless dogs. His reach is international. The man has a god complex, and has amassed enough followers to warrant his megalomania. Being so close to Elisa's execution is troubling enough. I'm paranoid to even walk the streets of L.A. It's only been 48 hours, but our faces are probably plastered all over the Cadence website," I said.

"If it helps you rest, they're not," said Grayson.

CHAPTER 38
REMEMBER?

The warm sun wrapped its life-giving arms around Maria. Black birds would perch upon her tattered sill and marvel. They enjoyed watching the Crystalline children, chirping sweet songs, while digesting their early morning catch. Sipping on a coffee, she stared toward the dawn and could feel Icarus touch her face through the rays. Though the outside air was blustery, her bedroom was engulfed in warmth. She envisioned herself resting beneath heaven's tiny microscope, while it cooked off the stress of her trying circumstances. Startled, her perfect morning was interrupted by the familiar voices of her spiritual roommates and a wooden breakfast tray.

"We have reason to believe the Cadence knows you're here," said Zane in a comforting, but concerned tone. "We found their calling card in our mailbox. Your name was on it," she paused, allowing Maria to swallow the news. "I don't know how they found you, but we can't risk staying here."

"We'll need to leave tonight," added Ben.

The whites of their eyes revealed the purity of their

intentions and sincerity of their plight. Catatonic, Maria gazed around the room. She was puzzled by the complexities of her irreversible odds. She knew they'd been cautious in preparing their move, determined to avoid pitfalls. Recalling their abrupt departure, her mind cycled and backpedaled through memories. Combing through the catacombs of Icarus's last days on earth, she wept.

"How did they find us?" Maria cried. Though accusatory, her frustration warranted her theatrics. "We cleaned the house and didn't leave a trace. We scrubbed our computers, threw away our belongings, and abstained from telling our families and friends. Have they been here, before?" she asked.

"We had been contacted, but passed over. Could you have been followed?" asked Ben.

"There must be another way they found me so quickly," said Maria.

"It's inconsequential. We have to leave, tonight," said Zane.

Maria sat up in her bed and brushed the whispers of madness from of her tangled black hair. Ben and Zane gave her the privacy she needed. Without a moment of debate, motherly instincts mobilized her from the comforts of fluffy sheets. Her swollen feet crushed the splintered floor, as she charged the shower. The water temperature seethed and the pipes squealed. Prepared to be baptized by the coming fire, she rinsed away her insecurities with scalding water. It beat against her back like the whips of the underworld. Her teeth gleamed, with a crazed and refreshed ferocity. She knew it was kill or be killed. She was intent to emerge a superhero.

After peeling off the dead skin and emerging from the glass enclosed cocoon, her first foot dramatically crossed the shower threshold and touched the cottage floor. She could hear the trumpets sound in her mind. She reached for her cape, dried off and proceeded to comfort her screaming infants in the bedroom. "They're not going to take you!" she said, leaning over the crib. The babies were comforted by her presence, but continued to wail. After caking on Zane's black eyeliner, she grabbed the children from the crib and entered the living room where Ben and Zane waited. They were debating exit strategy, unaware of her entrance.

"We shouldn't wait, we should go, now," whispered Ben.

Slowly cocking their heads they were amazed by the appearance of a living Santa Muerte. Out of respect, they both rose to address her and lassoed her with arms. They couldn't help but laugh at her metamorphosis, nor believe that a splash of holy water could magnify her beauty, and empower her to scatter the cobwebs of mental debris like ants.

"Do you have any weapons? There are going to be a lot of them," said Maria.

"There's a revolver in the top drawer of the bedroom dresser! It's loaded, be careful," said Ben.

"How do you know there will be a lot of them?" echoed Zane, from her bedroom.

"Icarus was given a vision. In the dream, the children were slaughtered by mob rule," said Maria.

"Jesus," said Zane.

"No, not even he could save us!" exclaimed Maria.

"If it *was* a vision, is it predetermined or can we alter the outcome?" asked Zane.

"I have no idea, but we're going to die trying. You have nothing to lose — I have everything," said Maria.

Demanding full attention, the phone rang, stifling the room's adrenaline-induced moment. Frozen by the possibility of who might await on the other line, they stalled to answer. As a second ring rattled their bones, Maria lowered the babies into the crib and reached for the nearby cord. On bended knee, she pulled the device from its wall mount and held it to her quivering earlobe. She already knew.

"I see you're awake, Maria. I presume you know who

this is?" asked a male voice.

Shaking and crying for The Council's mercy, Maria rolled over and pushed herself into the corner of the wall. Her new-found strength was quickly exhumed by the reality of their situation. Faint noises were returned through the receiver. Her words were replaced by heavy breathing, wheezing and gags.

"We've been watching! If you leave the home, you're dead." The disguised voice cut the line.

"What did they say?" asked Ben.

"They said, 'If we leave, we're dead,'" cried Maria.

Ben somberly seated himself at a nearby table and Zane knelt, comforting Maria. No one uttered a word. Blank stares did the talking. Hoping to part the clouds of the coming storm, their fogging minds were desperate for a bright idea. Flashes of terror paralyzed them. External noises faded to the furthest parts of their conscious minds. The clock's movement was amplified by the silence. They were trapped like rats, mere feet from the doorway.

"It was a receipt," offered Maria. "There were airline receipts in the apartment trashcan. That's how they knew I was here. When your phone rang, time stood still. Every moment of our last days in Greece became vivid. I remembered crumbling the papers and tossing them into the wastebasket. I didn't actually think they'd come and route through our trash. Shortsighted, I know."

"Don't blame yourself, Maria! They were following us, too," said Zane.

A rapt at the door disrupted their sentimental dialog.

"Nobody move," said Ben, prepping the firearm. "Be as still as church mice." He slowly reached for the door. The phone rang. In an anxious fury, he answered. "What do you want from us, you son of a bitch," he fired. His voice was hoarse and hand perspired, while settling the metal doorknob. "We've got infant children in here."

"You're not going to shoot the mailman, are you?" said the sinister voice.

Peering through the tiny peephole, Benjamin watched a jovial mailman skipping from the archway. Cautiously opening the door, he surveyed the premises, and noticed a package resting inches from his combat boots. He nudged the box into the panicked room and quickly locked the door.

"What does it say?" ask Zane.

"It doesn't say anything," said Ben.

"Please, be careful," said Maria.

Fearful of what lurked within, Ben left the ominous package at rest, while the tired sun set. With the long day slowly passing, Ben, Zane and Maria knew their eyes would soon shutter, and feared what evils awaited in the still of the night. Maria distracted her mind with maternal responsibilities, while Ben and Zane debated their options.

"Say we open the door and make a go at it — do you really believe they'll ambush us and leave us murdered in the streets?" asked Zane. "The sun hasn't completely given up on us. We may still...."

"That's exactly what they'll do," interrupted Maria. "Icarus dreamed this day would come. It's not the glowing eyes of a few bloodthirsty wolves out there, it's an actual gang. If we leave, they'll pounce and tear us to shreds. I'm not sure what's stopping them from breaking down the door. As unpleasant as it sounds, we don't really have any options. I'd rather force them to come to us. We have a revolver, and a better chance at trapping them in the doorway than scurrying into the wide open. They could be on the rooftops, in cars — you name it. If we scatter, we're dead."

"If we stay, we die!" proclaimed Zane.

"Right now, we have walls. It's better than being plucked off by a hot shot on the roof," said Maria.

Church bells clanked as the clock struck midnight. In the distance, they heard a chanting crowd approach. Startled, Maria had drifted. She knew what was coming. Their words were unintelligible, but their bravado was convicted, like the marching cadence of an army. A cracked window allowed a rush of cool air to whistle through the room. Sending shivers up Ben's spine, he clinched the barrel of his gun. Zane ran into the candlelit kitchen, scrambled through the silverware drawer and stockpiled knives. As the crowd neared, its chants cut through the hollow walls and their diction became clear.

"There's nothing new under the sun! You've got to hold on to your guns," barked the gang.

The town wanted their world to remain unaffected by the conspiracy they'd been sold. It was as if the entire provincial police unit had turned a blind eye. The civilian heroes had turned into villains. Even the kindest of spirits were hypnotized by Cadence of the Sun propaganda. They behaved like zombies; slaves to the Cadence's psychological prison. The depths of the trenches, carved by fear, were dug with the hands of groupthink and distorted by malleable reason.

"We're trapped! It's over." Maria cried.

"Why did you come, if you knew this would happen?" asked Zane, scared and assuming.

"Icarus didn't remember until we arrived. Interpreting The Council's dreams isn't an exact science — you should know! He warned me. We didn't realize we'd left a trail of breadcrumbs, leading directly to your doorstep. He was trying to protect us all – his family, friends and children. It wasn't until this morning, when you brought me breakfast, that I began to piece the puzzle together," said Maria, resigned. "I'm sorry!"

The babies cried, awoken by a thunderous pounding on the front door; their innocent mouths pleaded for calm. The chaos only intensified with the shattering of kitchen windows. A flurry of demonic paws clawed upon the exterior walls and the door handle rattled and creaked like the bits and hooves of the doomsday horseman. "You forgot to open your package," said a megaphoned voice. "Go ahead, enlighten us all!"

Benjamin picked-up the box and shook it.

"Just open it, for God's sake!" said Zane.

Picking up a sharp kitchen knife and conscious to keep a distance from its unknown contents, Benjamin stabbed the box. As he did, an odorless and noxious gas poured from the package, placing Maria, Zane, Ben and the babies under a spell. One by one, they fell like dominoes. A trio of masked men, dressed in black and tan trench coats, stormed the home and yanked the innocent children from their cribs. Maria, Zane and Benjamin were quickly silenced by single execution-style shots to the back of the head. The cottage was scorched. Just as prophesied, the babies were sacrificed. The words 'No Freedom' were carved into their tiny brows and the incident was documented. Their bodies were later tossed into the inferno. The photographs were forwarded to Dez; a new prize to hang in his museum of hate.

"Afire!" read a local news headline.

The town never spoke of its horrible crimes.

CHAPTER 39
THE TRUTH

Smoking a Kretek clove cigarette and swinging a Yankee's baseball bat, Grayson paced about his Brooklyn apartment — pondering. He wore a cliché straw writer's fedora. It was adorned with a black raven's feather. He was intent on flaunting his hipster credibility. His stained white t-shirt and blue jeans only added to the innocence resting comfortably inside the physique of a starving artist. He was constantly torn between his novel and his work.

"Deadlines, headlines, schmedlines..." he muttered, drifting in and out of consciousness.

Thrilled to accept its revolving door of human kindling, the dark underbelly of the Hallway of Sorrows flexed its living lungs and exhaled a horrid stench. Benjamin, Zane, Simon, Juno, Elisa and Magnus longed for the day The Program would reset and they'd return to the Earth's bountiful soil. They were the lucky ones. Knowing their day of judgment awaited, the damned could only pray they'd be chosen by The Lottery of Souls and spared a gruesome verdict. Icarus, Rand and Ash were far from the trappings of the underworld, leaving the writer, musician and murderer to write the final chapters of Grayson's never-ending story.

The air wreaked of sulfur, as tears gushed like a waterfall from dehydrated bodies. Night after night, the red and white birds interrupted Grayson's slumber. He'd awake, compelled to scribe out his visions. In his dreamscapes, he would communicate with his fellow Programmers and dictate their experiences. He would ingest sleeping agents to assure no stone was left unturned. Intent to flesh out their final entries, The Programmers were able to elucidate the minutia and lost dialogs. His only conciliation in seeing their tragic state was knowing that the Crystalline were sent to provide enlightenment. He hoped the living would someday learn and be spared a similar fate.

Starving for genuine rest, Grayson's work and diary kept him in a constant state of flux. By day, The Program's story continued to unfold. In the doldrums of night, it masqueraded about his subconscious. By morning, it had spiked his early morning cup o' coffee with anxiety. He kept his toiled-over book on a drive, locked in a safe beneath his kitchen floorboards. It was his dream to have it unearthed in his final days, or after his passing. He wasn't prepared to risk his journalistic credibility or willing to face pretentious scorn, over a tale that would easily offend the sensibilities of a sane man. Only a few blessed souls were ever made savvy to its existence.

The website had taken a backseat. With so many dead, he feared the only beneficiaries of its existence would use it against him. He knew it wouldn't be long before Dez's girlfriend would offer him a welcome distraction from his satirical New York City solitude and his writing. The gray bird had warned him of her arrival, but he was blinded by the merit of his calling. The truth was God's work.

Grayson made modest concessions for her arrival. Knowing her piece in the puzzle could save humanity, he accepted that her life and safety was more valuable than his book or his own. Patience forced him to wait and see where the jagged shards of reality fell. Exhausted by a long night of journalism, dreaming and cleaning, his tunneling hands and taxed mind continued to force his sanity to spiral out. The immediacy of his workload thwarted his countless attempts at a fully-rested reboot. If his heart skipped a beat, he knew he'd stop. Continuing to fade and lacking the wherewithal to interview another witness for his cover story, he was gratefully interrupted by the sound of a panicked mother.

"Grayson, I have made a huge mistake," said Crystal.

"Crystal? Please tell me you didn't call Dez! I know how these female riddles go," said Grayson.

"No, nothing like that. I called the strip club where I used to work. I was looking for a good friend of mine. My current phone number showed up on their ID. I may have compromised my whereabouts. We can't stay in Texas, any longer." She paused, awaiting rejection. "We are going to have to leave — now," said Crystal.

"Then get on the road. What are you waiting for?" asked Grayson.

"I'm sorry to spring this on you, but he has cult followers on every street corner," said Crystal.

"I'm tragically aware," said Grayson.

Grayson parted with any hope of his former life returning to a static calm. Crystal's fear trumped his focus. Protecting a child, likely to arrive and soil his suede living room couch, wasn't a hand he expected to be dealt. With only Neco to shoulder him, pawning off his ill-fated paternal role was no longer a romantic option. A tiny part of him welcomed the sense of purpose a selfless life would provide. He often gazed out his bay window and watched the zombified men and women being consumed by the city's pace, distracted by the complexities of societal desire and blinded from what The Council wanted for their lives. He knew these drones were already in the Hallway of Sorrows, but related to their appetite for distraction. It was the same ignorance he secretly wished to reclaim. As much as he sought the truth in a good story and depended on it for survival, he understood irreversible nature of knowing too much.

"The real sorrow lived in the ironic truth that our greatest gift was being born into ignorance," he typed. Smoke rose from behind his computer monitor. A singed index finger reminded him he'd forgotten to ash, and he might just be human after all. His mind stumbled over the juxtaposition of his calling and his recent epiphany about bliss. With his own pen, he realized he was taking responsibility for a future world's misery. It would be the curse of his unpublished memoirs.

With each somber keystroke, he typed, "I often wonder if these words will do more harm than..." he paused. His night had been spent writing an editorial piece on 'The Dangers of Leaking vs. Protecting Classified Information in a Digital Age.' Still toggling between his headline story and the Children of the Program book, he couldn't bring himself to type the final word of either. He surmised, immediate access to information can endanger the very freedoms a powerful country is sworn to uphold. The final word, hidden in plain sight, left the finality of his sentences lingering in quixotic debate. "Good was created by its beneficiary," he mumbled under his breath.

A peaceful wind blew through his aging pearly white curtains. Just beyond the window, he saw a dove perched on the reaching limbs. With the branches tickling of window screens, it was clear that the tree insisted on catching Grayson's attention. The bird sang a beautiful song, and lured him back into the dream he tirelessly fought.

"Grayson, Grayson, Grayson," called crazed voices.

The gray bird guided him back through the Hallway of Sorrows. His eyes welled. His friends' bodies gasped for the moisture his tears could provide their parched tongues. He informed them of The Program's status, his desperation, and asked for their guidance.

"Tell Neco, the world needs a hero! It needs to *believe*

in the impossible," said Simon.

"You've written our story. Remind the world of how powerful love can be," begged Juno.

His eyes flooded with emotions and memories. He had scribed their obituaries and taken detailed accounts, but never stopped to feel the longing of their hearts. In those moments, he relived the horrors of their final days. Being a journalist had taught him to disconnect himself from the words and to remain unbiased and unaffected. He realized the same methodology had left its footprint in his novel and that he needed to tell the whole story.

"Do not allow your mind to control your heart," screamed Magnus, longing for absolution.

"Nothing is certain. Free will is The Council's greatest gift and man's jagged little pill to swallow," cried Elisa.

Startled, Grayson awoke and looked at the clock. It was the witching hour. He lifted his fatigued forehead from the desk and realized he'd forgotten to finish his headline story for the New York Times. Heating a pot of burnt coffee, he sat before his computer screen, and took inventory of his lost time. He was surprised to find that all but one word of his account had been typed. With convicted hands and a chilled spine, he scrolled down and typed...

"Good."

CHAPTER 40
EAST

Joe's truck rattled the gravel. Camouflaged by the shadows of tall trees, he pulled into his winding driveway and prepared to nest. The whites of his eyes were bloodshot from the long trucking relays, but his tired heart was rejuvenated to find Crystal staring out of his paltry kitchen window. He longed for the day he'd have a stable woman to greet him; a girl he could call his own and would long for *his* return. Pushing the rickety screen door to the side, he teased the brass door knob. He was met halfway with her turn. He slunk across the threshold, too tired to smile. An exuberant Petey battled for a theater view of his best friend. As if knotted by the bonds of marriage, Crystal and Joe embraced. Forgetting the brevity of their odd relationship, he briefly paused to digest her threatened reality. He was reassured by the arsenal of fire power, lying dormant in his shed. His instincts longed to protect his woman, but therein lied his unconquerable obstacle. They were friends.

Crystal was anxious to reveal her news, but knew it was best to not interfere with the rhythm of his cycle. As if scripted, he would secure his tattered leather jacket on the coat rack, dismount from his compensating boots and sneer into the bathroom mirror, before addressing the household. He breezed past her and ruffled Petey's arching white feathers. Petey's eyes widened and his beak remained half-cocked, enjoying a healthy dosage of love and affection. Interrupting the calm, the stove let out an exasperated whistle. It was Crystal's cue to clue him in. Preparing a fresh pot of tea seemed like a soothing antidote for her folly and would serve its purpose in the coming hours.

"We have to leave, tonight!" Crystal insisted, pouring Joe the first cup.

"I'm not done with my shifts," he said, sipping, attempting modest eye contact.

"I made a mistake. We may be hunted, if we stay," she paused.

"We are hours from where I picked you up. What kind of timetable are we talking?"

"It depends. We may have hours, days or weeks. It's not worth our lives to find out."

"I..."

Pulling a chair for him, she controlled the cadence of their conversation with her deliberately submissive gestures, before revealing her missteps. Though his heavy eyes radiated like a nuclear meltdown, his commitment to her survival remained paramount and his lofty prayers for female companionship had been answered. He wasn't prepared to leave her side, despite the audacity of her claims. He owed God his gratitude.

"We can bring Petey," she offered.

"Like I said, it's best he stays," insisted Joe.

After a long hot shower and a home cooked meal, they loaded the diesel. Restless, Crystal fidgeted through his cluttered glove box, unearthing maps, condoms and pornographic magazines. It was of no consequence. He knew the way. The road was his veins and his body was the trampled ground beneath. Slowly, he turned the key of hope. Once the tractor engine sounded and the wheels began to spin, her obsessive fear diminished — eased by the trailing headlights disappearing from the rear view mirror. Relieved, they laughed and played road games, hoping to forget about the 23 hour drive ahead of them. Crystal wondered if the road was her safest bet. There was an undeniable freedom in never settling. It reminded her of the Cadence of the Sun — without the abuse.

"Why did you choose the road?" asked Crystal.

"When you don't have a home, the road chooses you," Joe offered, like a wise old cowboy.

"Sometimes, I wonder if there's hope for people lost without a trace. Maybe the vagabonds are happier staying off the radar, foraging from the land or simply crash landing their martyrdom into sky-scraping buildings. How else do you get God's attention?" Crystal paused, reflecting on her self-destructive club days. "We're like fallen angels. We're born to lose."

"People have all kinds of ways of dealing with their pain. Some self-medicate, others isolate themselves and others, knowingly or not, try to understand it, by hurting a world they feel has rejected them. You've embodied pain. Maybe it's time for someone to deal with you," Joe offered, pleading his case for love.

She liked the sound of his candor. No one had ever put her first. At times, the resurrection of her lost innocence would remind her of her stillborn youth. With his kind words, their joyful hearts harmoniously pulsed in tandem. As if heaven was listening, stars showered before the windshield. They danced in the iris of her eyes, as she tallied her wishes. Though thick lines rested upon her perplexed brow, her heavy blue eyes were calmed by his selfless words. His presence allowed her to rest and forget the mission. Her conscience, honeycombed by guilt, would someday have to learn how to swallow her sins and build a new life in New York City. After hours on the road, battling harsh elements, they stopped in Knoxville, Tennessee and sought refuge in an inconspicuous hotel.

"Grayson, we'll be there tomorrow," said Crystal, calling from a parking lot payphone.

"I knew it wouldn't be long. I will leave a key under my door mat. You're welcome to come in and make yourself at home. I apologize for my stark conditions. If you knew the prices out here, you'd understand that a modest living in New York is as close to godliness as you'll ever know. There *is* food!" Grayson said.

"Seriously, I can't thank you enough! Have you heard from Neco?" asked Crystal.

"Yes! They escaped," said Grayson.

"They?" asked Crystal.

"Yes, he's with a girl named Michelle. They're staying with a few of his friends in Los Angeles. I think he's trying to figure out their next move and how they can help us. Keep me looped, if anything changes. I'm so happy to hear you're safe and near. One more thing, don't let the Big Apple take a bite out of *you*! It's bigger than you think," offered Grayson.

"I think you've dealt with enough crazy people! New York should feel like home," joked Joe, overhearing their conversation.

After a long night's rest in queen beds, they awoke and forced down stale complimentary donuts with burned hotel coffee. By instinct, they fiddled through the brochures and stalled. The time had come. It was their last day on the road and wreaked of a long-lived farewell. Joe knew he couldn't live holed-up with Grayson, forever, without outstaying his welcome and losing his job. His heart sank to the bottom of his aggravated stomach. Battling carbohydrates, his mood dropped. He welled up and forced back the tears of another heavenly tease.

For the first time in years, he'd found someone to live for. It was gut wrenching. Without compromising his or her whereabouts, Joe knew he couldn't track or contact her and feared his sacrifice may leave him mopping up the devils from her past. He prayed for a safe return to Petey and for

God to someday send him another pregnant girl — a lass that would tell him the most unbelievable story ever told. It was a gamble he was willing to take, over and over again.

+++

Dez was poised to attack. His night terrors persisted, while his ability to harness his own twisted reasoning began to dwindle. Heightened brainwaves cooked off his sanity, as the lurking truth forced him to come to terms with the weight of Crystal's pregnancy. No longer could he hide in the shadows of doubt and no more could he wrestle with the notion of her eventual return.

"Max, I'm packing my guns and glory and heading to Texas. We've unearthed Crystal. I'll forward you the directions. It's mission critical that we find her. I need you to mobilize a small team and meet me there. Do not make a move until I arrive!" said Dez, with a hiss.

"What's the plan?" asked Max

"To kill the world's salvation!" Dez proclaimed, cryptically.

"I'll be on my way," said Max.

It was a brief conversation, but the orders were given.

CHAPTER 41
11:11

Her body, like mangled steel, struggled to pull itself from magnetic hospital sheets. The candy stripers would sympathetically visit, but knew the strain of her best friend's disappearance was a solace they'd never articulate. The drip of morphine soothed her torn body and teased her mind into a dreamlike submission. Weaning herself from the soothing medication meant injecting the reality of Rand's trip to The Beyond. Though she'd been given a backstage pass to his calling, she was suddenly forced to believe in miracles.

Begrudging and bewildered, she unlocked the clasps of her travel luggage, and prepared to take a trip into the unknown. The sound of her baby's cries sobered her from the lingering effects of the drugs and reminded her of her new child's importance to the world. Rand's parents did their best to encourage Isabella, but were torn between the birth of their grandchild and the loss of their own. Something in the blistering air assured the Backers that Rand was never coming home.

As mysterious as his trip to Arizona seemed, Mr.

Backer gave up on understanding the nature of his offspring. Witnessing his son's dramatic personality shift only reinforced what he felt about Rand's ramblings in the bar – his son had lost it. Mr. Backer wasn't psychologically equipped to validate the idea of Nephilim-inspired children. It mocked structure and sanity. Struggling to cope, a rush of guilt befell Isabella's falling face, as she stared in the bathroom mirror. Losing focus, she recalled the inexcusable nights of debauchery that lead to the conception of her first born. She recalled performing filthy sex acts on warehouse floors, orgies with Rand and common strangers and sharing heroin needles with cold and exploitative drug dealers. Returning to the same streets of chaos, where this new life had crawled, seemed equally as irresponsible as accepting a submissive role in her sexually abusive household. She owed the heavens a queen's penance.

"Sweetheart," interrupted Mrs. Backer. "Are you ready?" She pulled a convenience wheelchair into the hospital bathroom doorway and awaited her to snap from her stubborn gaze. A mother's instinct warned Mrs. Backer that it was best to leave her to tend her feelings.

"Yes. Just a minute," offered Isabella, attempting to avoid her lingering pause.

"It's OK, my dear," said Mrs. Backer. Carrying the weight of the world was more than her fragile bones could handle. Rand was her first and only child. She always sensed there was something special about his arrival, but wouldn't dare articulate it, for fear Mr. Backer would have her committed. She could almost hear Rand's story, buried deep within Isabella's heart and longed to know it.

Turning to look at the clock, Isabella recalled the numerology of angels. It was 11:11 am. It begged her peace. Comforted by superstition, she gathered her senses and descended into the wheelchair.

Mrs. Backer softly encouraged her through the bustling lobby area. Mr. Backer, adjusting an old war cap, led the charge. Approaching the automatic doors, they noticed a small group of young adult women, dressed in black, holding picket signs that read, 'Stop the birther,' and 'Alien Fetus!' Their angry rhetoric intensified Isabella's anxiety. Mr. Backer bulldozed through the war zone. Though Rand's threat to the Cadence of the Sun initiative was benign, the German sect never ceased observing the Backers and spreading their propaganda. Dez would have them killed for missing a childbirth. Scared by the protesters, Isabella wondered if the streets were her safe house.

When they arrived at the Backer house and settled, Isabella entered Rand's room and picked up an old gold framed picture. She pawed the outline of his face. A longing tear crept from her tired eyes. Though their child found a natural peace in the Backer's home, the chill of unanswered questions intensified her fury. Lying on Rand's bed, she prayed, before slipping under a spell of exhaustion.

Dreaming, she watched golden beings being sucked into a vacuum of brilliant light. Like the walls of a high school planetarium, they illuminated the otherwise non-existent universe around her. Stepping back, she could see the living constellations; everything known and unknown was defined by the light.

"I am with you, always and forever. I am in you, as you are in me," proclaimed Rand.

"Where are you?" asked Isabella.

"Take this locket and know!" said Rand.

Startled, she awoke to the cries of their baby. She noticed what felt like two hands softly cupping her throat. In a fog, she reached up to find a tiny sapphire choker necklace had been perfectly set around her neck. She knew it was of Rand. Before addressing her child, she wailed in joyful harmony. Excited by his presence, she instinctively threw open the blinds and looked toward the clear skyline.

"I love you," she motioned with her mouth.

Forming a heart, she connected the stars, before

running to grab their child. The baby instantly stopped crying. Rand's spirit radiated from the welcoming heavens. The fluorescent street lamps, blended with the blackest of nights, produced a radiant purple glow. It mimicked the hue pouring from their baby's indigo eyes.

"Love is love reflecting," Isabella thought. "Those were always Rand's favorite words."

As the weeks passed, it became frightfully clear that something was wrong with their child. Often by instinct, Isabella would awake and fear that Izzy had stopped breathing. His cheeks were always warm and flush. Cognizant of her arrival, the infant would gasp a telling cry. She always feared the worst, but was often hushed by the consolation of Mrs. Backer's experience.

"It'll pass," Mrs. Backer insisted. "It's just learning how to live on its own."

One night, the clock struck 3:00 am – the witching hour. Isabella gasped, shaken by a terrible nightmare. Thumbing through the dark hallways of the Backer house, and running toward the calling crib, she paused, listening for her newborn's living tells. Pulling Izzy from his slumber, she feverishly patted him on his soft back. She couldn't wake him, nor hear the tiny air escaping his perpetually stuffed nose. She panicked.

"Come on, come on!" Isabella quietly cried. Her baby's body felt cold and clammy, but she was convinced her mind was playing a virgin mother's trick upon her. She carefully laid him on the bed and grabbed a warm rag. When she returned, she bathed his skin and tried to open his clinched eyes, but they wouldn't budge. Rain began streaming down her cheeks, as she lifted the child's heart to her ear. It wasn't beating.

The lights flickered, reminding her of Izzy's cosmic relevance. Grabbing her sapphire stone necklace, she feverishly prayed to his absentee father. The reality of the situation broke her respectful silence. With a thunderous scream, she awoke the Backer's. She could feel a massively dark energy clouding the cooling room.

Mrs. Backer and Mr. Backer cautiously entered the nursery. Adjusting their robes and spectacles, they tried to make sense of their uncomfortable surroundings. "What is it, what is it?" screamed Mrs. Backer.

Pushing her aside, Isabella grabbed the phone and dialed an emergency unit. Hearing the click of an operator's connection, she spoke without question. "My child has stopped breathing. Please send someone, immediately."

It was no use. Izzy was gone, long before they arrived.

CHAPTER 42
THE HUNT

Into the void of night, the devil would roam — *again*! Dez's overused van sputtered to find a reason, just as his heart played tug-of-war with his mind. His grip was slipping. He coped by fueling his weakened ego with convenient store heists and mainlined shots of heroin. Losing his stronghold over the Cadence of the Sun made him detest mankind. He was determined to punish humanity for his shortcomings. With each passing mile, his energy weakened. The Council agitated his rest with visions of how things could have been. Rummaging through his darkest days, a moment of clarity showed him the canyon of unbridgeable guilt he'd dug. Being betrayed by the ones he trusted most was the only justification he needed for swiftly annihilating everything and everyone in his vicinity.

"I'm going off the rails on a crazy train," he barked, like a crazed madman.

Staring down the sonic highway, metal music blared through his quivering rubber speakers. Dodging cars with hesitant swerves, he tempted fate. His blurred vision was triple distilled with single malt scotch whiskey. His sanity obscured. He knew the Cadence still had the power to put him in the front seat of world domination, but their fire needed to be stoked. At times, he saw the unguarded desert cliffs as a misfired synapse between him and a Program reset. Haunted, his memories of the underworld sobered his crippled thinking — neither jail nor the afterlife were options worth entertaining. He needed to be the last man standing.

Dez spent hours contemplating his tragic final days with Crystal. Whether it was love or food poisoning, unacknowledged feelings erupted from his stomach like a volcano and manifested upon his sweaty brow. Though thoughts of beating his child from her stomach delighted his cry for retribution, somewhere, lurking deep within his twisted cavity, just below his ribcage, lived a forgotten soul. Grinding his teeth, his hard fought feelings were proof he still loved her. After hours on the highway, sickness brought his vengeful journey to a hurried pause. Pounding headaches and nausea won the hormonal grudge match that had plagued his drive with dizziness and uncomfortable tears. Lying, with his lazy eyes fixed upon a dirty area rug, he succumbed. Though alcohol, brownstone or a flu virus were all possible culprits, his instincts sensed his misery was coming from something *beyond* his control.

His derailment was Joe and Crystal's lifeline.

+++

After two days of slumber, he awoke, like a vagrant. He was delirious. Shoving aside the old rags he had rested upon, he crawled into the driver's seat, and finished the last leg of his trek to Joe's Texan home. The tired engine struggled, as a weakened battery sparked its final charge. It seemed poetic. He pulled from a truck station and adjusted his mirror. The sands of time were slipping through his calloused hands.

"Max, I'm here," said Dez.

"We're here, too. We arrived, yesterday. We're in a hotel – just a few miles up the road!"

"Page me at dusk! I'll survey the scene. I don't want to risk her slipping by our radar."

Dez pulled up to the mailbox at the end of Joe's long driveway and stared toward the empty lot. The house was dark. It agitated the boiling pit in his stomach. He knew he'd missed her. His heart, trampled under foot, longed to see her silhouette glide by the soft-lit cream curtains. Her spirit and perfume still seemed to linger in the dense air. The swaying trees above reminded him that life moves on, even when the mind is stuck in a moment. He slowly drove into the night and plotted his entrance.

A few hours later, Max and his clan arrived and waited. Dez returned. With their headlights dimmed and their engines cut, they drifted toward the driveway. The lot remained vacant, but a tiny kitchen lamp penetrated their doubt and called them to action. Surrounding the house, they awaited in the foliage for Dez's orders. With ominous sways, the trees continued to run surveillance. Tiny woodland creatures scurried from the camouflaged visitors. With eye contact and militant hand gestures, they confirmed their positions. Dez's cigarette lighter signaled Max, who signaled the troops. Split, two teams swiftly penetrated the home. One team entered through the front door and the other through the back. Their guns were drawn. With wide eyes and a sigh of relief, they intersected in the living room and lowered their weapons.

"Dammit! Where is she?" Dez screamed.

In a tirade, he began throwing couch cushions and tearing framed pictures from the pine wood paneling. Like Jesus in the temple, Dez toppled the homemade coffee table, made of cinder blocks and plywood, and smashed Joe's rabbit ear television set upon the thin and rigid industrial carpet flooring. Without orders, the anxious Cadence followed suit. No one dared to make a blip on the devil's sensitive radar.

"Tear this motherfucker apart. Go through the bedrooms, the dresser drawers, the bathrooms – all of it! I don't care if you have to reach down the goddamn toilet and pull her unappreciative ass out of the sewage drain," said Dez. He flipped the switch in Joe's makeshift office, fired up the computer and restlessly awaited the monitor to offer him a dial-up gateway to a Netscape browser. After a brief investigation of the search history, his heart raced to a stop. "She's *was* here!"

"What do you want us to do?" asked Max.

"Max, my dear, check to see if the water's been turned off. Look for clues," said Dez.

They tore the house to shreds.

"Dez, I've found this guy's old work schedule," said Max, pulling it from its weak magnetic hold on Joe's old lima bean green refrigerator. "They're not here! Judging by the dates, his last day of work was a little over a week ago."

Petey rustled from behind a black sheet. Alarmed, Max slowly pulled the cover from the free standing cage and unveiled the large white parrot to a demon possessed room. Innocently, it cawed and swayed on its wooden balance beam. Anxious for its visitors' attention, it batted his snow-driven faux hawk against the tiny prison bars.

"Petey play, Petey play."

"Petey, eh?" said Dez. "Does Petey want a cracker?" he sneered, making a fist.

Max began carelessly shaking the cage, unsure of how to free the feathered creature within.

"Take it easy," said Dez. "The bird isn't why we came!"

"Do you have any ideas where she might have gone?" asked Max.

"For all we know, she's back in New Mexico. Where are you hiding, Crystal?" he muttered.

"New York City! You're so pretty," chirped Petey.

"That's it," paused Dez. "She's heading to New York City to locate Grayson."

Determined to impress Dez, Max kicked over the birdcage. Agitated, Dez pushed Max aside, reached down, picked up Petey and placed him back in the cage, stormed through the unhinged front door and beelined to his van. Confident they'd follow, Dez never looked back. Max and his lemmings never second guessed his motives or connection to the Big Apple. Dez's wishes had a way of trumping reason, while his unapproachable demeanor handled the rest. Whistling and howling through the dead night, the hapless ghosts of combat settled into their black motorcade and paused for the procession to begin.

"There's a bar called The Monkey Bar, up ahead. Meet me there! Max, you owe us all a round o' Parrot Bay shots," he shouted. "Why, you'll ask? Because you've got zero class. If it wasn't for that harmless bird, we'd have nothing — *nothing*!"

Max's arrogant gesture had fallen flat. Dez was sure to maintain his dominance in the Cadence of the Sun with curt and frequent emasculation. Though they were sworn to his ideals and masqueraded as a unified front, he controlled the dogma of each day. His humiliating tone could rattle the core of even his most . confident follower. Once housebroken, he knew his dogs of war would continue to seek the praise chorus of their master.

"First rounds on you!" repeated Dez.

"OK, first rounds on me," said Max.

"Three cheers for the bird," mocked Dez.

"To the bird," they shouted back.

+++

They arrived at an old log cabin. It was the local watering hole of a notorious biker gang. A small crowd of rough and tumblers lunged and leered by the front door. They analyzed the merits of their traveling guests. Steering away any doubt that the club would be mistaken for a Hollywood movie set, the gang's authentic posture and bikes established an unmistakable cred. Assuming ownership of his sect, Dez approached the door with an alpha's pride and was quickly set loose — they were free to guzzle with the hogs! The energy in the room reminded the Cadence of their New Mexican compound.

Fatigued, Dez's unit sucked back whiskey shots, while the jukebox spun the distorted anthems of their youth. Their empowered bravado forced the locals to take notice. It wasn't long before the club sensed the aroma of the gang's territorial pissings. The surge of a coming bar fight was quickly quashed by the taratantara of a bartender's trumpet. Once the shotgun blast simmered the commotion and scattered the hangers-on, Dez shared his crazed reasoning for wanting to tackle New York City.

The further they slipped down the rabbit hole, the more Dez revealed about his weakening condition. In the bar lights, he paled. His graying skin and absent eyes seemed to apologize for his recent tantrums and issued Crystal's last rites. His stoic presence was noticeably shaken by his candor and the frequent coughing and wheezing between his stumbling sentences. An uncomfortable reality crept up Max's spine.

The Cadence of the Sun conferred until the wee hours of a cool Texan morning. The warm new day's sun caressed the skyline and awoke them. In the skunked wake of their poor decision making, they found themselves littered across the barren Monkey Bar parking lot. With a heave and ho, Dez mustered the remnants of his physical strength, rose and made concessions for their dire need for a clear direction. From his tattered jean pants pocket, his shaky hands pulled a crinkled piece of paper with the Children of the Program website information scribbled upon it. From another pocket he pulled a tiny Budweiser beverage napkin and added Grayson's email and telephone number, before handing them over to Max.

"You're going to have to carry the torch, m'boy," revealed Dez, barely able to speak. "I've got to get back to the bunker, before this sun murders me. I've got the symptoms of some type of bacterial infection or cancer. You should have everything you need. Just find Crystal, before it's too late to carry on."

"What happens if we don't find her?" asked Max.

"It's all I'm asking. Find her, or we're finished!" he said cryptically. "Shoot her."

"Dez?"

"Do you have a problem with that?" asked Dez, mustering the strength to stare directly into Max's trembling eye sockets. "She's carrying another man's baby. She's been in touch with a lunatic who protects these birthers. Even if she's not carrying an alien — please, do it for me! It's not my child. I'm begging you." His rant exuded his last drop of his mortal energy. Speechless and slow to turn, he walked toward the truck, and charted his course back to the compound.

CHAPTER 43
LIKE A DOG

Getting back east was important. It wasn't that I was avoiding my father's voice, I just didn't know how to bridge the gap. Our series of ups and downs had been exasperated by my lack of effort. With a universe of lost time to cross, I wasn't sure if he'd even accept my collect call or recognize my hoarse voice. Fearing his rejection made the weight of picking up a Los Angeles payphone receiver a Herculean feat. With my tail firmly tucked between my awkwardly tight denim, Michelle yanked the number from my hands, dialed and forced me to reach out and touch someone. Absorbing my nerves, she paced about the Santa Monica Pier, projected confidence and awaited a verdict.

"Dad."

"Neco!"

"I need to come home." I said, relieved by the grace in his tone.

Before I could even finish my awkward stammer, he offered a swift resolve. He locked his judgment in the reserves, only to resurface as a conversational piece, a joke or reason to leverage a future disagreement. With the few dollars he had to his name, he purchased Michelle and I two one way plane tickets to Baltimore-Washington International airport. In that moment, my hopes and his prayers had been answered. His only dream was that I'd return and be ready to lay a solid foundation in Maryland. With The Council's chaos unraveling, I knew it wouldn't be long before the word 'disappointed' reared its ugly head — *again*!

"You've got a ton of mail here. Have you been paying your car insurance and eating well?" he asked.

"We've been on the run. It's a long story, but it wasn't safe to salvage the car," I said.

"You can tell me about it at the airport."

"I'm looking forward to grabbing breakfast. Like we used to."

My words were followed by an awkward silence. Fond memories had a way of tearing open forgotten scars. Though it was likely just the Pacific condensation, I could almost feel his heavy tears falling upon my earlobes. He wasn't alone — the rivers forming in my eyes mirrored his longing for absolution. Our battle to see the world through similar eyes had lasted a lifetime. It wasn't that we didn't understand each other, it was that we were called to enlighten each other. He was sent to be my *rock* and me, the *roll*.

Had the circumstances been different, we'd have probably just thrown tiny verbal daggers, never taking a moment to notice the depths of our cutting sentiments. Luckily, too much time had passed for theatrics or posturing.

"There's a rather sizable package, here, from Ash of Scotland," he said.

"Oh my God!" I squawked.

"It may give you a little incentive to board your flight," he added.

The universe had been resting in our reckless hands for too long. I couldn't wait for the day I could explain my questionable logic and open his mind to the lunacy he had watched parading around the United States – like an acid tripping revolutionary from the 60's. Soldiering on, I knew we had to save Crystal and Grayson from the eyes of madness, or I'd never see the sunrise on that far off moment.

Ash's package was the piece of closure I needed to move on. Watching her house fill with smoke on Dez's surveillance monitors had left me feeling helpless, heartbroken and frozen in time. I could only hope she'd found her way *Beyond* it.

Michelle and I panhandled our fare, caught a cab to LAX and boarded the return flight. The entire tone of the trip was somber. Everything felt surreal. Though we'd learned to depend upon each other, there was still an unconnected landscape of memories and reasons living between us. Long hours on the plane reinforced our divide. Exhaustion made the simplest of dialogs a burden.

With my head in the clouds, I used my time to stare from my window seat and scribe song lyrics across the passing blue sky. Michelle rested, allowing her soul to sort through loss, regret and flashbacks. Though I was terrified of flying, my father's protective hands seemed to guide the wings and give me peace. When we landed, he was waiting. Despite the distance, our hearts shuffled off the emotional baggage and hugged. Sensing her discomfort, he wrapped his arm around Michelle and forced her into the family.

"Thank you, Dad."

"You're my son and my blood."

"Michelle and I plan on sticking around, but we do have to visit a friend in New York – *briefly*."

He wasn't surprised. Michelle continued to absorb the culture shock, as we charted our way home. Arriving at my old house for an all-too-familiar reunion, my instincts lead my itchy fingers directly to the bedroom telephone.

"Grayson! Has Crystal arrived?" I asked.

"Not yet. I expect them any day now," said Grayson.

"They?" I asked.

"She's on the road with some hopeless romantic. He offered to bring her here."

"Michelle and I are in Baltimore. We're going to get some rest, and head out in a couple of days. Dez doesn't know we are here, but I'm sure his wolves are sniffing around the door. I don't want to jeopardize my father's safety, any more than it already is. We've all been marked. My paranoia is convinced that Cadence binoculars are following my every move. Luckily, he has no reason to believe Crystal is saddled to your back, but you'd be wise to keep a healthy awareness," I said.

"I'm used to it. This city is crawling with freaks," added Grayson, before cutting the line.

Destiny paved a way for Michelle and me to connect. Fearing my father's house was being watched, we charted off course, and explored the tattered Baltimorean landscape. By moonlight, we exchanged campfire stories and fueled our tired minds with bottomless cups of diner coffee. We found our common thread was tied to a misdirected rebellion. We both wanted to destroy the poisoned world we were forced to accept, and we both wanted to find something greater than what we'd been taught and sold. Though the darkness seemed to shield us from societal expectations, it only perverted our hopes. In a world glamorizing self-aggrandizing behavior and autonomy, we'd foolishly neglected our soul's interconnected nature. The mere thought of building a new life together — on these revelations — made the tiny hairs on the back of our necks stand tall. We were falling in love.

+++

Michelle had all but forgotten Max. The truth could no longer be suppressed and the purity of my father's home lit a candle in her blackened heart. She spent countless nights repairing what the Cadence had tried to suppress and destroy in her. Using my ears as a soundboard proved to be the best remedy for her baggage. Long talks healed her more than her childhood psychiatrist, antipsychotic medications, stripping and the drug cocktails Dez had been giving her, combined. Injecting her heart with a positive faith, gave her a mainline to the Council of the Lords.

"We really shouldn't stay for too long," said Michelle.

Bundled in hoodies, while sitting under a tree in a nearby schoolyard, the blackbirds beckoned for notice. On a wooden bench we perched, built a stable nest and weaved our lives together with trusting words and stale cigarettes. Our names were carved into the tree. A tiny promise necklace was tied into the weeping branches. It was our very own museum, constructed with the purity of simplicity. It was a living love letter – our place in time.

"Neco, darling?" asked Michelle.

"I wish we could just turn it off and forget about this crazy world!"

"We can, and it'll quickly forget about us — *all of us*!

"I suppose."

Birds chirped. An orange sheen glimmered upon the dawning street. Talking ourselves into an unexpected sleep, we awoke, energized by The Council's call and covered in a cool morning dew. Saddling up our belongings, we soldiered up to my father's house, on top of the hill, and rehearsed our swan song. Slithering across the threshold, the still home offered us a way from the psychological cage we'd built — we could leave before the first rooster crowed. Parting the bedroom curtains, my tired father released a familiar sight of disapproval, and set us free, without ever uttering a damning word.

"I just couldn't," I said.

"Say, 'Goodbye'?" Michelle asked.

"I feel like my entire life has been a burden on his soul," I continued.

"Did you ever think, he feels equally as burdensome? Let's focus on Crystal."

+++

Before watchful eyes of fall and the bustling traffic, we planned for the coming war. On highway medians, we hitchhiked for rides, and arrived to the outskirts of New York City in record time. A bus station in New Jersey gave us time to make our final preparations, to connect and beg for bus fares — it was a small price to pay for a one way trip into the belly of America's beast.

"Grayson, we're here!" I said.

"How are you feeling?" he asked.

"Learning to survive is the closest a person will ever get to knowing God," I added.

"Do you guys have a place to stay? If you want to *get to know* sardines, we can try to find room," offered Grayson.

"We're going to remain in obscurity. If you're being watched, we'll need eyes on the outside," I continued.

As I slowly retired the dingy black payphone to its saddle, a homeless Jamaican fellow caught the corner of my eye — he was no stranger to survival. Buried in an ocean of curly black dreadlocks and wiry gray facial hair, the vacant soul haplessly raised his 40 oz. brown bag of freedom, and delivered the bottomless bottle into his dry and quivering mouth. He was society's truth. A derelict. A tired man crucified by unconquerable circumstances. I was forced to wonder, 'What are we fighting for?"

"You kids are almost out of time, aren't you?" he managed, cryptically.

There was something about his tone that made time stop and my spirit jump. My rational side made me think, 'Maybe he overheard the urgency in my call to Grayson?' or 'Maybe he witnessed us repeatedly looking at our watches.' Regardless, the entire world and its inhabitants seemed to be watching our lives unfold on a dystopian stage. Things like numerology, déjà vu and synchronicity amplified our suspicions, but guided us.

"The bus should be here any minute," he laughed, mocking my wide-eyed paranoia.

"That's what the ticket says!" I added.

"The early bird catches the worm," he grinned.

"They say," I said.

"Don't be modest, son, you know all about waking up with the birds – now, don't you?"

Turning to acknowledge him, he was gone.

"God?" I whispered.

CHAPTER 44
THE LONG GOODBYE

Crystal stared from the fingerprint smudged window. Her eyes, like a video camera, recorded the distance between her past and every passing moment. The road relentlessly sewed her story together. Unconsciously, she'd rub her tummy and replay the hurried conversation she'd had with Neco. She could almost feel the threat of the relentless New Mexican air, chasing after her. Lazy mile markers brought anxious butterflies to her stomach. Romantic visions of a life with Dez were nothing more than a passing flu — a small sacrifice to pay for the child growing harmoniously in tandem with the stars.

"What's your plan?" asked Joe, turning down an unpalatable Beach Boys song.

"I don't know," she said, trying to recall a time when anything went as such.

"I hope you'll stay in touch," said Joe.

"Promise me you'll keep Grayson's information handy. I don't intend to forget!"

Pulling into an intimidating Brooklyn neighborhood, a thick black cloud of finality descended upon the dark streets. His nervous lips quivered as he mouthed each residential complex number. His sadness made it impossible to produce an audible tone. Adding insult to his tragic fortune, a black cat crossed his path.

"Just my luck. I want you to take care of that baby!" he exclaimed, stopping his words short, aware of how fatherly he sounded. He had never felt so aged and unlovable. Adjusting the rear-view mirror, he couldn't help but watch his eyes well and his face fall.

"The future lives inside me," Crystal said, sensing his pain. She slowly cocked his head toward hers and gave him a long and gentle kiss. "I couldn't have done any of this without you," she added, never breaking eye contact. "Consider my world — our world — forever indebted to you! Take care of Petey, for me."

Joe knew he could stay, but didn't wish to extend his pain with a sleepover. Like a stranger in the night, Crystal descended from his trailer and approached a young and good looking gentleman. He seemed eager to take Joe's place. Draping his confident arm around her petite shoulder, Grayson looked back, smiled and waved him on. If only to break Grayson's assumptive contact, until Joe had managed his truck through the narrow streets, she shrugged him off, and laced her tall boots. Seizing the opportunity and missing the cue, Grayson grabbed her baggage and hurled it around his torso. They ascended into the complex and prepared for a long night.

"How long did it take?" Grayson asked, putzing around his tiny kitchen, distracted by a pot of coffee.

"Where do you want to start? If you consider all of the inane variables that lead up to this tiny moment, I guess you could say it took me over 20 years," she snarked, not prepared to let him in easily. "No sugar and no creamer," Crystal added, without being asked. "I should probably warn you, I can be a bit guarded."

"I understand. A cup o' black oil for the Snow Queen — coming right up!"

"OK, I assume you want the whole story." Crystal begrudgingly laughed. Settling into his divan, she parted with her pretension, and assumed the role of a mental patient, tasking Grayson with both journalism and psychiatry. Armed with a pen, he detailed her earliest days. His recorder picked up the scraps.

"So, stripping?" Grayson asked, welcoming the elephant into the room.

"I got into stripping because I needed the money — *period.* Dez provided me with a way out. He seemed a little crazy, but no more than exploiting my innocence for the hounds of hell. I got started when I was a teenager and found a small studio with my childhood friend, Michelle. My father was an absentee alcoholic. I'm not sure if he even realizes I'm gone."

"I'm sure he has," coaxed Grayson.

"He says my mother was a saint, and blames his spiraling on her passing. My early days were spent gazing into her old photos and wishing for a normal life. Often, I prayed for an early death, in hopes of hearing her voice. That's how connected I feel to her."

"She's with you."

"We're bad apples. This child has given me hope. The Program has given me purpose."

"Are you kidding? You're like a modern day Mother Mary. Your dark past makes it intriguing and poetic. Every word that falls from your ruby red lips sounds like a news headline," Grayson awkwardly professed, entranced by her back-story.

"Even if everything Neco told me was a total lie, it's a lie I'd choose to believe," Crystal quickly added, trying to distance herself from his innocent advance, and her heart's attraction.

Their eyes trembled to restrain the connection. Catching her cue, Grayson clicked his pen and folded the notebook. He couldn't shake his romantic feelings, but knew their calling was greater than his rush of hormones.

With grateful eyes, she offered him her cheek. Redirecting his intentions, he leaned down and gave her a friendly kiss.

"Thank you, Grayson," Crystal said.

"Do me a favor. Don't answer that door for anyone or anything. I'll probably be at work before you wake. I'll leave my pager number on the counter. If you so much as sense danger, please page me — *please*," instructed Grayson.

She nodded and slept. From the back of her eye lids, the gray bird appeared in the darkness and lead her through a cryptic New York City cemetery. It landed upon a shallow and unmarked plot. Holding her newborn child, she leaned over the empty hole. The bird was gazing upon an unrecognizable male frame. Face down, he appeared to be handsomely dressed and coated in the moist mud. His head turned. Disoriented, she awoke, screaming "Grayson!"

"What is it?" he asked.

"I was dreaming and displaced. I wasn't sure if I was in Brooklyn or Texas."

Grayson handed her a glass of water and headed back to bed. In the moonlit room, she stared, trying to envision herself in the comforts of Joe's living room. With strict focus, she could almost hear Petey's brash, but sweet, call. Fearing for his safety, she prayed.

Joe arrived to a ransacked home. Making a swift assessment, he was grateful to find Petey unscathed. None of his earthly processions could replace his only true friend. With hesitation, his tired heart slunk through the looted rooms. Sadness stirred the acids in his sullen stomach.

"New York City!" cawed Petey, from the kitchen. "You're so pretty!"

"That's it," thought Joe. "That's it!"

+++

Going through the motions of his new life, Grayson tied his noose, grabbed a tumbler and headed into the office. The copy room was manic with Cadence of the Sun and

NYC crime headlines. Assessing his timetable, he prioritized his assignments. Shuffling through litters of desk copy, he was interrupted by an origami pterodactyl flier.

"Are you planning to go to the Met Gala, tomorrow?" asked a flirty voice. It was Jessica Fisher, an accomplished and well respected editor. "I hear Princess Diana will be there! It seems like it's going to be a pretty big who's who. Being that you don't dare find the time to socialize with the underlings, a little hobnobbing might do your spirit good. I'm half-tempted to start stalking you myself – I want to know what you do in your free time. Maybe I'll write my own piece called, 'What Makes Grayson Miller Tick?'" said Jessica.

"If I have time and I'm asked," quipped Grayson. "I can't be distracted with finding an outfit."

"You don't have an outfit, nor a date," she joked, adjusting his tie. "I think we can arrange it, no?"

"Do I need to contact HR? It almost sounds like you're asking me out?" snarked Grayson.

"Please. I am asking you to stop being a square and to consider spending your evening with a woman! I'm sure there's a suit jacket lying around this pigsty. You don't want to miss an opportunity to relish in the posh pretension that is the Metropolitan Museum of Art, do you? You wouldn't want to jeopardize your counter-cultural integrity, by denying me this honor. So, you're going. If attire is your only concern, you'll look ravishing in one of my gowns. What could be more hip than gender bending before the princess?" poked Jessica.

"Gray, line one!" chimed a secretary.

"I'm sorry to bother. He's been here," said an emphatic voice.

"Who?"

"Dez flipped my house upside down," warned Joe. "He's heading your way. You've got to warn Crystal!"

Grayson disconnected, as if rattled by the thunder of god. "I've got to go! When is the Gala?" he asked.

"Tonight — Eight. Everything OK?" asked Jessica.

"I'm fine. If Silverstein asks, I'm following up on a lead for my feature story. I'll call, later."

Grayson swung on his Members Only jacket and left in a flurry. He arrived back at his home to find Crystal. She was still comfortably resting in his extra-large Weezer T-shirt. Her peace confused his racing heart. She wrestled with the idea of acknowledging his anxious presence, but was no match for her lazy eyes.

"We've got to get you out of here. We can't stay!" alarmed Grayson.

Despite her best attempts to avoid reality, his insistence woke the baby within.

"What's wrong?" Crystal asked.

"It's Dez. He knows you're here. Joe's home was destroyed."

"Petey!"

CHAPTER 45
THE MASQUERADE

"We made it!" exhaled Neco.

Neco and Michelle shuttled into New York City and set up a base camp in a Brooklyn pizza shop.

"It seems, everyone has 1,000 intentions, these days," said Neco, catching his wind. He was anxious to see Grayson and Crystal. "This whole spiritual war has been going on since the dawn of mankind. There are Program descendants walking amongst us. The inspired ones continue to brighten our world, while the damned seethe and thirst for man's destruction."

"Everybody wants to rule the rule!" said Michelle.

"Rule or ruin? Dez is a byproduct. Like a spider, he spins his unsuspecting victims into a web of lies, by tickling their curiosity and fanning the flames of their adolescent cries for rebellion — all while providing a roof, an identity and a peer group. He strips away accountability, and sells it as freedom. It's a sexy idea, but no one stood a chance. They're all pawns in a very dangerous game," sputtered Neco.

"I'll never forget the day Crystal and I met him. I knew

he'd laced our drinks, but was too vacant to care," said Michelle.

"While working undercover, I helped him administer strong doses of LSD to the trafficked newcomers. It killed me. All I could think was, 'How does an adolescent brain recover from this?' I say, 'adolescent,' but let's be honest, no one was completely innocent. Good, bad or indifferent, that's how the game is played. He's not the first. Where do you think the Hitlers, Stalins or Amin Dadas come from? They may not have all been Programmers, but they were inspired by the same spirit of megalomania. *Pride* is how the devil fooled the world and how we all found ourselves in checkmate," said Neco.

"It couldn't be more obvious, in this city. Look at these neon temples and the zombie class," said Michelle.

"We're not the first arrogant generation to believe the world centers around us and who believe it will end on our watch. Dez has a tried and true platform. Considering his success rate, it's feasible to think his messianic complex will sprout wings, if Crystal doesn't have his child," pondered Neco, aloud.

"Speaking of the devil, we should probably knock on a few doors and find Grayson," deduced Michelle.

"Right."

"There's a payphone just outside the door," said Michelle, thumbing Neco a quarter.

"I'm glad you called, Neco. I hit the panic button about an hour ago!" gruffed Grayson.

"What's going on, Grayson?" asked Neco.

"Long story short, I have a Gala to attend, and it's tonight. Joe, Crystal's driver, transporter or whatever you want to call him, called. Dez is tracking us. He's either here or on his way. My colleague offered us her place, for the night, but you'll need to seek a hospice or place to hide, until she can safely crown. Do you remember where our Program story is?" asked Grayson.

"Under the floorboards in the kitchen," said Neco.

"Perfect. We'll be better off keeping a distance and laying low for the next few days," closed Grayson.

Scribbling down Jessica Fisher's information, Neco hung up the phone and returned to the table. He couldn't shake the sense of foreboding that lingered in the damp air. "We need to find a shelter. The wolves have arrived."

"Don't you think 'wolves' is a little dramatic for a passing shower?" joked Michelle.

"Dez is tracking Crystal, which also means Grayson. He found them — *us*!" said Neco.

"She's got to be getting close to having his baby!" reminded Michelle.

With exhausted hearts, they left the pizza parlor. They soldiered across the Brooklyn Bridge to the New York City Public Library, and researched facilities able to harbor and protect a pregnant homeless woman; a damsel disenfranchised by circumstance. Though the traffic and crowds were impenetrably deafening, it couldn't silence the paranoid and strained voices in Neco's head; even the gargoyles seemed to stand watch — screams were the unnamed song of the city's streets.

"Neco, how about this? It's called the Covenant House. It's on 41st. We can drop her off. She can check in with an alias. The site says they don't discriminate, nor care about the circumstances surrounding their arrivals. Once she's in their custody, we should head back to Baltimore, and become invisible," said Michelle.

"Perfect! The less time we need to spend in this rotten city, the better," reassured Neco.

"Does it feel like Dez is watching our every move?" asked Michelle.

"Always!"

+++

Grayson escorted Crystal to the subway station. They headed toward Greeley Square on 34th street. "I've made arrangements for you to stay with a close friend of mine — Jessica Fisher. Neco and Michelle are on their way. We'll figure the rest out, tomorrow," Grayson said, hugging Crystal. Watching crowds of people pass them by, his attempts to make sure they hadn't been followed seemed futile. "You look flush, are you going to be all right?"

"Yeah, I'm fine. Have fun, Gray." Crystal kissed him on the cheek and followed her directions toward 28th street. Grayson walked nervously toward 1000 5th avenue, questioning his reason for leaving her side.

The Met Gala's stage was set for a masquerade. The guests adorned an undeniable mystique; masks were optional. Sequin dresses and harlequin hearts waltzed about the room, all hoping to be noticed by somebody as somebody. Their staunch attempts to keep the royal blood far from the grimy world living just beyond the museum's magnificent walls, provided an appetizer of adjectives for the swarming journalists. They wined, danced and used art history as excuse to flaunt their money and excuse adultery; an evening filled with enough sin and pretension to asphyxiate heaven's angels with the inferno's stoked smoke.

As the clock wound down, drunken party-goers staggered from the halls and took limo rides to costume-inspired sex parties, hosted by New York's finest penthouse suites. Consuming the last spoils of the evening, thirsty journalists compared notes. The streets were consumed by the Gala's scattered company.

Still overwrought by the coming threat, Grayson tried to drink away his woes. When the final whiskey and ginger was poured, he grabbed his spiral notebook and exited. Alone and inebriated, he stumbled toward to the subway station. Though sedated, his antennas couldn't help but notice the well-dressed wolves trailing behind. Blaming the congestion, he dismissed their presence as paranoia, until they boarded his train.

Blocks away, Crystal and Jessica bonded over stories of heartbreak and familial issues. Startled, Crystal saw a large pigeon perched just outside of Jessica's apartment window. She was speechless. Recalling the vision, she realized the handsome man, resting at the bottom of the grave, was Grayson. Fluttering her hand, as if smothering, she gasped.

"Grayson's in trouble!" insisted Crystal.

"What do you mean? He'll be in trouble if he didn't have a good time. I can't believe I missed the opportunity to meet *the* Princess Diana and have a possible nightcap with *the* Grayson Miller! This whole night's been a disaster," pouted Jessica.

"I had a dream, that..." said Crystal.

"Sweetheart, it was just a dream," she interrupted.

+++

Struggling to maintain his balance, Grayson surveyed the subway car for exits, trying to avoid eye contact with the suspicious characters. Approaching, they bobbed and weaved through the thick crowd. The car made frequent stops. He considered making a run for it, but couldn't risk getting lost in the downtrodden parts of New York City. The stress, whiskey and trains movement made his vision veer. Struggling to maintain, he passed out — cold. When he awoke, he was tied to a wobbly chair at the end of a dock. The legs of the metal chair kissed the ledge — one spry move would leave him swimming in the East River and writhing with the souls in the Hallway of Sorrows. His bow tie, taped into his mouth, thwarted his pleas. A stuffed nose left him convinced he'd smother.

"He's awake," said Max. He ripped the duct tape from Grayson's groaning mouth. "Before we push you into a mafia-grave, we thought we might just ask you a few questions. Sound good?" Max offered, teasing the legs of the chair with his Giorgio Armani shoes.

"Are you one of the Cadence cowards? The Sun's worthless derelicts?" asked Grayson.

Max unloaded a deadly blow to his face. The others took turns beating him, while blood squirted from his nose. Grayson squirmed, but was empowered by their hits. He knew they couldn't kill him — *permanently.*

"Now, where were we? Let me ask you again, where is she?" asked Max.

"I confess, your mother is handcuffed to my bed frame. Are you asking for the key?" Grayson taunted, hoping they'd push him into the blackened river. He knew he'd be murdered, no matter how he responded. "Where's your fearless leader? You know, the coward who created this bullshit cult that you lemmings have chosen to follow. Did it ever occur to you, he might be crazy?"

"I've heard enough from this disrespectful punk!" said one of Max's cronies.

Max turned Grayson's head and forced him to look at the dark waters below. "We will find her. When we do, we will kill her! I'm sure a minor investigation of your apartment will unearth everything we need. Who knows, maybe we'll even dig up information about your family, friends and coworkers. Don't think that your death exonerates you from your poor decision-making. Where is she?" Max ferociously screamed, pounding his face like a speed bag.

"If I die, you'll never find her." Grayson's mind was dizzy, his eyes were swollen — he watched blood drip from his busted gums. His shirt was a serial killer's prize. "You're going to kill me, either way. I know this will sound a bit like a cliché, but will you humor me with a last cigarette?"

Without hesitation, Max reached into his pocket, put a cigarette to Grayson's mouth and fired it up.

"Just listen to me — if you still want to kill me, after what I'm about to say, kill me. You have nothing to lose," Grayson said, yielding for a rebuttal. Without a word, he continued. "The man you are following is one of us. We are part of a group called The Program. We were sent to populate this planet with special children. We are not aliens.

Our children are not government engineered hybrids. They are the divine property of The Council of the Lords. They've been integrating, since the beginning."

"I've heard enough!" whispered Max.

"That's the problem, you're only hearing what justifies your means. Dez was one of the original 12. Since its genesis, he's been hunting us down. The Children of the Program website — my website — just made it easier for him. The Cadence is responsible for killing Juno, Benjamin, Zane and Simon. You tried to kill Ash, but failed," furthered Grayson.

"How do you know all of this?" Max asked, perplexed.

"Because I'm living it. I've been writing our story since we met in the Painted Desert. These children you killed will haunt you in the inferno. There's no recourse for your actions. Your war has disrupted the entire universe. If you stop now, you may have a chance at salvaging a little grace," offered Grayson.

"You're a fraud! This is all just clever rhetoric, pieced together by a very attentive writer," said Max.

"Am I? Go to the Children of the Program website. The password is the same — all one word! We'll see who is deceiving who, when the dust settles. I don't want to die, but you can't kill me. That's the beauty in all this, for Dez. He wants to rule the world. He doesn't care about you. When you die, you'll burn with the souls of the underworld. He doesn't die. He'll fall to earth for lifetimes to come. He's nearly succeeded. You have the power to stop him!" announced Grayson.

Turning to pace, Max ran his token black gloves through his black raven hair and fumbled with Grayson's words. His bloodthirsty henchman were unimpressed and thirsty for a sacrifice. Far from earshot, Max connected the dots and contemplated the value of Grayson's life and the merits of his plea.

"Why would I dedicate a website and attract awareness to a conspiracy that I'm involved in," asked

Grayson.

"Maybe you're clever," said Max.

"I've never been accused of that, and I've tired. Have you asked Dez about Michelle?" asked Grayson.

"What did you say?" Furious, Max's eye sockets filled with lightning.

"Dez? Michelle?" asked Grayson.

"How do you know about her? How?" asked Max.

"She joined us."

In a rage, and forced to stomach the depths of his malice, Grayson was pushed. Max felt betrayed, ashamed and angered by a reality he could no longer justify. A part of him believed Grayson, but couldn't allow his truth to dock in the harbors of his parting mind. Being used and disrespected by Dez was only eclipsed by knowing his girlfriend had joined the opposition to their revolution; forcing him off the scales of justice, in favor of blind anarchy — he was a revolutionary turned renegade.

No longer able to make heads of tails, Max was prepared to hunt Michelle to the ends of the earth. Dez had him addicted to adrenaline. Though he was unable to shake the sense of control and power the dark side allotted his ego, he refused to be brainwashed by a sociopath. In slow motion, with backs arched, Max's clan climbed through a chain link fence.

He would punish the world – everyone would pay!

+++

After a hard fought drive, Dez returned to the compound, fired up the underground, took inventory of his dwindling Program family and resumed his ministry. He was elated to know his top agent, Max, had carried the inferno to New York City, while the international Cadence of the Sun sects continued to dominate news headlines. His relative anonymity made him more of a villain than a murderer, which attracted the misdirected youth and inspired copycat killings.

"Another child has been killed, and another family grieves, as the Cadence cult continues to target — what they call — 'alien children.' With so many cells, a lot of the details and operators of this so-called 'revolution,' remain a mystery. Their only calling card is this Japanese symbol. They call themselves the *Cadence of the Sun*," said a television anchor, scrambling through the static. "As one police officer said, 'It's hard to handcuff a belief system.'"

"Who's next, what's what?" Though elated, his mind shuttered to maintain functionality. Hunched over, Dez shuffled and paced below the dirt. He clinched his revolver, but knew he couldn't put a hole in Father Time. One bullet ensured he'd force himself back to the Hallway of Sorrows. Even in death, he'd delight in how he had devastated The Council's plan. Scrubbed from the Book of Records, he'd be exonerated of accountability. "Two to go," he barked, before answering the phone.

"It's Max!"

"M'boy, have you found Grayson and Crystal?" asked Dez.

"We followed Grayson to a work event and dumped him in the East River," said Max.

"Excellent. How about Crystal?" Dez prodded.

"How about Michelle?" fired Max. The connection was instant.

"She's with Neco! He was a traitor. They escaped, just as I said," said Dez.

"You are one of them," he paused. "You're part of The Program, aren't you?" asked Max.

Dez paused. Being exposed was a possibility he hadn't planned for. His unveiling would destroy the Cadence. His followers' fury would reveal the compound to authorities. Without recourse, he reached into his hat and pulled out the only card he had left to play.

"It's your word verse mine. You came to me, with nothing, and I told you a story. No one made you follow me. No one made you kill, steal or rape those innocent people. It's what your heart wanted — it's what you are! And, just like you, the very people you think you'll sway from the Cadence of the Sun have the freedom to decide. They will turn on you, Max. There are three sides to every story — *three*. With the mountains of guilt and crime on your bloody hands, there's only one side that will sell — mine. If you died tonight, who would be the wiser? Who? You don't want to join Grayson, do you? Look around, m'boy!" rallied Dez.

"We killed for you! We believed in you," said Max.

"You did. Trust can certainly be a crutch, can't it? I didn't tell you to pick up the phone and assault my character, did I, Max? You were always a little too hot-headed for your own good. If I didn't know better, I'd think you wanted my job. My power. My respect. The guy you killed was a government terrorist," said Dez.

"What are you talking about?" asked Max.

"It doesn't matter! You'll believe what you want to believe — you've proven that. M'boy, do you think the authorities are going to give a damn about your sudden change of heart, when we're shot down in flames. With the lies you've told and the bodies you've buried, you blitzkrieg my character? I dare you, Max. Try me. The truth is, we're torn from the same cloth. We're mirror images of one another, and we both want the same thing — more life," said Dez.

"Who are you?" asked Max.

"Pleased to meet you, Max. Hope you guess my name."

CHAPTER 46
VISION OF THE BLACK BIRD (ISIS)

Dez's tired bones rested upon a yellow and sticky New York City bench. He listened to the arrival and departure announcements, as subway cars seamlessly roared by. Commuters went about their busy days, without noticing his rotten shambles of a life. Covered in layers of camouflaged clothing, long underwear, and a fitting beard, a tired old man awaited death's sting. The world had all but forgotten him. Going against the flow, he rose from the bench, slowly crossed through the turn stop and ascended onto the Manhattan streets. Dust and ash asphyxiated his lungs – a strange chemical burned his nostrils. The buildings were vacant and obliterated, and the hallucinated bustle passed. No one was left. Looking into the cavernous hole, from which his corpse emerged, the lights faded to black. Everything was cinematic.

Looking for signs of life, the man walked through the city, but could only find the lazy smolders of post-apocalyptic debris. He returned to the subway station, unable to accept the train's pause. Smeared on the wall, a bloodstained message indicated the station had been closed for nearly a decade. He couldn't help but think, 'This was the world that I wanted — the world I created.' Even in the wreckage, he could feel the spirits of discontent haunting him.

Placating his illusion of power had left him longing for love and genuine respect. Spending his entire life underground had disconnected him from how the real world operated. In defense, his mind had filled in the blanks, while reality penned a far more damning account. Consumed by his transgressions, he was mystified by the extent of his madness. He could sense the universe was unified in vanquishing his reign, and wouldn't rest until his immediate bloodline was punished with plagues, poverty and pain. It was sobering. He was powerless and unable to wage war upon The Council's creation.

He was then hurled into the void, stripped, ridiculed and hung by the hanging corpses in the Hallway of Sorrows. He stared into the inferno. Bodies pried at his shackles, hoping to toss him into the pit of eternal justice. He thirsted for the absolution of the fire. Agonizing, his lives flashed before his watery eyes — just as they had in the gathering circle. He could still feel the flames of past judgment, and vividly recall the generations of fathers who had stolen his virginity. The darkness forced him to relive each appalling affair. Purging with pain, he was then forced to watch the destruction he had waged upon The Program. He knew the underworld was equally as horrifying as being forced to walk the barren city streets; vacancy, in the aftermath of a cowardice victory. His shortsightedness hadn't planned for tomorrow.

He was then shown the world's beauty. He longed to dip his toes in the ocean and chase the seagulls. He longed to fall in love and know the eternal joy of raising a child. He longed to live, be forgotten and start anew. Allowed to awaken, his mind quickly recoiled back to the unforgettable plague of memories lurking within — they dashed out hope. He was just another human tragedy. In death, there was life, and in life there was death. He was nothing more than another proud soul, left to anguish in a self-generated cycle of earthbound hell.

"You are out of time," cawed Isis. "You will taste the fire. You will live with a regret so deep that you'll never truly love again. You will not be held responsible for your actions, by us — you will hold yourself in contempt. Should this child die, the stench of your arrogance will poison the very wombs your rebellious seed tries to harvest." It then pecked out Dez's eyes.

"You will not recall my words. The intentions of your heart must be heard by The Council."

"How can I stop this?" asked Dez.

"Listen to the silent voice buried deep within you. Break the cycle, and set yourself free."

Dez awoke shaking. He could remember the vision, but not understand its meaning. Struggling, he pulled himself from a dirty bunker mattress, and walked toward the control room. Looking at the screens, he saw a raven leering into the property's surveillance camera. It pecked at the tiny monocle of glass — his child was coming!

CHAPTER 47
FIREFIGHT

The arid New Mexican sun beckoned for Dez's attention. Adjusting his property camera, to ward off the pesky raven, he watched light waves refract off the desert plains and questioned whether a mirage was playing tricks on his mind. Kicking up dust, his paranoia was justified by the trace sounds of a creeping authority. Dropping a container of freshly brewed coffee, he anxiously shuttered through various camera feeds and assessed the unfolding situation from all angles. The lights in the bunker flickered and the ceiling shook from the movement overhead. Cracks in the bunker allowed tiny spurts of dirt to fall.

His smooth rhetoric and blackmail had failed — Max had betrayed him. The roar of aggressive police helicopters awoke the blood thirsty paparazzi. In moments, a swarm of patrol cars and journalists arrived and circled the lot. Every outlet was chomping at the bit to televise the final hours of an identified terrorist head and give the world a firsthand look at the compound the Cadence of the Sun called home. Vultures circled, awaiting the perfect moment to tear the pride from his bones. Disheartened, Dez walked toward an arsenal locker and pulled out a rusty old shotgun. Swallowing his fear, his shaky hands loaded his exit strategy. In a last stand of arrogance, he prepared to send a final salute out to his war.

"Ring around the rosy, pocket full of posies. Ashes, ashes, we all fall down," he mumbled. Flashbacks passed before his calloused eyes. His only regret was leaving the Cadence of the Sun at the mercy of Max's interpretation. With his final hours numbered, he accepted defeat — "If the cops don't finish this, Crystal will."

"This is the police. We have you surrounded," bellowed a distant bullhorn.

"Come out with your hands up," he mocked, under his breath.

Dez was determined to die a martyr. Cocking the shotgun and holstering his pistol, he prepared to climb the ladder of defeat and reveal himself to the world. As if cued by psychosis, the Godfather theme whistled through his dizzy head. Though he was betrayed, he refused to be robbed of his final blaze of glory. With a halfhearted shove, his weakened shoulder pushed open the shelter's hatch. His exasperated limbs turned gravity into a weapon, and pulled him back into the bunker.

+++

Settling into the Covenant House, Crystal awoke. "Oh my god!" Her heart raced and the birth pains began. Screaming for help, nurses flocked to her bedside. With cold rags and concern, they patted her forehead and adjusted her bed to an upward position. They fanned her with pamphlets, and encouraged her to breathe and relax. "This is it." Her cry echoed through the home's walls.

"From what you've told us, you can't be more than 28-32 weeks pregnant. If you have this child, tonight, it will have a much lower rate of survival. We've got to try and calm the oceans, darling. Just breathe and try to focus on the beautiful stars out that window. Count them for me," said Andrea Stevens, a staff nurse.

"This baby will have to take its chances. It means the world to me and you!" proclaimed Crystal.

"You're talking crazy, girl. I ain't raising no one else's baby. Just try and be still," Andrea said.

"What's crazy?" asked Crystal.

"Get her some meds," Andrea instructed a fellow colleague. "Now, do you think you can keep this feeling at bay for a couple of hours? At least until the sleep deprived doctor arrives? You'll want him awake, I promise."

"You don't know how hard I'm trying. I was in a deep sleep," she paused, breathing quickly, "when suddenly I saw a burst of bright light. My eyes flung open like a possessed madwoman. It's like, I've been awake for hours. I can't explain it, but something in my body is dying to get out — now! How does it have the strength to control me like this?" asked Crystal.

"Nature doesn't pay us no mind, my dear," said the nurse. "It never has. Life doesn't participate in the realm of reason — maybe, rhymes. Think of all those chaotic, fortunate or even horrifying events that had to happen for you to be lying here today. I know you've had a journey or you wouldn't be at The Covenant. If life was supposed to make sense, honey, it would." The nurse turned, filled a plastic cup with water and handed Crystal an aspirin. "I'll be back in a moment. Scream if you need me — I know you will," she smiled.

Crystal had never felt so alone. Though her isolation had the power to save an entire generation of mankind, she wanted to share her beautiful moment. From a small crack in the room's window, a cool gust blew through her feathering hair. She wanted to believe the Council of the Lords were stroking her head with sympathy. Softly, she prayed for Neco and Michelle's travels, hoping they'd meet again.

"He's got to survive," Crystal whispered.

+++

Dez's failed exit reminded him to baptize the premises with fire. He torched the rooms, before making his way back to the tunnel exit. His weathered eyes stung, as the smoke followed him through empty hallways. With one last heroic charge, he climbed the bunker staircase and threw open the steel doors; careful to stay out of view. A dust storm cascaded before the awaiting sun. Mere feet separated him from the saints in blue. Ceremoniously lighting a final cigarette, he carefully laid his shotgun in the stairwell and ascended with his right hand in view.

"Put both hands where we can see them."

"You can't kill me!"

Dez was surrounded. He was reminded of the gathering circle; now, center stage. Camera men swarmed like bees and law enforcement receivers buzzed. Slowly moving towards Dez, agents and officers were intent to take him alive. The thick atmosphere remained tense as he lethargically spit his cigarette. His lips parted, as smoke rings rose and haloed his head. Struck by awe and silence, no one moved.

"I have enough explosives buried on this lot to kill us all. I wouldn't suggest making another goddamned move," said Dez, calmly, revealing a tiny television remote, taped to the palm of his left hand. "You thought you had it all figured out, coming here, didn't you? The truth is, even in my death, the Cadence will continue. I will return. It exists, because people want us to exist — people just like you and me!" His fingers baited the remote.

The officers scrambled. "Don't move!"

+++

"Breathe!" Crystal's pain intensified, causing her consciousness to waver. Resting in a pool of blood and sweat, her body quaked with thunderous waves of contractions. Hoping to alert the mother within, an on-call doctor flashed his medical flashlight into her dilating eyes. Delirious, Crystal struggled to focus. Grabbing the handlebars, she tensed her sore muscles, pushed and gasped with a mother's fury.

"That's good, that's good. Andrea, prop her legs," said the doctor.

"I've got you," said Andrea, grabbing Crystal's hand. "No matter what happens, you'll be OK!"

An unspoken dialog, surrounding the child's chances of survival, lingered in the room. Andrea's wishful eyes locked with the doctor. She prayed his degrees could trump Crystal's cruel odds. Lights flickered, as a passing storm pounded through the region. With a flash, the lights faded to black. In the dark, the television turned on and dramatically played the National Anthem. The spirited room begged their attention, as a warbling hum cut through the silence.

+++

"What do you want?" asked an officer, holding a megaphone.

"What do I want? That's what you're missing. I don't want anything. I just want to be heard," said Dez.

"We hear you loud and clear!"

Reaching for his pocket, rifles clicked and clattered in tandem.

"Keep your hands up," urged the officer.

In a defining final moment, Dez lifted his shirt, reached for his waistband and allowed his symphonic tragedy to end. He had nothing left to say. His perfect stage had been set. The hounds of justice were unleashed, as a fury of shell casing danced across the desert floor. Dust clouds, from the frantic helicopters created a hurricane of excitement. Dez fell.

Crystal gasped, made a final push and delivered her child to an unsuspecting world. Sighs of relief brought closure to her exhaustive labor. Her child was quickly cleaned and taken to a neonatal intensive care unit on January 7th.

"He's arrived!" screamed Andrea, hugging Crystal. "Now, we pray!"

"He's got my mother's indigo eyes," cried Crystal.

As the dust settled, FBI units cautiously moved toward Dez's fallen body. Police reports and news stories determined that Dez had fallen into the compound and been vanquished by flames and explosives.

His body was never recovered.

CHAPTER 48
LETTERS TO THE LORDS

"A New York Times reporter's body was found and pulled from the East River. Now, back to the standoff unfolding in New Mexico." The television rattled and hummed. Patrons gathered in the lobby to catch a glimpse of the breaking news.

Michelle and I watched the reports unfold from the Old Town Pub in New York City. Visceral feelings bubbled to a head, as Dez's stalemate cast a long shadow over the entire city's rhythm. Barflies imbibed the drama and were mindful to keep their glasses full — fearful of losing their coveted view. As time slowed, we noticed a crowd forming on the streets; like big-eyed children, people wrestled to peak through the smudged glass and catch a glimpse. They were drawn, like mosquitoes to an ultraviolet light.

"If anyone realized our connection to the unfolding headlines, we'd be mobbed," I whispered to Michelle. Hearing the devastating news of Grayson's death meant unearthing his archived interviews and story, before returning to dock in Baltimore's industrial harbor. It also meant rolling the dice and risking a run-in with the Cadence, one last time. The day's events brought Michelle and me closer. Stewing in my suds, I couldn't imagine a life without her. Knowing the cult's ideology would mutate and continue to spread conspiracy theories and hate into the world, meant we needed each other. As the sun tucked behind the earth, we stumbled onto the glossy streets of surrealism.

"Where does he live, again?" asked Michelle.

"It doesn't matter, darling! Let's just walk."

We walked for a couple hours, contemplating the odds. We had a lifetime, or more, to come to terms with Dez's final moments. Elated, I shouted, "I have to write a song about it!" Like a chorus, my words echoed through the alleys. Aside from gathering Grayson's extensive notes and for once, there wasn't a next step. Our lives, consumed by adrenaline and anxiety, simply stopped. Luckily, the rest of humanity was moving quickly enough to keep the earth turning.

"I wonder if life has finally caught up to us and will spin us into its cocoon of purposeless years?" I asked.

"Only if we're lucky, Neco."

"It's strange. The future looks bland, but maybe that's OK."

Unknown to Michelle, we had circled Grayson's residence a dozen times. With a tired heart, I stopped her on the complex steps and kissed her — *deeply*. My racing heart pulsed on the tip of my quivering lips. My eyes were lost in the moment, as my soul dissolved into the emotional black hole I'd tried to swallow at the bar. The moon made silhouettes of us.

Turning the door handle with caution, we slipped into Grayson's modest apartment complex and let flickering wall lamps guide our steps. Grayson's presence oozed from the hipster paintings on his otherwise barren walls.

"He said it was under the floorboards," I motioned, scouring the ground for an entry point. Moving a tiny shag rug, resting in front of the sink, Michelle found a hook.

Lifting a heavy wood panel, I removed the large covering. It was roughly 2.25' x 3.75'. The aura in the room made it feel like we were opening the Ark of the Covenant. A tiny wind rushed from beneath the floor as I nervously reached into the void. Inside was a rectangular flash drive containing the contents of our lives.

"Is that really the Children of the Program story?" asked Michelle.

Cupping my mouth, I stumbled over the trivial nature of a response. My protective hands squeezed the tiny devise. It was as if Grayson had hand delivered our legacy – his aura seemed to pass through the room. Before the cool moonlight, I raised it to The Council, fell to my knees and cried. Michelle was there to catch me.

"We should probably get going, sweetheart," I said.

Like ships in the night, we lifted our anchors and sailed home — actually, we hopped a train. The entire ride felt like a metaphor. Dipping through dark tunnels, time raced by. It felt like we were passing through a wormhole and into a parallel reality.

+++

"Son, I'm glad you're home!" My father and I hugged, acknowledging our lost time. The burden of my ventures had been wiped clean by the bonds of unconditional love. He scurried to whip up a plate of scrambled eggs, nervously fearing I'd make another swift exit. I smiled, comforted by a choir of baby birds nesting below the deck.

"I'm not planning on going anywhere, Dad. We're done," I assured.

"You're both welcome to stay as long as you'd like. You were in such a rush, last time, you never opened your large delivery from Scotland. Curiosity almost killed this old cat. It's up in the attic, if you two want to go on one last adventure — together. At least I know where you're going and why," he laughed, pointing the way.

Lowering the trap, a hazy cloud of dust shimmered in the light cracks peeking through the roof joints and rusty nail pops. Ascending, like Goonies, spider webs and rickety floors ushered us toward a large square object. It felt like Christmas morning. Though she was gone, Ash wouldn't be content if she was forgotten. Gliding my hand across the smooth seams, I reached for a razor blade and separated the taped stitching. Michelle, offering a tiny flashlight and allowed her curiosity to smother away her jealousy.

"What do you think it is?" asked Michelle.

"It's about the size of a painting," I said.

"It's hard to believe she's gone, Neco. I'm sorry."

Opening the flap, I pulled a large framed picture from a tall wooden box. It was the 'Art of Darkness' canvas she'd painted and had auctioned to the public. The painting was worth millions of dollars. It was her life insurance policy, and I was the beneficiary. The frame was silver, rustic and designed with my tastes in mind. A tiny note on the glass casing begged my address.

"Should you receive this, I hope you'll know that I love you and have passed on. I want you to sell this piece and use the money to continue your music and writing. Your gift to the earth is your soul. You are a light — a beautiful spectrum of colors illuminating the darkness through blissful and uninhibited self-expression. I hope someday our hearts will collide, and breed a new universe. A place where inspired hearts and carefree minds no longer fear the dark. Forever yours, Ash," it read.

I wept.

Carefully, I slipped the beautiful painting back into the box and brought it down from the attic.

"What do you have there?"

"It's a painting of me."

"Of you?" asked my father. Gazing, his mind began connecting the dots of my crazy stories.

+++

Settling in my bedroom, Michelle and I used the light to reexamine *the gift*. The postage was dated three days after her horrendous house fire. Questions loomed. Flipping the canvas, I noticed a slight but deliberate tear in the paper lining. It begged my investigation. Pulling off the protective cover, I saw an address scribed on the frame. It read: "California Fertility Partners, Los Angeles, CA."

"She froze her eggs," I deduced.

"What do you mean?" asked Michelle.

"We had talked about the possibility of mass producing these Crystalline kids," I said.

"How?" asked Michelle.

"When our genetic codes mix with traditional human coding and true love, we produce Crystalline children," I explained.

"Right, and?" asked Michelle.

"If a couple are in love and are willing to pay a fertility clinic a large sum of money to create a miracle, than they already pass The Council's 'The one you hold most dear'-covenant. They are the perfect unsuspecting hosts," I continued.

"Right?"

"The problem with The Program is forging an honest union, under the pretense of an agenda," I said.

"So?" asked Michelle.

"In theory, The Program would no longer need to sustain on the works of fallen angels. We could harvest our own enlightenment. Once the public becomes savvy and witnesses the difference our unions can make, everyone will want to invest in the brightest stars The Council has to offer. Our genetically flawed human coding would soon be replaced with the eggs of Crystalline donors and future Programmers," I said.

"That is, if it works. Isn't that what Dez was trying to stop, in his own warped way?" asked Michelle.

"Dez was trying to manipulate the world and destroy

something divine. He was a monster," I said.

"You're talking about an assembly line of enlightenment. That's no less irresponsible than trying to stop it. You can't mess with The Council's will and we can't walk around the planet with god complexes. It's the same path that destroyed *Juno, Ben, Simon, Zane, Magnus, Grayson* and *Elisa*. You have to stop this," explained Michelle.

"Why?"

"I'm sure Ash was well-intended — I'm sure you both were, but you have to understand the complexities of this. Even if The Program fails, it fails naturally — because we allowed it to. Dez felt imprisoned and sought a dark recourse. He tried to control the future, but we are better than our fears of tomorrow. We have a greater responsibility to the salts of the earth — the people just trying to survive and enjoy the fleeting moments of bliss worth living for. Predestination isn't freedom, nor power — it's fear. It's the abandonment of responsibility. It's man-made arrogance. We must...," pleaded Michelle.

EPILOGUE
THE SONG REMAINS THE SAME

To this day, I still have no idea how we arrived back in Charm City — *alive*. It was as if I blacked out or was drugged by The Council. Deciphering Grayson's last words has haunted me. I never thought I'd be blessed with the opportunity to tell our story or go public with it. 'Nervous' doesn't even begin to explain my apprehension — lest we forget the snide comments and ridicule that await me. How does one live a life like this and sell it off to a publishing company?

Well, it is not for sale.

As you know, there were a few happy endings. Ash's beautiful baby girl, Akiane, was adopted by a family in the United States and Crystal's baby boy, Ari, survived. Amidst all of the tragedy, a Crystalline man and woman still walk this planet. Someday, they are going to find each other — that is, if I ever finish this monstrosity. It's amazing what is really going on out there, while we toil away our existence. We are mere pieces of an ever expanding puzzle.

Rand, Ash, and Icarus entered The Beyond.

Ben, Zane, Magnus, Juno, Grayson, Elisa and Simon

remain in the Hallways of Sorrows.

Dez is somewhere. I'm sure of it.

Then, there's me, Neco!

+++

A few years ago, I recall sitting on a blustery NYC park bench. I had settled into a new career, while the ethnic curbside florists of Chelsea were preparing for another beautiful sidewalk sale. The masses mindlessly went about their day. Synchronicity struck, while I sat reflecting on my hotel's name. Knowing my journey was far from over, the Hotel Indigo reminded me that I had a story to tell.

I am the only Programmer left. It's not something I have the luxury of taking lightly. Knowing my fallen friends are trapped in the hideous stench of the Hallway of Sorrows and awaiting my death — this book begs my attention. There are times when I think about pulling the trigger, joining my old friends and starting anew, but our story needs to be told. My biggest obstacle is, I'm not an author. I'm a writer, with a quirky outlook on life and a playful working knowledge of the English language — that's it.

I still look back on those days with a certain romanticism.

I've tried to carry the torch, by hiding our story in my dark songs. It's a tricky balance between keeping the music accessible and straining people to the point where they simply disconnect or won't bother. Souls use art and music to escape. We all want to believe in something greater than ourselves and are tickled when someone can show us the world from a new perspective. Music is a spiritual experience. It takes our hand and provides the soundtrack to our personal journey. It's our birthright.

You either steal their hearts or capture their imagination.

I always knew the day would come when I'd have to anxiously sit down and put this whole messy thing together.

I'm grateful to finally be in a position to do so. I still miss my brothers and sisters of The Program and continue to seek true love — *daily*! Perhaps, there's still hope for me — I don't know. My essence is fading. Perhaps, I'll come back with the next incarnation, find this book and get a good laugh.

Life is surreal. Our memories can really envelope us to a still, if we let them take the wheel. Now, imagine magnifying that tendency over multiple incarnations. The hardest thing we're forced to do is take another step forward and with this memoir, I hope I can finally put a few of my personal demons to rest.

Peace.

ABOUT THE AUTHOR

In a Nutshell:

My rock n' roll dream started when I was about 16-years-young. After releasing 13 full length albums, under various monikers and aliases, I wanted to expand my creative horizons and solder some of my manic metal musical musings with a fictional book. Years of scribing out lyrics, like a lawn gnome on a mushroom, made me quite *versed* in the art of word play and how to communicate through writing — yes, my tongue was firmly planted in my cheek.

For those of you who don't know me, I can assure you, I won't allow myself to be taken too seriously. I love sea lions, rock n' roll, fall weather and suds with my friends — oh, and a good story!

I attended Towson University and emerged with a Bachelor of Arts in journalism. Again, writing. So, to this day, I continue to tell the tale of a conflicted and often tortured spirit, bound by the conventions of a hypnotized society, longing to fly, but often settling for McDonald's french fries and a hot fudge sundae and content to forget it all. This story is my wings. I hope to someday find the courage to leave some of my hang-ups in a very dark place, maybe even a closet [sorry] — never to be opened again.

For now, this is my Ark.

Enter, if you dare...

Love,
Brad W. Cox

Made in the USA
Lexington, KY
04 June 2017